Praise for the novels of

CANDACE CAMP

"Camp has again produced a fast-paced plot brimming with
lively conflict among family, lovers and enemies."
—*Publishers Weekly* on *A Dangerous Man*

"Romance, humor, adventure, Incan treasure,
dreams, murder, psychics—the latest addition to
Camp's Mad Moreland series has it all."
—*Booklist* on *An Unexpected Pleasure*

"Entertaining, well-written Victorian romantic mystery."
—*The Best Reviews* on *An Unexpected Pleasure*

"A smart, fun-filled romp."
—*Publishers Weekly* on *Impetuous*

"Camp brings the dark Victorian world to life.
Her strong characters and perfect pacing keep you
turning the pages of this chilling mystery."
—*Romantic Times BOOKreviews* on *Winterset*

"From its delicious beginning to its satisfying ending,
[*Mesmerized*] offers a double helping of romance."
—*Booklist*

CANDACE CAMP

No Other Love

HQN™

ISBN-13: 978-0-373-77270-4
ISBN-10:   0-373-77270-X

NO OTHER LOVE

This is a work of fiction. Names, characters, places and incidents are either the product of the author's imagination or are used fictitiously, and any resemblance to actual persons, living or dead, business establishments, events or locales is entirely coincidental.

This edition published by arrangement with Harlequin Books S.A.

® and TM are trademarks of the publisher. Trademarks indicated with ® are registered in the United States Patent and Trademark Office, the Canadian Trade Marks Office and in other countries.

www.HQNBooks.com

Printed in U.S.A.

**Other newly released classics from
Candace Camp and HQN Books**

No Other Love

PROLOGUE

1789

HELEN BENT OVER THE SMALL BOY in the bed. He looked so small and helpless that it tore at her heart. His hair clung in damp ringlets to his head. He lay still, almost unmoving, his eyes closed, extraordinarily long dark lashes casting shadows on his cheeks. The only sign of life was the faint movement of the sheet as his chest rose and fell. Moments earlier he had been mumbling in his sleep, tossing and turning in the grip of a high fever. Now he lay still as death.

Helen brushed the wet strands of hair back from his forehead. *Don't let him die. Please, not now.* She had known him only two days, but already she could not bear to let him go.

Mr. Fuquay had arrived at the inn two nights ago in a post chaise with, oddly, this sick child inside. She knew Fuquay, of course. He had stayed at the village inn before, when Richard Montford had come with friends to visit his cousin, Lord Chilton, the Earl of Exmoor. It was whispered in the village that the Earl despised Richard Montford and would not allow him to stay at Tidings, the grand seat of the Montford family. Only now, of course, the old man was dead, and Richard Montford was the new Earl. It had seemed peculiar that Fuquay had come to the inn and not to Tidings.

It had seemed even more peculiar when she saw that he had two children with him. He had come to the door of the public room and motioned to her. She had cast a quick glance toward the tavern owner, then slipped out the door after Fuquay. He was an odd young man, handsome but very gaunt, with a peculiarly soft, almost dazed, look in his eyes most of the time. One of the other girls said that he was an opium eater, and perhaps that was true. But he had been kind and gentle to her, and it hadn't taken much persuasion on his part to induce Helen to warm his bed while he was at the inn. He had been generous, too, and she remembered him fondly.

He had taken her to the carriage and opened it, showing her two sleeping children inside. A girl, hidden in bonnet and coat, was curled up against the opposite wall. Across from her, on the opposite seat, lay a boy, wrapped in a blanket. His face was flushed and bathed in sweat, his body visibly trembling.

"Can you take care of him, Helen?" Fuquay had asked, fidgeting. "He's in a bad way. He won't last long, that's clear. But I can't just—no matter what he wants—"

He had paused at the end of this vague speech and gazed pleadingly into her eyes. He took a gold coin out of his pocket and pressed it into her hand. "I'll make it worth your while. Just stay with him and see him through to the end. You will do that, won't you?"

"What's the matter with him?" Helen had asked, unable to pull her eyes away from the small form. He had been so beautiful, so small and vulnerable.

Fuquay had shaken his head. "A fever. He's done for, but I can't—well, he ought to die in a bed, at least. Will you do it?"

Of course she had agreed. She had fallen in love with the child as soon as she set eyes on him. She had never been able to conceive—despite many opportunities—and she had always ached for a child, a secret, sorrowful desire that the other tavern girls had scoffed at. "You're lucky, you are," they had said, "never havin' to worry about gettin' in trouble."

And now here was this lovely child being handed to her, a gift, it seemed, from heaven. She had climbed into the carriage without delay, not asking any of the dozens of questions that tumbled about in her mind. Gentlemen didn't take to one prying into their affairs.

She had directed him toward her grandmother's cottage, for she had no intention of letting her precious gift die. If anyone could save the lad, it would be Granny Rose. It was a long drive, for Granny lived in a secluded cottage on the edge of Buckminster land, and Helen had had to walk the last part of the journey, carrying the boy in her arms, for there was no drivable road leading to Granny's cottage. Mr. Fuquay had let her out and handed her the boy with a profusion of thanks, but she had hardly paid any attention to him. Her thoughts were all on the boy and getting him to her grandmother.

Helen glanced up now and over at her grandmother. Granny Rose, as she was known to most of the local populace, was a short, rounded dumpling of a woman. Twinkling blue eyes looked out of a face so wrinkled and brown it resembled a dried apple. Despite her merry, almost comical appearance, she was a wise and highly regarded woman among the local people. She knew herbs and healing wisdom, and when Helen had staggered in, carrying the feverish boy, she had known just what to do.

For two days now she and Helen had been caring for

him, dosing him with Granny's decoctions, sponging his flaming body down with cool rags, and forcing little sips of water and soup through his parched lips. The fever had racked his body until Helen had cried for him, and it seemed with every struggling breath he took, Helen loved him more.

"Is he—" She stopped, her throat closing on the words. He looked so frightfully still and pale.

But Granny shook her head, a smile beginning to curve her lips. "No. I think he's past it. The fever's broken."

"Really?" Helen put her palm against the boy's cheek. It was true; he was definitely not as hot as he had been minutes before.

"What are you going to do with him?" Granny asked quietly, watching her granddaughter's face. "He's Quality, you know."

Helen nodded. That much was obvious. His fevered mutterings had been in the perfect tones of the upper class, and the clothes that he wore, though dirty and drenched in sweat, were of the finest cut and materials.

"I know. But he's mine," Helen added, setting her jaw. "We saved him, and he belongs to me now. I won't let them have him. Besides…"

She hesitated, not certain whether she wanted to admit to her shrewd grandmother what else she suspected about the child. She thought she knew who he was, but if her vague suspicions were correct, it might very well mean the boy's life if she revealed that he had survived. If she was wrong…well, then, she had no idea who the lad was, and it would not be her fault if she could not restore him to his proper family.

Either way, she told herself, the best thing to do was to remain silent.

"Besides what?" Granny Rose asked, her bright eyes boring into her granddaughter's.

"I don't know who he is. Where would we take him? And I—I don't think they *want* him to live."

"And what will you say if they ask you what happened to him?"

"Why, that he died, of course, just as they thought he would, and I buried him in the woods where none would ever see it."

The older woman said nothing, merely nodded, and did not mention the matter of the boy's return again. She, too, Helen thought, had fallen under the sick child's spell.

After the fever broke, the boy gradually grew better, until at last his eyelids fluttered open and he looked up at Helen with dark brown eyes.

"Who are you?" he whispered hoarsely.

Helen took his little hand in hers and replied, "I am your new mother, Gil."

"Mama?" he repeated vaguely, his eyes clouded, giving the word an inflection on the last syllable.

"Yes. Mama," Helen repeated firmly, stressing the first syllable.

"Oh. I don't—" His eyes teared up. "I can't remember—I'm scared!"

"Of course you are." Helen sat down beside him on the bed, taking him into her arms. "Of course you are. You have been very sick. But I'm here, and so is Granny Rose, and we are going to take care of you."

He held on to her tightly as tears rolled down his cheeks. "Mama…"

"Yes, dear. I'm right here. Always."

CHAPTER ONE

1815

THE CARRIAGE WAS DRAWING CLOSER to Exmoor's estate, and the thought filled Nicola with dread. *Why had she ever agreed to visit her sister here?* With every passing mile, Nicola wished more and more that she had not. She would have much preferred staying in London and helping Marianne and Penelope with their wedding plans. But Deborah had looked so unhappy and frail, even afraid, and Nicola had not been able to deny her plea. Deborah was, after all, her younger sister, and Nicola loved her. It was only her marriage to the Earl of Exmoor that had caused the bitterness and estrangement between them.

Nicola sighed and shifted on her seat. She hated to think of the quarrels that had followed Deborah's announcement that she was going to marry Richard. Nicola had done her best to dissuade her, but Deborah had been determinedly blind to Richard's faults. When Nicola had pointed out that only months before Richard had been pursuing *her,* Deborah had lashed out that Nicola was just jealous and unable to accept that a man might want Deborah instead of herself. After that, Nicola had given up trying, and for the past nine years, she and her sister had seen each other only occasionally. Nicola had refused to enter the Earl's house, and Deborah had grown more and more reclusive, rarely traveling to London or even venturing out of her house.

But when Nicola had seen Deborah last month at their cousin Bucky's house party, Deborah had begged Nicola to come stay with her through her fourth pregnancy. She had miscarried three times in her marriage, never managing to provide the Earl with a son, and she was terrified of losing this child, too. Looking into her haunted eyes, Nicola had been unable to refuse, no matter how much she hated the thought of living under the same roof with Richard Montford, even for a few months.

Deborah, of course, could not understand Nicola's hatred for the man. But Nicola could not escape the fact that every time she looked at Richard, she was reminded that he had ruined her life. That he had killed the only man she had ever loved.

The carriage lurched through a pothole, throwing Nicola across the seat and jarring her from her head down to her toes. She straightened herself, grimacing. It served her right, she thought, for not stopping for the night an hour ago, but insisting on going on through the dark. Little as she liked the thought of being at Tidings, she had wanted to get the journey over with, and they were only two hours from their destination. Impatience, she had been reminded often enough, was one of her besetting sins.

At that moment a shot boomed out, perilously close to the carriage, and Nicola jumped, her heart beginning to race in her chest.

"Halt!" a voice cried, and the carriage lumbered to a stop.

"I wouldn't if I were you," a male voice drawled in an amused tone. His accent, curiously, was that of the upper class. "You, dear friend, have only one blunderbuss, whereas we have six assorted firearms aimed at your heart."

Nicola realized, in some shock, that the carriage had been stopped by a highwayman—several of them, in fact, from what the man had said. It had been a common enough occurrence years ago in the outlying areas around London, but the practice had died down in recent years, and it was even more unusual so far from the City. Certainly such a thing had never happened to Nicola.

There followed a moment of silence, then the same man continued. "Excellent decision. You are a wise man. Now, I suggest that you hand your gun down to my man there—very slowly and, of course, the business end pointed up."

Carefully, Nicola lifted the edge of the curtain covering the window closest to her and peered out. It was a dark night, with only a quarter moon, a good night, she supposed, for men who operated in secrecy and furtiveness. The groom beside the coachman was handing down his blunderbuss from his seat high atop the carriage. A man on horseback reached up from below and took the firearm, tucking his own pistol into the waistband of his trousers and raising the newly acquired blunderbuss to train it on the driver and his assistant.

Several men ringed the carriage, all of them on horseback and holding pistols. Each of the men was dressed all in black, and, on their dark horses, they seemed to melt into the night, only the bits of metal on guns and bridles catching the faint light of the moon and the carriage lamps. Most sinister of all, every one of the men wore a black mask across the upper half of his face. Nicola drew an involuntary breath at the ominous tableau.

One of the men turned his head sharply at the sound, his eyes going straight to where Nicola sat. She dropped the curtain, her heart pounding.

"Well, now," the cultured voice said cheerfully. "A curious passenger." A certain note of satisfaction entered his voice, and he continued, "Ah, the Earl's crest, I see. Can I have been so fortunate as to have encountered the Earl of Exmoor himself? Step out, sir, if you please, so that we may see you better."

The man who had seen her was obviously the leader, and Nicola knew that he had noticed the family coat of arms drawn in gilt on the door. No doubt he was pleased to have stopped someone wealthy. She only hoped that he did not intend to seize her and hold her for ransom, assuming that the Earl of Exmoor would pay a great deal for his passenger's return. Under her breath, she cursed Richard's insistence on sending his carriage for her. A plain post chaise would have been a far better vehicle, upon reflection.

Drawing a calming breath, Nicola turned the handle of the door and opened it, stepping out with what she hoped was cool aplomb. She thought of her friend Alexandra's American habit of carrying a small pistol in her reticule. Everyone had looked askance at her for it, but right at this moment, it seemed a remarkably good idea.

She paused on the step of the carriage, standing ramrod straight, and looked at the leader with a steady gaze. She was determined not to appear cowed. The man on horseback stiffened and muttered a curse.

"Well done," Nicola said with icy sarcasm. "You have managed to capture an unarmed woman."

"No woman is unarmed," the man returned, his mouth quirking up into a smile. He dismounted in a smooth muscular sweep and stepped forward, making a formal bow to Nicola.

The man was tall and well-built in his dark clothes, a figure of power and even grace. Watching him, Nicola felt an unaccustomed quiver dart through her. Most of his face was covered with a soft dark mask, only the square jaw and chin visible, and a neat black goatee and mustache further disguised those features. But there was no way to conceal the clean-cut, compelling lines of his face—or the wide, firm mouth, now curved in a mocking smile. White, even teeth flashed in the darkness as he straightened and moved toward her, reaching up to help her down. His black-gloved hand closed around hers, neatly pulling her the last step down to the ground. He continued to hold her hand for a moment, his eyes boring into hers.

Nicola raised one eyebrow disdainfully. "Let me go."

"Oh, I will, my lady, I will."

In the dark night, his eyes were utterly black—soulless eyes, Nicola thought a little breathlessly. She could not tear her own gaze away from them. His hand tightened fractionally on hers. Then he released her.

"But you must pay a toll first, for passing through my lands."

"Your lands?" Nicola curled her hands into fists, struggling to keep her voice cool and slightly amused despite the strange torrent of sensations that was rushing through her. She made a show of glancing around. "But I thought we were on Exmoor property."

"In a legal sense."

"What other sense is there?"

"One of right. Does not the land belong to those who live upon it?"

"A radical notion. And you, I take it, claim to be the representative of 'the people'?"

He gave an expressive shrug of his shoulders, a more genuine smile parting his lips. "Who better?"

"Most of the people I know who live upon this land would not consider a thief a proper representative of themselves."

"You wound me, my lady. I had hoped we could be…civil." There was a faint caressing note in his low voice.

Once again something stirred in Nicola's abdomen, shocking her. "It is difficult to be civil when one is being threatened."

"Threatened?" He raised his hands in a gesture betokening innocence. "My lady, you shock me. I have made no threat to you."

"It is implicit, is it not, in stopping my carriage and demanding money?" She glanced around significantly at the men waiting silently on horseback, watching their exchange. "Why else are these men pointing guns at us?"

One of the men let out a soft grunt. "I am afraid she has you there, my friend."

This voice, too, came in the crisp accents of the upper class, and Nicola glanced in his direction, surprised. "What is this?" she asked, suddenly suspicious. "A group of town swells on a lark?"

The man who had just spoken chuckled, but the man before her said grimly, "No, my lady, it is no lark. It is business. So let us get down to it. Your purse, please."

"Of course." Nicola jerked open the drawstrings of her reticule and held it open to him.

He reached inside and deftly withdrew the leather money purse, gently bouncing it in his palm as if to measure its weight. "Ah, you do not travel lightly. A bonus for me."

"I suppose you want my jewelry, too," Nicola snapped, pulling off her gloves to reveal the two simple silver rings that adorned her fingers. If she exposed such valuables, he would not go searching for anything hidden. And she could not let him take the token she wore on a chain beneath her dress. It was worth very little, of course—except to her—but this obnoxious fellow would probably take it just to spite her.

"I am afraid I wear no bracelets or necklaces," she continued. "I rarely travel wearing jewelry."

"Mmm. I find it is usually carried on a journey rather than worn," he said, his tone amused, and made a gesture toward the carriage. Two of the men dismounted and swarmed up on the roof of the carriage, jumping down triumphantly a moment later, carrying Nicola's traveling jewel case and a small square strongbox, which they proceeded to stow on their mounts.

Nicola hid her relief at the thief's acceptance of her statement. He stripped off his own gloves and took her hand in one of his, and Nicola jumped at the contact. His hand was hard and warm, and as he slid the rings from her fingers with his other hand, her breath caught in her throat.

She glanced up and found him looking down at her enigmatically, the faintly jeering expression gone from his mouth, his eyes black and fathomless. Nicola jerked her hand from his.

"Now," she said bitingly, "if you are finished, I would like to be on my way."

"No. I am not quite finished," he replied. "There is one more item I would steal from you."

Nicola raised her brows questioningly. His hands

gripped her shoulders, and she sucked in a startled breath. A dark flame flashed to life in his eyes, and he pulled her to him, his mouth coming down on hers.

Nicola stiffened in outrage. His lips moved against hers, soft and seductive, searing her with their heat. Involuntarily, she went limp, her body suddenly hot and liquid. Wild, turbulent emotions bubbled through her, surprising and disturbing her as much as his insolent action had. Nicola was a beautiful woman, with a petite but curvaceous body, thick pale-gold hair and wide, dark-lashed eyes. She was accustomed to men being attracted to her, even to their making improper advances. But she was not accustomed to feeling such a response herself.

He released her as abruptly as he had seized her. His eyes flashed in the darkness, and Nicola was certain he had been aware of the way she had melted inside. Hot anger surged through her, and she reached up and slapped him sharply.

Everyone went still and silent around them, frozen in a tableau. Nicola faced him, certain that he would punish her for what she had done, but too furious to care. The man gazed at her for a long moment, his expression unreadable.

Finally he drawled, "My lady." Then, sketching a bow toward her, he turned and fluidly remounted his horse. He wheeled and vanished into the darkness, followed by his men.

Nicola watched him leave. Her lips burned from his kiss, and every nerve in her body seemed to be standing on end. Anger roiled inside her, making her tremble. The problem was, she didn't know whether she was more furious at the highwayman because the wretch had had the audacity to kiss her—or at herself for the way she has responded to his kiss.

"DAMN HIS IMPUDENCE!" The Earl of Exmoor slammed his fist down onto the closest thing to him, a small table of knickknacks that shook and rattled at the blow. He was a tall man, as all the Montfords were, and looked younger than his nearly fifty years. His hair was brown, graying at the temples, and his sharp features were generally considered adequately handsome. Today, however, they were distorted with rage.

Predictably, he had been furious when Nicola arrived and told him of the highwaymen waylaying her carriage. He had been striding up and down the length of the drawing room for the past few minutes, his face red and fists knotted. His wife, Deborah, had watched him with pale-faced anxiety, Nicola with a poorly suppressed dislike.

"Attacking my very own carriage!" Richard continued, disbelief warring with rage. "The effrontery of the man!"

"I would say that effrontery is something that man is not lacking," Nicola pointed out with cool amusement.

The Earl ignored her. "I'll have the coachman's head for this."

"It was not his fault," Nicola pointed out. "They had dragged a cut tree across the road. He could hardly have ruined his horses on it, even if the horses had not balked."

"What about the groom?" Richard swung around, pinning her with his piercing gaze. "I specifically put him up there beside the coachman with a gun to ward off such an attack. But he not only didn't fire a shot, he gave them his weapon!"

"I don't know what else you could expect. There were at least six men surrounding the coach. If he had fired it, both he and the coachman would have been dead in an instant. And then where would I have been? It would scarcely be doing their duty to leave me stranded and un-protected in the middle of the road, would it?"

Richard snorted. "Lot of protection they were."

"Well, I am here and unharmed, with nothing worse lost than a few jewels and some coins."

"I must say," her brother-in-law said resentfully, "you seem rather blasé about the whole affair."

"I am happy to be alive. For a few moments there, I was certain that I would be killed."

"Yes. Thank heavens you got here safe and well," Deborah put in, reaching out a hand to her sister.

Nicola moved nearer to Deborah and closed her own hand around Deborah's.

The Earl regarded the two women sourly. "Well, I am glad that you can regard it so lightly. But it is something I cannot ignore. It is a blatant insult to me."

"Oh, really, Richard! *I* am the one who was attacked!"

"You were traveling under my protection. It is a slap in my face. That blackguard is as good as saying that my protection is worthless. He clearly did it to humiliate me." He smiled grimly. "Well, this time the chap will find out that he has gone too far. I won't rest until I have his head on a pike. Thank heavens I had already sent for a Bow Street Runner. As soon as he gets here, I'll set him on this. Then that scoundrel will learn that he has been tweaking the wrong man."

It was typical, Nicola thought, that Richard would be much more concerned over the presumed insult to himself than he would be over his passenger's safety. She glanced at her sister, wondering if Deborah was still so blinded by love for the man that she did not see how cold and self-centered he was.

But, looking at Deborah's pinched, pale face, Nicola

quickly dropped all thoughts of Richard or of the attack. "Enough of this talk," she said crisply, going to her sister. "Deborah is obviously tired and needs to go to bed."

Her sister cast a grateful smile in her direction, though she demurred, "No, I am all right, really."

"Nonsense. It is quite clear that you are dead on your feet. Come along, I will take you up. Richard," Nicola said, casting him a perfunctory nod, "if you will excuse us…?"

Richard bowed back, barely sparing a glance for his wife. "Of course. I need to go out to question the coachman. Good night, Deborah. Nicola." He hesitated, then added with a wry twist of his mouth, "We are pleased to have you visit. I apologize for the inconvenience."

He left the room, and Nicola took her sister's arm and helped her up from her chair. They began to walk to the stairs. Deborah cast an anxious look toward the front door, through which Richard had disappeared.

"I do hope Richard will not be too harsh on the coachman. I—he would not be unkind normally, of course. It is just that this highwayman has him so upset."

"I could see that."

"It is because the man plagues Richard, you see. He—I know it sounds odd, but he seems to particularly delight in stealing from Richard. Tenants' payments, the shipments to and from the mines—I cannot tell you how many times those wagons have been stopped. Even in broad daylight. It is as if he were thumbing his nose at Richard."

"It makes sense. Richard is the largest landowner around here. It would stand to reason that much of the money the man takes would be from him."

"Oh, he stops other things—other carriages, the mail coach sometimes. But it is Richard who has been hit the hardest. It has cut deeply into his profits from the tin mines. Richard has been nearly beside himself. I think what bothers him the most is that 'The Gentleman,' as they call him, has evaded capture so easily. He comes out of nowhere and then melts back into the night. Richard has sent men out looking for his hiding place, but they have found nothing. He has put extra guards on the wagons and his carriage, but it doesn't stop him, just as it didn't tonight. And no one will come forward with any information about him. Even the miners and farmers who work for Exmoor claim to have no knowledge of the man. Do you think that is possible?"

"I don't know. It does seem somewhat unlikely that no one would know anything about him."

"Usually the people in the village seem to know about everything. Richard says they are deceiving him. Hiding the man's whereabouts from him. For some odd reason, the highwayman seems to almost be some sort of hero to the local people."

Having seen the fit of rage that Richard had pitched about the theft and the way he had blamed first the coachman, then the guard, Nicola could well believe that Richard's employees and tenants told him little. She had never seen Richard be anything but arrogant, even with his peers. With those he considered his inferiors, he was doubtless far worse. She suspected that the people around here were probably secretly pleased that the highwayman was harassing the Earl of Exmoor.

"What do you know about this highwayman?" Nicola asked, trying to keep her voice casual. "He seems an odd sort to be a thief. He spoke as well as you or I. And so did one of the other men."

Deborah nodded. "That is why they call him The Gentleman." They had reached the top of the stairs, and Deborah paused for a moment to catch her breath. "That and his manners. He is reputed to be invariably polite, especially to ladies, and it is said that he has not harmed anyone that he has stopped. He stopped the vicar once at night when he was going to the side of a dying man, and he didn't take a farthing from him, just apologized for stopping him when he saw who he was—and sent him on his way."

"Indeed." Nicola did not tell her that the man's behavior toward her tonight could scarcely be characterized as polite. Not, of course, that he had actually harmed her, but that kiss…well, it had been an insult, an effrontery.

"No one knows where he came from," Deborah added. "He started only a few months ago."

"It seems an odd place to choose. Thieves usually operate closer to London or on a main thoroughfare, not out in the country. How do you suppose he came to this pass? Do you think he really was gently born? A son who disgraced his family and was disowned?"

"Or a wastrel who squandered his fortune," Deborah offered. "That is the theory that the vicar's wife proposes. Or perhaps he was merely someone who was well-educated but poor, a tutor or a fencing master, or someone of that sort."

"A tutor?" Nicola couldn't suppress a giggle. "A history scholar who takes to the highways?"

Deborah grinned, too. "That does seem a little absurd. Richard says that he is merely a 'damned actor' who has learned how to ape his betters." She sighed. "And perhaps he is. No doubt we make him seem a more romantic figure than he is."

"No doubt." Nicola remembered the touch of his hand on hers, the searing pressure of his lips, and a shiver ran through her.

"I am sorry." Deborah, holding her arm, felt the faint

tremor, and she turned toward her, frowning in concern. "I should not be speaking so lightly of him when you have just had such a dreadful experience. It must have been awful."

Nicola smiled. "I am all right. No doubt you remember that I am not a very sensitive woman. I rarely have the vapors."

"But meeting a ruthless criminal would cause even you to feel some qualms, no doubt. Let us not speak of it any longer."

Deborah had come to a stop outside a door, and now she turned the knob. "This is your room. Mine is right next door." She motioned to the next door down the hall. "I hope you like it," she continued. "If there is anything that you need, just let me know."

The room beyond the door was spacious and well furnished, with two sets of windows upon the back wall, the heavy drapes now drawn to close out the night. A fire had been banked in the fireplace, and an oil lamp burned low on the bedside table. A maid was running a warming pan between the sheets as they came in, and she curtsied and left the room.

"It's lovely," Nicola said, looking around the room.

Deborah smiled. "I am so glad you like it. It has quite a lovely view during the day—the garden below and the moor rising in the distance."

"I am sure it is beautiful."

"Come see my room," Deborah urged, taking her hand and leading her out of the bedroom and down the hall.

Deborah's bedroom turned out to be quite similar to the room she had allotted to Nicola—spacious and attractive, it was a very feminine room, full of ruffles and frills, with no sign of masculine occupancy anywhere, not even a pair of men's boots against the wall or a shaving stand. It did not surprise Nicola that the Earl and his Countess had separate sleeping quarters; it was quite common among the aristocracy. However, it did strike Nicola as a trifle odd that there was no sign of even Richard's occasional presence.

Nicola glanced at her sister, who was happily talking about her plans to put the baby's crib beside her bed and a cot for the nurse in the dressing room once the baby was born. She wondered if Deborah still loved Richard as she had when she married him, or if she had come over the years to see him for what he really was.

Deborah sighed, still looking at the spot where the baby's crib would stand, and Nicola could see the fear and sorrow mingling in her face. No doubt she was remembering the other babies whom she had hoped to place there.

"I am sure it will be a wonderful arrangement," Nicola said quickly, going to her sister and putting her arm around Deborah's shoulders. "And the baby will love it."

"Really?"

Nicola knew that her sister was actually asking for reassurance that this baby would not meet the fate that its siblings had. So Nicola smiled at Deborah, putting every ounce of confidence she possessed into her expression. "Of course. You'll see. Now, you must not worry. That will not help the baby at all."

"I know. That is what everyone says. But it is so hard when—"

"Naturally. But rest assured that I am here, and I will help you. If there are problems with running the household or anything else, I will take care of them. You know what a bossy soul I am."

Her sister smiled and relaxed a little against Nicola, and

Nicola knew that the ingrained habit of a younger sister to depend on an older one had worked its magic.

"It is so wonderful to have you here," Deborah said, and there was such a sad, yearning look on her face that Nicola felt guilty that she had avoided visiting her for so long. "I—I know you and I disagreed on—a number of things. But we can put that behind us now, can't we?"

"Of course we can." Nicola knew that it had never been her differences with Deborah that had kept her out of this house. It was Richard—and the things that he had done ten years ago. "Let us not worry about that. All that need concern us is your health."

"I am tired," Deborah admitted. "I seem to have so little energy these days. And the morning sickness is much worse this time." She brightened, smiling at her sister. "But the doctor says that is a good sign, that it means this is a healthy baby, not like the others."

"Doubtless he is right," Nicola replied, even though she personally thought doctors were often woefully ignorant. It was one of her many opinions that made others in London Society term her "eccentric"—or worse. "And I am sure he told you that you needed to get plenty of rest, as well, didn't he?"

Deborah agreed, smiling. "Yes."

"Then let me ring for your maid to help you undress so that you can go to bed."

"But I want to hear all about Cousin Bucky's engagement!" Deborah protested.

"We shall have ample time for that tomorrow. I promise I will tell you all about it—and Lord Lambeth's, too."

"Indeed? He is marrying, as well?" Deborah's eyes widened with interest. "But who? I thought he was a confirmed bachelor."

"I suppose it only takes the right woman," Nicola replied. "But it is far too long a tale for now. I will tell you all about it tomorrow."

With a rather tired smile, Deborah agreed. Nicola gave her a peck on the cheek and left the room, going down the hall to the room Deborah had prepared for her. She closed the door behind her with a sigh and looked around the pleasant room. The glow of the lamp was welcoming, but it could not dispel the chill in her heart.

She hated it here. She wished she were miles away, back in London, in the life she had built for herself there. In London she was content. She had her charity work with the poverty-stricken women of the East End, the kitchen that dispensed food and clothes for those bitterly in need. There was the social round that she kept up with when and if it pleased her, the little flirtations that no one took seriously, the intellectual discussions at her small, intimate dinners. Even the arguments over her causes with various members of her social set were a bracing part of her life. She was useful and busy, and there were the pleasures of the opera and theater to be enjoyed.

But here...here she felt unsettled. She hated being in this house with Richard. And there had been that dreadful confrontation with the highwayman...that kiss....

Nicola shook her head as if to clear it. *It was so stupid to be thinking about that kiss; she would not do it.*

She walked to the window and parted the heavy drapes, peering out into the dark night. The trees and shrubbery of the garden were dark shapes in the moonless night. Nicola closed her eyes and leaned her head against the cool window as a sharp yearning pierced her, so fierce she almost cried out. *Oh, Gil!*

It had happened like this before, a swift, unexpected

pain in her chest, as if the wound were brand-new, not years old, and when it did, she would ache for Gil with a sorrow that threatened to smother her. But it had not happened for a long time now; it had, after all, been ten years, and usually when she thought of Gil it was in a sweet, sad way, a remembrance of his smile or his laugh, or the way he walked, that made her smile as much as it made her sigh with regret. But this—this yearning that swept over her—was bitter and painful, cutting into her almost as it had ten years ago.

The thought of him had kept popping into her mind all evening. As her carriage had pulled into the yard, she had remembered suddenly the first time she had seen him. It had been here at Tidings, as she and the rest of a large party had returned from a hunt. He had come up to her horse, reaching up to help her down, and she had looked down at him, taking in with a jolt his handsome face and laughing black eyes, the thick shock of dark hair that tumbled across his forehead. Her heart had been lost to him at that moment, though she had fought it for a while.

Thoughts of him had kept intruding all through her talk with Richard and later with Deborah. Now that she was alone, she could not hold them back. Memories came flooding in. She supposed it was because she was here at Tidings, where she had first met him, or perhaps it was being around Richard, whom she had done her best to avoid for ten years. Whatever it was, her heart ached with a pain and hunger that she knew would never die, only recede now and then until the next time they welled up.

With a half sob, she left the window and threw herself down on the bed. She turned on her side, gazing into the glowing red coals of the fireplace, and, curling up like a child, she gave herself up to thoughts of him....

CHAPTER TWO

1805

NICOLA WAS SIXTEEN WHEN SHE MOVED to Dartmoor with her mother and younger sister, Deborah. Her father had died, and while he had left them well-provided for, the estate upon which they had lived was entailed and passed automatically, along with the title, to a second cousin. The cousin had politely offered to let them continue to live at home with him, his wife and their brood. He had little feeling for them, but it would have looked bad for him to do otherwise. However, Lady Falcourt, who had as little liking for him as he did for her, and even less liking for his efficient, energetic wife and noisy pack of children, declined his offer with equal politeness and removed herself and her children to the house of her sister, Lady Buckminster.

Lord Buckminster, her nephew, familiarly known as Bucky, was a friendly, easygoing sort who welcomed them to stay as long as they wished. Nicola, frankly, found herself happier at Buckminster than she had ever been at home. While she mourned her father, he had been a distant sort of parent who spent most of his time in London. Lady Falcourt was given to various illnesses, and so, from an early age, much of the decision-making for the household had fallen upon Nicola.

But here at Buckminster, Lady Buckminster's house-keeper was a supremely competent woman who ran the household with little more than a vague nod of approval from Lady Buckminster. Lady Buckminster's abiding passion was horses, and as long as she was not inconvenienced or distracted from her riding and breeding and hunts, she paid little attention to the house or to the behavior of anyone in it. Freed from a governess for the first time, with the weight of household management off her shoulders, and under Lady Buckminster's less-than-watchful eye, Nicola found herself more or less on her own, free to do as she wished.

Therefore, she spent most of her time riding about the countryside, meeting the people who lived there. From childhood, Nicola had always felt at ease among the servants and tenants of her father's estate. Her mother had usually been feeling too "invalidish" to spend much time with an active youngster, and Nicola had received the bulk of her love from their nurse and had returned it with all the enthusiasm of her nature. Her "family" had grown over the years to include most of the other servants, from the lowliest groom or upstairs maid all the way to the imposing figure of Cook, who ruled the kitchen with an iron hand.

It was Cook who had inspired her interest in herbs, explaining to her the properties of each herb or spice she put into the food, while Nicola sat on a high stool beside her, watching with great interest. It was the healing properties of the herbs that most appealed to Nicola, and before long Cook was teaching her to grow herbs in a garden, as well as identify and pick them in the wild. She had learned how to dry them, mix them, how to make tinctures and salves and folk remedies of all sorts. Nicola had broadened her knowledge as she grew older by reading and experimenting, and by the time she was fourteen, she was called upon to cure this illness or that almost as much as Cook herself.

It had cost her a good many tears to leave behind the servants when they moved to Buckminster. However, once there, she quickly began making friends wherever she went.

The only problem in her new existence came in the form of the Earl of Exmoor. As the only other member of the aristocracy in the area, he was invariably present on any social occasion, and given the looser restrictions of country life, Nicola, though only seventeen, was usually often included in those events, as well. She was undeniably the belle of the area, sought after by the vicar's pimply son, down from Oxford, as well as the Squire's son and his frequently visiting friends. She didn't mind such boys and their usually awkward attempts at flirtations. The Earl was another matter altogether. Mature and sophisticated, he courted her with all the smoothness of an accomplished rake. Without appearing in any way overbold in the eyes of her mother or Lady Buckminster or any of the older ladies present, he managed to find numerous opportunities to touch her in some way, and he talked to her in a low, silky way, with unmistakable gazes of passion, that both irritated and alarmed Nicola.

She had no interest in the man. However, to her mother, as to most of the world, he seemed a marvelous catch. "Goodness, Nicola," she responded when Nicola protested her inviting him on some outing, "I would think you would be flattered by his attentions. He is quite a catch, you know. Splendid family, the Montfords—wealth, a title. Why, you're even friends with his cousin—what is that mousy little girl's name?"

"Penelope," Nicola replied through gritted teeth. "And she's not mousy, merely quiet. Yes, I like Penelope, and her grandmother, too, but that has no bearing on how I feel about Exmoor. I don't like him. I don't like the way he looks at me or talks to me."

"Oh, my dear," her mother replied with a chuckle. "You're simply too used to callow youths."

"Well, I prefer callow youths to an old man!" Nicola flared.

"Really, Nicola, the way you talk… The Earl isn't old. He's in the prime of his life."

"He must be close to forty! And I am only seventeen, in case you have forgotten."

"Please, dear, there is no need for you to be rude," Lady Falcourt said with a martyred sigh. "He is in his late thirties, but that's scarcely too old to marry. Many men are quite a bit older than their wives. Your father, for instance, was sixteen years older than I."

Nicola bit her lip to hold back the sharp retort that sprang to them. It had been clear to everyone that her father had married her mother for her youthful beauty and then had found her a dead bore once the infatuation had worn off. That was why he had spent most of his time in London.

"It doesn't matter" was all she said. "I have no wish to marry anyone. I don't plan to marry for a good many years yet, certainly not until I find someone I love. Grandmama left me a pleasant portion so that I would not have to marry at all if I didn't want to."

Lady Falcourt gasped and sank back weakly against her chair. "I don't know where you get these radical notions."

"Yes, you do. From Grandmama." Her grandmother had been an outspoken and independent woman who had always looked somewhat askance at the fluttery, vapid woman who was her daughter. Her grandmother had been forced by family pressure into a loveless marriage, and she had made certain that none of her own three daughters had been compelled to do the same. She had often spoken to Nicola about following her own heart, and when she died, she left both her and Deborah sizable enough inheritances that they would be able to live independently if they chose to.

"Yes. And you get them from your aunt Drusilla, as well," Lady Falcourt agreed darkly. Her sister Drusilla had never married, but had lived with their mother in London, where she maintained a social salon of great note and wit. Lady Falcourt understood her even less than the horse-mad Adelaide, Lady Buckminster. "Drusilla is no one to pattern your life after. A spinster…no children to brighten her days, no husband to look after or home to keep."

Nicola sighed. This was a favorite theme of her mother's, even though Nicola had rarely seen her mother lift a finger to organize the household or raise a child. "I have no intention of not marrying, Mama. However, it will be when and to whom I want. And that certainly will not be now or to Lord Exmoor."

Still, there was little way to avoid the man unless she wanted to become a social recluse. He was bound to be at any local party or dinner; having an earl in one's house was considered a feather in any matron's cap, even one as supposedly unworldly as the vicar's wife. Worse, her mother insisted on accepting any invitation he sent their way.

So it was that Nicola attended the hunt at Tidings, the Exmoor estate, and trotted into the yard, flushed from the activity, her hair coming loose in little tendrils around her face. As the Exmoor grooms rushed out to take the reins of the horses, Nicola looked down and found herself staring into one of the handsomest faces she had ever seen.

He was larger than most of the grooms, taller and leanly muscled. Dark, mischievous eyes gazed out from his tanned face, framed by a mop of thick black hair. A smile widened his mobile mouth as he gazed up at Nicola. Nicola stared back, feeling rather the way she had the time she fell out of the oak tree when she was little, as if the world had somehow stopped and she was floating free from it, as if her lungs no longer worked, but her heart was skittering double time.

He reached up his hands toward her, black eyes dancing. "Help you down, miss?"

She could not answer, simply pulled her foot from the stirrup and twisted off the sidesaddle, leaning down to him. His hands grasped her waist, lifting her down effortlessly, and she braced her hands on his shoulders to steady herself. She could feel the heat of his body beneath the rough woolen shirt, the hard stretch of bone and muscle. For an instant they were close, his face so near hers she could see the thick, dark fringe of lashes that shadowed his eyes. Then she was on the ground, and in the next instant, the Earl was there, stepping around the groom to take her arm and lead her into the house.

Nicola scarcely heard a word he said—nor much of any of the rest of the conversation through the hearty post-hunt brunch. Her thoughts were on the groom. She wanted to know his name, but she could think of no way to inquire about him that would not sound exceedingly strange. And even if she could have phrased it acceptably, she knew that it was doubtful that anyone would know who he was, even the Earl, who employed him. Servants might as well have been part of the furniture to most people of her social set, she knew, and though they knew the name of the most important ones— the butler, the housekeeper, their personal maid or valet—it was rare that they knew the names of the multitudinous footmen, maids and grooms. So she was forced to leave later without having learned anything of use to her.

After that, her mother no longer had any difficulty in persuading her to attend a function at Tidings. When her mother suggested they pay a thank-you call the following day, she acquiesced without a murmur, causing her mother to glance at her oddly. The next week she agreed to attend a small dinner party at the Earl's house, and when he suggested a picnic up on the moor, leaving from his house, she smiled and agreed that the idea sounded lovely.

But despite all her efforts to be at Tidings—which had cost her a great deal of inner squirming—she did not catch even a glimpse of the groom. She surmised that he was not important enough in the line of command in the stable to be allowed to interact directly with guests unless there were such a large number present that they needed all the grooms, such as at the hunt.

She told herself that it was foolish to be so interested in the man. She had, after all, seen him only for a moment, and just because she had had that odd response, it did not mean that he was anyone special or significant. It could have been just some odd physical twinge, indicative of nothing.

She could not even have said what she hoped to accomplish by seeing the man again. All she knew was that she was restless and unsettled, that she had to see him.

Oddly enough, it was not at Tidings that she came face-to-face with him again two weeks later. It was at Granny Rose's cottage.

Not long after she had moved to Buckminster, when she had administered a tonic to one of the upstairs maids for a head cold and given a salve to the gardener to ease the pain of his reddened knuckles, people had begun to tell her about an old woman in the area. Everyone called her Granny Rose, though Nicola surmised that no one was actually related to her. She was known throughout the countryside for her remedies. There were even those who superstitiously considered her a witch. It was said that she knew more about plants and their medicinal properties than anyone, and for miles around, people had long relied on her potions to ease the pain of childbirth or protect a wound from infection. Even the old Lord Buckminster himself, who had suffered terribly from the gout, had availed himself of her remedies to ease the disease.

Nicola immediately wanted to meet the woman, and after some cajoling, she got one of the maids to lead her through the woods to the woman's cottage, nestled in a pleasant spot sheltered by a group of trees cupped like a hand around the little house. It was a small structure of wattle and daub, with a thatched roof, and so overgrown with ivy along one side that in summer it almost blended in with the green trees behind it. A small garden of herbs grew beside the house, tinging the air with scent.

Granny herself seemed almost as ancient as the house, her skin creased and browned like a withered old apple, and her hair a pure snow white. But her eyes were merry and younger than she appeared, and her smile, though gaptoothed, was so warm that one had to respond to it in kind.

Nicola took to the old woman at once, and Granny Rose had an equal affinity for Nicola. Nicola was soon riding over to the little cottage frequently, where Granny taught her far more about herbs and medicinal plants than Cook had ever known—although it took her a little time to understand Granny's thick Dartmoor accent. Nicola helped her with her garden of herbs and plants and walked with her in the woods, where Granny searched for wild plants, pointing them out to Nicola and explaining all their uses and dangers. She taught her how to decoct her potions, how to dry and cook and steep and grind, what proportions to use. Nicola diligently wrote down each step of her recipes, adding them to her collection. Granny, who told her that her own daughter had never been interested in learning her secrets, was happy to entrust them to Nicola to use and preserve.

Granny was wise in many other ways, too, and Nicola often stayed to chat with her over a cup of fragrant tea. She had told her about her father and his death, about her mother, even about the persistent pursuit of the Earl of Exmoor. Granny frowned at this and shook her head.

"A bad 'un, that 'un. Ye best be stayin' away from him," she said grimly.

"Bad?" Nicola looked at her, faintly surprised. Though she had not liked the Earl, she had not attributed it to any sense of evil in the man. "But no one has said that he has done anything wrong."

"Mayhap they don't know it," Granny pointed out, with a sage nod of her head. "Mayhap he's good at hiding it from his own sort. But them that works fer him, they see, and they know. There's no kindness in the man."

"Well, I shan't be marrying him," Nicola assured her. "No matter what Mother thinks."

After that conversation, she was a little embarrassed to tell Granny that she had gone against her own judgment and had been to Tidings as frequently as she had been able to the past two weeks. Besides, she found herself reluctant to reveal her desire to see the groom again. Granny would no doubt find it as odd as any of the people in her own class would; ladies did not mingle with grooms, even ladies as pleasant and down-to-earth as Nicola. Moreover, Nicola found herself reluctant to share anything about the feeling that had swept over her; it was something she had hugged to herself for two weeks.

As they drank their tea, Nicola noticed that Granny Rose kept glancing out the window with some frequency, and finally she realized that her mentor seemed to be waiting for someone. So Nicola drank a last sip of her tea and rose, taking her leave. Granny smiled and patted her arm, and Nicola thought with a faint sense of hurt that Granny was happy for her to go. She told herself that Granny's visitor was probably someone who did not wish to be seen visiting the local medicine woman, which also meant that it was probably some member of the local gentry whom Nicola would recognize. The thought made her feel a little bit better.

She slipped out the front door and started down the path, then stopped abruptly when she realized that there was a man standing beside her horse, running his hand down the animal's neck and talking to it in a low voice. He turned at the sound of the door closing, and his brows sailed upward in surprise.

Nicola simply stood, stunned into a breathless silence. The man looking back at her was the groom from Tidings. He was dressed in his Sunday best today, though he had taken off the dark jacket and had it slung over his shoulder. His shirt was white against his browned skin and open at the throat, the sleeves rolled up against the heat of the day.

He smiled now, the same cocky grin that he had worn the other day, as he sauntered toward her. "Well, now, if it isn't the lady. And what would such a high-born creature be doing coming out of Granny Rose's cottage?"

He stopped only a foot away from her and looked down at her, one eyebrow arching in amusement. His eyes were as dark as she remembered them, the dimple in his cheek just as deep. Nicola suddenly found it difficult to breathe.

She lifted her chin a little. She was not about to let him know that he had a drastic effect on her. "Why shouldn't I be?"

"They usually send their maids...unless, of course, they're seeking a remedy for something they can't let anyone know about."

Nicola's eyes widened as she realized his implication, and she drew a sharp breath at his audacity. She was about to let fly with a withering retort when he laughed and made a sweeping bow.

"But of course that could not be the case with a young lady as innocent and beautiful as yourself," he continued in a light voice, blurred by the local accent. "Ye'd have no need of beauty creams or love potions, obviously. Half the men in Dartmoor must already be at your feet."

"And you obviously have no need of any charm yourself," Nicola replied, unable to keep from smiling. "You are already too smooth by half."

He let out an exaggerated sigh of relief, his black eyes dancing. "Whew. I'm glad to hear ye say so. Me gran'd have me ears if I offended one of her customers."

"Your gran?" Nicola asked, intrigued. "Do you mean to say she really is your grandmother?"

He nodded. "Me mother's grandmother."

"I'm surprised I've never seen you before," Nicola commented.

"I live at the stables, you see, at Tidings. 'Tis part of me job. I visit Gran every Sunday, on me day off."

"I see."

There was a moment's pause, during which Nicola realized that she had nothing to stand here talking to this young man about. Desperately she searched for something to say to prolong the moment.

"Ma and I lived in Twyndel," he said suddenly. "But last year, when she died, I moved back to be near Gran. She's gettin' on, ye see."

"I am not from the area, either," Nicola volunteered. "We are staying with my aunt, Lady Buckminster."

"Ah." The grin returned. "We had a right interestin' talk, Lady Buckminster and me, about her mare."

"I am sure it was," Nicola said with a chuckle. "My aunt is not prone to talk of anything else. Had you not taken good enough care of her?"

"You wound me, miss." He put on a pained air. "She'd injured her fetlock, so Lady Buckminster came to the stables to leave the mare, as we were nearer than Buckminster. I put one of Gran's salves on it, and the mare was right as rain the next day when she came to see about it. 'Twas the salve she was wanting to talk about."

"Oh. Well…" Nicola glanced around. She could think of no reason to linger, yet she wanted very much to stay right here, talking to him. "I suppose I should be leaving."

Was that a flash of disappointment in his eyes? "Oh. Yes. Of course."

Nicola began to walk toward her horse, her steps lagging. He strolled along with her.

"Do you…come here often?" he asked casually.

Nicola glanced at him. There was nothing casual about the intense interest in his eyes. "Yes. I am interested in herbs and remedies. Your grandmother has very kindly taught me a great deal. I come here to learn and to purchase supplies from her. She has let me have a corner of her garden for my own."

He looked at her in surprise. "You are growing them yourself?"

"Why, yes. I dry and grind and mix them, as well," Nicola responded tartly. "I realize that you think I am a useless, shallow slip of a girl, but I do have interests outside of my dress and my hair."

He had the grace to redden a little beneath his tan. "Indeed, miss, I did not think you useless and shallow. It is just a little unusual."

"If you knew me, you would find that *I* am a little unusual."

He smiled. "I could already tell that. Not many ladies would stand about chatting with grooms."

"Mmm. My mother tells me I am deplorably egalitarian," Nicola agreed lightly.

They had reached her horse, and Nicola turned to him. "Well. Goodbye, then. I—it was nice to see you again."

"Thank you." He paused, then said quickly, "I come to visit Gran every Sunday."

"Do you?" Nicola's heart began to pound a little harder in her chest. *He was telling her that he wanted to see her again, wasn't he?* "I—uh—" She had to pause and clear her throat, which seemed suddenly swollen. "Then perhaps I will see you here again."

She ended her statement on an upward note, sneaking a glance up at him. To her explosive relief, he grinned.

"Perhaps you will," he agreed. "Let me help you up." He nodded toward the horse.

Then, to Nicola's surprise, instead of cupping his hands

to give her a leg up, he placed his hands on either side of her waist and lifted her to her saddle. He stepped back, looking up at her. Nicola took up her reins in trembling fingers. She could feel the imprint of his fingers against her flesh, as if they had burned into her.

"I—I don't know your name," she said softly.

"It's Gil, miss. Gil Martin."

"Don't call me 'miss,'" Nicola said quickly, something in her rebelling against the subservience in this common form of address from servants.

"All right," he said slowly, watching her. "What should I call you, then?"

"My name is Nicola Falcourt."

The smile that crept across his face this time held none of its former amusement, only a kind of heat that stirred Nicola's blood. "All right. Nicola."

HE WAS THERE AT GRANNY ROSE'S the following Sunday when Nicola arrived. Nicola saw the faint consternation on Granny's face when she opened the door to find Nicola on the step, as well as the uneasy way she glanced over at her grandson. Though she and Granny talked easily enough together, as equals, she supposed that Granny must be uncertain about her being thrown together with a servant.

Gil rose from his seat at the table, his eyes intent on Nicola's face. Nicola looked at him, and a wave of heat washed through her, so fierce that she blushed with embarrassment.

She sat down at the table with Gil and Granny Rose, and Granny politely offered her a cup of tea. The three of them sat and drank tea together, their conversation awkward and stilted. But later, he walked her halfway home, strolling along beside her as she led her horse by its reins. They talked about any and everything, from Granny Rose and her home medicines to Nicola's father to a foal that had been born two days ago at the Tidings stables. Nicola found herself telling him things she had never told anyone before, even her sister Deborah, her innermost feelings and thoughts. When at last they reached the point where he must turn off for Tidings, they hesitated, unwilling to part.

"Will ye be comin' to the main house this Friday, then?" he asked, glancing at her, then away. "His lordship's dance, I mean."

"What?" Nicola was looking at him, watching the play of the sun on his crow-black hair and fighting the sudden urge she felt to reach up and sift her fingers through it. It took a moment for his words to register. "Oh. Yes."

She grimaced. She no longer had any desire to go to Tidings now that she had found Gil. But she could hardly tell her mother that, so she had had to accept the invitation.

Gil looked away, seemingly studying intently a rock on the ground at his feet. "The others are sayin' that he's sweet on ye."

"Exmoor?"

He nodded. "'Tis common gossip about the house."

Nicola sighed. "He seems to be."

"And you?" He looked up abruptly, his dark eyes boring into hers. "What do ye feel for the man?"

"The Earl?" Nicola asked in some astonishment. "Why, nothing. What would I feel?"

"There's those sayin' ye'll be acceptin' him."

"Never."

Gil relaxed a little. "Well, then…that's all right."

"I beg your pardon?"

Gil smiled faintly. "Never mind. I'd best be going. Almost anyone could happen by."

He hesitated, his eyes going to her mouth, and for a brief, dizzying moment Nicola thought that he meant to kiss her.

But then he swung away, moving swiftly down the track toward Tidings, turning back once to raise his hand in a farewell wave. Nicola watched him go, her insides in a turmoil. *Had he wanted to kiss her? Had she wanted him to?* When he had asked her if she was attending the Earl's ball on Friday, she had felt an instant's leap of hope, a vision of his leading her onto the floor in a waltz, before she had realized how foolish that idea was. If she saw him, it would certainly not be on the dance floor, but in the drive in front of the house, helping with the horses and carriages. That was the last thing she wanted, she thought, after this afternoon—to see him in the context of servant, with her the guest, and with Exmoor, her mother and all the others around.

Nicola turned and led her horse to a low stile, where she could climb up and remount him. She scrambled up and turned the gelding toward home, sunk in her thoughts. She had never felt this way before, so confused and torn and giddy. She had wanted Gil to kiss her; she was too honest to deny that fact, at least to herself. She had wanted to taste his lips, and she wished with all her heart that he could be one of the local swains at the Earl's ball, that she could twirl around the floor in his arms, swooping and turning to the grand strains of a waltz.

But she was no fool. However well she might get along with the servants and the villagers, however much she might think that the common folk she knew were as good

as or better than her fellow aristocrats, she also knew that
the gulf between her and a stable boy was vast—even unbridgeable. There could be no future for them—nor, if she
was honest, could there be much present, either. *What
could they possibly have except a few afternoons together
like this? What could happen except that both their hearts
could be broken?*

Her thoughts brought her to tears, and she knew that she
was already halfway to falling in love with Gil. It would
be foolish, disastrous, she told herself. She could not go
on in this headstrong, impulsive way.

By the time she reached home, she had made up her
mind that she would not go to Granny Rose's next Sunday,
however much she wanted to. It would be better all around
if she did not let anything develop between them.

NICOLA MAINTAINED HER RESOLVE all week. She tried everything she could think of to get out of going to the Earl's
ball, but her mother was adamant, and Nicola realized that
nothing short of a serious illness was going to be enough
for her mother to let her stay home. Deborah, a year
younger and not yet allowed to go to adult parties, offered
to take Nicola's place, then retired to sulk in her room
when her mother told her shortly not to be silly.

Finally Nicola agreed to go, telling herself that it was
unlikely that she would even see Gil, let alone come face-
to-face with him. Yet she found herself, unreasonably,
taking special precautions with her dress and hair. She was
aware of a drop of disappointment in her stomach when
their carriage pulled up in front of the house and a footman
came to open the door. A quick glance around showed her
no sign of any groom, only footmen leaping to open
carriage doors and help the passengers down.

Nicola went inside, telling herself that it was all for the best. It would be kinder for both of them if she did not see him.

The party itself was the usual fare here in the country—a few guests of the Earl's down from London, the local gentry, dazzled at rubbing elbows with the sophisticated members of the Ton, and the Buckminsters, Lady Falcourt and herself. Lady Buckminster, of course, was soon engrossed in a deep discussion of bloodlines with an equally horse-mad fellow who made up one of the party rusticating at Tidings. Dutifully Nicola danced the opening quadrille with the Squire, and as it was a long dance and the Squire not much of a conversationalist, it was a rather boring half hour. Exmoor claimed her first waltz, and she acquiesced; she could hardly refuse the host. She could see her mother's eyes gleaming, for it was a distinct honor and an indication of interest on his part.

Her dance card was soon full, but rather than enjoying the evening, Nicola was acutely bored. The men from the city seemed pretentious and condescending, the local boys unusually callow and tongue-tied. She wished she were back home with Deborah, playing some silly child's game or reading a novel. As the evening progressed, the room grew stifling, despite the open windows, and Nicola seized the excuse of the heat to slip out onto the terrace.

She made her way quietly into the side garden, hoping that her mother had not noticed her escape, and popped around the corner of a hedge so that she was out of sight of the terrace. She could still hear the music from the ballroom, even though she could no longer see the house, and she hummed as she strolled along, the moonlight strong enough to navigate the beaten dirt path.

At a crossroads, she turned toward the right. A man spoke from behind her, "Wrong way, miss."

Nicola gasped and whirled around, her heart beating rapidly. Gil stood a few feet away from her in the middle of the path she would have taken if she had turned left instead. "Gil."

She could not keep the note of pleasure from her voice. "I didn't expect to see you," she continued, starting slowly toward him.

"Ye'll break my heart," he teased. "I was thinkin' ye were out here lookin' for me."

"I had no idea you'd be here," Nicola responded, choosing not to notice that she had not denied the idea.

"Surely you didn't think I'd let the evening go by without seein' ye."

"I didn't know."

Less than a foot away from him, she stopped. The moonlight silvered his face, throwing his long-lashed eyes into shadow. He smiled, showing even white teeth, and it occurred to Nicola that there wasn't a man at the ball who could compare to him in looks. He was dressed in his best, black hair combed back, and there was a gleam in his dark eyes that set her pulse pounding.

"We shouldn't be here," she said breathlessly, looking up into his eyes. "Someone might come out at any minute."

His lips curved. "We're safe here."

The orchestra inside struck up a waltz, and Gil swept a grand bow to her. "Would you care to dance, my lady?"

Nicola giggled. It was wonderfully, delightfully absurd. She bent deep in a curtsey. "I would love to, sir."

He held out his hand, and she took it, and he pulled her into his arms. She did not know how he had learned to waltz; it was a dance of the aristocracy, with most of the common folk being content with jigs and country dances. But he followed the steps correctly, if a little clumsily, and somehow moving in his arms was much more wonderful than dancing with any other man, no matter how skillfully he waltzed. Nicola laughed with sheer pleasure as they swooped and dipped across the lawn, dodging flowers and bushes and twirling around hedges.

A lively country dance followed, and by the time it was over, the two of them collapsed on the nearest stone bench, out of breath and laughing with the sheer pleasure of the moment.

"You know, my gran warned me away from you," Gil said lightly.

"Warned you?" Nicola turned to look at him, surprised and a little hurt. "But why? Granny Rose—I mean, I thought she liked me."

"Oh, she does. She says you're a wonderful young lady—smart and good and eager to learn."

"Then why? I don't understand...."

"She says we don't belong together. It's dangerous, moving outside your class like that...wanting something—or someone—you can never have."

"But who is to say that you can't have it?" Nicola protested.

At her words, something sparked deep in his eyes, something hot and primitive. He crooked his finger and put it under her chin, tilting up her face to his. Nicola's breath caught in her throat. She knew that she ought to flee, but nothing could have made her leave this spot at that moment. His face loomed closer, and then his lips were touching hers, soft at first, then harder and deeper. His hands settled on her shoulders, steadying her more than holding her, but it was Nicola who moved closer, curling her fingers into his jacket, pressing up into him, astounded by the pleasure of his mouth.

At her response, he wrapped his arms around her, pulling her into him, and his mouth claimed hers. They clung together, lost in the moonlit night, heat mingling with heat, bodies alive with sensations, hearts pounding so loudly they could not distinguish one from the other. It was a moment that seemed to hang in eternity, endlessly breathtaking.

At last Gil raised his head and looked into her eyes, his own dark orbs flaming. And Nicola knew at that moment that none of the conventions mattered—nor their stations in life or their families' wishes or Society's shocked exclamations. There was only one man in the world for her.

"I love you," Nicola breathed.

CHAPTER THREE

1815

TEARS GLITTERED IN NICOLA'S EYES, turning the coals of the fire into a red, wavering curtain. *She would never love like that again.*

She sat up, wiping the tears from her eyes in quick, almost angry gestures. It seemed unfair that that old pain should come sweeping in on her like this, slashing through her chest, reminding her of her loss as if it were a fresh wound, as if Gil had died only last week instead of ten years ago.

After all, she was content with her life now. She had accepted the fact that for her there would be no wedding day, no children, no growing old together. That part of her life was over, even if she was only twenty-seven years old. She had moved on. She had developed things in her life that were pleasing to her. She helped women in the East End; she gave them some hope, she thought. She matched wits with others at her eccentric aunt's salon. She danced at parties and went to the opera and flirted when she felt like it with certain men to whom she knew it meant no more than it did to her.

Her life was full—or full enough, she reasoned. There were other women who had less than she, aristocratic women who had married as they were expected to and lived in loveless unions with nothing to interest them except clothes and gossip. There was her own sister, for instance, tied to a man like the Earl of Exmoor, miserably childless and panicked by fear that she would once again miscarry.

Better by far the life she had. Nicola swallowed hard and stood up from the bed, straightening her dress. She was foolish to wallow in her old grief, she told herself sternly, going to the dresser and pulling open drawers until she found where the maid had stowed her nightdress. She laid the gown out on the bed and began to undo the buttons of her dress.

No more thinking about her lost love. No more feeling sorry for herself. It was an isolated instance, she reasoned, brought on by being back here at the place where it had all happened. But she had grieved for Gil for ten years; she had long ago gone through the dark pit of despair and come out without losing her sanity or her life. She had learned to live the life that had been given to her. And she was not going to let herself be overwhelmed by old grief just because she was at Tidings.

On that firm note, she slipped out of her clothes, neatly laying them aside over the chair, and pulled on her nightgown. Extinguishing the oil lamp on the small bedside table, she climbed into bed and settled under the covers. But even though she determinedly shut her eyes, it was a long time before sleep crept over her, and when it did, tear tracks stained her cheeks.

"ISN'T IT A LOVELY MORNING?" DEBORAH asked, setting down her teacup and gazing happily around her at the small garden. "I am so glad that you suggested taking tea out here."

It was midmorning, and she and her sister were sitting in the little garden beside the house, sheltered on one side by the looming house and on two others by an outside wall. It was a mild winter's day and pleasantly warm in the small area. Winds did not reach here, and though in the afternoon it was cast deep in shadows, in the morning, the sun shone brightly in it. Two stone benches had been placed here long ago for enjoyment of the sheltered location, and a small fountain and delicate green bushes enlivened the area.

Nicola smiled at her sister. Deborah looked much better this morning. Obviously she had had a good night's rest—more than Nicola herself could say—and just being out of the house had brought a little bloom to her cheeks. Nicola was glad that she had suggested coming out here to have their cup of tea while they chatted.

"Yes," she agreed. "It is pleasant. I am so happy to see you looking well."

Deborah grinned. "Not as happy as I. It is wonderful having you here. Now…" She leaned forward, eyes alight with curiosity. "You must tell me all the gossip from the City. Mama wrote me that that plain little Penelope Castlereigh has caught our cousin Bucky. Is that true? And is Lord Lambeth really marrying an adventuress?"

Nicola made a face. "That certainly sounds like Mother's version of events."

After Gil's death, ten years ago, Nicola had left the area, unable to bear the constant heartbreak of living where she and Gil had loved. She had moved to London to live with her aunt, and her mother, angry with her at the time for having turned down Lord Exmoor's offer, had been happy to let her go. But after Deborah had married the Earl, Lady Falcourt had relocated to the City herself, where she had insisted that Nicola come to live with her. Anything else "looked odd," she explained. Nicola suspected that it was simply that she wanted someone to listen to her recitals of her many illnesses and their symptoms, and to offer her the appropriate sympathy and errand-running. She had resisted for some time, much preferring life with her forward-thinking aunt, but at last she had given in to her mother's tears and whinings, as was usually the case, and had moved into her mother's house.

While Nicola ran the household, her mother rested, kept up a voluminous amount of correspondence with people all over the country, and received the calls of her numerous middle-aged female acquaintances. As a result, though her mother rarely left the house, she knew all the gossip about everyone in Society—not only in London but in the whole of England.

"The truth is, Bucky simply woke up to Penelope's wonderful qualities." Nicola grinned, adding, "However, Marianne and I helped to lay a little trap."

"Marianne? Oh! The beautiful red-haired woman at Bucky's party?"

About a month earlier, Nicola had come with a number of other guests to her cousin's estate for a house party. Among them had been Penelope Castlereigh, a distant cousin of the Earl of Exmoor, as well as Nicola, Lord Lambeth, and a beautiful woman named Marianne Cotterwood, whom Bucky at that time had been pursuing. Deborah had attended the ball Lord Buckminster had given during the weeklong house party and had met the guests, even though she had left early due to her "delicate condition." She had, therefore, missed the tumultuous conclusion to the party, which had included a kidnapping and shooting.

Nicola looked at her sister, wondering how much of the story she had heard from Richard. Nicola suspected that Deborah's husband did not tell her everything, especially any events that might reflect badly on him.

"Yes. That is Marianne."

"Isn't she the one whom Lambeth is marrying?"

Nicola nodded. "Yes, but she is not an adventuress, as Mother said."

"Then who is she? Tell me about her. I had never seen her before—or even heard of her."

"No one had, until Bucky tumbled knee-deep in love with her. It is quite a tale." Nicola looked at her sister's bright eyes and rising color and decided that a bit of gossip was doing her a world of good. "I met her only a week or two before Bucky brought everyone down to his estate for the party. The fact of the matter is, she is the whole reason that Bucky even had the party. He was quite enamored of her. Bucky and Penelope met her at a crush of Lady Batterslee's, and Bucky urged me to invite her to a soiree Mother and I had the next week. Of course, I did; I was dying of curiosity to see who this 'Mrs. Cotterwood' was. Bucky could talk of nothing but her. I liked her immediately, but I was a little concerned because Bucky was so head-over-heels.

"Frankly, I was a trifle worried, too, that she might be an adventuress," Nicola continued. "Besides, I knew how much Penelope loved Bucky, and I kept hoping that someday he would wake up and realize what a treasure he had right there in front of him. So I was quite prepared to dislike Mrs. Cotterwood. But once I met her, I couldn't help liking her, just as Penelope did. Marianne had no interest in Bucky. In fact, she is the one who came up with a delightful scheme that cooled Bucky's fever for her and threw him right into Penelope's arms." Nicola smiled at the memory. "I wish you could have seen her performance.

Whenever Marianne was around him, she played the most shallow, self-centered creature in existence, making sure always to leave him with Penelope for comfort and advice. Eventually, even Bucky saw that he was pining after the wrong woman. And Lord Lambeth, as you know, won Marianne's hand."

"When are Bucky and Penelope to be married?"

"Soon. They are going to be married here in the village church in a month. It seemed only right, what with an alliance between a Buckminster and a Montford." The Montfords, the family to which the Earl of Exmoor belonged, and Lord Buckminster's family were the noble clans of the area.

"That's true. Penelope's mother was a Montford," Deborah mused. "I sometimes forget that Lady Ursula and her mother are Richard's cousins. We see them so rarely."

Nicola carefully made no comment. It was a well-known fact that Penelope's grandmother, the Dowager Countess of Exmoor, had little liking for the man who had inherited the title when her own husband died. Though the Countess sometimes wintered in the Dower House, which was also in the area, Nicola doubted that she called on or received the Earl of Exmoor.

"The Countess is in her element, let me tell you," Nicola continued, sliding past the subject. "Preparing the whole thing as if it were an army going to battle. She and Penelope and Marianne will be driving up to the Dower House in a couple of weeks to oversee the preparations. I can hardly wait for you to get a chance to talk to Marianne."

"But I cannot imagine Lady Ursula letting anyone else arrange Penelope's wedding," Deborah protested, mentioning Penelope's overbearing mother. "And do you mean that the Countess is taking on Marianne's wedding, also?"

"Even Lady Ursula will back down in the face of money. The Countess knew that Penelope would not get the wedding she wanted if Lady Ursula was in charge of it. So Lady Exmoor told Ursula that she would pay for the entire cost of her granddaughters' weddings—but she made it clear that her word was the one that would be final in all matters. You know what a skinflint Penelope's mother can be. She gave in—though you may be sure that she does her best to try to run the thing, anyway. As for Marianne's wedding—well, that is the most fantastical thing of all. I wonder that Richard hasn't told you about it."

"Richard? But why would he? Men have little interest in nuptials, I find."

"Yes, but I would think he has quite a bit of interest in Marianne. You see, it turns out that *she* is Lady Exmoor's granddaughter, too—Richard's cousin."

"What!" Deborah stared at Nicola, her jaw dropping. "You're joking!"

"Not a bit." Nicola shook her head. "She had been lost to the family for years. That is why no one knew her. But she is one of Lord Chilton's children."

"Lord Chilton? The Countess's son? But he—didn't he and all his family die years and years ago? I mean, that is why Richard inherited the earldom, is it not? Otherwise Chilton would have been Earl after the old Earl died."

"That is what everyone has believed all these years." Nicola shrugged eloquently. "But it turned out that the children escaped. It was only Lord Chilton and his wife who died."

"But…this is fantastical! How could Lady Exmoor not know? What happened to them?"

Nicola knew that she was treading on shaky ground here. She could hardly tell Deborah what the Countess believed had happened without bringing Richard into it. And she could not bring herself to tell her sister, especially in the condition she was in right now, what a thorough blackguard her husband really was.

"I, uh, I'm not exactly sure about all the details," Nicola hedged. "But apparently the children were rescued by a friend of Lady Chilton's, an American."

"I see. Then she took them to the United States?"

"Yes, one of them. The boy, John, died of a fever he contracted on the journey. But the other, Marianne, uh, wound up in an orphanage."

Nicola knew that Penelope and her grandmother believed that it was Richard who was responsible for the fates of both the children. When the children had been brought to London by Lady Chilton's friend, she had turned them over to the Countess's companion, a woman named Willa, because the Countess was prostrate with grief, believing her son's entire family dead—and all this right on the heels of her own husband's recent death. But Willa had confessed on her deathbed that she had given the children to Richard. She had been enamored of Richard and knew that the little boy John was the rightful heir to the title and estate of the late Earl, and that Richard had inherited only because Chilton and his son were both believed to be dead. Richard had then hidden the children away, sending the boy no one knew where, though Willa said that he had died not long after, and giving the little girl to one of his henchmen to get rid of. The man had put her into an orphanage.

"No! Oh, how awful! You mean, all these years, she didn't know who she was?"

Nicola nodded. "This all came out a few months ago when the baby, the one taken to the United States, came here to visit and the Countess met her. It so happens that she looks exactly like her mother, and the Countess knew she must be a relation. Eventually it emerged that she was Alexandra, the youngest of Chilton's children. After they were reunited, they set out to find Marianne."

"How exciting! This is like a novel."

"Yes. It even had a romance. Alexandra fell in love with Lord Thorpe, and they were married. The Bow Street Runner they hired finally tracked down Marianne—at Bucky's party."

"Was that when that awful man was killed? Richard told me about that, how the man was threatening one of the guests with a gun and Richard had to save her by shooting him?"

"Yes," Nicola replied dryly. "He was threatening Marianne. The man who was killed had…had something to do with Marianne's being placed in the orphanage."

"The villain! Well, I am glad Richard shot him. It—it sounded so awful. I was very glad Richard had already sent me home earlier in the carriage."

"It was awful," Nicola agreed shortly, biting back the words she longed to say—that she suspected that it had been Richard's own neck he was trying to save, not Marianne's. "But even then, none of us knew, you see, *why* he had tried to kill Marianne. It seemed utterly senseless. Then the Bow Street Runner arrived the next day and revealed who Marianne was."

"My!" Deborah's eyes widened in wonderment. "How could Richard not have told me! Men are so silly sometimes. They think the dullest things are fascinating and then forget to even mention really exciting things."

"The Dowager Countess has been happier than I have seen her in years," Nicola went on. "She and Alexandra are ecstatic at being reunited with Marianne, and of course it was a dream come true for Marianne, finding her real family after all these years."

"I should think so. What a wonderful story! And to end with a double wedding…" Deborah released a sigh of happiness. "I can hardly wait until they come to the Dower House and I can meet them. I—I see so few people here."

"You should get out more," Nicola urged. "You should come to London with Richard instead of staying here, rusticating."

Deborah looked at her, her face falling into a look of sadness, and Nicola thought that she was about to say something, but at that moment a male voice came from behind them. "That is what I keep telling her. Perhaps she will listen more to a sister than to a husband."

The two women turned around to see the Earl strolling along the dirt path toward them, smiling. He was followed by another man, a stocky, plainly dressed individual whose face looked as though it had never been visited by a smile.

"Richard!" Deborah smiled. "I didn't realize you were there."

"Hello, Richard," Nicola greeted him coolly. She could never see him without thinking of Gil's death, and though he had said it was an accident, she held him responsible. Now that she had learned from Penelope about the wicked things he had done, she was even more certain that he was a man driven by evil.

"I came out here to introduce my new employee to you. Ladies, this is the Bow Street Runner I told you I had hired.

His name is George Stone. Mr. Stone, my wife, Lady Exmoor, and her sister, Miss Falcourt."

"Milady. Miss." Stone's smile seemed carved out of granite, and he offered them a stiff little bow. He was not a tall man, but he was powerfully built, with a thick chest and arms that made his jacket fit him poorly.

"Mr. Stone wants to speak with you about the incident last night, Nicola," Richard added. "He needs all the information you can give him to help capture this blackguard."

"I am afraid I cannot tell him very much," Nicola replied blandly. Little as she liked the highwayman, she had no good feeling about Mr. Stone, either, and she liked the Earl least of all. She found that she was not much inclined to aid Mr. Stone in finding the man who was tweaking Richard's nose.

"You saw him, miss," Stone said stolidly. "Surely you can tell me something about him."

Nicola turned her most aristocratic gaze on the man, raising her eyebrows slightly as if amazed to find that someone such as he had dared to address her. "It was dark," she said dismissively. "And he wore a mask. I cannot imagine what I could tell you about him."

"What size man was he?"

"He was on a horse, Mr. Stone. How could I tell his height?"

"The coachman says he dismounted, miss, that he was standing in front of you part of the time. He says as how you slapped the man, miss."

"Indeed, I did. I have no stomach for impertinence," Nicola snapped, casting the man a significant look.

"I'm sure not, miss, but what I'm saying is, you must have gotten some idea of how tall he was then."

Nicola sighed. "I suppose he was average height. Average build."

"The groom says he was a large man, miss."

"I presume he would seem so to the groom," Nicola replied. "Jamie is a rather small man." Her eyes flickered significantly to the top of the Runner's head, indicating without saying anything that she found Mr. Stone rather lacking in inches, also.

"Yes, miss, I noticed." Stone's face turned even more expressionless, if that was possible. "Were there any distinguishing marks on the man? Anything about his clothing or his manner or his walk?"

"He spoke like a gentleman," Nicola offered, knowing that this fact was already well-known. "As for his manner, his walk—I am sorry to disappoint you, Mr. Stone, but I was in fear for my life at the time, and I am afraid I did not notice many details."

"Yes, miss. Thank you." Stone sketched a rough bow toward Nicola, then turned to Richard, saying, "I shall look into the matter further, sir."

Richard watched the man walk away, then turned toward Nicola. Raising his brows, he said lightly, "You seemed a trifle obstructive, dear sister-in-law."

"Obstructive? Don't be absurd, Exmoor. I don't like Mr. Stone. I found him impertinent. But I told him all I know. The highwayman was dressed all in dark clothes, as were his men. They wore masks, and their horses were dark-colored, with no marks. They seemed to have put a great deal of effort into making themselves as unidentifiable as possible. Besides, as I said, I was in fear for my life."

"You, my dear Nicola? I don't believe you have ever been in fear of anything."

"What nonsense. Of course I have. Just ask your wife.

She will tell you I have an absolute abhorrence of rats." She paused, then added, "Especially the two-legged variety."

Her gaze remained steadily on Richard's face. He allowed a thin smile to touch his lips. "Of course. Well, ladies, shall we go inside? I believe it is almost time for luncheon. Perhaps afterward we can have a pleasant visit. I am rather free for the day."

"I'm sorry," Nicola said quickly. She had no desire to be stuck in her brother-in-law's company all afternoon. "I have already made plans to go down to the village."

"Visiting the peasants again?" Richard asked sardonically. "Don't you find such nobility of soul rather wearing?"

"It is not nobility of soul. I enjoy the local people. They welcomed me when we moved here, and I shall never forget how kind they were to me."

"What else would they be? You were Buckminster's cousin."

"I don't mean they were polite and afraid to offend me, Richard. I am talking about real warmth and liking. That cannot be forced or caused by fear."

"I must confess, I find your affinity for the lower classes rather odd. But I do trust that you will partake of luncheon with us before you set out."

"Of course." Nicola bared her teeth in a smile.

Richard returned one that was equally false. "Splendid." He pivoted toward his wife, offering her his arm. "Come, my dear. Let us go in."

Deborah rose and took his arm, and they started toward the house. Nicola, with a sigh, fell into step after them. She had known it would be difficult to live in the same house with Richard—she had acceded to her sister's wishes only because Deborah seemed so desperate—but she was realizing that it was going to be even more difficult than she had thought.

She made it through the noon meal by talking little and smiling frequently, doing her best to tune out Richard's conversation and face. Afterward, she went upstairs and got her kit of remedies, a bag that contained the salves and tonics for which she was most frequently asked. A few weeks ago, when she had been at Buckminster for her cousin's party, she had been besieged by requests for healing remedies when she visited Bucky's tenants and the villagers. Since Granny Rose had died, they had suffered without her wisdom and care, and they had turned to Nicola as her student to help them out. She had made certain to bring all her supplies with her this time, anticipating their requests.

With her kit strapped onto the back of her horse, and after firmly refusing the accompaniment of one of the grooms, Nicola left Tidings, taking the back trail through the fields. It was a little more difficult riding, but it cut at least a mile from the journey, and Nicola had always been at home on a horse. Of course, in London she had to be content with a morning's ride along Rotten Row, but when in the country, as now, she loved to ride.

She breathed deeply, pulling in the fresh air, so different from the City, and felt the tensions of dealing with Richard ease from her shoulders and back. She didn't know how she was going to get through the following months with Richard. Every time she saw him, she felt as if a serpent had crossed her path. Yet she could hardly leave. Deborah had been so pathetically eager for Nicola to come stay with her, and Nicola had seen this morning how much better Deborah felt with her here. She could not desert her sister in her hour of need. She wished that she could take Deborah back to London with her, but that was clearly impossible, even if Exmoor would have allowed it. Given Deborah's condition and her past history of miscarriage, a jolting two-day journey would be the worst thing for her.

But such worries gradually melted away as she trotted through the countryside, taking the occasional low stone wall with ease. By the time her mount approached a fence, she and the horse had grown accustomed to each other, and they soared over it. Exhilarated, Nicola emerged onto a lane lined with trees and dappled with winter sunshine. She paused, looking up the lane toward the right. If she went left, she would reach the village sooner. To the right lay the road to the top of Lydford Gorge, where Lady Falls poured down in a torrent. If she went to Lady Falls, she could then take a different path to the village. It would add perhaps an hour to her ride, but she would still have ample time to visit. *Of course, there was no reason to go there....*

Nicola turned to the right, urging her horse back to a trot. She had to see Lady Falls again. She realized now that it had been in the back of her mind when she had decided to visit the village; after her thoughts the evening before, she knew she could not rest until she had seen the Falls again.

She hardly noticed the countryside now as she rode; the bold upthrusts of rocky tors might have been the green grass of Hyde Park for all the attention she paid to them. All her concentration was on the place to which she was riding.

After a time, she came to the narrow River Lyd and followed it to the spot where it tumbled suddenly down into Lydford Gorge. Her pace slowed, and her heart began to pound. She had not been here since the day after Gil's death, so many years ago. She dreaded seeing it again. A few weeks ago, at Bucky's house party, she had accompanied the rest of the group on a picnic to Lydford Gorge below, and even that, looking up at the Falls from the gorge, had filled her with an almost unbearable sorrow. This, she knew, would be worse—to stand at the top of the Falls, in that spot so filled with beautiful and painful memories—yet she had to do it. She could not rest until she had.

She heard the roar of water, faint at first, then growing louder. At last, ahead of her, she saw the idyllic spot where she and Gil had often met during those magical few weeks of love—the tumble of rocks and the greenery growing rampant at the edge of the water, the delicate mist rising from the Falls, creating a dancing rainbow of colors in the air.

Nicola pulled up her horse and dismounted, leading it the last few yards. Finally, close to the edge, the mist from the tumbling spray caressing her face, she stopped and looked around, her heart swelling with emotion.

It was here that she and Gil had often met after the dance at Tidings. They had sat beneath the shade of the trees a few yards from the Falls, and they had talked and kissed, making plans for their future. They would go to America, they said, when Nicola reached eighteen and could marry as she chose. There, Gil had heard, people did not care about one's birth and a man could make his way on his own merits. He had given her a ring, a heavy, simple man's ring that was, he said, the only inheritance he had. His mother had given it to him before she died, saying it was his father's, but she would not tell him more than that. It was their betrothal ring, and Nicola wore it on a chain, hidden beneath her dress.

Nicola closed her eyes, yearning sweeping through her.

She remembered sitting on the ground, leaning back against Gil's chest, his arms wrapped around her from behind, enfolding her with love, and the memory was so real it was a fresh stab of pain.

"Oh, Gil!" The words tore from her in a sob, drowned by the rush of water.

She had never felt so alive as she had in his arms. His kisses had been like fire, and his caresses had awakened sensations in her that she had never dreamed existed. They had lain beneath the tree, kissing and stroking each other, exploring their eager, youthful passion until they were almost frenzied with desire, yet always Gil had pulled back finally. He refused to dishonor her, he said; no matter how difficult it was, they would wait until she was his bride.

Nicola had wanted to continue, arguing with him that she did not care, teasing him with her mouth and body. That last day, she remembered, she had unbuttoned her bodice and pulled the sides apart, glorying in the heavy-lidded, greedy way Gil stared at her, his breath rasping in his throat.

"Don't you want me?" she had whispered.

"Sweet heaven, girl, you're killing me" had been his husky answer, and he had reached out and cupped one breast, his thumb brushing her nipple and making it harden eagerly. "Don't you know I want ye more than life itself?"

His dark eyes were lit with an inner flame. He moved his hand across her chest, pausing to touch the ring that lay nestled between her breasts. "To see you…to see my ring there, warmed by your flesh—knowing that ye are mine and I'm yours…"

"Then take me," Nicola had said boldly, covering his hand with hers, her eyes glowing up at him. "Make love to me. I want to feel you, to know—"

"No! I won't be plantin' my seed in ye and ye not bearin' my name. It's what happened to my mother, and I will not put that shame on ye. Or on my child."

He had bent and lightly touched his lips to her pink nipple. "Now cover up, girl, before ye drive me to distraction."

"And if I won't?" Nicola had asked saucily, leaning back on her elbows, her eyes filled with challenge.

"Well, then, I'll just have to make ye, won't I?" He had reached for her.

At that moment a roar had split the air, sounding even over the rush of the water, and Nicola and Gil had whirled around to see the Earl of Exmoor standing only a few feet away from them, his face thunderous.

Gil scrambled to his feet, but Richard reached him before he was completely upright and swung his fist, connectedly solidly with Gil's jaw and sending him tumbling backward. He turned toward Nicola, and his eyes dropped down to her open bodice, and he stopped as if struck. "What is that? A ring?"

"Yes. Gil gave it to me," Nicola told him, rising and pulling the sides of her bodice together to hide her breasts. "I am going to marry him."

"Marry? Marry a groom?" Before she realized what he was doing, Richard reached out and grabbed the ring, snapping the thin chain that held it. He held the ring up, looking at it for a long moment, then murmured, "I'll be damned...."

"Give that back!" Nicola cried. "That's mine! How dare you interfere?"

With a great roar of rage, Richard hurled the ring toward the Falls. "You'll never marry him!"

Nicola shrieked and ran after the ring, stopping helplessly at the edge. Behind her, Gil got up and rushed at Richard, crashing into him, and the two men fell to the ground. Nicola stared down at the tumbling water, spilling down the side of the cliff to crash into the gorge below and rush onward. *Gil's ring was gone.* She could never hope to find it again. She whirled, angry words on her lips, then stopped at the sight of the two men locked in a silent, furious struggle.

She'd seen two men fight before. Once, when she was young, two of the grooms had squared off in the yard, and one of them had knocked the other down before Nicola's governess hustled her back inside. But that angry exchange scarcely resembled this intense battle. The two men rolled across the ground, punching and grappling, silent except for an occasional grunt or atavistic growl.

"Stop it! Gil! Exmoor!" Nicola realized that she might as well have been speaking to herself for all the good it did.

The men inched perilously close to the edge of the Falls, so close that the mist from the spewing water enveloped them. Nicola started toward them, shouting of the danger. At that instant, the edge of the cliff beside the Falls began to crumble. Nicola froze, a shriek tearing out of her lungs, watching in horror as the men's feet were suddenly dangling in air. Realizing what was happening, Gil and Exmoor crawled toward safety. But the ground gave way beneath Gil's legs, the rocks and earth flowing from beneath him almost like a river, and he slid backward, his hands scrabbling for purchase.

"Gil!"

Richard, who had reached stable ground, turned around as Gil slid slowly over the lip of the cliff, the spray from the Falls beside him rising around him like a cloud. Richard crawled over to the edge and peered over it.

"Hold on, I'll help you!" he shouted, reaching one arm over the side.

Nicola prayed frantically as she watched. The muscles in the earl's back bunched, and she could see his shoulder move. Then there was a brief cry, and Richard went limp, his arm still dangling over the side.

Nicola's stomach fell to her feet, and she sat down hard, her knees suddenly too watery to support her. She could not speak. Slowly Richard edged back from the cliff and rose to his feet, turning around.

"I am sorry," he told her. "He couldn't hold on. I tried, but he slipped out of my grasp. He is gone."

CHAPTER FOUR

NICOLA TURNED AWAY FROM THE FALLS, her eyes blinded with tears. The memory of that day ten years ago was as clear as if it had happened yesterday. She could still remember the sick, empty feeling in the pit of her stomach as she sat there, staring numbly at the cliff's edge. Shock and disbelief had swamped her. Her heart was already stricken with grief, but her mind could not yet grasp the facts. *Gil couldn't be dead!*

Then a new thought had entered her mind, and she had jumped to her feet, shaky but filled with hope. "Maybe he didn't die! Maybe he's down at the bottom of the gorge—hurt!"

"Impossible. He could not have survived the fall. You know the rocks around there."

"But there is water, too! He could have fallen into the water."

"No. You must not go down there. It would be too horrible a sight."

But she had ignored Richard, running to her horse and clambering onto it to ride down and around to the entrance of the gorge. Once she reached the mouth of the gorge, she rode back up its length to Lady Falls. It was the only way to get to the area below them; the walls of the gorge were too precipitate beside the Falls. But it took an inordinately long time, and by the time she reached the spot below the cliff where Gil had fallen, it was late afternoon, and the high walls of the gorge cast deep shadows all around the pool where the waterfall emptied.

There was no body on the rocks or ground, though she and Richard, who had insisted on accompanying her, had searched all over, clambering over rocks. Nor could she see Gil's body in the pool, dug deep by years of erosion.

"Nicola…let me take you home. This is fruitless. Surely you can see that. His body is either at the bottom of the pool or it was swept downriver. In either case, the boy is long since dead. If the fall didn't kill him, he surely drowned. Please…"

"He's not dead!" she had shrieked. "He's not! I know it! I would feel it if he were. He's alive! He fell into the water and must have been swept down the river, but he could still be alive. He just got out farther downriver."

They rode back through the gorge at a much slower pace than they had taken coming in, searching the narrow river and its banks for sign of a man. There was no sign of him. It was almost dark by the time they reached the mouth of the gorge, and Nicola had allowed Richard to escort her home. "I am sorry," he had said as he helped her down from her horse at Buckminster. "I was angry, yes, but you must know that I never meant him to die."

Nicola had nodded numbly.

"I tried to save him. You saw that. But our hands were wet, and we couldn't hold on. He slipped out of my grasp." When Nicola said nothing, he went on. "I will send for the magistrate and tell him what happened. Don't worry. I will make sure that your reputation isn't harmed by it. We cannot let anyone know that you were out there with a groom."

"I don't care about my reputation!" Nicola had snapped. "And he's not dead! I know it."

"Of course."

He had spoken quietly to her mother, who later insisted that Nicola drink some nasty tonic that a doctor had given her. Nicola had then gone to her bedroom, certain that she would never be able to sleep, but wanting some blessed solitude while she waited out the long, dark night. She had been surprised to find that she went to sleep almost immediately, and the next day, when she woke up, it was almost noon. She realized then that her mother must have given her some of her laudanum, doubtless on the Earl's suggestion.

Shaking off her grogginess, Nicola had ridden back to the gorge and searched it from one end to the other in the daylight. But there was no sign of Gil. She went back home, hoping that there had been some word from Gil that he was all right, but there had been no message for her. She refused her mother's tonic that evening and as a consequence spent a long, restless night, remembering each detail of Gil's plunge off the cliff and repeating to herself all the reasons why Gil might still be alive. *He was young and healthy, and obviously he had fallen into the water instead of onto the hard rocks. The pool was deep, so he would not have hit the bottom. And he had told her that he was a strong swimmer. He had to have survived. He had to.*

But as the days passed and no word had come from Gil, the knowledge that he must be dead had weighed more and more heavily upon her. If he were alive, she knew that he would have contacted her somehow. She had managed to think of reasons why he might have delayed contacting her—he was delirious, perhaps, or lying unconscious somewhere, or had broken his arm so that he could not write. But as time went by, even those gloomy hopes faded.

Day after day she had waited, and no message had ever come. Nicola knew then that Gil was indeed dead. She had sunk into depression, not eating, not sleeping, refusing some days even to get out of bed.

The magistrate had come and asked her a few gentle questions, and she had told him that yes, the Earl had reached down to grab Gil, but he had slipped out of Richard's grasp, that yes, it had been an accident. She had realized after a time that the magistrate believed that Nicola and Richard had been out for a ride together, with Gil along to take care of the horses. She had started to protest, but then she realized that it didn't really matter. *Nothing mattered anymore.*

One day, two weeks later, her aunt had come for a visit and swept Nicola back to London with her. At first Nicola had not wanted to go, still clinging to a faint, desperate hope that one day Gil would get in touch with her. But her aunt had refused to take no for an answer, and Nicola had realized finally that she could not continue to stay here, soaking in her misery, surrounded by all the places and things that reminded her of Gil and their brief love.

She had taken one last ride up to Lady Falls to say her farewell to Gil. She had stood for a long time at the edge of the Falls, looking out over the green gorge, then down, following the silver spray of water to where it splashed into the gorge below. Finally, she turned away, and as she did so, a flash of gold just below the rim of the gorge caught her eye. She looked again, her eyes focusing on the small, thorny bush that grew out of the cliffside less than a foot below the edge. She spotted the wink of gold again, and she dropped down onto her knees at the edge of the cliff, her heart beginning to pound. There, caught in the thorny foliage, was the ring Gil had given her. When Richard had torn it from her neck and tossed it away, it must have fallen into this bush and caught. It had been here for all these weeks, just waiting for her!

Almost sick at the thought that she had almost missed the ring, Nicola lay down flat on the ground and inched forward, reaching down over the edge of the cliff until she could reach the little bush. Her fingers closed around the ring, and she wriggled backward, clutching it in her hand. This much, at least, she had of Gil; she would always have it.

She had pocketed the ring, her heart less heavy than before, and had ridden back to Buckminster. The next day she had gone to London with her aunt.

NICOLA TURNED AND WALKED AWAY from the Falls, her hand going unconsciously to her pocket, where the ring lay. It had been her habit through the years to wear the ring hidden from the eyes of others on a long chain underneath her dress, except when she wore a dress, as she did today, that would have revealed the ring. At first it had served as a kind of talisman, a reminder of Gil that comforted and strengthened her, helped her through the worst days of sorrow and pain. Now she had worn it so long that it had become almost second nature, something she rarely thought about.

Leading her horse to a rock, she mounted and rode away from the Falls. She turned toward the village, riding cross-country until she reached the country lane that led to the village from the south. She stopped at the vicarage first, politely calling on the vicar's wife. But she kept her visit short, know that the amiable, gentle vicar's wife would have no answers to any of the questions she was filled with.

As she was leaving, the housekeeper came around the side of the house to intercept her. It seemed that the cook had come down with catarrh, and the scullery maid had a bad case of chilblains. Nicola went around to the side door and gave the cook a tonic containing hyssop and elder flowers, and the maid a small tin of arnica cream.

"Yer a sweet girl, Miss Falcourt, and that's the God's truth," the housekeeper said, smiling broadly. "Me sister Em told me how you cured the itchin' on her feet for her last month, and I told Cook as soon as I saw ye this afternoon that ye'd do the same for her."

"Your sister Em?" Nicola asked. "Are you Mrs. Potson's sister?"

Nicola wouldn't have thought it possible that the woman's smile could broaden any more, but it did. "That's right! Ain't you the downy one?"

"How is your sister?"

"Feeling pretty well these days, though she gets down in her back sometimes, but that comes from lifting too much. I tell her, time and time again, to let that girl of hers do more of the work, but she lets that Sally twist her round her little finger, she does. Ah, well…" She shrugged expressively. "There's no tellin' her."

Nicola smiled. She wouldn't have thought anyone could twist the redoubtable Mrs. Potson around her finger. She certainly ran her large, quiet husband and the rest of the household, as far as Nicola could see.

Her first stop after the vicarage was the inn. It was owned by Jasper Hinton, a man as thin and small as his wife was tall and large. They were unalike in most every other way, as well, he being a nearly silent man with more liking for numbers than for people, and his wife Lydia a gregarious soul who would rather talk than eat—and it was obvious that she enjoyed her food a good deal. The inn and adjoining tavern were a natural location for local gossip and news, and Lydia's consuming interest in people and everything they were doing made it even more of an information center.

It would also be a natural place to rest and drink something refreshing after her ride—and there was always a serving girl or ostler or scullery maid who was ill and in need of one of her remedies.

When she turned into the yard, Nicola was greeted with a great roar of delight from the head ostler, who hurried across the yard, shoving one of the boys out of his way so that he could help Nicola down himself. "Miss Falcourt! I heard you was up at Tidings these days, but I didn't believe it. Not there, I says, never known her to go there, and she were here at Buckminster only a month ago."

"I know. But I came back to visit my sister."

"That's good of ye. Here, Jem, come take the lady's horse—and rub him down good, I'm tellin' ye. I'll be checkin' to see how ye've done." He handed the reins of Nicola's horse over to the youngster he'd shoved aside and walked with Nicola toward the door of the inn. "How is your sister? She's a good lady, though we don't see her much."

"No. I am afraid Deborah doesn't get out a lot." Nor had Deborah ever had the same interest in the common people that Nicola had had, though she was offhandedly kind and reasonable with the servants. "How is your eye, Malcolm?"

The older man looked immensely pleased. "Now, isn't that just like ye to remember a little thing like that? It's fine now, thanks to that salve you give me. Worked like a charm, it did."

"I'm glad to hear it."

"There's no one with your touch with cures, miss—not now that Granny Rose is gone, God rest her soul."

"I'm afraid I will never know as much as she did."

The ostler nodded. "She were that good. Why, she could walk through the woods and name every flower and plant in it—and what you could use it for. Learned it from her mam, and her mam from hers before that, and so on. They were always healin' women."

They reached the front door, the end of the ostler's domain, and he bade Nicola a cheerful goodbye, turning back to the yard and bellowing an order at one of his hapless charges. Nicola smiled and went into the inn. Lydia Hinton was already hurrying down the hall toward her, wiping her hands on her apron, her face wreathed in smiles.

"Miss Falcourt! Bless the day! I never thought to see you back so soon. When that chit Susan told me you were in the yard, I didn't believe her. Come into the private parlor and rest."

Mrs. Hinton believed in the proper order of things, and she would have been horrified to have sat down with Nicola in the kitchen for a good gossip. A young lady belonged in the private parlor, and she would never think of sitting down with Nicola until Nicola let her bring her food and drink—and then only if Nicola insisted on her doing so. So they went through their usual ritual, with Mrs. Hinton helping her off with her cloak, bringing her tea and cakes, and not making a move toward a chair at the table until Nicola asked her to join her and overrode her first refusal. Then, at last, as they had both known she would, Lydia settled down in the chair opposite Nicola for a cup of tea and a nice hour of gossip.

There were the usual amenities to be observed first—Nicola inquired about Mr. Hinton and their children, and the workers at the inn, listening with interest to the other bits of local gossip that Lydia found of particular importance—before Nicola could get down to the question that burned in her mind. But at last there was a pause in the conversation as Lydia sat back in her chair and took a sip of tea.

Nicola set down her own cup and asked casually, "And what of this highwayman, Mrs. Hinton?"

"Highwayman?" Lydia repeated innocently, and Nicola could almost see her mind racing behind her carefully blank eyes.

"Yes. The highwayman," Nicola repeated a bit wryly. "He stopped my carriage last night, you know."

"No!" Mrs. Hinton set down her cup with a clatter, looking genuinely shocked. "Now, he hadn't ought to have done that, Miss Falcourt. Not to you. I mean, it's one thing when it's *his*—" She stopped abruptly, then added lamely, "Well, there's no call to be stopping a lady like yerself."

Nicola smiled faintly. "If you are worrying that I might tell the Earl anything you say to me, you needn't. Exmoor and I are not on the best of terms."

"It's clear you haven't visited them before all these years…" Lydia admitted. "But blood is thicker than water, they say—"

"Exmoor and I share no blood!" Nicola snapped, her gray eyes suddenly silver with emotion. "My sister's foolish decision to marry the man does not bind *me* to him in any way. I think you know me well enough to know that I have no interest in hurting anyone. Did I ask how young Harry got shotgun pellets in his thigh last month when it was clear as day that he must have been poaching? Did I tell Lord Buckminster or his gamekeeper that I had given him salve after his father had dug out the pellets and left him with a raging infection? I did not. I put it on and bound him up and never said a word to anyone. And Bucky is my dear cousin—if I did not tell him, you can be sure I would never reveal anything detrimental to Lord Exmoor, whom I despise."

Lydia flushed. "It's that sorry I am, miss. I know you wouldn't be tellin' on anyone. It was just, well, you know, you are livin' at Tidings now, and your sister is his lady."

"I know." Nicola smiled at her. She understood the woman's innate distrust of a member of the aristocracy. No matter how well one might get along with the common people, there was always the possibility that, when it came to something important, one would revert, would come down on the side of one's "own kind." "But I'll tell you this: even though he robbed me, I did not give a good description of him to the Bow Street Runner."

"Runner!" the other cried, alarmed.

Nicola nodded. "Yes. The Earl has hired a Runner to investigate the highwayman and his gang. His name is Stone, and I talked to him this morning. He looks a hard man. I did not like him."

The other woman shook her head. "The Gentleman shouldn't be taking such risks. I knew he'd go too far one day and his lordship would go after him. The Earl's not a man to be crossin', is what I say."

"No doubt you are right about that," Nicola agreed. "You sound as if—do you know this man? Have you met him?"

Lydia shifted in her chair, looking uneasy. "I don't know him, exactly. I've, uh, well, he's *known* around here."

"I don't understand."

Lydia sighed, then straightened, looking Nicola in the eye. "He is liked, miss, that's what I'm sayin'. He's done things for people. He helps them out."

"You mean gives them money?"

Lydia nodded. "Aye, he does. You know Ernest Macken, miss. He's got a wife and five little ones, and he's worked in the tin mines all his life. Well, he come up sick and couldn't go to work for weeks. His lordship let him go, and he owns the house they live in, too, miss, and he was ready to turn them out 'cause they couldn't keep up the rent with Ernest not workin'. But one night they hear a thump at the door, and Jenny, she gets up and goes to the door, and there's a sack lyin' there, and when she looks inside, it's got coins in it. Enough to pay their rent for six months and buy food and clothes, too."

"And it was the highwayman who gave it to them? How do they know?"

"Who else? There's none around here that has that much money to hand, except for the Earl or the Squire or Lord Buckminster, and none of them were riding about at night droppin' off sacks of coin."

"No, I am sure you are right."

"It has happened to others, too. Some more, some less. Faith Burkitt, when her man died? His lordship would have turned her out, too. She got money at her door, too, but she got a look at the man when he left it, and she said he was dressed all in black, with a mask on his face."

"He is a sort of Robin Hood?"

Lydia nodded vigorously. "That's how people round here feel, miss. He helps them out, which is more than you can say for anyone else, and he hurts the Earl only, and there's none as would cry over *that*."

"No, I am sure not. I would not imagine that Exmoor is a

good landlord or employer." As the Earl of Exmoor, Richard had inherited not only tin mines but a good deal of the land in the area, both farms and much of the village, as well.

Lydia made a face. "The old Earl wasn't a bad sort, and they say his father before him was the same. But when the new Earl came in…" She shook her head gloomily. "The wages at the mines are a sin, and that's God's own truth, miss. Not long after he got hold of them, he cut the wages. Says they weren't makin' enough profit. It was enough profit for the old Earl, now, wasn't it? Then he raises the rent that the mine workers who live in his houses have to pay. It's hard enough on the farmers, especially when they have a bad year, but what about the miners? He's payin' them less, and they're havin' to pay him more. It's a sin, that's what it is."

"Yes, it is," Nicola agreed. It was this sort of inequity that filled her with righteous indignation and had fueled her venture into charitable projects in the East End. It had also gotten her into enough arguments with others at parties that she was generally termed a radical and a bluestocking by her peers. "It is not surprising that the people have no qualms about his being robbed. Lady Exmoor told me it was mostly his wagons that were preyed upon by the brigands."

Lydia nodded. "Aye. Oh, a carriage now and then that's traveling through. But not local people much. Once he stopped the doctor when he was driving in his new gig to see a patient, and when he saw who it was, he just waved him on, didn't take a cent from him."

"He sounds like a saint."

"Oh, I'm sure he's not that, miss. He's a man, after all, and I've never met many of them that were saints. But he's after the Earl only—there's no mistakin' that."

"I wonder why."

"Why? After what the Earl's done? Who better?"

"I'm sure that is true, but thieves are not usually so selective. It sounds as if he has something against the Earl personally. Is he from around here?"

Lydia shook her head. "No. He moved in a few months ago. At first there was just him and the men that came with him, but after a while, some others joined him."

"You mean local men?"

Lydia nodded, her gaze measuring.

"Oh, dear." Nicola frowned. "I am afraid of what might happen to them. The Earl is dead set on catching him. Now with the Runner trying to find him..."

"I wouldn't worry too much, miss. 'The Gentleman' is a slick one. There's none that know where he lives. The local men meet him at a certain place, but that ain't where he and the outsiders stay. There's four of them, and they live someplace hidden. He's never told a soul."

"What—what is he like?" Nicola looked down at her cup as she spoke, turning it idly.

"Like? I'm not sure, miss. I've never seen him but the once." She edged closer and lowered her voice to a confidential whisper. "One night Ste—that is to say, a man comes to the inn, and he won't speak to anybody but me Jasper, so Jasper goes down there, and I gets up to see what's what. So I creeps down to the landing, and I'm sittin' there in the dark on the stairs, where no one can see me. Well, Ste—this man—says to Jasper that he needs a tot of whiskey for someone outside. It was rainin' and blowin' something fierce, not a fit night out for man nor beast. So me Jasper says why can't the man come inside, it's a sight dryer, and he says he just can't, and finally Jasper goes and pours a glass of whiskey. Then I hears the sound of boots and spurs on the stones outside, and the next thing you know, this man steps into the doorway. I next to keeled over with terror, I'll tell you!"

Mrs. Hinton pantomimed her shock, one hand going to her chest, her eyes widening and her mouth dropping open. "He was a big man, like to fill the doorway, towering over me Jasper and this other man. And he's dressed all in black, he is, from his head to his toes, and he's even wearing a black mask over the top half of his face. Well, I knew who he was, of course, as soon as I saw him, and I was that scared for Jasper, because, well, no matter what everybody said about him, you just never know, do you? Then in this elegant voice, he says, 'Thank you, sir, I won't trouble you to bring this outside on such a stormy night as this.' And he took the glass from him and knocked it back—and paid him with a gold coin! I nearly fell off the stairs when I saw that. Then he bids a very polite farewell to Jasper and turns to go, but as he turns, he says, not even looking over at me, 'And good night to you, too, Mrs. Hinton.' I couldn't believe it! He'd spotted me in that little bit of time, but neither of the other two had caught sight of me the whole time they were standing there."

"So you've never seen his face? Has anyone?"

"Not me, miss. Some of the girls in the village say that he's handsome, but they're just silly romantic chits. I dare swear they've never seen him even in a mask, let alone without it. He stays to himself, he does. I don't know anyone who knows anything about him—not even where he comes from."

Nicola was sure that if Mrs. Hinton didn't know anything, then no one did. "I wonder if he is really a gentleman," she mused. "He certainly sounded it."

"His hands aren't those of a gentleman," Lydia said decisively, shaking her head. "I saw 'em when he pulled off his gloves to take his drink. They're big and callused and scarred—the hands of a man who's worked all his life. Not even a gentleman who rides without his gloves has hands like that."

"Then how did he learn to speak like that?"

The other woman shrugged. "He's a mystery, Miss Falcourt, and that's a fact. Personally, I think he likes it that way. He don't want people to know about him."

"Mmm. I suppose that the less anyone knows about him, the less likely anyone would be able to turn him in."

"Oh, won't no one turn him in, miss, I'll tell you that. He's a hero here."

"Even if Exmoor offers a reward?" Nicola asked. "There is always someone in a town willing to talk then. I'll venture that it won't be long before Richard turns to that. He is determined to capture him. He takes the man's acts as a personal affront."

"Well, be that as it may, he'll have a hard time catchin' that one. And anyone who does turn him in better watch his backside around here."

"I hope you're right. I should hate for any of the locals who ride with him to be caught. It would mean hanging for them, you know."

"Aye, I know." Mrs. Hinton looked somber for a moment, but then her ready smile was back. "But they won't get caught. I'm tellin' you, he's canny."

Having exhausted Mrs. Hinton's store of knowledge on the subject of the mysterious highwayman, Nicola turned their conversation to other matters. Finally, Mrs. Hinton rose, saying that she'd taken up enough of Nicola's time.

"But, if you don't mind, miss," she asked, knowing the answer as well as Nicola did, "some of the girls complain about their 'time of the month,' and Granny Rose used to give them something that fixed them right up. Would you be knowing the recipe?"

"I do indeed. I brought some with me, if you'll have someone fetch my bag from my horse."

"Of course, miss. You're a good woman, if you don't mind my bein' so bold as to say that. Granny Rose would be proud of you."

"Thank you, Mrs. Hinton. That makes me very pleased."

So for the rest of the afternoon Nicola stayed in the private parlor of the inn, listening to the ills of first the servants, then various other townspeople who had heard that she was there and dropped in to seek her help. She dispensed advice and remedies, and when she did not have the decoction that she thought would best cure an ill, she made a note of it and promised to send something to them the next day. Several people came for loved ones who were ill at home, and these Nicola accompanied back to their houses to see the patients and take note of their symptoms herself.

The afternoon lengthened, then died away, and it was growing dark when she turned away from Tom Jeffers's house, where she had gone to see his mother, who lay frail and shriveled in her bed, slowly drifting away from life. Nicola had known at once that there was nothing she could do for the woman except give her a tonic to ease the pain the old woman was suffering.

She walked back down the street toward the inn to retrieve her horse, but before she reached it, she saw a man's figure hurrying down a side street toward her, and instinctively she knew that he came for her.

"Miss! Miss!" he gasped, short of breath. "Wait! Don't go."

She stopped, letting him catch up to her. "Why, Frank." She smiled at the man, whom she recognized now as the husband of one of the former housemaids at Buckminster. The couple had been married five years now and had four children. "How are you?"

"Not good, Miss Falcourt, not good." He stopped, breathing heavily. "I'm sorry, miss. We just heard you was here. It's the baby—he's sick. He don't sound good, like he can hardly breathe. Lucy was up all night with him, but he just keeps getting worse. Can you come? Lucy fair brightened up when she heard you was here. 'The young lady can fix him,' she says. Can you, miss?"

"I'll come, of course." She smiled, hiding the sinking sensation in her stomach. She didn't have Lucy's touching faith in her skills. She knew that illness in children was worse; they were so small, so fragile. A fever that an adult might endure could carry a child off.

She followed the man to his cottage, where he ushered her into the low-ceilinged room. It was dim inside, lit only by a guttering tallow candle and the fire, which provided heat for the house, as well. A woman sat on a stool before the fire, a small child about two years old wrapped in a blanket in her arms. She rocked back and forth, crooning tunelessly. When she saw Nicola enter the door, she jumped to her feet, a smile spreading tremulously across her face. "Miss Nicola! Oh, thank you!"

Tears began to fall from her eyes, and she hurried forward, holding the child up for Nicola to see. "You'll help him, won't you, miss? You won't let him die!"

"I will do my best. Now, what's the matter with him?" Her question was almost unnecessary, for it was easy to see the flush of fever on his cheeks, and as Lucy handed him over to Nicola, he coughed, a harsh, deep, barking sound.

"It sounds like the croup, Lucy. I think he will be all right. We just need to keep that little throat from closing up on him. Put some water on to boil, will you?"

Lucy nodded wordlessly and went right to work. Nicola sent the father for a small blanket, while she paced up and down, holding the child and murmuring soothing noises as he continued to cough. When the water was steaming, she had Lucy pour it into a bowl and put it on the table. Then, forming a small tent with the blanket, she sat down and held the child so that his head was under the tent. As the child breathed in the steamy air, his cough began to quiet, then subsided.

Lucy began to cry again, mopping away her tears with the corner of her apron. "Oh, miss, I knew you could help him."

Nicola smiled. "Just do this when he gets an attack. The steam opens up his throat so he can breathe better. Put warm poultices on his feet tonight. I'll give you a bag of wild plum bark for you to make him tea. Give it to him several times a day."

Lucy nodded fervently, repeating "yes, miss, oh, yes, miss" like a magic incantation. When the baby's cough had died away, she took the child and put him tenderly to bed, then returned to Nicola so she could demonstrate how to make the hot poultices for his feet. Lastly, Nicola dipped out a small amount of dried bark into a sack and handed it to her.

"I shall send you more if you need it. I have given out all the rest of it this afternoon, but I can get more when I get back to Tidings. So let me know. Any time he has another coughing fit, you be sure to put him under the tent with steam."

"Oh, I will, miss, I will. Lord love you, miss." She

grabbed Nicola's hand and would have kissed it had Nicola not pulled her hand away and given Lucy a hug instead.

"Send for me if something happens," Nicola told her. "Promise me."

"I will. I promise."

After several more protracted thank-yous from Lucy and her husband, Nicola managed to leave. Frank insisted on walking her back to the inn's stable, just to make sure she was safe, for it was late in the evening by the time Nicola finished.

The ostler at the inn seemed equally troubled at the idea of a lady riding back to Tidings in the dark evening, but Nicola brushed aside his offer of an escort. She knew that no one who lived around here would do her harm, nor was she afraid of the legends of fire-breathing hounds and ghostly carriages that kept most local people firmly inside their houses after dark. There was the highwayman, of course. The thought of him sent a strange chill down her spine. But, she reasoned, he would not bother with such paltry game as a lone female rider. It was a trifle chilly, but her cloak would keep her warm.

She left the village, letting her mare pick her way, for the sliver of new moon provided little light. It was a cloudless evening, and the stars were already shining brightly in the sky. Nicola rode along, letting her thoughts drift as she contemplated the dark velvet sky. She felt tired, but satisfied. It was always rewarding to be able to help someone, especially when it was a child's life at stake. Lucy's baby, she thought, would recover, though it might take a while for the illness to run its course.

Ahead of her a copse of trees lay beside the road, and as she neared it, a man on horseback rode out from the shadows beneath the trees. Nicola sucked in her breath, her heart beginning to pound, and pulled back automatically on her reins, stopping her horse.

The man rode toward her without haste, and Nicola watched him, her mouth dry. He was dressed all in black, and under his hat his face was unnaturally dark. She knew without a doubt that it was the highwayman. So she had been wrong. He would stoop to accost a lone woman. Her hands tightened on the reins as she debated whether to turn and flee toward the village, but she could not bear to play the coward in front of this man. Besides, she reminded herself practically, his horse looked powerful, and she suspected that he would catch up with her if she did run. *Better to stand and face the danger.* That had always been her way.

She waited, chin lifting unconsciously. The man stopped a few feet from her and swept off his hat, bowing to her. A smile played on his lips. "Well, my lady. A bit dangerous for you to be out this late, isn't it? Alone? In the dark?"

CHAPTER FIVE

NICOLA KEPT HER VOICE EVEN AS SHE replied, "I haven't been afraid of the dark since I was a child."

"Nevertheless, I think I should escort you home. We would not want any harm to befall you while you were out playing Lady Bountiful, now would we?"

"Since you are the only person around here who would harm me, I see little point in your escort."

"I? Wish you harm? You wound me." His teeth flashed white in the dimness.

"What else would you call stopping my carriage and robbing me at gunpoint?" Nicola responded tartly.

"But I offered no harm to your person. Surely you realize that."

Nicola shot him a hard look. "You forced yourself upon me."

"Forced myself!" He began to laugh. "My dear lady, stealing one little kiss is hardly 'forcing myself upon you.' Besides, I believe you paid me back well enough for that." He rubbed his cheek ruefully. "You pack quite a wallop."

"What nonsense. I didn't hurt you."

"Oh, but you did. Imagine my wounded pride after you gave me such a setdown—and in front of all my men, too."

"Is that why you are here? To exact revenge on me? To salve your pride?"

"You are an exceedingly suspicious woman. I thought I had established that I was not here to harm you but to make sure that you get home safely."

"Oh, yes. Silly of me to think otherwise."

Nicola glanced sideways at him. He looked the personification of wickedness and danger, masked and dressed all in black, yet the way her pulse quickened was not entirely due to fear—there was a strange sort of excitement coursing through her, as well, a tingling, eager feeling that unnerved Nicola even as she relished it. She felt quite sure that this was not the kind of reaction she should have to a man like this. His height and the breadth of his shoulders, even the husky rumble of his voice, should inspire fear, not this unfamiliar heat deep in her loins.

As if he could sense the direction of her thoughts, the highwayman turned toward her and smiled—a slow, almost taunting smile.

"Who are you?" Nicola asked abruptly, seeking a subject, any subject, that would break the thrum of sensual tension his smile set off.

"Do you really expect me to tell you that?"

"It seems absurd to call you nothing. It would be better to have a name to put to your face—or, I should say, your lack thereof."

A brief dip of his head and a wry smile acknowledged her thrust. "God help us, a clever woman."

"No doubt *you* prefer a foolish one."

"Oh, no, my lady, not a foolish one. Indeed, you are to my liking, wit, temper and all. I am a man who likes to live on the edge, you see." He paused, then added, "One could say the same for you."

"Nonsense. I am sure the edge would be much too uncomfortable for me."

"Ah, yes, you are such a conventional—one might even say timid—sort. Running about the countryside alone on horseback after dark."

"Being in a carriage with a driver and groom did not exactly help me last night, did it? I would say I am as well off on my own. And no one around here would harm me, anyway—present company excepted, of course."

"I believe that most women would have elected to stay indoors today—and especially this evening—if they had had such a harrowing experience as being stopped by a highwayman last night."

"I presumed a highwayman would not bother with a solitary horseback rider, particularly one who is not on the main road…if anything hereabouts could be considered a main road. You know, it strikes me as a little odd that an accomplished thief such as yourself would be roaming about the wilds of Dartmoor. One would think that the London area would be a much more profitable place—Blackheath Moor, for instance."

"Ah, but the days of Dick Turpin are dead now. Blackheath Moor is no longer a healthy place for those of my profession."

"Still…Dartmoor? How many carriages do you stop a week?"

"You are concerned for my welfare. I am touched. However, you need not worry. We manage to get by."

Nicola grimaced. "You persist in misunderstanding me. I have no concern for your welfare. I merely wonder why you would choose such an out-of-the-way place as this for your thievery."

"Less opportunity, perhaps, but also less chance of getting caught. And the mines provide a steady stream of cash and goods being transported."

"One might almost think that you have a personal vendetta against the Earl of Exmoor."

"I? How could anyone carry a grudge against such a pleasant man as the Earl of Exmoor? So kind to his workers, so understanding with his tenants."

"I realize that he is an easy target. It is difficult to feel sympathy for the usurer when he is robbed, too. Still, it *is* theft, pure and simple. And when you are caught, you will hang just as readily as if you had stolen from a saint. Nor, I think, will you be quite such a hero to the local inhabitants when some of their own men are hanged with you."

"Ah, but that makes the assumption that we shall be caught. I do not intend for that to happen."

"I am sure few criminals do," Nicola retorted. "But they are nabbed, anyway. You will be, too."

"How can you be so sure?"

"How can you be so full of yourself as to think anything else? You delight in tweaking Richard's nose. You think he will not come after you? He is a very powerful and wealthy man."

"Let him come after me," her companion said, his voice rich with satisfaction. "I would delight in meeting him."

"You think he will come after you personally? Don't be absurd. Men like Richard hire other men to do their dirty work. It is they who will hunt you and your men down like dogs. But he *has* hired them. He doesn't mind the cost. You have insulted him, practically dared him to stop you. It is infuriating enough to him that you have been stealing his money. Last night, when you stopped his own carriage, it was like rubbing his nose in it. He won't rest until you are swinging from a gibbet. He has already hired a Bow Street Runner."

"Has he indeed?" His voice was thoughtful.

"Yes. I met him this morning. His name is Stone, and he looks to be a man to live up to his name."

"Well. That makes the game more interesting. Still, I think I can hold my own against a Bow Street Runner."

"Don't you understand? Richard will not stop. Maybe you can handle this Runner—elude him, kill him, whatever you plan to do. But it will not end with Stone. If he fails, Richard will hire more. He will put out rewards for your capture. Someone, sometime, will betray you for the money, no matter how highly the people around here regard you. He will put guards on his wagons."

"He already has." The highwayman's teeth flashed whitely in the dark. "Yet still I have come away with the strongboxes."

"Then he will hire more—and ones who are not terribly concerned about killing a man over a strongbox. Why won't you see? Richard Montford is not a man to cross! He is willing to do anything to protect his possessions."

"I am sure he is. No doubt you are one of his prize possessions."

"I?" Nicola swiveled sharply to glare at him. "How dare you! I am no man's possession."

"No? I dare swear your husband would look at it differently."

"He would not," Nicola retorted sharply. "If he did, he would not be my husband, I can assure you."

"I would not have thought the sort of man you would marry would be so...advanced in his views."

"The sort of man I would marry? How would you know anything about the sort of man I would marry? You don't know me at all."

"I know you are the sister of the Countess of Exmoor," he replied. "The cousin of Lord Buckminster. A woman firmly entrenched in the aristocracy. A woman of name and beauty…therefore one who doubtless made an excellent marriage. I *had* thought you were the Countess of Exmoor."

"I? Married to Richard? Hardly. That is my sister."

"So my men told me. But I would assume that you made an equally advantageous marriage—even better. Perhaps a duke? Have I erred in calling you 'my lady'? Should it have been 'your grace'?"

"Neither." Nicola bit off the word. I am *Miss* Falcourt."

The highwayman glanced at her sharply. "You are not married?"

"No, I am not. It is hardly so astonishing. There are women who do not marry."

"Rare for a woman of your beauty and background. That is the purpose of a lady's life, is it not? To marry for alliance? To gain the best position she can, given her natural assets?"

"You make marriage sound like a business proposition."

"Is it not?" he answered, his voice cold and sharp as a knife. "A noblewoman is the same as any prostitute, selling her wares to the highest bidder. The only difference is that the buyer pays with a wedding ring instead of coins of the realm."

Nicola's hands clenched her reins tightly, and she felt again the compelling urge to slap this man, but she struggled to control herself. "You, sir, are a fool. It is your prerogative, of course, but I do not have to stay and listen to you. Good day."

She started to dig her heels into her horse, but the man lashed out with one hand and grabbed her upper arm tightly, holding her in place. "I'm no fool, *Miss* Falcourt.

I was once, but no longer. I found out what motivates a woman to choose a husband, and it is not love or even desire. I know whereof I speak."

"You know nothing. You only think you know. Obviously some woman disappointed you, but only a fool would paint all women with the same brush."

"Not all women. Noblewomen. I know many a common woman whose heart is large and warm. But a lady's heart is a cold, hard stone."

"Then a lady's heart must be something like your mind," Nicola shot back.

Much to her surprise, the man laughed. "A fair shot, my—I mean, *Miss* Falcourt." He released her arm, and their mounts started forward again.

"You are utterly infuriating."

"Indeed, I have been told that."

"I must say, I wonder why you should choose to ride along with me, despising noblewomen as you do."

"Once a man understands what they are about, he can partake of—" his eyes slid appreciatively down her body, leaving little doubt as to the underlying meaning of his words "—the pleasure of her company without being so foolhardy as to lose his heart. Or his head."

"That is typical of a man—noble or low. 'Tis not the same for a woman."

He let out a bark of laughter again, but this time it had little amusement in it. "Women would have us think so."

"Oh, and I suppose that you know better than I how a woman feels or thinks?"

"I am more honest about it."

"Your arrogance is astonishing."

"It isn't arrogance to speak the truth. Women like to pretend that they feel no desire unless their heart is engaged, that they marry for love, not wealth or position. The truth is that they marry for well-calculated reasons, and their passion can burn quite hot without the spark of love."

"Then I must be an odd woman indeed, for it is not that way with me."

"You lie through your pearly white teeth," her companion responded without heat.

"How dare you imply that—"

"I imply nothing. I say it outright. You are not speaking the truth, and you know it. Do you feel love for me?"

Nicola quirked an eyebrow at him. "Hardly."

"Yet last night you responded to my kiss with passion."

"What nonsense." Nicola could hear the lack of conviction in her own voice.

"You and I both know that it is not." He reached out and grasped her bridle, pulling her horse to a halt with his. He leaned toward her, his face unnervingly blank, half-covered as it was with a mask, in contrast to the hot spark in his eyes. "I kissed you, and you kissed me back, even though you did not love me—indeed, were not even acquainted with me. You did not even know my name, yet your lips quivered and melted beneath mine."

"A man's capacity for self-deception is boundless." Nicola's stomach fluttered, though she strove to keep her tone cool and unconcerned. "I slapped you, if you will remember, yet you term that response passionate? Passionately angry, perhaps."

His hand curled around her wrist as he held her still, staring straight into her eyes. "How much of that anger was at me—and how much at yourself?"

Nicola could not conceal the shiver that shook her at his touch. "You presume too much."

"I presume no more than you feel." He leaned even closer to her, his face only inches from hers. Nicola wanted to look away, to pull her arm from his grasp, yet she could not. She could only gaze back at him, exerting all her will to keep her eyes steady and cool.

"No."

"Kiss me, then, and tell me you feel no passion. No desire. Show me how only love moves your body."

"I do not wish to kiss you," Nicola protested, knowing as she did so that she was lying. A strange heat flooded her insides even as her hands turned freezing, and all she could think about was his mouth, exposed beneath his half-mask, the bottom lip full and eminently kissable, hinting at passionate delights. She remembered how his mouth had felt against hers, and deep down she knew that she wanted to feel it again.

He smiled in a knowing way, and in the next instant, his mouth met hers. It was just as it had been the night before: his lips were warm and velvety, searing her with heat and a strange, shivery delight. She could not conceal the long shudder of pleasure that ran through her, and he made a sound of satisfaction deep in his throat at her response. His arm went around her tightly, lifting her from her saddle onto his horse in front of him. He wrapped his arms around her, pressing her into his chest, as his mouth continued to conquer hers. Nicola leaned against him quiescently, a trifle stunned by her own response.

She had told herself that last night had been a fluke, that she had kissed him with a fervor that had been somehow born of that time and place and would never happen again. But she had been fooling herself, she knew now. This kiss touched her like fire, too, a strange fire that both consumed and fed her, that made her burn not only where his lips touched her but deep inside herself, as well. It was both wonderful and frightening, magical in its effect. Nicola felt a stranger to herself, yet she could not bring herself to want to return to the woman she knew.

Her arms went up and encircled his neck, and his kiss deepened, all lightness and mockery vanished in the flaming heat of passion. His lips dug into hers, opening her mouth to him, and his hand came up to anchor itself in her hair, holding her captive to his marauding lips and tongue. But she had no desire to escape him, only to taste more and more of the delight his mouth offered. She pressed her lips against his, her tongue meeting his in a delicate, sensual dance. She felt the shudder of his response as he let out a long, yearning sigh, and it stoked the fires of her passion even more.

His other hand slipped between the edges of her cloak and roamed up her body to cup her breast. His thumb circled her nipple through her dress, and Nicola made a noise of surprise and pleasure at the sensation that rippled through her. His fingers kneaded and caressed the lush orb, and his breathing grew harsh and heavy. Nicola moaned, her fingers digging into his shirt, as the things his hand was doing set up a hot, thrumming pulse deep within her abdomen.

His hand left her breast, and Nicola made a small noise of protest at the loss, but he moved it only to slip beneath the neckline of her dress, delving down inside the garment until he found the soft curve of her naked breast. Nicola gasped and jerked, stunned by the jolt of pleasure that shook her as his fingers slid down on either side of her nipple, capturing it between them. Gently he pressed and squeezed, his movement narrowly constrained by her dress, which somehow made the sensations he aroused even more titillating. Nicola's nipple hardened and tightened, aching for his fuller caress.

He lifted his mouth from hers and gazed down at her with glittering eyes. His arm went behind her back, and she leaned against it, her head lolling back, as she luxuriated in the pleasure his hand aroused in her. It was all he could do not to rip her dress down the front to gain full access to her breasts, but he controlled himself, teasing them both with the soft grazing of his fingertips over her nipple. He was rewarded when Nicola's hands came up and began to unbutton the top buttons of her dress, opening herself to him.

She did not think about what she was doing or how brazen and licentious she must seem—such thoughts would come later. But right now she was aware of nothing but the hunger coursing through her, the fiery grip of desire that clenched her vitals, wanting more and more....

With the barrier of her dress undone, he cupped her breast more fully, caressing and stroking the supremely soft skin and manipulating the nipple until it was a hard, pebbled button. He tugged gently at the nipple with his forefinger and thumb, and was rewarded by a soft moan from Nicola's lips. With a gentle, caressing movement, he pushed down the neck of her chemise, shoving aside her dress and revealing the soft mounds of her breasts. He paused for a moment, gazing down at her, his eyes as black as the night around them.

"You don't know how I have—" he began in a gravelly voice, then stopped abruptly. He bent and gently kissed the pink center of one breast. Nicola drew in her breath sharply and sank her hands into his thick, springing hair. She could not speak, could barely even think with his lips upon her, laving and caressing and teasing her nipple. He played with the little bud, pulling it finally into his mouth and sucking gently as he teased it with his tongue.

Heat flowered between her legs, increasing with each tug of his mouth upon her. Nicola dug her fingers into his scalp, hurtling toward something she did not comprehend. She only knew that she had never felt such fire or such urgency.

"Please…" she murmured.

He lifted his head, and she looked straight into his glittering eyes. "Is that not desire inside you now?" he asked huskily. "Are you not moaning with passion? Yet I warrant you feel no love for me."

Nicola came to her senses with a jolt. Suddenly she was aware of the cold evening air on her bared breasts and of the fact that this man, this complete stranger, still held her breast, cupped brazenly in his palm. Shame flooded her, and her face blazed red. She shot up, away from his supporting arm, her hands going to her dress and chemise to jerk them back up to cover her. With a hard shove against his unyielding chest, she jumped down off the horse and ran over to where her own stood grazing placidly. She hastened to button up her bodice with fingers that still shook, rage and embarrassment warring within her. *How could she have been so foolish? So easily seduced? Whatever was the matter with her?*

She felt as if she were a stranger to herself. Whenever this man was around, she acted like a different person. *It was no wonder that he held such a low opinion of her!* Nicola wasn't sure whether she hated herself or him more.

Grabbing her horse's reins, she glanced around for some low wall or rock or fence on which she could stand to mount him. To further her embarrassment, she saw nothing at hand. She turned and strode past the highwayman, her face averted from him. She could sense his eyes on her. Then he dismounted and followed her.

"Go away!" Nicola snapped, not looking back at him.

"I was going to give you a leg up," he responded evenly.

"I do not need any help from you."

"So you plan to walk back to Tidings, leading your horse?" The amusement in his voice exacerbated Nicola's already raw feelings.

"No, I do not. I shall find a place to mount before long."

"It would be much easier if I helped you. Come, put aside your pride at losing our little bet, and—"

"We did not have a bet!" Nicola whirled to face him, her face white with fury. "And I am not angry because my pride has been damaged. You are right—I don't know whether I am angrier at you or at myself, for acting in that low, vulgar way! It makes me sick that I even allowed you to touch me."

"I am sure it was much worse with me than with one of your highborn gentleman friends."

"No gentleman has ever touched me like that! No man at all!" Her mind touched briefly on Gil and his sweet, drugging kisses. His hands had caressed her through her clothes and even opened her dress to touch the bare skin beneath. *But it had been different with Gil. They had loved each other, and it had been beautiful—nothing like this sordid episode!* She shoved the thought of Gil from her mind and went on. "You act as if I had allowed any number of men to do such things, and I have never—I would never—" Tears of anger rose in her, threatening to burst forth, and Nicola had to stop talking to hold them back. She refused to let this man see that he had made her cry.

She swallowed hard and struggled for a moment to bring her voice back under control. "I was a fool," she said bitterly. "I acted like some silly, will-less woman, the sort whom men have to protect from themselves. But I can promise you that it will never happen again, least of all with you."

He crossed his arms over his chest, studying her. "Are you sure?"

"Yes, I am sure!" Nicola hissed. "Just the thought of your touching me again makes my skin crawl. You are the lowest of creatures. They call you 'The Gentleman'— what a joke! You are no gentleman at all. You are nothing but a common thief, no matter how you like to dress it up. You may have all the locals fooled as to your motives. They see in you a great Robin Hood. But I see you for what you really are—a robber who uses everyone around him to gain what he wants. Oh, yes, you so kindly give this poor widow a few coins to get her through the winter or help that unfortunate man who is too sick to work anymore. You do it to endear yourself to them. It's no noble motive that pushes you, only the desire to bind the villagers to you so that they will help you, hide you, even join your gang! You care nothing for them—you care only for yourself. What is it to you if they get caught with you and face the gibbet? What is it to you if they lie for you and obstruct the law for you?"

"I ask no one to do those things for me!" he shot back.

"You do not need to ask. You know that they will, because you have convinced them that you are a noble defender of the people—when the truth is that you are greedy for money and too lazy to work to get it. No, you'd rather steal from someone else, and no doubt it is doubly pleasurable to get it from someone for whom you carry some personal grudge. It is all about you and what you want, and you don't give a damn about anyone else!"

"I bow to your expertise in that matter." His voice was tight, his mouth drawn into a thin line. "You like to help the people around here, but it is all for your aggrandizement. You love to hear their praise. You love the reverence in their eyes. You enjoy making them believe that you are a friend of the people. But you are a parasite on the earth, like all the other aristocrats, and when it gets down to the nitty-gritty, you won't step out of your way for the common people. You stick with your own kind, and the rest of us be damned."

"How dare you! You know nothing about me. You have no idea what I think or feel or why I do things!"

"I know you as well as you know me," he retorted, stepping closer.

Without warning, he reached out and seized her by the waist, and Nicola gasped, suddenly frightened by his strength and anger. He heaved her up and tossed her onto her saddle. His lip curled, and she knew that he had read the fear in her eyes.

"By the way," he continued with cold sarcasm, "my name is Jack Moore, in case you wonder to whom you almost gave yourself tonight."

Nicola's cheeks flared red, and she dug her heels in. Her horse took off like a shot, leaving the highwayman behind them.

REGRET FLOODED NICOLA AS SHE rode towards Tidings. Reaching into her pocket she took out the ring Gil had given her and fastened it around her neck, almost defiantly. By the time she reached the estate she had composed herself. She found Tidings ablaze with lights and the stable yard busy with grooms saddling horses. Richard was already mounted, with the Runner, Stone, on another horse by his side, and he was shouting out orders to the hapless grooms. The head groom turned, saw Nicola and let out a shout of relief.

"Miss Falcourt! Look, my lord, there she is."

Richard turned and saw her, and his scowl grew even darker. "Good God, Nicola, what the devil do you think you're doing? Do you realize what time it is? We were just about to mount a search party for you."

"I know. I am sorry," Nicola said with all the contriteness she could muster, for she hated apologizing to Richard. "I should have sent someone with a note explaining that I would be late. I didn't think—I am so used, you know, to being on my own."

"If this is your behavior in London, I shouldn't wonder if your mother is prostrate with worry half the time."

"Oh, Mother has quite given up on me," Nicola replied lightly. "But I truly do apologize."

"Your sister is practically hysterical," Richard said sourly. "You had best get in and let her see that you are all right. She was certain that you had been kidnapped by that damned highwayman."

Nicola was glad of the darkness to hide the rush of color in her cheeks at the very mention of the highwayman. "No, I was perfectly safe."

"You cannot be sure of being safe," Richard pointed out. "I should think you would have more sense than to ride about alone, especially after dark. You have already been stopped by the man."

"I did not presume he would bother with a lone rider," Nicola pointed out, sliding down off her horse and handing the reins over to the groom. It was galling to explain herself to Richard, as if he had some right to oversee her behavior. Yet she knew that she had been rude and thoughtless to stay out so long without letting her hosts know where she was, so she forced herself to answer politely. "And since he took my jewels and money yesterday, I shouldn't think he would find me much of a prize to stop."

"There are worse things than thievery, Miss Falcourt," Mr. Stone added darkly.

"No doubt. However, I had not heard of this man attacking women."

"You cannot be sure with a scoundrel like that, miss."

"Next time you had better take a groom with you," Richard ordered.

"I was only a little late," Nicola said impatiently. "I really do not think it warrants quite this much fuss. Now, if you will excuse me, I must go calm Deborah."

To her annoyance, Richard dismounted and followed on her heels into the mansion, walking with her to the drawing room, where Deborah sat, twisting and turning her handkerchief.

"Nicola!" She jumped to her feet when her sister entered the room. "I was so worried! Isn't this wonderful, Richard, that she is all right?"

"Wonderful," he agreed dryly. "She came riding in as we were about to leave on a search party."

"I am sorry for worrying you," Nicola told her sister, doing her best to ignore Richard. "One of the villagers had a sick baby, and he caught me just as I was about to leave. I had to go see the child."

"Really, Nicola," Richard said. "Why do you bother with them? It isn't as if you have any responsibility toward them. This isn't even your family's land."

"That does not remove my human obligation," Nicola replied frostily. "Perhaps if you treated your workers and tenants more humanely, they wouldn't consider The Gentleman such a hero."

Richard's eyebrows rose. "Indeed? And where did you hear that?"

Nicola realized instantly that in her irritation she had

made a dangerous mistake. She shrugged. "I don't remember specifically where. There is gossip all around the village about him. Everyone wanted to talk about it, because they had heard that he stopped me last night."

"So they all revere the man?"

"No, of course not. Why would they revere a thief? I merely heard that there are those who regard him as a sort of Robin Hood."

"And who are those people?"

"How should I know?" Nicola countered. "No one would tell me who says such things. After all, they know that Deborah is my sister."

"Yet you are such a *friend* of the common people. I would think that many of them opened their hearts to you."

"Don't be absurd." Nicola had no idea whether he believed her, but there was no way that he could make her tell him who had talked to her about The Gentleman. "They appreciate what I do for them, of course, but I am still the aristocracy. They are not going to reveal any secrets to me."

"Mmm. I am surprised. I thought you mingled with the lowborn quite freely."

Nicola knew that he was making an oblique reference to her love for Gil years ago, and a shaft of pain lanced her with such ferocity that she could hardly breathe. Tears filled her eyes, and her hand slipped unconsciously to where the ring lay beneath her cloak.

Richard's eyes narrowed, following the movement of her hand. She turned away, saying in a stifled voice, "I am sorry. I am afraid I am quite tired. Please excuse me."

"Of course." Deborah, frowning with worry, stood and started to follow her sister, but Nicola waved her away and strode out the door.

The Earl watched his sister-in-law leave. He turned

thoughtfully toward Deborah. "Did you see that gesture she made?"

"What?" Deborah looked at him blankly.

He raised his hand in imitation. "This."

"Oh. Yes. I have seen her do that before. She used to wear a ring there a long time ago."

"When?"

Deborah glanced at him, puzzled. "Why, I don't know. Years and years ago, before we were married. Some talisman, I suppose. Perhaps that old woman gave it to her, that Granny Something-or-other. She used to visit her frequently. That is where she learned her herbal knowledge. It was an odd old ring, quite simple and plain, not the sort of thing one would cherish."

"When was the last time you saw her wear this ring?"

"What?" Deborah looked at him oddly. "Why, I don't know. Why do you care?"

"It is just…something I am curious about. I shall tell you another time."

Deborah, accustomed to her husband's frequent secrets, simply shrugged. "I suppose the last time was, um, at our wedding. I am almost sure she had it on, and the neckline of her dress was too low, so she had to take it off and push it down into her bouquet.

"Our wedding. Then it was after…"

"After what?"

He shrugged. "After that summer, when the stable boy died at Lady Falls."

"Oh, yes. That dreadful time."

"Well…" Richard shrugged. "It is scarcely important, anyway. Now I think it is time that you were in bed."

Deborah smiled at him tentatively. It seemed a long time since she and her husband had conversed this much.

"Yes. No doubt you are right." With a hope she could not quite stifle, she took his arm and let him lead her from the room.

SHE HAD BETRAYED GIL THIS EVENING! Nicola threw herself into the chair beside her bed, flooded with guilt and shame. *How could she have let that man kiss her? How could she have enjoyed it so?*

Ever since Gil's death, she had remained true to him. She had not loved another man. Oh, she had engaged in little flirtations, had even allowed a kiss now and then, but they had never been anything but harmless diversions, and she had never felt the powerful passion that she had experienced with Gil. When she had told Jack this evening that for a woman passion and love were inextricably entwined, she had meant it, for that had been her only experience. She had loved Gil, and his kisses had filled her with desire; she had neither loved nor desired since him. But tonight…!

She had never experienced anything like what had happened with Jack. She barely knew the man, had no liking for him whatsoever, yet when he kissed her, the earth seemed to open up beneath her. She had been lost, swept up in passion. *How could it have happened like that?*

Nicola could not understand it. She still loved Gil. Why, just last night she had sat in this very room and cried at the ten-year-old loss of him. Yet this evening another man—a loathsome, horrid stranger!—had kissed her, and she had responded to him as if Gil had never existed, as if her heart did not lie in a grave.

Was it because she had been thinking so much about Gil these past two days? Had the memory of his love, his kisses, made her vulnerable to another's kisses? Had his kiss somehow carried her back to those days with Gil, and had the passion she felt been the old desire for Gil?

She knew immediately how absurd that thought was. The highwayman was so unlike Gil in every way that she could not imagine how his kiss could evoke the memory of Gil. Gil had been gentle and loving, and his kisses had been sweet, whereas this man was rude and unkind, his kisses hard, almost punishing. He did what he wanted, took what he wanted, with no regard for her or her feelings, which was in no way like Gil's loving tenderness. Gil had spoken like a member of the lower classes and had worn the rough clothes of a groom, yet he had possessed the essential qualities that belonged to a gentleman—he was honest, loyal, kind and noble. On the other hand, the highwayman acted and talked like an aristocrat, yet he was a cruel, sardonic thief. He did not even resemble Gil physically. This man was taller and heavier than Gil had been, a powerfully built man rather than a lean boy. His dark eyes held none of the warmth that Gil's had; they were hard and cold through the slits in his mask.

No, Nicola could see no way to blame her lapse on his touching the chord of love in her for Gil. She had been seized by an inexplicable lust, an overpowering physical response over which she had seemed to have no control.

Guilt and shame burned in her, and she told herself that it would never happen again. She would not allow it. Hopefully, she would never see the thief again, and if by some strange chance she did run into him, she would be on the watch this time. She would keep a stern grip on her emotions and desires. She refused to succumb to her basest instincts. Nicola thought of the way he had laughed at her, that knowing glint in his eyes, as if he had been fully confident that he could make her respond to him with desire even though she did not like him. She was *not,* she vowed, going to give him another opportunity to look at her that way.

CHAPTER SIX

NICOLA WAS NOT SURE WHAT AWAKENED HER—the faint scrape of a shoe, the click of the door—but something invaded her sleep and brought her suddenly, instantly awake, with the heart-pounding feeling that something was wrong. Her eyes flew open. There was a man in her room.

He was tall and dressed all in black, with a mask over his face. He stood in front of her vanity table, bending over and quietly searching through the things that lay scattered across its top.

"What are you doing!" Nicola demanded, anger surging through her.

The figure turned toward her, startled, then ran for the door. Nicola jumped up to intercept him, not thinking of the danger but only of her anger and indignation that he dared to come into her room and mess about with her things.

"Stop!" she shrieked, reaching out and grabbing his sleeve. "Stop!"

The man jerked his arm away and swung out at her, catching her cheek hard with the back of his hand and knocking her down. Then he flung open the door and rushed out into the hall.

The blow and the fall dazed Nicola, and for a moment she sat, stunned, where she had fallen. Then she scrambled to her feet and darted after him, shouting, "Help! Stop him!"

There was no one in the hallway or on the stairs. Nicola ran to the top of the stairway and peered down it to the dark foyer below. Behind her a door opened, and then another. She turned and saw Deborah standing in her doorway. Further down the hall, Richard, clad in an elegant brocade dressing gown, came out into the hall.

"Nicola? What happened? Did you scream?"

"Yes. I—something woke me, and I saw a man standing in my room."

Deborah gasped, and Richard exclaimed, "What!" He strode rapidly toward her, saying, "No one could have gotten into the house. It must have been a dream. Are you sure you weren't dreaming?"

Nicola opened her mouth to retort hotly that she knew very well the difference between reality and a dream, but then she saw the meaningful look Richard gave her and the way he nodded his head subtly toward his wife.

Nicola glanced at Deborah and saw that her face was white with fear, her eyes wide, and she realized her mistake. Swallowing her bile, she managed to say, "Oh…oh, yes, perhaps it was a dream. It seemed so real, but you're right. I was probably asleep and didn't realize it."

She was rewarded for her lie by the immediate look of relief on her sister's countenance. "Oh, thank goodness, Nicky. I was so scared!" She breathed out a tremulous sigh.

"I am sorry to have scared you. You should go back to bed now. Your feet will get cold, and we can't have you getting sick," Nicola added.

"Yes, no doubt you're right." Deborah glanced down

at her bare feet. "But I can't leave you when you've had such a fright."

"It's all right, Deborah." Impatience tinged the Earl's voice. "I will talk to Nicola until she is feeling calmer."

"Yes. You go on to bed," Nicola agreed, smiling at her sister. "I shall be fine."

"If you're sure." With a doubtful glance back at Nicola, Deborah turned and went back into her room.

Richard watched her until the door clicked behind her, then swung around to face Nicola. "Thank you for going along with that little charade. It is imperative that Deborah not be upset. Now, what happened? Did this intruder threaten you? Harm you?"

"No." Nicola shook her head. "Well, I mean, he did knock me down, but that was after I screamed and tried to stop him."

"He hit you? Are you all right?"

"Yes, although I may have a bruise tomorrow." Nicola reached up to touch her cheek gingerly. "He caught me on the cheek, I'm afraid, and it knocked me down."

"The blackguard. It was that damned highwayman, no doubt."

"That is what I thought at first," Nicola admitted. "But I'm not so sure now."

"Why not? Who else could it be? We aren't exactly overrun with thieves around here."

"I don't know. It just, well, it didn't seem like him. There was something different."

Nicola realized that she could scarcely tell the Earl that she doubted the highwayman would return for a visit when he had just talked to her earlier this evening. If she did, she would have to hear a lecture from him about her reckless ways, and then he would doubtlessly insist that she take a groom with her every time she went riding. Nor could she explain to him that the highwayman would be more likely to linger and exchange words with her than to knock her down and rush out the door. There was an exciting air of danger about the highwayman, but it was different from the menacing chill she had felt when she saw the intruder lurking in her room.

"Different how?" Richard asked impatiently. "You told me you could scarcely describe the highwayman."

"I'm not sure. He just—moved differently, or something. Besides, why would The Gentleman return to paw through my vanity when he had ample opportunity to steal everything I own yesterday when he stopped the carriage? Why risk coming into the house with servants all about?"

"To tweak my nose!" Richard replied bitterly. "It is exactly the sort of impudent gesture he revels in. Well, it won't happen again, I assure you. I shall send the servants out to search the house and grounds right now. Henceforth, there will be a patrol at night." He set his jaw, and his eyes flashed. "I shall send Stone to talk to you tomorrow morning. Perhaps you might be able to add something to your description of the man now," he added dryly.

"I don't know how, since it was dark, and he wore a mask. Besides, I told you—I don't think it was the same man."

"Nonsense. Who else could it be?" He paused, then added shrewdly, "I realize that you have no desire to help me, Nicola. Ever since that unfortunate incident at the Falls, you have regarded me with—"

"Unfortunate incident!" Nicola exclaimed. "You killed the man I loved, and you call it an 'unfortunate incident'?"

"It was an accident. You know that. We were struggling, and he fell. I regret that it happened, but I can scarcely go on atoning to you for it for the rest of my days."

"I don't ask that you atone to me," Nicola retorted. "Whatever happened is between you and God. But you can scarcely expect me to regard you with liking after what you did."

"No, I have realized that. However, I would think you would care about your sister and our unborn child. This fellow disturbs her, and you know how delicate her health is. The slightest thing could bring about another tragedy."

"Are you suggesting that the highwayman's larcenous escapades could bring about another miscarriage for my sister? Really, Richard, I think that is carrying it a bit too far."

The Earl's brows drew together in a haughty look. "I must say, Nicola, this work you do among the fallen women of London has brought a certain coarseness to your speech. I must hope that you do not speak so bluntly in front of your sister."

"No, I protect Deborah as much as I can from the harsh realities of life. However, I see little need to shield *you* from them, as well. Whatever the reason my sister has lost each of her babies, it has had nothing to do with this highwayman. It simply tramples your pride that he manages to elude you."

"I might have known that you would make a hero of him, too." Richard's voice dripped acid. "The man is nothing but a common thief. One would think that this evening's incident might have demonstrated that to you. But you remain stubbornly woolly-minded."

"I have not made a hero of him." Nicola's eyes flashed, and her hands doubled into fists. "And I promise you that I am not in the slightest woolly-minded. However, the man in my room tonight was *not* the highwayman. Now, if you will excuse me, I would like to return to my slumber…and I believe that you said something about searching the grounds?"

"Yes. Of course. Good night." Richard offered her a small, stiff bow and whipped around to start down the stairs.

Nicola grimaced and stalked back to her bedroom. She had never felt less like sleeping, but she needed to get away from the annoyance of her brother-in-law and think. Inside her room, she lit a lamp and quickly checked her vanity and dresser. She could find nothing missing from her things. She could also not find a key to the door anywhere, even though she searched all the drawers and even climbed up to look on top of the large wardrobe.

She did not relish the idea of going back to bed in a room that she could not secure. She glanced around, then picked up a small straight-backed chair and hauled it over to the door, propping the top of it under the handle. Nicola was not sure that it would jam and prevent the door opening when pushed, but at the least it would create a great deal of noise when it fell, and she would wake up.

With that task done, she pulled on a dressing gown over her night rail and stepped into her bedroom slippers, tasks she had overlooked in her rush to catch the intruder. Then she walked over to the window and shoved aside the curtain to gaze out at the dark and think.

Richard obviously wanted to blame the highwayman for what had happened tonight; she would never change his mind. However, she was equally certain that her intruder had not been Jack. The problem, as Richard had pointed out, was that there were no other likely candidates for the role.

This was a quiet country area, not a city teeming with burglars and footpads. It was unusual for a highwayman to be operating in such a place; the thought that there might be a house thief here, as well, was patently absurd.

The second problem was that even if she admitted the

far-fetched possibility of such a thief breaking into Tidings, it would have been the height of foolishness on his part to sneak into the room of a young woman in search of valuables. An unmarried woman, even a wealthy one, rarely had jewelry of any value. She, for instance, had nothing other than a cameo or two on ribbons, a string of pearls, and a few earbobs of jet, pearl or opal—and even these had been taken by the highwayman. The only jewelry she valued was Gil's ring, which hung warm against her flesh beneath her nightgown. She would have been immensely sad if it had been stolen, but even then, it was not particularly valuable in the world's eyes. Any self-respecting thief would have gone straight to the silver and gold plate downstairs, or to the safe, where Richard doubtless kept the family heirlooms. And if anyone in the house were so careless as to leave valuable jewels lying about, it was much more likely to be in the Countess's room—though that thought was enough to make Nicola shudder.

Such reasoning applied to the highwayman as well as any other thief—even more so, since he would know that Nicola had no jewels, having taken them himself the night she arrived in Dartmoor.

So if thievery were not the aim, what was? Being logical, Nicola knew that she must consider that the man had been after herself, not any jewels or money. He could have broken in to rape her. Nicola had seen the aftermath of such attacks too often among women in the East End to not know that it could happen. *However, if that had been his intent, why had he been standing in front of her vanity?* It would be more logical to go straight to her sleeping form on the bed, she thought. There was also the fact that when she woke up, he ran, rather than rushing to her to subdue her. Though she admittedly had little knowledge of the workings of such a man's mind, his actions made little sense if he were intent on harming her…in any way.

Yet he must have been there for some reason. *If it was not to hurt her or kill her or steal from her, what was it?* No matter how hard she racked her brain, Nicola could come up with no reason.

She decided to go at the problem from another direction. If she could not figure out *why,* perhaps she could work on *who.* Because of the mask and his height, her first thought had been of the highwayman, but she had discarded him as a suspect. It would be far easier and safer to enter her room, she thought, if one was already inside the house rather than having to break in. It could have been a servant—one or two of the footmen were perhaps tall enough. Of course, it would be foolhardy in the extreme for one of them to be caught in her bedroom for whatever purpose, but perhaps if they were driven enough by greed or lust…but again the same problems came to the forefront. Any of the servants could get much more money from taking some of the silver or some other valuable object in the house—and it would be much less risky for them to do it in the daytime, anyway. And if it was lust, again, why would he be hanging about her vanity instead of her bed?

Mr. Stone came to mind. She had not liked him, and she could well see him in the role of intruder. He was not staying here, but rooming in the inn in the village. However, he had been in the house a good deal and could have jammed a door or window so that he could reenter easily. However, he was not as tall as the man she had seen. And there was Richard, whom she could readily cast as a villain. He was tall enough to have been her intruder and had easy access to her chamber, being only a few yards down the hall. She had seen him come out of his room, but there might have been enough time for him to run to his room, discard the mask and throw his dressing gown on over his clothes, then make his appearance, looking innocent and surprised. She had, after all, been dazed and had sat for a moment, then struggled to her feet. *How long had it been before he had emerged from his door after she went into the hall?*

Nicola wrinkled her brow, trying to recall, then sighed and dropped down into her chair. *This was all absurd. It didn't really matter whether Richard could have done it, because the fact remained that there was no reason for him to.* Richard least of all would have been after any valuables, and while he had once greatly desired her, surely he would not do anything so foolish as to try to force himself on his own wife's sister! Only driving, obsessive lust would cloud his judgment so, she thought, and she had not seen any sign that he regarded her with anything except cynical antagonism. In all these years that she had been forced to be around him at parties or with her sister, he had never once importuned her with even a kiss or caress. He could perhaps have wanted to search her room for some reason—to discover evidence that she knew something more about the highwayman than she let on, perhaps? He seemed a trifle suspicious in that regard. However, Nicola knew that it would have been far easier for him to have searched her room this afternoon while she was out of the house than to sneak in at night while she was lying right there, easily awakened, and then rummage about in the dark.

It was all so unlikely that it was enough to make her wonder if she really had dreamed the whole incident,

Nicola thought with a grim twist of humor. However, the throbbing in her cheek was enough to remind her that the incident was all too real. The intruder had hit her; she would be lucky if she didn't have a bruise the next day.

And *that,* she reminded herself, was ample proof that the intruder had not been the highwayman. She was certain that he would not have hit her. Why, he had not raised a hand to her when she had provided him with much more reason by slapping him. Her intruder had been both un-gentlemanly and cowardly, two things the highwayman definitely was not.

A faint smile played upon Nicola's lips. Well—perhaps the highwayman had not acted in a precisely gentleman-like manner. She leaned her head back against the high-backed chair and let her mind drift to earlier this evening. He had behaved reprehensibly, of course, and she hoped never to see him again—and if she did, she certainly would not act in the fuzzy-headed way she had this evening. However, she could not help wondering about the man. *Where did a man like that come from? What had set him on this course? Was he a gentleman, a knave, or something in between?*

And, most of all, why did he alone, of all the men in England, have such an effect on her?

AFTER HER ADVENTURES THE NIGHT BEFORE, Nicola rose rather later than usual. She found, when she moved aside the chair and opened the door, that the maid had come and, being unable to open the door, had left a tray with a pot of tea and a plate of toast. The tea was still warm, and Nicola drank a cup of it, then dressed and went forth to find her sister. Deborah was not in the dining room, but Nicola paused long enough to have a rather fresher cup of tea and a few pieces of toast with butter and mouth-watering strawberry jam.

One of the maids informed her that her sister was feeling "low" this morning and had remained in bed, so after her light breakfast, Nicola went upstairs to Deborah's room. She opened the door quietly and poked her head inside. Deborah was awake and lying on her side in the massive dark bed, her eyes huge and shadowed, as though charcoal had been smudged beneath them.

"Nicky…" Deborah gave her a wan smile. "I am afraid I'm not feeling quite the thing this morning."

"His little lordship is making his presence known today," a woman's voice said crisply, and she stood up from a chair on the other side of Deborah's bed.

Nicola refrained from remarking that the baby must be remarkably like his father, then, if he made his presence known in such an obnoxious manner. She studied the woman, who was well past middle age, with iron-gray hair severely clubbed back and pinned. Her clothes were gray, with starched white collar and cuffs, and her eyes, too, were the hue of a winter sky, so that she seemed to be all one color. She was tall and stiff-backed despite her age, seemingly almost in defiance of it, and she had a face that Nicola wagered had rarely been visited by a smile.

"Oh, Nicola, I'm sorry. You have not met Nurse Gregory," Deborah said quickly. "This is Nurse Gregory, the Earl's nurse when he was a child. Nurse, this is my sister Nicola Falcourt. Nurse comes to sit with me when I am not feeling well," Deborah said in explanation.

"His lordship was so kind as to give me a cottage on the estate to retire to," Nurse said in a heavy, formal tone. "I can do no less for him than to care for his heir."

Nicola thought that this formidable woman was the last

person she would want to have sitting with her if she felt ill. Deborah looked rather intimidated by the woman, frankly. Nicola gave the nurse a brief, cool smile.

"It is nice to meet you, Nurse Gregory. It was very kind of you to help my sister. But now that I am here, I shall sit with her. Shall I read to you, Deb?"

Deborah brightened. "Oh, yes, that sounds nice." She turned uncertainly toward the older woman. "If that's all right with you, Nurse?"

"I am sure Nurse Gregory would welcome an opportunity to rest," Nicola said, not giving the woman a chance to speak. "It was kind of her to come, but doubtless she would prefer to be under her own roof."

Nicola turned her gaze on the other woman, as flat and ungiving as the older woman's. Nurse Gregory had little choice but to give in, which she did with little grace, packing up her knitting bag and marching out with only a perfunctory goodbye to Deborah. Deborah watched the door close behind her and sighed.

"Oh, dear, I hope she isn't angry. Richard does so dislike it that I have never warmed up to his old nurse."

"Having met her gives me more of an insight into why Richard is the way he is," Nicola commented dryly.

A giggle bubbled out of Deborah, and she looked fractionally better. "Oh, Nicky, you shouldn't say such things. But she *is* grim, isn't she?"

"Very. Nothing at all like our nurse."

"Oh, no!" Deborah's face warmed even more as she remembered the plump, apple-cheeked woman who had cared for her and Nicola when they were young. "Nurse was such a dear. Always so cheerful. Remember how she used to sing to us? And the hot chocolate she made? Mmm, I'd love some of that now."

"Would you? Then I'll ring for a maid and have Cook make you a cup. I am sure it will not match Nurse's, but it will cheer you up a little, don't you think?"

"Oh, yes. I am sorry that I'm so blue. It's silly of me, I know. Other women go through this all the time—and so much more easily than I."

"Nonsense. It doesn't matter what other women do. You *are* the only one I worry about. You are my baby sister, and you must let me coddle you."

Nicola pulled the bell cord for a maid, and when she arrived, bobbing a curtsey, ordered a small pot of hot chocolate and a plate of toast for her sister.

"You know," she said, after the maid had left, "I just had a thought. Why not write Nurse and ask her to come stay with you and care for you?"

A smile broke across her sister's face like sunshine, then just as quickly vanished. "Oh, no, I could not do that. Nurse Gregory's feelings would be hurt, and Richard would not like that."

"I shall talk to Richard," Nicola replied. "I am sure that your husband would want you to have the person who made you feel the most comfortable and happy. After all, it is not only his wife, but his heir, at issue here. I am sure he wants only the best for you. He doesn't know that you would prefer your old nurse unless you tell him. He probably thinks you are quite happy with Nurse Gregory, but that is scarcely the truth."

"Oh, please, you mustn't…."

"Don't fret," Nicola reassured her quickly. "I won't upset Richard, and it will be he, not you, who tells Nurse Gregory that your old nurse is coming to take care of you. There is nothing for you to worry about. Once Nurse is here, you will feel ten times better, I promise you."

Doubt warred with pleasure on Deborah's face. "It would be nice to have Nurse here...."

"If Richard doesn't approve of the idea, it won't happen, will it?" Nicola remarked. "So you needn't worry about it. Now, why don't I read to you for a little while? Your chocolate should be here soon, and then you might take a little nap."

"Yes, that sounds nice," Deborah agreed, happy to let go of the other problem.

The maid brought the pot of chocolate and the toast, and Deborah, propped up on pillows and listening to Nicola, managed to get down most of it. Later, Nicola tucked her in and left her sleeping peacefully, with one of the maids to watch over her in case she awakened and needed anything.

Nicola went back to her room and quickly pulled on her riding habit, then set forth on a few errands of her own. First she rode over to call on her aunt, Lady Buckminster. It was only polite to pay her respects to her aunt now that she was staying nearby, but Nicola had a further plan in mind, which required her aunt's complicity. Lady Buckminster, a pleasant, easygoing woman, was happy to see her niece and just as agreeable to the scheme Nicola suggested.

Afterward, Nicola rode to the village to check on the child she had treated the day before. The boy was doing much better, as were his parents, and Nicola rode back to Tidings, glancing around now and then as she rode. She half expected the highwayman to pop up somewhere—though, of course, that was *not* why she had come, she reminded herself—but he did not appear. Nicola could not deny the faint sense of disappointment she felt. It was, she told herself, only because the highwayman provided a certain excitement.

She spent the rest of the afternoon reading to her sister again, and the two of them ate a private supper from a tray in Deborah's bedroom, with Nicola teasing and cajoling her sister into eating a little chicken and bread. Nicola went to bed early that night, positioning the chair under the knob as she had the night before, but she found herself unable to sleep, tossing and turning and thinking about the highwayman.

The next day Deborah was feeling better, her morning sickness subsided, and she dressed and came downstairs to the sitting room in the afternoon. Lady Buckminster came to call on them, bringing with her the vicar's wife, which brought Richard in from his office to greet the ladies.

Nicola smiled to herself. So far her plan was working perfectly. They alluded in a genteel way to Deborah's health, then Lady Buckminster said cheerfully, "You know what would be just the thing for you, Deb? You ought to send to Larchmont for your old nurse. That would make you feel much better."

"My nurse has been taking care of Deborah," Richard proffered. "She is quite good."

"Of course she is, but Nurse Gregory's getting up in years, there's no denying that. She would probably be grateful for a little relief. Besides, there's nothing like one's *own* nurse, is there, Deborah?"

Deborah glanced a little nervously toward her husband. "I am sure that Nurse Gregory is quite good," she demurred.

"Oh, don't be so missish, Deb," Lady Buckminster replied in her hearty way. "You know you want your own nurse. Men don't understand these things, I'm afraid." She glanced at Richard. "I'm sure you'll agree, Exmoor.

I know my own dear husband just gave me carte blanche to do what I wished during my 'times.'"

"Of course. If that is what Deborah wishes..." Richard gave Lady Buckminster a perfunctory smile.

"Good. Then that's settled," Lady Buckminster said with a decisive nod. "I'll send for her as soon as I get home. What was her name?"

"Owens. Gladys Owens," Nicola supplied smoothly, smiling to herself. She had been certain that there was nothing that Richard could do but comply to the request, coming as it did from Lady Buckminster and with the vicar's wife present. To have done anything else would have seemed churlish.

Nicola turned and saw Richard watching her, a small, sardonic smile on his lips. Later, after her aunt and the vicar's wife had left, Richard turned to her and said mildly, "Really, my dear sister, you did not need to engage in such stratagems to get your old nurse installed here."

"Stratagems?" Nicola asked with supreme innocence. "I don't know what you are talking about."

"Come, come, you mustn't take me for such a fool as to believe I think that Lady Buckminster would ever think of sending for Deborah's nurse to care for her—unless, of course, Nurse Owens were a noted horsewoman. This has your handiwork all over it."

"I shall tell her not to, if you don't want her to come, Richard," Deborah offered.

"Nonsense. If your nurse would make you feel better, by all means send for her. If I had known that you did not like Nurse Gregory, I would not have—"

"I do not dislike her," Deborah began, looking distraught. "It is just that my nurse is, well, so familiar."

"Of course." The Earl shrugged and smiled. "I understand perfectly. And that is exactly who you should have. But there was no need for the secrecy." He turned toward Nicola. "Someday, Nicola, you are going to have to stop casting me as the villain of your little scenarios."

"Villain!" Deborah gasped. "Oh, no, Richard, you must not think that—"

"Really, Deborah, I know *you* do not think so." Impatience tinged his voice, and Deborah quickly subsided. "It is your sister who makes me out to be one."

"Oh, no, Richard, you mistake me," Nicola said in a voice as light and brittle as glass. "I do not *make* you anything. You are as you are, without any effort on my part."

Richard smiled tightly and started to respond, but at that moment the butler stepped into the room, and instead Richard turned toward him.

"Mr. Stone to see you, my lord," the butler announced. "I have seated him in your study."

Richard nodded in response, then turned and bowed slightly toward Nicola and Deborah. "Ladies, if you will excuse me? I am afraid I have business to attend to now."

He left the room, and Deborah turned toward her sister. "He wasn't angry with me, do you think?"

"Of course not, Deb. I am sure he thinks I am an interfering busybody, but I don't care about that."

"Good. I'm glad that Nurse is coming. I know I'll feel better with her here."

"I am sure you will, too." Nicola paused, then added casually, "Mr. Stone certainly seems to be here a great deal."

Deborah made a face. "Yes. He was here just last night. Richard said he might let him stay in that empty room off the kitchen. I wish he wouldn't. I don't like the man."

"I don't, either. Do you think that he will succeed? Find the highwayman, I mean?"

Deborah frowned. "I don't know. Richard says Mr. Stone is quite competent. He seems cold to me, but I presume that would help one do his job. Mr. Stone suggested that Richard hire extra men to guard the wagons, and Richard agreed."

"Really? You mean, men with guns?"

Deborah nodded. "Yes."

"Oh, dear. I hope no one gets hurt." Nicola had a vision of the highwayman toppling from his horse, a red stain blossoming across his shirt. She clenched her hands in her lap. "I think perhaps some of the villagers may have joined the highwayman's gang."

"That is what that man Stone thinks. I heard him tell Richard so. He thinks that a bribe will bring one of them to betray The Gentleman. Richard said that they would try it if the extra guards did not work."

It occurred to Nicola that her sister had apparently overheard a great deal of the conversation between the two men, and she wondered if perhaps Deborah had stood with her ear glued to the door to Richard's room.

"I could not understand everything they said," Deborah added naively. "But I think there is a shipment tonight, and the extra guards will be there. I hope nothing happens...."

Nicola could not rid herself of the thought of extra guards with guns on the wagon tonight. She tried not to think about the highwayman getting shot, but she could not keep from picturing it in her mind.

That evening, after supper, Richard was called away. Nicola and Deborah, still sitting in the drawing room, heard his raised voice in the study. She could not understand what he said, but the tone was definitely angry. In a few minutes the study door opened and Mr. Stone walked down the hall, followed by the sound of the door slamming behind him. Nicola pressed her lips together to suppress a smile. Richard was furious, and that could only mean that the highwayman had not been killed or captured.

"Oh, dear," Deborah murmured worriedly. "Perhaps… perhaps we should go on to bed."

"You're absolutely right," Nicola agreed with alacrity, her heart amazingly lighter.

She went upstairs with Deborah and walked down the hall to her room. There she went through her nightly ritual of hooking the chair beneath the knob before she turned and sat down in front of her vanity to take down her hair. Absentmindedly she pulled out the pins from her thick golden hair and let it fall to her shoulders, all the while wondering what had happened tonight. *Had Jack pulled off the robbery despite the extra guards?* She felt certain that he had not been killed because of Richard's reaction, but that did not mean that all of the men had escaped harm. She hated to think that someone from the village had died tonight—or that one of the guards had, either.

She picked up her silver-backed brush and began to run it through her hair with long strokes. Her head was down, her thoughts far away, when she heard a faint rustle. Her head came up sharply, and in the mirror she saw the image of a man behind her before he closed the gap in one long stride and clapped his hand over her mouth, pulling her up out of her seat and back hard against his body.

CHAPTER SEVEN

For an instant, Nicola froze. Then she began to struggle. The man's other arm went immediately around her body, pinning her arms to her sides and effectively circumventing her, but she was able to kick back with her heel and was rewarded by a soft grunt of pain.

Then she felt the smooth touch of satin against her ear as he hissed, "Dammit, vixen! Stop it. I am not going to hurt you. I just don't want you to scream and bring the whole bloody household in."

Nicola recognized the low rasp of his voice even as she opened her eyes and saw in the mirror that the man standing behind her, bending down to whisper to her, wore a mask over the upper portion of his face, a sort of black satin scarf that wrapped around his face and over the top of his head, pirate-like, and tied in the back. Only intense dark eyes and the bottom portion of his face showed, but she recognized him, just as she knew his voice.

"Jack!" She stopped struggling. "What the devil are you doing here?"

"Tsk, tsk…such language from a lady." His husky voice brimmed with amusement.

"Oh, stop," Nicola said disgustedly. "Really, I have had enough of your foolish games. Was it you who came into

my room the other night? You have a great deal of nerve
coming back here."

"Came into your room?" he repeated. "What are you
talking about? I didn't—there was a man in your room?"
His voice roughened, and his arm tightened around her.

"You are cutting off my breath," Nicola protested. "Yes.
I awoke the night before last, and there was a man in my
room—wearing a mask."

"The devil!" He released Nicola and spun her around
to face him. "What happened? Did he harm you?"

"No. I frightened him off."

"If you were able to scare him off, then you must know
it was not I," he retorted with a grin.

Nicola grimaced. "I assumed it was not, since he lacked
your arrogance."

"What was he doing here? Did he try—"

"He didn't try anything. He was looking at my vanity
table."

"What?" Jack glanced down at the table, then back at
her. "Why?"

"How should I know? I woke up and saw him, then I
shouted at him, and he ran out the door."

"He was wearing a mask?" he asked, then went on. "No
doubt it was someone who wanted to implicate me—your
esteemed brother-in-law, for instance."

"That was his sole purpose—to make everyone think you
had broken into my room? Then why was he lurking about
the vanity? What good would it do to break in here, anyway?"

"To steal something from you. To harm you—and make
it look as if I was the one who had done it."

"Why bother, since you apparently are quite willing to
break in here yourself?"

His mouth tightened. "Not to hurt you."

"How am I to know that?"

"I should hope you are not enough of a fool to think that I—" He stopped abruptly and released a sigh. "Bloody hell! You are the most irritating woman. The fact is, I came for your help."

Nicola raised her brows. "You are certainly going about it in an unusual manner. Insults are not typically the way to get someone to help you."

"It isn't I who needs you, actually. I wouldn't have come to you if that were the case. It is one of my men— he was wounded tonight."

"Oh, no! One of the villagers?"

"No. One of the men who came with me—my friend. He was shot in the chest, and I am afraid he's in bad shape."

"He has a ball in his chest?" Nicola gasped, and the man nodded. "Then you should take him to a doctor. I cannot— I have never—I merely concoct tonics and salves and such."

"I would not turn him over to a doctor—that is as good as a death sentence. You can do it. You've seen it done."

"What?" Nicola asked, surprised. "Why would you think that I—"

"They tell me that you studied with Granny Rose. They say that she was magical at healing—that she could cut and stitch better than any doctor."

"Yes. I have seen her do that. I assisted her a time or two…." Nicola stopped, frowning. She had helped Granny Rose once when she had dug a ball from a gameskeeper's musket out of an unfortunate poacher's arm, even though it had turned her stomach. And Granny had described to her how she had done the same sort of thing with a piece of a tine from a farmer's hayfork. She had even once herself pulled out the broken-off end of a knife from the chest of a man in the East End when he showed up at her kitchen, asking for help.

Nicola shook her head. "But that is not the same. I couldn't dig about in a man's chest searching for a musket ball! What if he dies?"

"He will die for sure if I let a doctor have at him. At least you can prevent him from dying from a fever afterward. That is what the villagers say—that you can cure pus in a wound and the fever that comes with it." He paused, then added, "Surely you won't let him die just because he is a thief, will you?"

"Of course not!" Nicola responded indignantly. "That's not it at all. But I am not sure—"

"The only sure thing is that he will die if you don't help him." His dark eyes were steely as they gazed into hers. "Are you willing to let that happen?"

"No. All right. I will come. But how—" She glanced at the door into the hall. "How will we leave? How did you get in, anyway?"

He looked at the door, with the chair propped under the knob. "Actually, your apparatus wasn't there when I came in. I was already inside the room. But I came by way of the window."

"The window!" Nicola stared. "But that is a sheer drop!"

"There are niches and jut-outs here and there—enough that I managed. However, I don't expect you to go down that way. I brought this."

He crossed to the window and drew out a coiled rope from behind the chair. "We'll use it to get down."

Nicola cocked an eyebrow at the rope. "You may be agile as a squirrel, but I can tell you that I can't go scaling walls in full skirts, even with a rope."

He smiled faintly. "You won't have to. You'll see. Just get your medicines. We need to make haste."

Nicola nodded and pulled out the bag she used to carry her supplies. Quickly she took out some of the bottles and herbs that she would not need and made sure that she included such things as meadowsweet and comfrey, as well as ample bandages and tweezers. When she was ready, Jack swung the strap of the bag over his shoulder and picked up the rope. He tied one end around the sturdy post of her bed, which stood next to the window, and the other around his waist, then tested both knots. He opened the window and peered out, and when he was satisfied that no one was about, he grasped the rope, sat down on the windowsill and slung one leg out. He turned to Nicola, holding out his arm.

"All right. Now, you come and hold on around my neck as hard as you can."

"What?" Nicola looked at him with misgiving.

"Come on," he said impatiently. "I am not trying to seduce you. I am going to rappel down the wall, and I will carry you. That's all."

Nicola looked at him, considering, then sighed, wrapped her cloak about her shoulders and walked over to him. Tentatively she put her arms around his neck, clasping her forearms with her hands. She was only inches from him. She could feel his warmth and smell the mingled scents of horse, leather and man.

He wrapped his arm around her, pulling her tightly against his body, lifting her up and into him as he reached around to grasp the rope with both hands. He shoved them out of the window with his foot, and for a breathtaking moment they were dangling in the air. Nicola clung even closer to him, unsure whether her pulse was pounding from the danger or from being pressed against him all the way up and down her body. She hung on, burying her face in his chest, as he planted his feet against the wall and began to "walk" slowly down it, moving his hands along the rope as he slid down.

Nicola held on to him, scarcely breathing, trying not to think about how high in the air they were—or how his hard body felt against hers, or how strangely exciting the satin touch of his mask was against her face, or how strong his arm was around her. It seemed as if everywhere her mind skittered was worse than before.

With a thump, Jack dropped the last foot to the ground. He held her tightly against him for a moment before he lowered her to the earth and stepped back. He turned away from her, unknotting the rope from his waist. Leaving the rope dangling from the window, he took her hand and led her along the wall, his eyes constantly roaming the grounds. When they reached the back of the house, he stood still as a statue, looking around him. Then he gave her hand a tug and began to run lightly along the path away from the house, pulling Nicola along with him. He made his way through the garden, careful to stay close to the trees and large bushes, until they were out of sight of the house.

They hurried along a path until at last they came upon Jack's horse, tethered to a tree and patiently waiting. Nicola came to a halt and turned toward the highwayman.

"What am I to ride?"

"You will ride with me. We cannot risk going to the stables to get you a horse."

Nicola thought about riding on the horse with Jack, her body necessarily close to his. "It will be much faster if I have my own mount."

"We haven't the time to waste. God knows if he will even be alive by the time we get back. Now, are you going to get on that horse, or shall I put you on it?"

Nicola made a face and put her foot in his cupped hands, letting him toss her up onto the horse. Jack climbed on behind her, so that she sat between his legs, resting so intimately against him that it made her blush. Then he pulled a black scarf from his pocket and reached up to put it around her head. Nicola pulled back from him.

"No! What are you doing?"

"You have to wear a blindfold."

"What? No!"

"Yes. I cannot let you see the route I take. You could lead the Earl straight to our house."

"I wouldn't do that," Nicola protested.

"I can't take the chance," he replied stonily. "If you don't wear the blindfold, it will mean you cannot leave our hideout."

He looked straight into her eyes, his gaze stony, and Nicola shivered. "All right."

She closed her eyes as he wrapped the scarf around her head. The cloth was cool and soft, reducing her world to darkness. She felt vulnerable and a little frightened, but there was something strangely exciting about it, too. It was as if the darkness separated her from reality, relieving her of responsibility for herself or what happened. And, as if to compensate for the loss of her sight, she was suddenly very much alive to all other sensory stimuli. The silk scarf was luxuriously soft against her cheek, the touch of the breeze on her face delightful and unexpected. She was enveloped by Jack's male scent and his warmth, his chest flush against her back, his arms around her as he held the reins, his legs firmly cupping her bottom.

It was a heady sensation, as sensual as if he had caressed her body with his hands, and her breasts and loins grew warm and heavy, almost tender, and she realized with a sense of shame that she wished he would touch her. She hoped he could not feel the rush of heat that invaded her body.

In the darkness, and with the double weight, they could not ride swiftly. Nicola could sense her companion's impatience in the rock-hard tautness of his arms and in the rise and fall of his chest behind her back. His nerves sizzled within him, creating an almost tangible air of tension, which only increased the jangling of Nicola's own nerves.

She was intensely aware of all the sounds that came through the hush of the night—the call of an owl or the rustle of bushes as an animal skittered away from them, the jingle of the horse's harness, the soft thud of his hooves upon the dirt path. She was also all too aware of the heat of Jack's body, the strength and hardness of it against her own. The horse's gait moved her against him in a way that both embarrassed and aroused her. She wondered if he was as conscious of it as she was—she did not see how he could be ignorant of it—and if it raised the same sort of sensations in him that it did in her.

Nicola was amazed at this wanton streak that had sprung up in her of late. She had never in the past had the least trouble controlling her actions or, indeed, the feelings upon which those actions were based. *How was it that now it had become so difficult?* Even now, as she took herself to task for her lack of will, she was distracted by the scent of him so close to her. She shifted, trying to pull her mind back, but that had the unfortunate result of rubbing her bottom against him even more than the horse's gait was doing. She felt an answering movement, a prodding that she realized with a wave of embarrassment was his physical response to her motion. She blushed, glad of the covering darkness that would hide her red face. *Would he think she had done that on purpose? To entice him?* Clearly there was no way she could explain without thrusting herself deeper and deeper into embarrassment.

She tried to hold herself away from him, but that stiff posture was impossible to maintain for any length of time, and soon she was leaning against him again, her body fitting naturally into the curves of his. The ride seemed to go on forever, and all the while her blood ran hotter and hotter through her veins. Their gait grew slower, and it seemed to Nicola that the horse and its rider were picking their way. Now and then he shifted a little in the saddle behind her, and his arm would leave her momentarily. Nicola became aware of an earthy aroma of damp, plants and decay, and she suspected that they were traveling through trees deeper into the woods. Her hunch was confirmed by the occasional soft touch of a tender branch or leaves against her cheek or shoulder. The light touches, the ripe scent of the forest and the velvet darkness added to Nicola's sensual awareness, already heightened to the boiling point by the horse's rocking gait as she sat cradled between Jack's legs. Once, breathlessly, she was certain she felt Jack's hand slide down from where it clasped her waist and move onto her thigh, and another time she felt a whisper touch of something on her hair and heard the harsh rasp of his breath closer to her ear.

There was a distinct note of relief in the highwayman's voice when at last he said, "There it is! We're almost to it."

Moments later the horse came to a halt, and Jack slid

down from behind her. His hands went to her waist, pulling her down from the saddle. He set her down, and she stumbled, sightless. His arms went around her more tightly to steady her, and for a moment she was pressed against his body, his heart a steady pounding in her ear. Then his hands went to her shoulders and he turned her, guiding her around the horse and up two steps. There was the sound of a door opening, and his arm around her moved her inside. The door closed after them.

Nicola could see edges of light around her blindfold. He fumbled with the knot and pulled the cloth from her eyes. Nicola blinked in the sudden light, though it was only a single squat candle, guttering low. She saw that she was in a tiny foyer. Jack lifted a longer taper from a small table and lit it from the candle, then fitted it into a candleholder.

"Come with me." He did not give her a chance to do anything but obey him, taking her by the arm with his free hand and leading her up the stairs.

It was even darker upstairs, the only illumination besides Jack's candle being a sliver of light coming from beneath a door at the end of the hall. It was toward this door that they walked, Jack's steps growing faster and faster until he reached it. He opened the door softly, though, none of his impatience showing, and entered, leading Nicola in after him.

The scene inside was dimly lit, but horrifying nonetheless. Heavy drapes covered the only window, and the air was close inside the room, thick with the scent of a poorly drawing fire, sweat, blood and whiskey. A man lay on the narrow bed, eyes closed in his unnaturally pale face, his chest laboring to breathe. The covers were pushed aside, and his dark shirt had been opened, revealing his bare chest. A bulky bandage lay over one side of his chest and shoulder, heavily stained with blood. His face was spotted with sweat, and his hair was dark with moisture. A man sat in a chair beside the bed, his elbows on his knees and his hands thrust through his hair, his face turned downward. A bottle of whiskey stood on the small square table between his chair and the bed, along with an oil lamp, which provided the feeble light in the room. On the other side of the bed stood a young woman, wringing her hands. Her eyes were wide with fear, and tears ran down her cheeks.

"Oh, dear, oh, dear," she repeated over and over in a dreary monotone. She turned at the sound of Jack's footsteps on the floor. "Jack! Thank God you're here!"

The girl ran across the room to throw herself against Jack's chest, sobbing. Nicola watched with distaste as Jack tried to untangle himself from the girl's clinging arms. "How is he? Dirk?"

The other man raised his head. He looked haggard. "It ain't good, Jack. He's having trouble breathing."

Nicola knew that this was not good news. If the ball had pierced his lung and it was filling up with blood, there would be little she could do to save him. However, when she saw Jack look to the bed, his body taut as a wire and an unmistakable flash of fear in his dark eyes, she said quickly, "It is no wonder that he would have trouble breathing, as close as the air is in this room. Open the door. Can we not crack the window? And I scarcely think we need a roaring fire right now, especially one that fills the room with smoke, as that one does."

Jack relaxed, a smile coming to his lips as he turned toward her. "Never one to mince words, are you, my dear Miss Falcourt? Allow me to introduce Dirk. He has been watching over my friend while I went to fetch you. And this is Diane. She, uh, is with another of my men, and she takes care of the house."

He had succeeded in detaching the girl from himself as he said this, but she continued to look at him in a way that made Nicola suspect Diane was far more interested in him than in any of his men—or his house. Whatever she was to Jack, she certainly was not of much use in a sickroom.

"This is Miss Falcourt," Jack said, talking to the man and woman. "She is here to help Perry. You are to do what she asks."

Dirk nodded, gazing at her with bleary interest, and the girl cast her a sullen look before nodding her understanding.

"So put out the fire, Dirk," Jack said crisply. "Draw the drapes and open the window, Di."

"But what about the light?" the girl asked, looking disgruntled. "Anyone could see it. 'Sides, everyone knows the night air's not good for a sick man."

"He isn't sick, he is injured," Nicola told her. "There is a difference. You are adding to his troubles by making him sweat and breathe fetid air. We need to help him, not make it harder for him."

"Do as I said, Diane," Jack added in a voice that brooked no disobedience. "Leave the shutters closed and little light will get out, while some air gets in. The trees will hide it, too, and if it is discovered…" He shrugged. "I will not let Perry die so that we can remain undetected."

He turned to Nicola. "What else should we do?"

"I have to clean the wound. I need the purest water you have. Granny Rose used distilled water, as she did for her decoctions and infusions, but we haven't the equipment or time for that now. I have one bottle of distilled water—I will use that. But we need more. Boil some and let it cool.

That will leave some of the impurities on the bottom of the pot. I'll need more light. I can barely see the patient, let alone find a ball in his wound."

Jack nodded and went to turn up the lamp. He added his candle to the table beside the lamp, then went in search of more lamps. Nicola walked over to the table and looked down at the man lying in the bed. Her eyes went first to his wound, covered by the lumpy, amateurish bandage. It was soaked with blood, but it was brownish and much of it dried, rather than fresh, which indicated that at least the bleeding had stopped. She feared that when she pulled off the bandage to look at it, the bleeding would start afresh, so she decided to wait until more light arrived.

Her eyes went to the man's face. Like Dirk and the girl, he wore no mask, and Nicola could see that he was a rather good-looking man in his late thirties or early forties, with a Norman nose, long face and reddish-blond coloring. He opened his eyes as she stood there.

"Hullo." His voice was thick and weak. "I would swear you were an angel, but I doubt that would be the place I've gone."

Nicola smiled. "You are far too ready with your tongue to be approaching either heaven or hell right now, sir. My name is Nicola Falcourt, and I am here to help you, if I can."

"Ah…Nicola Falcourt…" The man's eyes wavered. His face was flushed, and an overpowering smell of whiskey hung over him.

Jack walked into the room, carrying an oil lamp in each hand, and Nicola turned to him accusingly. "Is this man drunk?" She cast a critical glance at Dirk. "This one certainly seems to be. Not exactly the one I would entrust a wounded man to. Did you all sit around drinking before you came to get me?"

"No," Jack answered. "I gave Perry a shot or two of whiskey for the pain, and I will give him more before you begin to work on him. But most of the smell of alcohol comes from his wound. I poured whisky on it. I have seen it done before to cleanse a wound."

"It sounds as if you have had more experience than I in that regard," Nicola replied. "Perhaps you should be the one who digs the ball out."

"I will if I have to," he replied evenly.

Nicola nodded and turned back to her patient. "Perhaps you had better give him a drink, then, for I need to remove the bandage. I am afraid it will stick."

Without a word, Jack took the bottle in one hand and cupped the other behind the wounded man's head, lifting it. "Here you go, old boy. Take a drink. It will make it seem easier."

"But I don't want him drunk to the point of vomiting," Nicola cautioned. "That will only make it harder on all of us, including him."

The man in the bed took a slug of whiskey, then another, and Jack eased him back down onto the pillow. Nicola glanced at the girl, still standing beside the opened window, then at Jack. He nodded briefly in understanding.

"Go down to the kitchen and boil a pot of water for Miss Falcourt, Diane. Dirk, you go down, too, and send one of the other men up…one who hasn't been nipping at the whiskey bottle the past hour or two."

"Yes, sir." The other man gave Jack a hangdog look. "I'm sorry, sir. I didn't mean to. Only—it was hard just sittin' there watchin' 'im try to breathe."

"I know. It's all right. But I think we need someone with a steadier hand and eye right now. So send Saunders up, will you?"

The other man nodded and left the room, taking a reluctant Diane by the arm and hauling her out with him. Jack and Nicola turned back to the patient. He lay now with his eyes closed. His breathing was still heavy, but Nicola was relieved to hear none of the gurgling sounds that would indicate blood in his lungs.

Taking the bottle of distilled water out of her bag, she poured some of it on the bandage, dampening the crusted blood to soften it and cause less tearing when she took it off. Then she carefully peeled the bandage back. The patient drew in a sharp breath of pain as the bandage came off with a tug. Nicola sucked in her breath almost as sharply at the sight of the red, puckered wound. Fresh blood welled up out of it.

Nicola poured more of the water on one of the rags she had brought, then began to gently wash away the dried blood all around the wound. With the same care, she poured more of the water onto the man's chest, letting it flow down across the wound. She knew that it was painful, but she also knew that it was imperative to leave nothing in the wound. Granny Rose had always stressed that. Any bit of foreign material left in the wound was an irritant to it, she had said, and would work against the healing, creating an angry, pus-filled wound.

The water washed out a tiny fragment of black cloth, probably his shirt, and a few grains of gunpowder. Nicola continued to clean the wound with cloth and water until the pink-stained water ran clear of any other matter.

"Hold a lamp as close to the wound as you can," she told Jack, and when he did, she leaned down to examine the torn flesh. "I can't see the ball. I will have to probe for it."

She swallowed, her stomach roiling at the thought of

what she was about to do, and looked at Jack. His face was a trifle pale, too, she thought, but he merely nodded. "Saunders will help hold him down."

The man named Saunders knocked on the door and entered a moment later. Nicola took her tweezers from her bag, doing her best to ignore the jangling of her nerves and the icy fear in the pit of her stomach. She knew that this procedure would be incredibly painful for her patient, and the less skillful she was, the worse it would be. She could not let her hands shake, could not allow herself to feel or show doubt.

Saunders sat down on the patient's legs and took the lamp from Jack, holding it as close as he could to the wound. Jack went around to the head of the bed and leaned over the wounded man, placing his hands firmly on the man's arms. With the patient thus pinned, Nicola leaned over the bed and began to probe for the ball with her tweezers.

A bellow escaped the patient, and he began to twist and jerk, trying to get away. Jack and his helper clamped down even harder. As Nicola continued to feel for the metal ball, the man's eyes rolled up in his head, and he passed out. After that, it was easier.

Nicola could feel the beads of sweat rolling down her face and neck. Blood was welling up out of the man's wound now in a seeming flood. Her instrument clicked on metal. Biting her lip until it bled, Nicola manipulated the tweezers until she could clamp down on the bit of metal. Carefully, slowly, she lifted the tweezers, scared that she would make a false move and the ball would fly out of her grasp.

But now the tweezers were free of the wound, and clamped between them was a misshapen lump of metal.

Nicola drew a shaky breath that sounded very much like a sob and dropped both tweezers and the mangled ball of lead onto the bed. She sat down on the side of the bed, for the room was suddenly spinning around her, and lowered her head to her hands.

"You did it." Jack's voice was low and close to her ear, and his arm went around her shoulders, pressing her close to him.

As if his very warmth had brought home to her how cold she was, Nicola began to shiver. Quickly he stripped off his jacket and wrapped it around her, holding her in his arms and rubbing his hands up and down her arms.

"It's shock," he told her. "The aftermath of danger."

He nodded toward his man, who sprang up and poured a shot of whiskey into a glass, the bottle rattling against the rim. Jack took the glass from him and pressed it to Nicola's lips. "Here, drink this. It'll help you."

"I can't. There are still things I have to do." She turned vaguely toward the patient.

"You'll feel better if you take a drink of this."

Obediently she took a sip of the amber liquid. It roared like fire through her mouth and down her throat, bursting in her stomach. Nicola gasped and shuddered.

"Are you insane?" she managed to squeak out.

He chuckled. "Perhaps. A little. Take another sip."

It did not taste quite as bad this time, and Nicola realized after a moment that her trembling had ceased and she no longer felt as if she were freezing from the inside out. In that same instant she realized how close she was to Jack and how good and warm it felt to have his arm draped around her shoulders, protecting and soothing her.

She stood up abruptly. *This was not at all the sort of thing she should be thinking.* "Thank you."

She turned back to the man on the bed. Once again, she washed the wound clean, then held a bandage against it to stop the bleeding.

"Hold this here, hard," she told Jack, turning over the bandage to him, and went to her bag. Taking a vial of oil and a small pot, she returned to the bed. "Has the bleeding stopped?"

Jack nodded, lifting the bloodied cloth so that she could see. "What are those?"

"This is a cream of marigold mixed with marsh wound-wort," she explained, holding up the small pot and taking out a dab of it, which she applied carefully to the wound. "It helps prevent pus from forming. The other is oil infused with comfrey, to help it heal quickly."

When she had applied the remedies, she stitched the wound and placed a clean, soft folded cloth on the wound, and, while the two men held the patient's torso up off the bed, she wrapped a long strip of cloth around the man's chest to hold the bandage in place. Then she pulled the covers up over her patient's chest and stood for a moment looking down at him.

"That is all I can do right now," she told Jack. "He may get a fever. They often do. I will leave some powdered meadowsweet, which you can steep in hot water for a tea. It will ease his fever and pain. Change his bandage at least once a day—I will give you some clean ones. Reapply the marigold cream and comfrey oil when you change it."

She glanced back at her patient and sighed. "I am afraid it could be some time before he is out of the woods. He is still in a great deal of danger from fever and infection. If he does get delirious from fever, you will need to hold him down to keep him from reopening his wound. He will have to be watched round the clock." She frowned, thinking of the girl who had been set to look after him before she came; she had little faith that Diane would make an adequate nurse. "If you care for this man, you will make sure that someone competent is looking after him."

"I do care for him," Jack replied. "That is why you are going to stay."

CHAPTER EIGHT

NICOLA SIMPLY STARED AT HIM. "Excuse me? What did you just say?"

Jack turned toward Saunders and jerked his head toward the door. Saunders left without a word, and Jack turned back to Nicola. "I said that is why you will have to remain here. To nurse Perry."

"You cannot be serious." When he said nothing, just gazed back at her blandly, Nicola went on. "I cannot stay here. It's impossible."

"Of course you can. Nothing easier. There is an extra room down the hall. It even has a lock—in case you doubt my intentions. You and I can take turns keeping watch. And you will be here to change the bandage and give him whatever medicine he needs."

Nicola cut in on his words. "Now I am certain of it— you are indeed mad. I am *not* remaining here."

"Why? Because it will damage your reputation?" he asked sarcastically. "Does your reputation matter more to you than a man's life?"

"Of course not. I was not thinking about my reputation. But I cannot simply disappear. Have you forgotten that I am staying with my sister and her husband? Do you think they will not notice when I don't come downstairs tomorrow morning? That no one will wonder what happened to me or where I am? My sister's health is precarious and my disappearance might aggravate her condition. Also, I might point out that you will be the first person Richard blames when I turn up missing. He already would love to have your head on a platter, and he will be more than happy to add kidnapping to your list of crimes."

"I am sure he will. But it cannot be helped. It is more important that Perry have the proper care."

"If you are so concerned for your friend, perhaps you should have thought of his welfare before you pulled him in on this escapade of yours," Nicola retorted. "Exmoor hates you, but I can promise that his efforts to find you so far are nothing compared to what he will do when he realizes that you have abducted me."

"Oh, I am certain that he will move heaven and hell to find *you*," Jack spat back, his mouth twisting bitterly.

"What is that supposed to mean?" Nicola asked, indignation rising in her at his tone.

"Why, that the Earl if very fond of you, of course," he replied. "Any man would be."

"I must say that you work very hard at being insulting. Whatever you are implying about Exmoor and me, I can assure you that it is not true. However, I am his wife's sister. Abducting me out of his very house is tantamount to spitting in his face. He will not rest or spare any expense until he finds me. Nor, I think, will you find the people in the village quite as reluctant to talk about you when he tells them that you have kidnapped me. For all any of them will know, you could have killed me. And, however much *you* may despise me, I can tell you that I am not without friends in the village."

"They may tell him all they want, but none of them knows where we are. I have taken great pains not to let them know the location of my home. None of the villagers has been here. And I have made sure that this house is very difficult to find."

Nicola crossed her arms and looked at him. "You are a reckless man, but heretofore you had not struck me as a fool. Do you think they will not comb these woods? Do you think that no one will remember the existence of this house? Someone built it. Someone used to live in it. You may think that you have hidden yourself from everyone, but I'll warrant there are one or two people in the village who have some idea where you live. It may take them a few days, but I can assure you that eventually they will find it. With Exmoor and my cousin offering rewards—as they are sure to do—they will make the effort."

He faced her silently, arms crossed over his chest. After a long moment, he said, "In that case, you will simply have to write a note to your sister and her husband. Tell them that you have gone to visit a friend."

"In the middle of the night?"

"Your friend is ill. She sent for you to come posthaste."

"And exactly why did I barricade my door and leave by my window?" Nicola shook her head. "No one would believe that, even if my door were not locked. I would have awakened someone and told them I was leaving. Indeed, the person who brought the message would have had to awaken someone to gain admittance to the house."

"I can get around all that," he told her confidently. "I shall return to your room and leave it as if you had been called away suddenly. And I will see to it that one of the servants will say that they opened the door to the messenger."

"You have the Earl's servants in your employ?" Nicola asked, amazed.

"Not in my employ. But I do have connections. Exmoor is not a popular employer—nor a very generous one."

"You are serious, aren't you?" Nicola studied him. "You are willing to risk everything so that I will stay here and take care of your friend?"

The highwayman shrugged. "He has been a good friend to me for many years. More than that, he showed me that not everyone is treacherous."

"This is absurd. You will never be able to pull the wool over their eyes." Nicola sighed and turned away from him, gazing down at the man in the bed. Finally, she said, "All right. What if I agree to look after him? But first, you take me back to Tidings, where I will tell my sister that I am going…somewhere for a few days. Perhaps my aunt's. That would be reasonable, and Deborah won't want to go over there in her condition…although she might not want me to leave her for that long."

"There is always the friend-in-need story," Jack suggested wryly.

"I suppose I could invent something—no, wait, I've got it. I will tell her I'm going to fetch Nurse. Aunt Adelaide was supposed to write her, but I can say that I have decided to go in person to convince her. Instead, I shall come here. No, wait—" Nicola frowned. "Exmoor will probably insist on sending somebody with me for protection, thanks to your stopping me the other day. And he will make me take the carriage and coachman. I cannot do that."

"Then I will do what I intended in the first place."

"Don't be so hasty. I have it. I will tell them that I am going to visit Aunt Adelaide. That way the Earl's carriage and coachman can take me over there and leave me, then return and get me. I can ride from Buckminster on one of Aunt Adelaide's horses. I shall tell her I am going to get our nurse. *She* won't think twice about my riding there on horseback, and she will gladly lie to cover my absence, should anyone ask. I will tell Deborah the same thing, but I shall explain that I am leaving from my aunt's because I don't want Richard making me take the coachman and a groom for protection. She knows me well enough to know that I would not like that at all. So she will be happy, knowing I am going to get Nurse, Richard will be satisfied because I will take the coach to Aunt Adelaide, and Aunt Adelaide will be blissfully unaware. It should all work out fine as long as you do your part and bring our nurse back."

"There is one further problem," Jack pointed out.

"What?"

"How do I have any assurance that you are actually going to do this? Suppose I take you back tonight? Who is to say that you will come riding in here tomorrow? Or that if I tell you how to get here, you won't tell your brother-in-law?"

Nicola cocked her eyebrow and regarded him coolly. "If you are afraid that I will reveal the location of this house, then I will meet you somewhere and you can blindfold me again and lead me here. You can wait for me on the road from Buckminster to the village."

"Too crowded. I will meet you on the path that runs from Buckminster to Lady Falls. Do you know it?"

"Yes. I know it," Nicola replied evenly. "Where would you like to meet?"

"There is a large rock, about seven feet tall, looks like three rocks stacked together, a few yards from the path. It comes along not long after the group of three oak trees."

"I know the rock," Nicola replied shortly. That was the spot where she and Gil used to part when they had spent time at the Falls. "I will be there tomorrow afternoon. It will take some time to go to Aunt Adelaide's, then get away. I doubt I will be there before midafternoon. As for whether I will show up... I don't know how I can convince you that I will, except to say that I came here tonight to help your friend."

"You knew I would have carried you here if you had refused."

"I could have screamed. I could have kicked. I could have made it much more difficult."

"I would have simply tied you up and gagged you, and your journey would have been a good bit more uncomfortable. I imagine you were aware of that."

"Actually, I didn't think about it. But since you are determined to see only the worst in me... Yes, you could have forced me to come here. But you could not have forced me to use my knowledge and my skill. I could have dissolved into hysterics and been unable to pull out the ball. I could have refused to give him anything. Or given him the wrong thing. Would you have known if I did not give him the right remedy? I could have given him something that would kill him instead of help him. I still could, for that matter. So you see, you simply have to trust me about some things. This is one of them. I will meet you tomorrow afternoon where we said."

The highwayman looked at her with a long, unblinking gaze. "I appear to have little choice, don't I?" he said finally. "If I keep you here, I will, as you explained, increase the danger to my men and myself. And, as you so smoothly implied, you could kill Perry in retaliation rather than heal him."

"I didn't say that!" Nicola protested.

"Not in so many words. But there was a clear message in what you said." Jack's eyes were dark and unreadable.

Nicola wished that she could rip aside the mask so that she could see his expression.

"You are the most suspicious man I have ever met!" Nicola exclaimed.

"I have good reason to be. I learned long ago the perfidy of women."

"Oh, that's right. Blame it on a female. That is always the easiest thing, isn't it? 'A woman made me sin.' The truth is, you are suspicious because it is your nature," Nicola retorted. "No doubt you suspect everyone else because you yourself are so full of secrets. It is you whom no one knows, whose face is never revealed, who lets no one learn his hiding place or true name."

"It is safer for everyone that way."

"It seems to me a hideous way to live—trusting no one, confiding in no one…."

"I am accustomed to it."

"Accustomed? I think not. What you are is embittered and hardened."

"You're awfully cocksure in your opinions, given the fact that you know me not at all."

"It does not take more than meeting you to see your bitterness," Nicola shot back. "It comes oozing out of your every pore. I would have to be deaf, dumb and blind *not* to be aware of it."

"Well, that is very edifying, Miss Falcourt," the highwayman began dismissively. "However, it—"

He was stopped by a groan from the man on the bed. Both he and Nicola whirled around to look at Perry. He turned his head on the pillow, letting out another groan. They waited anxiously, watching him, but he did not move or make more noise. Nicola moved closer to the bed and laid her hand upon his forehead.

"No fever yet." She looked at Jack. They both knew that the odds were that there would be a fever later.

"We had better leave. The sooner you get home, the better. You will need some sleep if you are to carry out your plan tomorrow. I will get Saunders to come watch over him while I'm gone."

Nicola nodded and started toward the door. As she passed him, the highwayman reached out and wrapped his hand around her wrist, pulling her to a halt. She looked at him in cool inquiry.

"Should you think about not following through with your plan...remember how easily I got into your room tonight."

A tremor ran through Nicola, more at the touch of his hand upon her bare skin than from any fear. "If you think threatening me will cause me to do what you want, you are sadly mistaken, sir," she said, returning his gaze unblinkingly. "I will do as I said because I told you I would. It is the concern for another human being that impels me, not your threats. And if I were you, I don't think I would try entering my room that way again."

She waited, gazing at him in the same icily unconcerned way until finally he released her wrist and stepped back, allowing her to walk past him to the door. He followed her down the stairs.

Saunders came from the kitchen into the entryway at the sound of their footsteps, and Jack tersely told him to watch Perry while he was gone. "Don't let him move around and reopen that wound. And for God's sake, don't entrust his care to Diane. She's a fool. I will take over when I get back."

The other man nodded his understanding and, with one quick glance at Nicola, turned and ran lightly up the stairs.

Jack pulled the black scarf from his pocket and came toward Nicola, folding the scarf into a blindfold. Nicola grimaced, but closed her eyes and stood passively as he tied the thing around her head, annoyed by the way her pulse sped up at his nearness. The man was infuriating, and there should be nothing that stirred her about his tying the scarf over her eyes.

After all, she reminded herself, she resented it; it was humiliating and unnerving. Yet she could not keep from recalling, as the soft silk settled upon her skin, the sensuality of the ride over here this evening—the heightening of all her senses, the feel of the cool night air against her skin, the rougher touch of his jacket, the smell of leather and horse and the man whose arms encircled her, the warmth of his body and the deep rumble of his voice, which she both heard and felt as she leaned against his chest, the sexual suggestion of her position between his legs, the unmistakable quickening of his manhood against her buttocks, the rhythmic rocking of the horse. Her nipples tightened at the memory, and she realized with a small jolt of shock that she was looking forward to the upcoming ride with a kind of excitement, even pleasure.

Heat rushed to her cheeks, embarrassment mingling with excitement. Nicola hated it that she felt like this—as if she were the sort of weak creature men often painted women to be, controlled by their emotions and desires, easily tempted and even more easily giving in, the sort of being who must be protected not only from others but from herself, as well. She was both angry and humiliated at the way her nipples swelled and grew tender when Jack's fingers brushed against her face as he wrapped the scarf about her eyes…at the warmth that blossomed between her legs in anticipation. She wondered if he had any idea of the effect he had upon her. *No doubt if he did it amused him terribly!*

Jack wrapped his hand around her arm, and he guided her out the door, his voice low and warm in her ear. "There's a step down here." He held her arm firmly as she made her tentative way across what seemed to be a porch. "Now two more steps. There. Wait a moment while I untie my horse."

She waited, listening to his voice murmuring to his mount as he untied it and the low answering neigh from his horse. She recognized the familiar sounds of a horse moving and shaking its head. Sternly she told herself that the ride back to Tidings would be different. She would hold herself aloof. She would not give in to the sensual thoughts and feelings that had overtaken her on the way here. It had been nonsensical of her to do so the first time; it was not like her at all. She was not a cold person—indeed, she was quite warm and loving with those she cared about—but with men she had a certain reputation of being disinterested, even cool, a woman who might flirt with one, but who would never be inclined to a little dalliance.

She felt Jack's hands at her waist, lifting her up onto the horse. An instant later, he was up behind her, settling her against him and wrapping his arms around her as he had before. Nicola found herself fitting into her spot all too easily, and heat flooded her as his strong thighs cupped her buttocks, her stern resolutions evaporating in the reality of his touch. It amazed her that she had so little control over herself. She did not understand what was the matter with her, why she was acting so unlike herself. *How could her body respond so to a man she did not even like?*

They made their way slowly through the night, the soft brush every now and then of leaves against her shoulder or face confirming her supposition that they were winding through trees. Her body shifted with the movement of the horse, rubbing her subtly against Jack, and a low noise escaped him, muffled quickly against her hair. Nicola felt the heat of his body rise, engulfing her.

She cast about desperately in her mind for something to say, to do, that would take her thoughts away from the tumult in her body. "I, um, I left a bag of meadowsweet for the fever, did I not?"

"Yes. You left your whole kit of herbs and potions there." His breath ruffled her hair and touched her ear, sending a shiver of primitive response straight down through her to her loins.

"Oh. Yes, of course." It had made sense to leave it, since she was coming right back, but Nicola knew that she had not made any conscious decision to do so. She had merely forgotten it, something she could not even remember doing. Jack Moore had a lethal effect on her mind as well as her senses, apparently.

He shifted a little in the saddle, pulling her back even more tightly against him. Nicola had to press her lips together to suppress a little gasp at the feel of him hard against her. His arms tightened around her, and she felt his head move against hers. She realized that he had buried his face in her hair at the crook of her neck. He said something, his voice muffled by her hair; she thought it was her name. Desire stirred in her, turning her loins soft and waxen.

His hand came up and pushed her hair back from her neck. He bent and pressed his lips against the tender flesh. Nicola knew that she should protest, should push away from him, but she could not make herself move. She felt languid and heated, dazed at the rush of sensual pleasure his lips evoked in her. His lips were warm and soft, the merest touch like a butterfly's wing, yet they seared her like fire. She leaned back, her body melting involuntarily against him. The movement seemed to add fuel to the flame of his passion, for his hand slipped inside her cloak, pulling it apart, and he began to caress her body, his hand sliding back and forth across her waist, then drifting up until it brushed the undersides of her breasts.

Her nipples blossomed, swelling with heat, and Nicola had to bite back a most unladylike moan of hunger. Somehow, the fact that she was blindfolded made the situation even more sensual. Each new touch, each kiss, came as a surprise, and her lack of sight seemed to increase the sensitivity of her other senses, so that each sensation was heightened. Her breasts tingled with anticipation, eager to feel his touch. It was an embarrassing sensation, but at the same time, it was far too enjoyable to stop. All she could do was wait, barely breathing, for what he would do.

His hand slid down again, and she felt a dip of disappointment, but in the next instant his hand was roaming down past her waist onto the flat plane of her abdomen, touching her in a way that no one ever had. Nicola's breath rasped in her throat, quick, almost panting. He explored her body boldly, moving all over her stomach and abdomen and down onto her thighs, and with each touch, Nicola felt herself melting more and more inside. There was a tingling heat between her legs, a prickling sensation that made her want to clamp her legs together to ease it, yet at the same time open up to him.

The last thought sent a flush of embarrassment rising to

her cheeks that made her glad it was dark. She knew that he must assume her to be a wanton, the way she let him caress her so freely without even a protest. It was a humiliating realization, but she could not tell him to stop. There was a pulsing hunger inside her, a desire to feel all that she could feel, and that hunger was far stronger than any other emotion.

His hand slid up and down her side, the base of his palm brushing the side of her breast, and she trembled every time he grazed the soft orb. She ached for him to touch her breast; her hand tightened into a fist to keep from reaching out and pulling him to her. His lips moved up her neck and back down, onto the bony plateau of her collarbone, teasing and caressing, sending the flames roaring higher within her.

Just when Nicola thought she could stand the tension no longer, that she would have to beg him to take her breast in his hand, he did exactly that, cupping the underside of one breast. It gave her a certain amount of satisfaction to feel the shudder that ran through his body when he did so, for obviously it affected him as strongly as it did her.

He pressed his lips against the soft skin of her neck, nibbling and kissing, his breath a blast of hot air upon her flesh, while his hand gently squeezed her breast, his forefinger finding her nipple beneath the cloth of her dress and caressing it. Nicola could not hold back her soft groan at that. Gently his fingers played with her, digging gently into the supremely soft flesh of her breast, circling the hard button of her nipple, then squeezing it gently between his thumb and forefinger. His hand crept up over the top of her dress onto the sliver of soft breast above the neckline. He tried to slip his exploring fingers down beneath the material, but the dress thwarted him.

166 NO OTHER LOVE

With a low noise of frustration, he went to the buttons down the front of her dress and began to undo them. His fingers were clumsy with haste, and two of the little buttons popped off, flying into the dark night. Then he was touching her bare breast, his skin sliding over her flesh, pushing down the thin barrier of her chemise. Her nipple tightened as the cool air touched it, and she could feel his response to the sight in the insistent throb against her hip. His hand covered the white orb, sliding gently over it to cup it from beneath, delighting in the heaviness in his palm. His thumb moved over the little bud of her nipple, stimulating it to a harder, tauter state. Her breasts felt swollen with desire, her nipples supremely sensitive, and with every motion of his hand, her passion flamed hotter.

His teeth nipped at her neck gently, his tongue tracing delicate patterns on her skin as his lips pressed like fire into her skin. And all the while, his hand aroused her breast, caressing and kneading, bringing every nerve in her body to life. Nicola had to fight the urge to turn and wrap her legs around him, to press the hot center of passion against his.

Now his hand was moving lower, undoing more of her buttons, delving down beneath her petticoats, fingertips gliding over the bare skin of her abdomen. Nicola drew a sharp breath. Never, even with Gil, had she felt such sensations. Hot, insistent desire pulsed between her legs; she felt swollen and hot, flooded with the moisture of desire. It was humiliating, she told herself, that he should see her this way, that she should crumble so completely beneath his assault on her senses. Yet she could not protest, could not tell him to stop. She wanted to feel this way, ached to feel it. His hand slipped over her satiny skin and through the prickle of hair, then into the hot, slick folds of her femininity. Nicola groaned, shaken to the core of her being. She had never dreamed that anything could be like this. His body was like a furnace against hers, his breath coming in harsh, fast pants. He buried his face in her neck, moaning her name.

"Lie with me tonight," he murmured. "Here. I'll make a bed on the leaves. The trees will shelter us." He drew a shaky breath, his mouth trailing up her neck to her ear. His lips touched the silk of her blindfold, and he reached up, impatiently shoving it off and flinging it away. He pushed her hair back from her ear and pressed his lips to it.

"Let me love you. I want to be in you, part of you. I have dreamed…"

His voice trailed away as he rubbed his face against her hair. His voice, his words, were as sexual as a caress, creating a scene of such realism that Nicola shivered with desire. Yet even as the vision sent a shaft of longing spiraling through her, it made her think, with a piercing ache, of Gil and the long, delicious hours they had spent lying beneath a tree or sheltered by rocks, kissing and caressing, talking in low murmurs of their love. The heat had been fierce then, too, though never carried this far, never reaching the act of completion. Their caresses had been slow and tender, their time together moments of love, not the fire and rush of lust as this was.

Guilt and contempt sliced through her. She was betraying Gil, soiling his memory, with her low, lascivious passion for this man. She did not love Jack Moore; why, she barely knew him. There was nothing between them except sheer carnal hunger—and she knew that if she lay with him, she would be unfaithful to Gil and to their love as surely as if she were a married woman running to her lover.

"No!" She jerked away from him, leaning forward and

pulling the sides of her gaping dress together. "No, I cannot." Hurriedly she began to do up the little buttons that fastened the front of her dress.

For a moment, he did not move. She didn't dare glance back at him. Then he straightened and took a firmer grasp of the reins. His arm curved around her back—it had to for him to hold the reins—but it was hard as iron now and held as far from her skin as possible. He nudged the horse forward with his heels.

Anger radiated from him with all the force of his frustrated passion, and Nicola found herself uneasily explaining, "I'm sorry. It would be wrong."

"Of course it would." His voice was light, at odds with his stiff posture. "A lady may dally with a peasant, but it would soil her to give him the pleasure of her body."

"That isn't it at all!" Nicola retorted hotly.

"Ah, so you are saying it is your high morals?" His sneering tone made clear what he thought of her moral level.

"Yes, it *is* my morals—and my honor. I am scarcely in the habit of jumping into the nearest bed of leaves with a man I do not know."

"I wouldn't have guessed that when you were melting against me and moaning a few minutes ago," he replied.

Humiliation flared bright red in Nicola's cheeks, and she was furious to find that tears sprang into her eyes.

"Or was that merely an act, Lady Virtue?" he added. "Were you only teasing the buffoon to see how hot and desperate you could make him? Is that how you get your pleasures?"

"Stop it! I did not begin this. It was you who—"

"No, but you entered into it readily enough, didn't you?"

"I will admit that. But fortunately I came to my senses!" Nicola spat out.

"Is that what you call it? I would have said it was you remembering your station."

"It wasn't remembering my station. It was remembering who I am—which is not a common trollop."

"Common you are not," he agreed in an infuriating drawl. "But I think you have the same heat in your blood as any maid in a tavern. A heat I can relight any time I wish."

"Please…spare me your male braggadocio. You caught me in a strange moment of weakness. I am not your easy prey."

"Is that right?" He chuckled in a way guaranteed to raise Nicola's hackles. "Would you care to lay a bet on that?"

The desire that had melted her bones was completely gone now, burned up in the fire of her anger. "You think that I am going to wager on my virtue?" Nicola twisted around to face him and found that it was even more irritating to address that masked face, the upper half hidden and smooth, the lower half marked by a mocking sneer.

"You are a despicable man, and it would serve you right if I did not return tomorrow."

"Ah, but you made a promise…." he reminded her.

"Yes, I did, and for that reason—and for your friend's sake—I will do all I can to help him. But you can rest assured that I would rather spend several days in a house with a snake than be there with you! If you think that I am going to give in to your blandishments, you are fair and far off. I have no intention of sleeping with you, and, indeed, it is my wish to see as little of you as possible the whole time I'm there."

"I have equally little desire to spend my time with a tease—worse, a sanctimonious tease."

"Good. Then I suggest that we avoid each other."

"I will do my best."

"I, too." Nicola turned and faced forward, her back as straight as a board and as far away from him as she could manage on a horse.

They rode the rest of the way in silence.

CHAPTER NINE

NICOLA AWOKE LATE THE NEXT MORNING, heavy-lidded with lack of sleep and feeling somehow more tired than she had when she crawled into bed. It had been not long before sunrise when she and Jack reached Tidings. Jack had climbed back up to her room with an effortless grace that she could not tear her eyes away from, no matter how hard she tried. Once inside, he had unbarricaded her door so that she could sneak into the house through the kitchen and up the backstairs to her room. She had been racked with fear that Richard might step out of his room and find her sneaking down the hall, fully dressed and obviously up to no good in the middle of the night.

She had breathed a sigh of relief when she stepped inside her room, but it had quickly turned to a curiously hollow feeling when she realized that Jack had already left without even a goodbye. She had undressed, leaving her clothes in an uncharacteristically messy heap on the floor and put on her nightgown, then collapsed on the bed.

It seemed she had barely closed her eyes when the sound of the maids' voices in the hall awakened her. She sat up, yawning, and saw that it was already almost ten o'clock. With a sigh, she slid out of bed and rang for a maid and bathwater. Much as she would have liked to sleep on, there was much to be done today, and she could not delay. She could perhaps catch a few winks in the carriage on the way over to Buckminster Hall.

Once she was bathed and dressed and fortified with tea and toast, she felt a good deal better, and she went into her sister's bedroom to set her plan into motion. It took little convincing to get her sister's approval of her going to fetch their old nursemaid. Aunt Adelaide, she agreed, might not even have written the note yet if she had gotten distracted by some more important, horse-related matter. She understood, too, Nicola's subterfuge of going to Buckminster Hall first, for, after the incident upon Nicola's arrival, she knew that Richard would insist on sending an escort, and she also knew her sister's fierce independence.

Richard was a somewhat tougher proposition. In a jollying tone, he chided Nicola for deserting her sister so soon, but there was a suspicious narrowing of his eyes as he looked at her. Deborah hastened to assure him that she understood and was in complete agreement, for Aunt Adelaide would doubtless be in desperate need of help with the upcoming wedding preparations. Exmoor, as aware as anyone else of Lady Buckminster's inattention to things domestic, shrugged, and after Nicola and Deborah launched into an exhaustive account of all the things that would need to be done for the approaching nuptials of the lord of Buckminster Hall, his eyes began to glaze over and he dropped the subject, other than to say he would tell the servants to bring the carriage around to take her to her aunt's.

Nicola returned to her room to pack, eschewing the services of a maid, who would doubtless have found it extremely odd to see the amount of herbs, bandages and medical supplies that Nicola stuffed into her bags. Clothes were a minor consideration. She had little space, for she dared not appear to pack for more than a few nights' stay.

Besides, whatever luggage she took would have to be carried on horseback from Buckminster to the highwayman's lair in the woods.

It was still early in the afternoon when she climbed into the carriage to drive to her aunt's house. Her sister watched her go, waving and smiling a trifle wistfully. Nicola managed to sleep much of the way over there, despite the bumpy ride of the carriage, so she arrived at her aunt's house feeling somewhat refreshed.

The butler smoothly hid whatever astonishment he felt upon seeing the coachman unload Nicola's luggage on their doorstep and showed Nicola politely into the informal sitting room, where the family was wont to gather. Her aunt came in a few minutes later, dressed in an old dress that ended above her ankles and equally worn boots, to which bits of mud and straw still clung. It was obvious that Adelaide had been in the stables, though from the lack of riding habit, apparently not riding.

"Nicola!" she said with sincere delight, striding in her mannish way across the drawing room to enfold her niece in an embrace. She stepped back, looking guilty. "Did I know you were coming?"

"No, Aunt Adelaide. It was a spur-of-the-moment thing."

The older woman's brow cleared. "Ah, good. Well, why don't I ring for tea? It's a bit early, but I am famished. Been out since dawn helping Carson—my favorite mare's foaling, and having a difficult time of it, too, I must say."

Nicola smiled. Her aunt's blunt way of talking doubtless raised more than a few eyebrows, but Nicola had always found Aunt Adelaide refreshing. She cared little for what other people thought, unless they happened to be experts on horseflesh, and while she would uphold all the proprieties, she often tended to be unaware of exactly what those were, as they had nothing to do with horses. Nicola often wondered how Aunt Adelaide and her other aunt, the intellectual and rather iconclastic Drusilla, could be related to their sister, Nicola's mother, who was on the whole as dull and Society-bound a woman as one could find.

"I'm sorry to hear that," Nicola sympathized. "I am sure you must be worried."

"I am. Carson says he'll have to turn the foal, but that's no easy matter—painful, too." She sighed.

"I am sure that you are not desirous of company, then," Nicola said. "So I shall not keep you long. I came to find out what you had done about locating our old nurse."

Aunt Adelaide looked blankly at her, then remembrance touched her eyes, and she smiled. "Oh, let's see, when was that we talked about it?" She wrinkled her brow and thought. "You know, I don't believe I did write her. I am sorry."

"It's all right," Nicola said quickly. "I had been thinking that I should visit Nurse myself and urge her to come to Deborah."

"That would be perfect," Aunt Adelaide agreed. Then her brow furrowed and she said, "Are you—are you wanting me to go with you?"

"I would not dream of taking you away from your mare," Nicola assured her. "I am quite capable of getting there on my own. But I would like to borrow a horse from you, if I may."

"Of course." This was a topic nearer to Lady Buckminster's heart, and she launched into a thorough discussion of precisely which mount would suit her niece's purposes the best.

Nicola was happy to go along with her aunt's decision on the matter and told her so. "The only problem is Exmoor," she told Aunt Adelaide. "If he knew I was going, he would insist on my taking his carriage and a full armed escort. He has become absolutely maniacal on the subject of this highwayman. But I am sure that he will not accost me again. And it would be so pleasant to ride. I don't want to be cooped up in a stuffy old carriage."

Aunt Adelaide, who felt the same way about vehicles as opposed to horseback, nodded sympathetically. "But you will have an escort of some sort, won't you? I don't think riding cross-country by yourself would be quite the thing," she mused in a massive understatement.

"Of course," Nicola lied without a qualm. "I will take one of the men from the village. The head ostler at the inn."

"Oh? Yes, he's good with horses," Aunt Adelaide said in approval.

"The thing is, what if Exmoor were to come to call and find that I had gone to Nurse's without telling him?"

"Humph!" Lady Buckminster made a disdainful noise. Though she had always been polite to Lord Exmoor, as was necessary with such a close neighbor, she had never had any liking for the man since the day she had seen him hitting his mount with his riding crop in a paroxysm of fury because the animal would not take a fence. "Damned fool," she had sniffed. "It was his bad form that made the horse hang back. That man could ruin any animal."

"As if he has a right to know where you are," Adelaide said now. "Don't worry about it. I shall instruct Huggins to say that you are out if he should have the audacity to come check up on you."

"That would be a perfect solution!" Nicola exclaimed, feeling a twinge of remorse at deceiving her aunt this way.

However, there was a man's life at stake, she told herself, and that had to take precedence.

An hour later, she was mounted on the mare her aunt had decided on, her bags tied behind her, and riding the familiar trail to the rock where she was to meet Jack. It was an unmistakable landmark, big and layered, as if it had been built out of three rocks stacked one on top of the other. Nicola had met Gil there many times on a Sunday afternoon, and just the thought of meeting anyone else there, for any reason, made her heart constrict. It seemed somehow another disloyalty to Gil, a small betrayal to add to the weight of the large one she had committed last night by melting beneath the highwayman's heated caresses.

Nicola didn't know what had come over her. Certainly her behavior had been totally unlike her. Never before had she given in to such lust—indeed, never before had she *felt* the kind of unbridled passion that she had last night with Jack Moore. Only Gil had ever stirred her senses, and she had been in love with him; it had been no merely physical attraction. Since Gil, she had been interested in no man. It seemed bizarre that this stranger, this man whose face she had never even seen, should arouse such feelings in her.

But whatever the reasons for her extremely atypical behavior, Nicola was determined that it would not happen again. She was a better person than that, more moral, more devoted to her long-dead love. Moreover, she thoroughly disliked Jack, and she would not give him the satisfaction of knowing that he could control her in that way. She would be aloof to him, speaking to him only when necessary, concentrating her time and attention on helping his friend get well. That was the only reason she was going back, after all—to help the wounded man. It had nothing to do with seeing Jack Moore; indeed, she reminded herself, his presence made her *not* want to go back to the house deep in the woods.

As she drew nearer and nearer to the rock, Nicola was aware of a growing sense of anticipation in her stomach. She felt edgy and jumpy, faintly excited. That, too, she assured herself, had nothing to do with Jack Moore. It was simply that she was looking forward to using her skills, to doing battle with sickness and death.

She passed under the spreading branches of three oak trees that grew beside the road, and, once beyond them, she could see the rock ahead of her, looming beside the trail. There was no sign of anyone waiting there, but when she was almost there, she heard the unmistakable whinny of a horse, and a moment later there was the sound of feet sliding on smaller rocks. She looked up to see a man coming lithely down the slope behind the rock. He disappeared from view for a moment, then came around the rock, leading a horse. Tall and broad-shouldered, dressed all in black, his face as always half-obscured by the mask, he was intensely masculine, tinged with an air of mystery. Nicola's pulse speeded up involuntarily.

She pulled to a stop in front of him, irritation at her own response making her voice sharp, "Do you wear that mask everywhere? Is your face so fearsome?"

He grinned, his teeth gleaming white against his dark skin, and swung easily up onto his horse. "Indeed, Miss Falcourt, it is a terrible thing, my visage, the sort that sends children screaming. Worse, 'tis a thing you could identify for the authorities."

Nicola snorted inelegantly. "Has it not occurred to you

that if I had a mind to turn you in to the authorities, I could have simply brought them with me today?"

"Aye, it occurred to me. That is why I scouted out the whole area before I settled down here, to make sure there were no men with guns waiting to seize me. It is also why I chose this point. It's higher than the trail. From back there—" he gestured toward a pile of rocks several yards behind the landmark and quite a bit higher "—I was able to see the sweep of land behind you for a good distance, in case there was anyone riding discreetly along behind you."

Nicola cocked an eyebrow. "I would hate to be the sort of man you are, trusting no one, always suspicious."

He shrugged. "'Tis better than being dead or in gaol, I can assure you."

"You make it sound as if those were the only choices in life. Surely you could have done something else with your life besides rob people."

"Mmm," he replied noncommittally. "Probably. But it would not have been as exciting."

"You are impossible."

"No doubt." He turned and started along the smaller path that bisected the one Nicola had taken, curving around the rock and over the shoulder of the hill. Nicola urged her horse after him.

"What? No blindfold today?" she asked. The sarcasm helped, she found, kept away the odd humming awareness of him all through her body.

Jack grimaced. "To what effect? Considering the fact that you were not blindfolded most of the way last night."

Nicola blushed, remembering the way he had torn off the scarf from her eyes as he kissed his way across her face to her earlobe. He glanced sideways at her. "I warrant you could find your way at least back to the woods. Am I right?"

His statement surprised Nicola. She had always been quick at finding her way, her sense of direction excellent, but it was odd that he should assume so. She had found that men invariably assumed a woman was poor at such things.

"We came out of Blackfell Woods, I think—the north end. Inside the woods…" She shrugged, thinking it was just as well to let him assume that she was uncertain, though the fact was that she thought she could have made her way at least a hundred yards into the wood, as well.

He nodded. "As I thought. When we get to the woods, I shall blindfold you again. Safer that way."

"Mmm." She did not look forward to being blindfolded, but it would be easier today. At least she would not be forced to ride on the same horse with him. However, she did not like not being in full faculty of her senses or giving up control of herself to another. That was why she intended to try this time to figure out their path. She had already determined to do so; the fact that it was daylight should make it easier.

"How is the patient today?" she asked.

"He came to early this morning for a little while, but he has slept since then. He seemed a trifle hot to the touch when I left. That was a good two hours ago. I gave him the medicine you told me to."

"The feverfew?"

He nodded. "I hoped it would keep him from growing worse while I was gone. There is someone there watching him, but…"

"You do not trust him?"

"Oh, I trust him. He would do nothing to harm Perry.

But he is no nursemaid. I will feel easier when you are there."

"You surprise me. I thought you considered me a frivolous, characterless member of an evil class—and a weak, wicked woman, to boot."

He glanced at her expressionlessly. "With you it is just the opposite of Saunders. I would not trust you in the slightest. But I know you are a wizard with herbs."

"You certainly know how to take back any sort of compliment," Nicola commented dryly.

"I said you were a wizard with herbs. Hardly derogatory."

"As long as one does not mind being considered a dead loss as a human being."

He grunted softly. "I don't imagine you are that, either. Many of the villagers think highly of you."

"You, I am sure, reserve your judgment on that."

"As you said earlier, I am a suspicious man."

"Was the woman who hurt you a noblewoman?" Nicola asked impulsively.

He turned sharply to look at her. "What? What makes you say that? I never said—"

"You did not have to. It is obvious from the things you say that you were badly hurt by a woman. Why else would you be so bitter, so quick to label women treacherous and deceitful? And—" she went on determinedly, overriding his voice as he started to protest "—you are equally contemptuous of the nobility. The conclusion was easy."

"But not necessarily true."

"Am I wrong?" Nicola asked challengingly.

After a long moment, he said quietly, "No. You are not wrong. It was a woman of high station who betrayed me."

"Betrayed you in what way?" Nicola asked, curious about what drove this man.

He gave her a cool look. "Someday your curiosity will get you into serious trouble."

"Oh, it already has, many times," Nicola replied lightly. She added, "You know, not all noblewomen are alike, any more than are all people of any group. 'Tis a bit unfair, don't you think, to paint us with the same brush?"

"Is it?" His dark gaze remained steadily on her face, his eyes, so often bright and mocking, now very serious. "What about you? Did you never betray a man who loved you?"

Nicola opened her mouth to answer "no," then suddenly thought about the night before and the way she had given in to this man, about the guilt she had felt, the fear that she had been unfaithful to her dead love, and she blushed, turning her face away from his.

His chuckle was humorless. "You see? You did it, too."

"But it wasn't—I mean—" She struggled to convey the difference between the guilt she felt at the thought of giving in to this man's caresses when she still loved a man long dead and the sort of faithlessness that she felt sure he meant. "I was not unfaithful…."

"There are many ways to betray a man," he pointed out shortly. "It isn't only lying with another man, though that is common enough. Isn't it just as wicked to turn one over to one's enemies?"

Nicola raised her brows. "Is that what happened to you?"

His eyes were intent on her face, and she thought she saw a flicker of some indefinable emotion flicker across his face at her words. Obviously whatever had happened still pained him after all these years.

"Yes. It is. I was enjoyable for a while, but then I became…an inconvenience."

Nicola thought she was beginning to see the story. He had dallied with some noblewoman, probably someone married to a dull old lord, a woman eager for the excitement and danger that an affair with a highwayman brought. Then, when she grew tired—or he grew importunate—she had simply informed the authorities of his whereabouts.

"I'm sorry," she said simply. How he must have loved this woman, to still carry his hurt like an open wound. "But not all women are like that."

"You would do the same," he said tightly, "given the same circumstances."

"I would not!" Nicola retorted hotly, feeling on much firmer ground now.

"Liar," he replied without heat, and there was a darkness in his eyes that was ancient and impenetrable. He dug his heels into his horse and moved in front of her.

Nicola started to go after him to argue her case, but then she stopped. It was foolish; Jack would believe what he wanted to believe, what fit with his perception of things. There was no way that she could prove that she was unlike the woman he had known—and really, she thought suddenly, why did it matter? What Jack Moore thought of her was immaterial. They were nothing to each other, brought together only by peculiar circumstances.

So she hung back, following him without further conversation.

After a time, he left the path that led to Lady Falls, taking a narrower track that before long gave way to less traveled land. They rode through a meadow and over a stream, and gradually the trees grew thicker around them. Soon they reached Blackfell Wood, still riding in silence.

He pulled his horse to a halt, turning around to face her. "It is time for the blindfold."

"All right." Nicola accepted his words calmly. She knew where she was and what direction they were traveling. With a bit of effort, she thought that she would be able to figure out where they went. It wasn't so much that she cared where the hidden house was. She had no intention of going there again—and she certainly would never reveal to anyone where it was—but she disliked very much not knowing where she was going, being led and manipulated by someone else.

He wrapped the blindfold around her head, fastening it from behind, but since they were both on horseback, it was a little more difficult this time, a state to which Nicola contributed by gently nudging her horse so that it moved restlessly. The scarf was not tight, and when he took her reins from her and moved his horse ahead to lead hers, Nicola seized the opportunity to push the scarf up just a trifle, so that now she could see the ground on either side of her horse beneath the blindfold. It was not much, but she was afraid that if she moved it up more, he might notice. She thought that this would be enough, for the main thing she wanted was to be able to keep her sense of direction, which was entirely lost to her when her world was utterly dark.

Concentrating on which way they went, where they turned and how much distance they traveled each leg of the way made the trip pass quickly. They crossed a stream, and Nicola took extra care to look for landmarks there, even sneaking her hand up to push up the blindfold from one eye for a moment to glance around. Fortunately, Jack was still facing ahead and did not notice her. Until then, they had changed directions only a few times, but on the other side of the stream, they went through a dizzying series of twists and turns that sorely tested Nicola's ability. When at last Jack halted and came around to help her down from her horse, Nicola was not certain about the specific location of the house.

As Jack set her down on the ground, his strong hands gripped her waist for a moment longer than necessary, holding her close to him, and he leaned down until his lips were by her ear and whispered, "Surely you did not think I didn't notice what you were doing."

Chagrin sent a stain of red into Nicola's cheeks. *He had seen her surreptitiously lifting her blindfold and looking for ways to mark her path! Had she been so clumsy?*

"I don't know what you're talking about," she lied, annoyed that the stiffness of her tone cast doubt upon the truth of her words. "What do you think I was doing?"

He chuckled but made no reply, just took her arm in his hand and led her up the steps and into the house. Nicola itched to jerk her arm away, but that, of course, would have been not only impossible but also foolish, as she wouldn't have dared to walk forward without his guidance.

"You must be the most suspicious man alive," she said crossly.

Again he leaned close, so close to her that his breath ruffled her hair, and it sent a shiver down her spine. "My dear girl, I know—" He paused, then said, "I know your sort."

"My sort! And what is that?"

"Always poking and prying. Having to have the last word. Step up here." With his hand on her arm, he guided her up the two steps to the stoop.

"What nonsense!" But Nicola knew it was true enough. It was simply infuriating that he could guess her personality that well. "Besides, what makes you think that you outsmarted me?"

"Last word—you see?" he murmured. "Frankly, I don't

know whether I outsmarted you. That keeps the game interesting, don't you think?"

"I am not playing a game."

"No?" He opened the front door and eased her inside, then unfastened the knot holding her blindfold. "What are you doing, then?"

"I'm not sure," Nicola replied honestly, blinking a little in the indoor light. She looked up into his face and wished, not for the first time, that that impenetrable mask was gone so that she could read his expression.

There was the clatter of feet on the stairs, and a moment later a man appeared, looking relieved. "There you are, sir! It's right glad I am to see ye, too." His eyes flickered a little warily to Nicola, then back to Jack. "Perry's looking worse."

"Bloody hell." Jack hurried up the stairs, Nicola right behind him. "What happened?"

"Nothing 'appened, exactly. 'E just is 'ot, and 'e's started mumblin', like."

"Is he delirious?" Nicola asked.

The man glanced at her, then at Jack. "Wot?"

"Is he talking crazy?" Jack explained.

"I can't tell wot 'e's talkin' about. Just words and mumbles, and sometimes 'e moves around, all restless like."

Jack opened the door to the sickroom, standing back to allow Nicola to enter. She went straight to the bed and looked down at her patient. When she left the night before, he had been deathly pale and still. Now there was a faint flush on his cheeks, and he was moving—turning his head from side to side, twitching an arm or throwing a leg out from under the covers. As she stood looking down at him, he sighed and threw his arm up over his eyes, muttering something unintelligible.

Jack joined her at the bedside and cast her a worried look. He knew as well as she that the healthier-appearing color in his friend's face was actually a sign of fever, not recuperation.

Nicola bent over the bed and laid her hand against Perry's forehead. It was, as she expected, much warmer than it should be.

"Let's give him some more feverfew," she suggested. "When did you last give it to him?" She looked at the man who had been with Perry.

He gazed back at her blankly. "I didn't give 'im, nothin', miss."

"The last he had was what I gave him before I left," Jack told her. "You can go now, Quillen."

Nicola went around the bed to the small table beside it, where her bag of medicines sat. Taking out a vial of ground powder, she mixed it in a glass of water and turned back to the bed.

"You will have to help me. Hold him up, and let's try to get some of this down his throat."

Jack did as she told him, putting his arm beneath the man's shoulders and lifting him up to an upright position. Perry opened his eyes and looked around vaguely, his gaze lighting on Nicola. He frowned.

"Who're you?" he mumbled.

"Nicola. I am here to help you. You will feel better if you drink some of this." Nicola held the cup to his lips, and he began to drink, but by the time he had taken two sips, he made a face and turned away.

"No. You have to drink it." Nicola put one hand firmly at the back of his head and turned it back, pouring the liquid into his mouth again. He made a feeble protest, but drank several sips before he turned away.

"Blast it all, Perry, drink it!" Jack ordered, taking the man's chin firmly in his free hand and holding it steady.

Perry did so, though not without protest. Jack continued to prop him up while Nicola unwound the bandage wrapped around his chest. Then Jack laid him back down, and Nicola carefully lifted the pad from his wound. Perry winced and cursed softly when the pad stuck to the wound. She looked at it, holding the candle closer. The wound was still raw, and the skin around it was red and a little puffy. Nicola applied a cream of woundwort and marigold to the wound.

"Good gad, woman, are you trying to kill me?" Perry gasped.

"No, save you."

"Stop whining, now, old man," Jack said jokingly. "If it weren't for her, you'd probably be dead by now."

"With the—pain—I'm feeling, I might wish I were," Perry panted out. His eyes narrowed as he looked at Nicola. "I say, are you Jack's lady?"

Nicola's brows rose, and Jack said hastily, "Hush, Perry. You're acting dicked in the nob." He glanced over at Nicola. "I think you're right. He *is* delirious."

"He sounded quite lucid to me," Nicola retorted. She turned to the patient. "I am my own lady, sir, not Jack's nor any other man's."

Perry grinned faintly. "Yes, ma'am." In an aside to Jack, he added, "I like the cut of this one's jib."

"I am so honored," Nicola added sarcastically. "Now, then, I intend for you to get well, sir, so I suggest that you lie back and go to sleep. It's the best thing you can do for your health."

Perry merely nodded, his eyes beginning to drift closed already. Jack looked at Nicola. "How is he doing?"

Nicola shrugged. "Too early to say. His wound is angry-looking, but there is no pus formed yet. Nor is his fever raging. I am hopeful that there will be no infection. Still, it has not been very long. We must simply wait and see." She suited her actions to her words, sitting down in the straight-backed chair beside the bed.

Jack stood there for a moment, then pulled another chair from the far wall over to the bed and sat down across the sickbed from her. Nicola raised her brows slightly.

"There is no need for both of us to be here," she told him. "I came here to take care of him. No doubt there are other matters that require your attention—loot to divide, carriages to stop, people to rob...."

"My, but you've developed a wicked tongue."

"Developed? I think, Mr. Moore, that you would find that I have always had one."

"Somewhat at odds with all the stories I hear about your kindness and generosity."

Nicola moved her shoulder in a gesture of dismissal. "Odd...I hear similarly glowing stories about you."

She surprised a flicker of a smile from him.

"Perhaps," she continued a little less tartly, "the difference is less in us than in the person who perceives us."

"Perhaps."

Nicola looked at him, his upper face hidden by the enigmatic black mask. It was most irritating, the way he kept his face secret from her, and she had to wonder at the motive. *What did it matter if she could recognize him?* Surely he must realize after all this that she was not about to turn him in to the constable, no matter how much he annoyed her. She had too little liking for Richard and too much fondness of the people in the village for that. The village would suffer if the highwayman went down, and that was the last thing Nicola wanted.

She wondered if it was because of some scar or deformity that he kept his visage covered. *Did he conceal himself from everyone?* She remembered Lydia talking about how he concealed himself and kept away from others. That would seem to argue in favor of some hideousness that he was reluctant to reveal. However, the lower half of his face, the visible part, belied any notion of ugliness. His jaw was firm and straight; she could see that much even though it was a trifle hidden by the dark, neatly trimmed goatee and mustache that adorned his lip and chin. His lips were full and firm, well cut, even, she had to admit, somewhat arousing.

Nicola remembered the feel of that mouth upon hers last night, the brush of his beard and skin against her face. Heat blossomed in her at the memory, and hastily she turned her mind away, seeking another subject.

"Tell me about yourself," she said into the stillness.

Jack looked at her oddly. "I am a highwayman."

"Is that the sum of your parts?" Nicola responded. "Surely you come from somewhere, have done other things. You have a family, a past."

"Aye," he answered laconically. "I do. I did. No longer. I see little point in talking about them."

"It will help to pass the time," Nicola pointed out. "I shall be here for some time with your friend, and since you seem determined to stay, you might as well do something to alleviate the boredom."

"My life was surpassingly dull," he said lightly. "I do not think it would pass your time well."

"Why don't you try me?"

He shrugged. "My family was quite small, all dead now. I left home several years ago. I was in the Royal Navy."

"The navy? Really? You do not seem like a sailor."

"It was not by choice, I can assure you. I was taken by a press gang. When I awoke with a sore head, I found myself in the bowels of a ship. That is where I met Perry."

"That's awful!" Nicola exclaimed. "I have heard tales of such, but I have never met a man who actually—"

"Few of them are free and alive to be telling their tales. But Perry and I and some others escaped."

"Others? You mean the rest of your men?"

He nodded.

"I see. So then the lot of you decided to go into the business of thievery on the highways?"

"After a time. We tried some other things first. It was something I wanted to do. The others went along." He grimaced. "Obviously I did Perry a disservice."

"Yourself as well. If you are caught, you will be hanged."

"I know." He looked at her. "Perhaps it is time to be thinking of getting out."

"I would say past time."

"No doubt you are right." He sighed and rose, walking to the small window. He leaned against the wall, looking out. "I suppose that I have accomplished all I can hope to here."

"What was it you wanted to accomplish?"

The glance he shot her was brief and fierce. "To destroy the Earl of Exmoor."

Nicola's brows rose. "I am afraid it would take more than the depredations of a highwayman to do that."

"I know." His mouth twisted bitterly. "I am more like a bee stinging him than the sword that lays him low, as I would like to be. I cannot make him feel the pain I felt, for there is no one and nothing that he loves—other than himself."

"What did he do to you to make you hate him so?" Nicola asked.

"He destroyed my love."

Nicola's eyes widened. "He killed the woman you loved?" She frowned. "But I thought you said that—"

"No. He did not kill her. He killed our love." He turned to look at her, his dark eyes bleak. "He turned her against me. Used her to get rid of me. And in doing so, he ripped my heart out."

Nicola sucked in a breath, moved by the pure despair in his voice. "Oh, Jack…"

"He took away even the feelings, the memories, so that I had nothing left."

"I am so sorry." Nicola stood up, pulled toward him by her sympathy.

He turned away abruptly. "It doesn't matter. You are right. It hardly requires both of us to watch over Perry. I will relieve you in a few hours."

With those words, he walked away, leaving Nicola staring speechlessly after him.

CHAPTER TEN

NICOLA STOOD UP AND LOOKED DOWN at her patient. He seemed a bit more flushed, she thought. She had been sitting with him for more than three hours. For a while he had been quiet and somewhat cooler, but now he was moving restlessly again, and his arm, when she laid her hand upon it, seemed warmer. She put her hand on his forehead. It was damp with sweat and definitely hotter than before, hotter, she thought, than when she had first come in.

She turned to the stand beside the bed, where a bowl of water sat. She dipped a rag in it and wrung it out, then wiped his face with it. Again she swished the rag through the water, wrung it out and folded it to lay across his forehead. This was a process that she had done several times during the last few hours. It helped somewhat, but it was only an extra measure. What he needed was another dose of feverfew, and she thought that she would add some meadowsweet this time.

The problem was, she would have to mix the powders and get him to drink, and it had been clear last time that getting him to drink required at least two people. She would have to call Jack, and that was something she had been putting off for the past half hour.

He had left in an obviously black mood, but it was not his temper that made Nicola nervous. She was not a person who feared much, and she had faced an angry man before. It was more that she no longer knew how to act around Jack. His revelation about Richard and the pain that had tinged his words had aroused her sympathy. Up until now, she had maintained an adversarial status with him; even through their passionate kisses, there had been some sort of battle raging between them. But the bleakness in him tonight had touched some answering chord in her; she had felt not only sadness for him, but a sort of kinship, as well. Jack, for all his mocking, irritating ways, had dwelled in the same depths of sorrow and despair as she had, his life ripped and trampled beneath the feet of another. It was even the same man who had ruined them both. She understood his pain on a wordless, visceral level.

And now she no longer knew how to treat him, how to act with him. *Had they reached a sort of understanding? Would he talk to her? Or would he revert to the sarcastic tone he had used with her before? Would he be embarrassed at how much of himself he had revealed and therefore become even more distant?*

However, she could hardly stand by and watch her patient's temperature climb just because of her uneasiness at the idea of finding Jack and asking for his help. So Nicola squared her shoulders and walked out into the hall. It was night now, and the hallway was dim, lit by a couple of sconces along the wall.

"Mr. Moore?" She walked along the hall and peered down the stairs to the floor below. It looked rather dark down there, so she continued along the hall toward an open doorway, through which a flickering shaft of light fell. "Jack?"

She reached the door and stopped, looking in. Jack was standing before the washbasin, stripped to the waist and washing his face. He was turned away from her, so that she could see only his back, but that was enough to hold her eye. His back, padded with muscle and browned by the sun, broadened from a slender waist and hips to wide shoulders. His dark hair was damp from the washing and a trifle shaggy across the back of his neck. Nicola was aware of a primitive impulse to run her hands over his back, and the heat that flooded her abdomen at the thought set her back a little. *Was she so weak that the mere sight of his naked torso filled her with lust?*

It was then that she saw the network of fine white lines that crisscrossed his back. Nicola realized, with a little indrawn breath of horror, that the lines were scars, and she could think of nothing that would make such scars but a whip. Given his involuntary time in the navy, she felt sure that she was right about the whippings.

He must have heard her involuntary gasp, for he glanced back toward the door, still rubbing his face with the towel. When he saw her, he let out an oath and swung back around, hastily dropping the towel and picking up the mask that lay on the stand beside the washbowl. He put it on even before he reached for his shirt, lying over the back of a chair.

He slipped on the shirt and turned back to her, saying crossly, "Bloody hell, woman, don't you know better than to sneak up on a man like that?"

"I was scarcely sneaking," Nicola retorted. "I called your name. Twice."

"Has something happened to Perry?" The irritation in his voice was replaced by worry, and he crossed the room in three quick strides, not pausing to button his shirt. "Is he worse?"

"A little. Nothing to alarm us yet, but I should give him another dose to bring down his temperature. I need your help." Nicola was intensely aware of the bare skin of his chest, ridged with muscle, that was exposed between the open sides of his shirt, and she looked away.

"Yes, of course."

He strode off down the hall, and Nicola had to hurry to keep up with him. Inside the room, he went straight to Perry's bed. Nicola entered behind him and began to mix the feverfew powder and water.

"He is not improving, is he?" he asked.

"He is not failing, either," Nicola reminded him. "It has been only a day, and I imagine that he lost a lot of blood."

"Yes. It was a long ride back," Jack agreed. "And we could not keep the bleeding stemmed."

"Lift him up," Nicola told him, coming to the bed with the glass of medicine.

Jack complied, and she began to pour the liquid into Perry's mouth. He drank thirstily at first and downed more than half the dose before the bitter taste registered on his tongue. He turned his head, cursing, and once again Jack and Nicola had to hold his head still to get the rest of it down him. When Jack laid his friend back down on the bed, he looked over at Nicola.

"You look done in," he said. "Why don't you lie down and sleep for a while? I will watch over him."

"But that is what I came here to do," Nicola protested. "I am sure you will have ample opportunity to do so over the next few days. But you will be better able to help him if you are not dead on your feet. I will wake you if his condition worsens."

Nicola cast a glance at the patient. She knew that it was likely that he would come to a crisis before much longer. It made sense to snatch whatever sleep she could now. After all, she had had a tiring day and little sleep the night before. "All right."

"Take the bedroom next door." Jack nodded toward the far wall. "No one will disturb you."

Nicola nodded and left the room. The next room was small, but clean, as was the bed in it. She pulled the pins from her hair and shook it down, easing the beginning pains of a headache. She took off her shoes and lay down on top of the bed fully dressed, spreading out a blanket over her. She was asleep almost instantly.

SHE WAS LYING IN HER BED, NOT here or at Tidings, but she knew it was her bed. A man lay in the bed beside her, his hand stroking her body. She turned to look at him, and she saw that it was Gil. She smiled and relaxed, stretching her arms above her head and giving herself up to the pleasure that Gil was creating in her. His hand was gentle and warm, callused. She had never felt anything as pleasurable. His hand roamed all over her, arousing her until she moaned and stirred. Her breasts were tight and full, aching for his touch, and between her legs passion throbbed, hot and demanding. He began to kiss her, murmuring her name....

"Nicola...Nicola...wake up. Nicola."

She was pulled reluctantly from sleep, her body alive and tingling from her dream, her mind still befogged. A man stood beside her bed, looking down at her. *Gil!* For a confused instant, her heart leapt within her, and her arms lifted toward him.

Then it registered on her sleepy mind that a mask covered half the man's face, and she remembered suddenly who he was and where *she* was. Her arms dropped to her sides, and her face flamed with embarrassment. She sat up, pushing the blanket from her, but it had twisted around her as she slept, and now it seemed to tangle worse and worse the more she struggled.

Jack reached down and hooked a hand in the blanket, peeling it aside and freeing her. Nicola felt even more the fool, and she hid her face by swinging off the bed and bending down to pick up her shoes and put them on.

"What's happened?" she asked curtly, hoping that if she were matter-of-fact, he would respond in kind. But inside her mind was racing. *What had he seen?* She could remember the details of her dream all too vividly. *Had she moaned aloud as she had in her dream? Had he heard her? How long had he been standing there watching her sleep? Could he tell what sort of thing she was dreaming about?*

She called herself ten times a fool for not locking the door. *Imagine—at Tidings, she barricaded herself in her room each night, but here, in the midst of a gang of thieves, she had not even thought of locking the door!* It had doubtless been because she was so tired, but still…it seemed to her that anyone with the least common sense would have been afraid to fall asleep here unprotected.

"He has taken a turn for the worse," Jack explained, his voice and face giving nothing away. "His fever is high, and he's thrashing about and talking nonsense. I had to hold him down for fear he would reopen his wound."

Nicola hurried out of the room, not taking the time to pin up her hair, and it floated in a pale cloud about her shoulders, soft and golden. When she entered Perry's room, she found him struggling to sit up, cursing softly.

"Damn him! I'll not be dictated to!" he exclaimed, his eyes wild, his voice even more accented in the tones of wealth and privilege.

"Of course you won't," Nicola said agreeably, coming around to one side of the bed and taking his arm in both her hands, gently pushing him back down. "But you really must lie down, you know."

"I don't want to lie down," he answered pettishly. "I have to—to talk…" His voice trailed off, and he lay back with a weary sigh, his eyes closing. "Tell him."

"I will. And later you may tell him yourself."

"Arrogant bastard."

Nicola made a soothing noise, brushing his hair back from his forehead and feeling for herself how hot his skin had become. She reached for the washcloth and dipped it into the bowl of water.

"Thank God for you, Netta," Perry continued.

"Mmm." Nicola smoothed the damp cloth over his face. "There. That feels better, doesn't it? You should rest now."

Perry nodded, mumbling something unintelligible, and soon the evenness of his breathing showed that he was asleep again. Nicola looked across the bed at Jack.

"What was that about?"

He shrugged. "I know little more than you. I think Netta is the name of his sister. He does not talk about his family much. They are estranged. I believe his father threw him out because of his wild ways. His mind is ten years in the past. How bad is he?"

"I don't know. Obviously he's delirious. He is quite hot. All we can do is try to bring down the fever and keep him still so he doesn't reopen his wound." She wiped down his sweating face and chest, carefully staying away from the bandage over his wound, then rinsed the cloth and wrung it out and started over again.

"I'll bring up a pitcher of water from the barrel outside," Jack said. "It will be cooler." He left the room, taking the bowl of water with him, and returned a few minutes later with an empty bowl and a pitcher of water, chilled from sitting in the evening air.

Nicola repeated the process with the cooler water, then

laid a damp cloth beneath his neck and another over his forehead. She left Jack with their patient to make sure he did not hurt himself by thrashing around again, and she went downstairs to the kitchen to heat water for a cup of meadowsweet tea. When the herb had steeped, she carried the pot and a cup upstairs. She found Jack leaning over the bed when she entered, holding his friend down.

"He keeps insisting on getting up," Jack said grimly. "If we are to get that cup of tea down him, I had better call for reinforcements."

He went to the door and yelled for Saunders, returning to help Nicola press Perry back flat on the bed. Within a few minutes, Saunders, the man who had helped them the day before, joined them.

It took the three of them to get the cup of fluid down Perry's throat. Perry was delirious and shouting imprecations at them, using the sort of language that would have made Nicola blush had she not heard it all before from the women she worked with in the East End. After a few minutes, the meadowsweet began to work on his fever and he subsided into a restless sleep, still hot enough to soak the sheets with his sweat, but at least no longer raving and seeing things that were not there.

They stayed with him throughout the night. Jack's man made a pallet on the floor and went to sleep there, rising when they needed him to hold Perry down. Otherwise Jack and Nicola watched over Perry, keeping his fever down with cool cloths and holding him still whenever he began to try to get out of bed or to flail around.

It was a long, desperate night. Nicola forgot about eating, and there was no question of sleep. All her attention was focused on her patient. Jack worked quietly and well with her, doing whatever she asked of him. All sarcasm and teasing had disappeared in the face of his worry about his friend. They changed Perry's bandages and applied new salves of woundwort and comfrey. They fought his fever with cooling cloths and forced feedings of meadowsweet, feverfew and water. Perry, in pain and delirious, was not an easy patient, and it required strength, forbearance and patience to nurse him.

Now and again Jack looked over at Nicola, his eyes narrowed and thoughtful. Finally she snapped, "Must you keep looking at me like that?"

"Like what?"

"In that cold, assessing way. It is most unnerving."

"I did not mean to make you uneasy. I was just thinking...I am surprised. A little puzzled by you."

"Puzzled? What do you mean?" Nicola, wiping Perry's face with a cool cloth, glanced at him.

"You are very determined, very hardworking."

"You did not think I was determined?" A smile quirked the edges of Nicola's mouth as she turned away to drop the cloth back into the washbasin. "That, if nothing else, would make it clear how little you know me."

"Stubborn, yes. That is easy enough to see. Accustomed to getting your own way, naturally. But this willingness to work, to sacrifice...it surprises me."

"Your opinion of me constantly amazes," Nicola told him dryly. "If you thought that I was such a fluff, so unwilling to do anything, merely selfish and stubborn, it is a wonder that you asked me—no, I should say, *commanded* me—to come take care of your friend. What did you expect to have to do, hold a gun to my head to force me to treat him?"

"No. I knew only that you were good with herbs and remedies, and I knew that whatever you would do would be more than what he had without you."

"Careful. Such high encomiums might turn my head."
Nicola sat down beside Perry's bed with a weary sigh.

"Obviously I was wrong," Jack said stiffly. "You have
done more than I ever imagined, and I thank you."

Nicola glanced at him. She had some inkling of how
much those words had cost him. Nor, if she was honest,
how could she really blame him for supposing a woman
of her station in life would be unlikely to devote herself
with great energy to healing a common highwayman. After
all, she was a stranger to him. So she relented enough to
give him a smile.

"You are welcome."

He looked as if he might say more, but at that moment
Perry groaned and started to roll onto his side. Nicola and
Jack jumped up to catch him and gently, but firmly, make
him stay on his back.

"These bed linens are soaked," Nicola commented. The
patient's profuse sweating, as well as the wet cloths they
had been applying, had done their damage. "We cannot
have him catching a cold, as well. We must change them."

Jack cast a worried glance at his friend. "You want to
move him? I suppose Saunders and I can do it."

"No. We can manage, I think, with him in the bed, if
you will help me. First, I need fresh linens."

"Of course." It was obvious from the blank expression
on his face that he hadn't a clue where they were, but he
left the room and returned a few minutes later with a pile
of fresh bedding.

Quickly and efficiently, Nicola undid the sheets on one
side of the bed, then helped Jack pull the patient on the
loose sheet over to the other side of the bed. She remade
half the bed with clean linens, after which, they pushed and
squirmed and tugged Perry as gently as possible back to

the clean side, and Nicola finished replacing the wet sheet. They laid a fresh blanket atop him, which Perry, of course, immediately pushed down.

"At the risk of incurring your wrath yet again, I must say that I am surprised at your skill in making a bed."

Nicola laughed. "I admit that that is something I did not know how to do until the past few years. But in my house in the East End, I have pitched in with work as well as money."

"Your house in the East End!" He looked at her oddly. "You never lived there!"

"Oh, no, not I. 'Tis the unfortunate women I take in. Several of them live there, and we feed as many others daily as we can."

"Who lives there? Why?"

"Women who have no other place to go," Nicola said simply. "At first I intended it only for pregnant women who needed a roof over their heads—girls tossed out by angry fathers, tavern maids and serving girls whose jobs were taken away when they began to show, even prostitutes who got careless and were too afraid of the butchers to get rid of it."

Jack stared at her, dumbfounded. "Haymarket ware?" he asked. "Tavern wenches? You created a home for them?"

"Yes. It isn't nearly adequate." Nicola got up and went to the basin to wring out a cloth and wipe Perry's sweating face.

"I am astonished that you even know about them, even speak of such things, let alone—"

"Oh, you would find that I am quite ostracized by many members of the Ton," Nicola said with no sign of regret. "I have offended many a matron by talking about such things. But what is the point of hinting around the subject? I haven't the time or the energy, not when there is so much that needs to be done. Some women, I have found, are more relieved than anything else by my plain speech. It can grow quite wearisome always talking around a subject. And just as many as those who won't speak to me give me money to help me with the work." She grinned, thinking about her money-raising efforts. "Indeed, there are one or two women who won't speak to me in public because of their husband's wishes but who give me money in private."

She wet the cloth again and wrung it out, then folded it and placed it on Perry's forehead. "My house has grown considerably. I soon found that there were many other women who needed help, women beaten by their husbands or fathers—or the men who run them as prostitutes. I could hardly turn them away, especially when they had children with them. The house is bursting at the seams, and now I have to turn away all but the most needy. We have purchased a second house, and we are in the process now of making it habitable. I have help, of course. Penelope— my good friend—helps me when she can, though she has to keep it secret from her dragon of a mother. The assistant vicar at St. Swithin's has made it a project of his church's, and some of the women from there help. One of the women who I took in, one of the 'Haymarket ware' as you called them, has proved to be remarkably capable, and she has taken over the daily running of it—with an almost terrifying efficiency, I might add. Needless to say, I have bullied money from everyone I know."

Nicola cast him a teasing smile as she said, "Perhaps you would like to donate some of your ill-gotten gains to it."

"Perhaps I will." He shook his head wonderingly. "I confess, you astound me, Nicola."

His use of her name surprised her. It was the first time he had called her anything except "Miss Falcourt," in that mocking way he had. But her first name had slipped out effortlessly, familiarly, and somehow the sound of it on his tongue made her heart turn in her chest. She did not wish him to know that, however, so she kept her head turned away from him, ostensibly watching their patient.

"Why? Because I have a heart? Or the wit to do something about it?"

"I don't know. I only know that you are not what I expected."

"What you expected?" She looked over at him at that, puzzled. "Why would you have expected *anything* of me?"

He hesitated, then shrugged. "From what I heard of you. What the villagers said. 'The kind and gracious Miss Falcourt.' I thought you must be either a saint or one of those patronizing females who come now and then and cast a few treats at the peasants, collect their groveling thanks and return to your luxuries. When I met you, of course, I realized right away that you were no saint, so that left only the 'noble lady of the manor.'"

"Never a consideration that I might be simply a person who does what she can to help, was there? I must say, Mr. Moore, that you are an absolute morass of prejudices and assumptions."

He grinned unexpectedly. "Your acid tongue was something of a surprise, as well, though I must say, I derive a certain enjoyment from it."

"I won't!" Perry said loudly, making them both start, and they turned to look at him. His eyes were wide open and staring wildly, his face flushed and beading with sweat. He reached up and felt the cloth that lay across his forehead, then crumpled it up and flung it across the room with an oath. "I'll be damned first!"

At his roar, Saunders woke from his pallet on the floor and jumped to his feet, looking around. "Wot the devil?"

"It's all right, Saunders. Our friend is simply getting a trifle loud," Jack said, but his face was more worried than his light tone implied.

Nicola, too, felt a piercing thrust of fear. Perry was clearly delirious, and his fever seemed to have spiked suddenly. She stood up and reached over to feel his wrist, but he twisted his hand around and grabbed her arm, his fingers digging in.

"What the devil do you think you're doing?" he snapped. "I'll see you in hell before I—"

Jack was by her side in an instant, prying Perry's fingers from her arm. "Leave off, Per. She is trying to help you. We all are."

Perry swung at him, his fist thudding ineffectually into Jack's wide chest, and he let out a string of oaths. He turned his head away, his voice fading out, and his eyes closed.

"Are you all right?" Jack asked, turning to Nicola, reaching out to take her arm and inspect it.

"I am fine," Nicola said shortly. She despised the rush of satisfaction she had felt when Jack sprang to her aid— and, even more, the tingle of pleasure that the touch of his fingers on her arm had brought. She pulled her arm out of Jack's grasp and turned toward the man in the bed. "He is growing worse quickly."

"What can we do?"

"What we have been doing. I—I know of nothing else." She cast Jack a worried look. "I wish Granny Rose were here. I am afraid that I have reached the limit of my skills."

"Then they will have to do," he replied grimly. "Saunders..." He turned toward his man. "Fetch more cold water." He swiveled back to Nicola. "All right, let's get to work."

Through the remainder of the night they worked on Perry, fighting to keep his fever from soaring, as a battle raged in the man's body. He had reached a crisis point, and Nicola was unhappily aware of how close to the edge the man lay. The infection could gain too strong a foothold, the fever roar out of control, and his body might not be strong enough to overcome it, even with the help of the poultices and oral remedies that Nicola had been giving him.

They kept cold cloths on his forehead and the back of his neck constantly, changing them as his body heat warmed them, and they bathed his chest, neck and face with cool water, over and over, no longer pausing to sit or rest. Saunders and Jack lifted him and kept him still as Nicola forced him to sip water or meadowsweet tea or the bitter mixture of feverfew.

Nicola's back ached from standing bent over the bed, and her head pounded from fatigue and lack of food, for they had been too preoccupied with their patient to eat an evening meal. It seemed as if their task was never ending. But she called on her reserves of strength and stubbornly worked on.

Numbed and tired, she moved so mechanically through her routine that it was some minutes before the change in the patient's condition registered on her weary brain. Suddenly she realized that while they had been working, Perry had subtly, gradually, become cooler.

Nicola stopped in mid-motion, looking down at her patient. He was lying quietly, his chest rising and falling in even breaths. "Jack!"

He turned toward her from where he stood at the wash-basin, pouring in fresh cold water to use for their rags.

"Look!" Nicola whispered, scarcely daring to raise her voice. She pointed to Perry. "I think his fever has dropped."

"What?" He came closer to the bed, seeing, as Nicola had, that Perry's labored breathing and restlessness had grown calmer, his face less flushed. Jack wrapped his hand around the other man's wrist. He turned to Nicola, wonder dawning on his face. "You're right. He is cooler."

"He passed the crisis!" Nicola cried, tears springing into her eyes. "I think he is going to be all right!"

Jack let out a laugh. "Saunders, go tell the others. Perry's improving!"

"Yes, sir!" Saunders was already hurrying to the door.

Jack let out a whoop and startled Nicola by picking her up off her feet in a bone-crushing hug and whirling her around. "You did it! You saved him!"

Nicola clung to him, giddy at the way he was spinning her about the room, and laughed with joy. Jack stopped and set her on the floor, giving her a resounding kiss of sheer exuberance. They parted and stepped back, suddenly aware of their close proximity, of the impulsive touch of their lips. His gesture had been natural, an overflowing of relief, excitement and joy. But now, as they looked at each other, other sensations, other emotions, shimmered on the edge of their consciousness. Arousal, suppressed and displaced for the past day, now hovered, on the verge of exploding into passion.

Footsteps pounded on the stairs, accompanied by the babble of excited voices. Nicola whirled and moved away from Jack; a moment later the door opened, and three men and Diane poured into the room. Jack laughed, saying that Perry was not up to a party yet, but indulgently watched them crowd around their friend's bed.

They remained for a few minutes, until Jack shooed them away, and then once again it was only the two of them. Nicola could not help but think of that moment before the others came in, of the desire that had boiled up in her. It had been the excitement, she told herself, coupled with weariness, that had made her let her guard down. It would not happen again. Not looking at Jack, she resumed her seat beside Perry's bed, curling her hand around his wrist to feel his pulse, no longer so tumultuous, and his temperature, still noticeably cooler than it had been. She leaned upon her arm, her eyes on Perry's face.

The next thing she knew, light was streaming through the window and she was awakening with a jerk. She sat for a moment, blinking and trying to orient herself. A glance at Perry's face reminded her where she was. It was morning, and obviously she had fallen asleep sitting by his bed. Guiltily, she reached out and touched his arm. It was cooler, and he was sleeping deeply, his breathing calm and even. He was better, his body healing itself in blessed sleep.

Nicola sat up stiffly. Her arm, upon which her head had been resting, had gone numb, and now tingles were shooting through it. Her neck, bent at an odd angle, was stiff, as was her back, and she stood up slowly, rolling her head and bending this way and that.

She looked across the bed. Jack was still there, seated on the other side. He, too, was asleep, leaning against the high back of the chair, his face relaxed and vulnerable. Nicola stood for a moment, watching him. Outside the birds twittered and chased one another. She heard a man's voice and the closing of a door.

Perry was doing well enough now that one of the others could watch him, she thought. Indeed, he had been doing well enough on his own the past few hours, with her and Jack sound asleep. She could call to one of Jack's men and instruct him to watch Perry, and she could go to her room for a few needed hours of sleep. She thought with deep satisfaction of stretching out on a soft bed for the next few hours.

She looked back at Jack, thinking that she should wake him, as well. He needed sleep just as much as she did. She thought again, as she had yesterday afternoon, that he was even more handsome in the daylight, for the lines of his face were clean and strong. Her eyes flickered over the neatly trimmed goatee and mustache, and the firm, wide mouth that centered them. His jaw was shadowed by a night's stubble, as black as the curling hair on his head. Her eyes roamed upward, taking in the straight nose and the high curve of his cheekbones, disappearing beneath the black mask. She wondered, as always, what the mask hid and why, and as she stood there watching him, it occurred to her that while he slept, she could push up the mask and see the features he kept hidden.

Curiosity filled her, drowning out a faint voice of guilt that objected to this invasion of his privacy. She tiptoed around the edge of the bed, her heart pounding. Trepidation and eagerness swelled within her, setting her fingers trembling and her pulse pounding. Quietly, she stretched out her hand to him. Her fingers brushed the lower edge of his mask.

Suddenly his eyes flew open and his hand wrapped around her wrist like a steel band, imprisoning it. "Don't."

His voice was even harder than his touch, and his eyes glittered darkly through the mask. Nicola let out a little squeak of surprise, a flush rising in her cheeks at being caught in such an ignominious position. She tried to straighten up, but he would not let her. For an instant, they stood locked in the tableau. Then, as quickly as a snake striking, he jerked her down into his lap, his other arm going out to encircle her, and his lips fastened on hers.

Nicola did not know what she had expected—anger, jokes, recriminations—but it was not this. Desire exploded within her at the touch of his mouth, hot, hard and demanding. She felt the same passion bolt through him, and her body flared with heat. Thoughts of resistance—indeed, thought altogether—fled from her mind, and she trembled, pressing into him with equal fervor.

They kissed until they were breathless, consumed with flame. Jack stood up abruptly, sweeping her up into his arms, and started toward the door. Nicola made a feeble resistance, waving in the general direction of Perry's bed and murmuring, "Wait. What about—"

He closed her mouth with a brief, hard kiss and flung open the door. Striding down the hall with her in his arms, he bellowed, "Saunders! See to Perry!"

Then they were inside his room, and he kicked the door shut behind him, setting Nicola down so that he could pull her into his arms once again. Hungrily they kissed, his hands sliding over her body, as they inched their way toward his bed. All the touches, the looks, the teasing flickers of desire that had occurred over the past two days, flamed into life now, sending a consuming fire roaring through them. Nicola trembled, her hands curling into his shirt.

"Nicola," he murmured as his hand found and cupped her breast. "God, it's been so long. Sweet Nicky."

Pain lanced through Nicola at his use of the nickname Gil had often called her. She jerked away. "No! Oh, no!" She turned away blindly, her hands going to her face. "No, I cannot."

"Bloody hell!" He reached out and grasped her wrist, whipping her back around to face him. "What sort of game are you playing? You want me—I felt it in you. Do you want to drive me mad? Make me beg for you?"

"No!" Nicola started to cry. "I am sorry. Truly. I did not mean—I swore I would not let anything happen. I don't know what is the matter with me!" She looked at him, her eyes wide and filled with unshed tears. "But I cannot do this with you. I cannot be unfaithful."

A red light flared in his eyes, and his grip tightened painfully on her arm. "Unfaithful!" he thundered. "What do you mean, unfaithful? You said you were not married."

"I'm not! I never have been."

"Then what—"

"I was in love! I love him still."

"Who?" His voice was quiet now, and more chilling than the rage. "Who owns your heart?"

"A boy. He is dead. He died long ago." The tears spilled out of her eyes and down her cheeks, and she looked up at him pleadingly. "I don't know why I feel this—this *lust* for you. But it is not enough. I will not break faith with him."

He dropped her arm, and his voice was filled with scorn. "You expect me to believe that? That you remain true to your former lover? A man who has been dead for years?"

"Yes!" Nicola straightened her shoulders and glared at him. "Why shouldn't you believe it? It is the truth. I loved Gil. I'll never love another."

"Gil," he repeated, his face as hard and unreadable as stone. "You have had no other man since him."

"No, of course not. He was all in all to me." Her voice caught on a sob.

"A very pretty tale."

"'Tis not a tale!" Nicola retorted hotly. "How dare you—"

He reached up behind his head and pulled at the ribbons of his mask, untying it. His hand dropped, taking down the mask and revealing his face for the first time. He looked at Nicola unwaveringly.

Nicola stared back at him. Suddenly there seemed to be no air to breathe, and noise roared in her ears. She crumpled to the floor in a faint.

CHAPTER ELEVEN

"Nicola?"

She heard a voice saying her name, and slowly her eyes fluttered open. A man knelt beside her, his face looming above her, dearly familiar and yet very different, too. It was Gil's face, but older, with sun lines around his eyes and a goatee and mustache obscuring his chin, as well as a small scar on his cheek that had not been there before.

"Gil!" Joy rushed up in Nicola, and she sat up, throwing her arms around his neck. "Oh, Gil, it's you! You're alive!"

She began to cry, a reaction more of nerves than any sort of sadness, and she said his name again and again, punctuating it with little kisses all over his face. She reached his mouth, and this kiss was long and deep. It was him, and it was Jack, and suddenly she understood her immediate, intense response to this man. Her heart and body had recognized him, even though her mind had been too rational to even consider the possibility. She cried harder, clinging to him.

"I can't believe it! How could I not have known?" She leaned back, grasping his shoulders, and looked up into his face. "But—you are taller! And bigger. And your voice—no, I suppose that was just the different way you talked, the gentlemanly accent."

"I grew another couple of inches. I was only twenty, after all. And I filled out as I got older. It happens."

"But why did you hide from me?" In her instantaneous joy and excitement, the thought had not occurred to her at first. But now pain lanced through her as she realized that Gil had purposely hidden himself from her, worn a mask so that she could not see his face and recognize him. "Why didn't you come to me? Tell me who you were? Why did you wear that mask?"

She pulled back from him, questions flooding in on her. "For that matter, where have you been? Why haven't you let me know where you were? It's been ten years, Jack! Gil. You see, I don't even know who you are anymore!"

"Everyone calls me Jack now. I am used to it. I stopped using my name ten years ago."

"But why? Why didn't you write me? Why didn't you tell me you were alive all those years? Don't you know how I worried? Didn't you care?"

Nicola was swept with cold as she realized the implications of his years of silence, and suddenly she felt quite remote, even numb. "You didn't love me."

"Didn't love you!" Jack rose in a swift, angry motion. "Good God, woman, do not try to turn this around on me! I am no longer a love-blinded fool whom you can twist around her finger. Why should I write you? Why in the hell would I think you would want to know whether I was still alive? So you could tell Exmoor?"

"Exmoor! Why would I tell Exmoor?" she asked, confused and frustrated by his words. "Why are you acting like this? What happened to you?"

"You happened to me! One betrayal was enough. I am not slow to learn."

"Betrayal! What are you talking about? Are you saying

that I betrayed—" She stopped abruptly, her mind going back to something the highwayman had told her about his past. "Are you saying—was what you told me the truth? Exmoor had a press gang kidnap you and put you on a naval ship?"

"Of course. Did you not know how he got rid of me? Perhaps you didn't care to know the details as long as the problem was removed."

Nicola stared at him, bereft of speech for a moment. "And that girl you told me about, the one who soured you on women—that was me? The one you said betrayed you to your enemy?"

He looked at her oddly. "Of course. I was rather surprised you did not recognize your own story."

"My own—what are you talking about? I never betrayed you."

He grimaced. "Don't bother lying, Nicola. There is no way you can talk your way out of this. You told Richard where I was, asked him to get rid of me so that I would not plague you anymore."

"What?" Nicola rose to her feet, her hands going to her head as though to hold inside the tumult of thoughts rushing around her brain. "Have you run mad? How could I have betrayed you to Richard? I didn't know where you were. I didn't even know you were alive! You went off the Falls, and we searched and searched for you, but we couldn't find you. I never heard from you again. I thought you were dead!"

"I sent you a letter. I am not mad. I know what I did. What you did. I sent you a letter, telling you how a farmer had found me, half in, half out of the river, clinging to a tree root. I told you where I was so that you could come to me. So we could marry and leave this place. Imagine my surprise when who should show up? Not you, my 'beloved'…" His voice was thick with scorn. "But the Earl of Exmoor himself. You had sent him, he said, because you had realized what a fool you had been—how you had lowered yourself by dallying with a peasant. You could see that I would be a problem for you, and you wanted to be rid of me, so you had told him where I was and asked him to 'take care of the problem.'"

"And you believed *him?*" Nicola asked, anger rushing up through her chest. "The man who had just come to fisticuffs with you? Who had let you slip off the Falls?"

"Let me slip?" Jack snorted. "He pushed me."

"Even worse! You knew he had tried to kill you, yet you believed what *he* told you? You did not even think to check with me?"

"There was no need to 'check'!" Jack retorted, his eyes blazing. "How else could he have known where I was? Only you—and that farmer's family—knew. And since the farmer and his family knew neither you, me, nor the Earl of Exmoor, I doubt that they went straight to him with the news."

"Someone else had to know!" Nicola insisted. "You sent the letter to me somehow. You entrusted someone with it. They betrayed you, not me."

His face was like granite. "Don't lie to me, Nicola. You cannot squirm out of this. I sent the farmer's son with the letter. As I told you, he would have had no idea to take it to Exmoor. Those living at Exmoor thought I had fallen off the Falls, and I did not enlighten them. I thought the less they knew, the better for them."

"Then Richard must have somehow intercepted it, taken it from the boy. I never received it."

"The boy told me he delivered it," Jack replied, his voice laced with contempt.

"Not to me!"

"No, not to you," Jack admitted grimly. "I put your letter inside another letter, which he delivered, and he brought me back a note from her saying she had received it and would give your letter to you. I sent it to Granny Rose." He looked at her with bitter eyes. "Do you think Granny Rose betrayed me?"

Nicola stared back at him. She felt as if the ground had suddenly turned to quicksand beneath her feet. *Had he gone mad? Had she?*

"No," she replied, her voice shaky. "Of course not." He was Granny Rose's grandson; she had loved him more than life itself. One might as well believe that pigs could fly as that Granny Rose would have told Gil's enemy where he was.

She sat down on the bed, her knees suddenly weak beneath her. Her whole life had been turned upside down the past few minutes, so that she no longer knew what to think—or even what she felt.

"But something must have happened," she protested faintly. "I got no letter. Did Granny Rose know that Exmoor had tried to kill you? Perhaps he went there, hoping to find you, and she told him—not thinking that—"

"For God's sake, Nicola!" Jack exploded. "Of course I told her he shoved me off the Falls. She knew. She had always known him for the blackguard he was. Why do you keep up this pretense? We both know that you sent Exmoor. You might as well admit it."

"No," Nicola said, struggling to keep her voice even. "We don't *both* know that. I don't know what happened, or how Richard came upon that information. But I never got that letter. Why won't you believe me?"

"Why would I? You were a Judas before. I would be a fool to trust what you tell me now."

"You talk in circles." Nicola jumped to her feet, her arms stiff at her sides, her hands fisting. "You say that I lie now when I tell you I did not betray you, and your proof is that you think I betrayed you back then!"

"This is absurd!"

"Yes, I suppose it is." Nicola struggled to hold down the sobs rising in her throat, the scalding tears battering her eyes. "To think that I loved you all these years, held my heart locked away from other men, because I knew I would never love anyone but you. But you did not love me enough to trust me, as you loved and trusted Granny Rose. You knew it could not have been she who betrayed you. Why did you not believe the same thing about me?"

He stared back at her, his face suddenly blank.

Nicola turned away, her voice raw with unshed tears. "Go away. I cannot bear to look at you."

NICOLA AWAKENED FEELING AS IF she had hardly slept, even though she could tell from the way the sun slanted through the window that it had been several hours since she had fallen asleep. Slowly she sat up, pushing her tangled hair back from her face. She had given way to a long storm of crying after closing herself in her room, with the result that her head ached and her eyes were swollen. Her heart felt equally battered. The onslaught of emotions earlier, swinging from the heights of joy, when she realized that Gil was still alive, to the depths of pain as it dawned on her that he had hated her for years, had left her numbed and bruised. She wasn't sure what she felt, besides a pervasive sadness.

She crossed to the small dresser, where the few toiletry articles she had brought with her sat. One look in the mirror confirmed the swollen, blotchy state of her face after a bout of tears. She washed her face in the basin, then began the laborious process of brushing out her hair. When she had it free from tangles, she pulled it back and coiled it up on the back of her neck in a simple style. Finally, she slipped off her wrinkled dress, which she had slept in, having thrown herself across the bed in a paroxysm of tears, then fallen asleep as she lay. A quick wash and fresh clothing made her feel a trifle better, and when she looked in the small mirror above the dresser, she thought that she looked presentable. At least she did not look like a wild woman who had spent the morning crying.

Crossing the room, she opened the door and peered out into the hall. It was empty, though downstairs she could hear the sound of a woman singing and the clatter of dishes. Her heart was pounding in her ribs. Drawing a deep breath, Nicola walked down the hall toward the sickroom. With every step, she was tinglingly aware that she might run into Jack, and she didn't know what she would do if that happened. But she had to see her patient, didn't she? she argued to herself.

She opened the door to Perry's room and stepped inside. Perry lay asleep in the bed, propped up slightly by pillows. Jack sat beside the bed. He had shaved off his goatee and mustache, she saw, and he looked even more like his old self. Nicola stopped, her heart jumping up into her throat.

Why had she thought that she was numb? At the sight of Jack, she was filled with such rushing, conflicting emotions that she thought she might explode. She wanted to look at him forever, drinking in each feature, finding all the achingly familiar things like the dark arch of his eyebrow or the curve of his cheekbone, examining all those things that were different, like the small arc of a scar high on his cheek or the deeper lines that fanned out from his eyes. She wanted to cling to him, and at the same time, she was aware of a very strong urge to slap him. Thrilled, appalled, giddy, furious, she ached with love, desire and hurt. He had sent her world crashing, and now everything she knew or felt lay in shards on the ground, splintered, scattered and mixed-up.

He stood up as she entered the room, his eyes searching her face, and for a long moment they simply looked at each other. Finally Nicola cleared her throat nervously and came forward a few more steps.

"Why didn't you send for me?" she asked. A thousand questions and recriminations vied for release, twisting her stomach into knots, and so she asked only the simplest, least meaningful question that came to mind.

"You were sleeping. I didn't want to disturb you. And Perry was doing all right. I stayed with him. I would have called you if anything seemed amiss."

"Then you must be very tired," Nicola said, speaking almost as she would to a stranger. She walked around the bed to stand on the opposite side, near the foot. "I can relieve you now so that you can get some sleep, too."

He hesitated, then said, "All right. Thank you. I will be down the hall if you need me. His temperature has been much cooler, and he has not been so restless. I gave him some meadowsweet tea a while ago. He was awake and drank it with only a little support from me. He was weak but rational."

"Good. It sounds as if he is past the worst, then."

"Yes, I hope so." He paused. "Nicola…"

She looked at him with a clear, cool gaze, her eyebrows raised slightly, much the way she might deflect the questions of an impudent stranger. "Yes?"

He started to speak, then stopped, shaking his head. "Nothing."

Jack turned and walked out of the room, and when he had closed the door behind him, Nicola sank down into her chair with a shaky sigh of relief.

"So he told you." A voice spoke weakly but clearly, and Nicola jumped, startled, and looked at the bed. Her patient lay with his eyes open, watching her. He was wan and obviously weak, but there was an undeniable spark of interest in his pale blue eyes.

"What? Oh. Yes, he told me."

The man nodded. "About time."

"I agree." Nicola stood up and leaned over the bed, feeling his forehead. "You are doing better."

"Thanks to you."

"Well, I don't want to see any of my handiwork undone, so I suggest that you rest and let your body go about its business of healing."

"But I want to hear about what happened," he protested, even though he was obviously having trouble keeping his eyes open.

"Later. I will tell you all about it later. But I won't have you tiring yourself."

"Promise?"

Nicola smiled. "Yes. I promise. Now go to sleep."

He nodded, his eyes closing, and Nicola sat back down in her chair. She wondered how much Jack's friend knew about her and her past with Jack. It was embarrassing— as well as irritating—to think of the sort of picture Jack had doubtless painted of her.

There was a soft tap, and a moment later the door opened, and Diane, the woman whom Nicola had met the other day, entered the room quietly. She carried a tray, from which emanated such a savory smell that Nicola's mouth began to water. She realized suddenly that she was starving to death. It made sense; she had not eaten since almost this time yesterday.

"Jack told me to bring you some food," the girl said, looking no more friendly than she had the other night. "It is only stew."

"Stew would be wonderful. It smells delicious," Nicola told her honestly, standing up and reaching out to take the tray. "Thank you."

The girl shrugged and handed it over to her. Nicola wondered why the girl seemed antagonistic toward her. Perhaps she felt slighted that Jack had not trusted her to care for his friend but had sent for Nicola. Or, she thought, more likely she simply resented the intrusion of another female into this cozy den—especially when Jack had brought in the intruder. Nicola did not doubt that the girl had probably woven some pleasant fantasies with Jack at their center.

Or perhaps they were not fantasies.

Nicola was surprised at the sharp stab of jealousy that pierced her at the thought. It would not be unusual, no doubt, for the leader of the gang to have the only woman at the hideout as his mistress. He had said that the girl belonged to one of the other men, but perhaps that had been merely a pretense. Just because she had remained faithful to their love did not mean that he had. Jack was, after all, young and virile, and it had been ten years since she had seen him. It was absurd to think that he might have lived celibately all that time, especially given the fact that he despised Nicola and thought her a traitor to their love.

Nicola dismissed the girl rather more sharply than she normally would have and returned to her seat, putting the tray on her lap. Even her pique was not enough to erase her hunger, and she devoured the food. Whatever else the girl might be, she was a wonderful cook; even the rough brown bread with its slab of pale butter was ambrosial.

As she ate, Nicola's mind was a turmoil of thoughts. What did Jack want here? How did he feel about her? Obviously he had come back for revenge on his nemesis, Exmoor. But that did not explain the fact that he had kissed her. If he hated her so much, why had he pursued her? She was adept at healing, which might be adequate to explain his overcoming his dislike enough to ask for her help for his friend. But it certainly did not take care of his reasons for following her home from the village. Nor did it explain his passionate kisses and caresses. No matter how much he despised her, he seemed to want her still.

Or perhaps those kisses had simply been his way of proving that he had mastery over her, that he could control her by using her own desire. He had made her respond to him against her will, and what could prove his power more than that? *Had his lovemaking been nothing more than a way of getting back at her?* That was a lowering thought indeed.

Even more confusing was the fact that Nicola did not know how she felt about him. She had loved him more than anything, had never given her heart to another man— or even been interested in one. She remembered the way her heart had leapt in her chest this morning when she saw his face and realized that Gil was alive. But the fury that had swept her when she understood that he had let her believe for ten years that he was dead was also branded into her heart and soul, as well as the searing hurt and loss when she saw how low he had rated her love. *Could she love a man who thought her capable of such treachery?*

Was Jack Moore still the man she had loved, or had he changed beyond all recognition?

She spent a good part of the afternoon on such gloomy considerations, so that it was something of a relief when Perry woke up later, complaining of thirst, and she had something to do besides dwell on unproductive thoughts. She brought him a glass of water and helped him sip it, glad that with him conscious, she could manage to help him raise his head enough to drink without calling Jack for help. The less she saw of Jack, the better.

After that, she made her way downstairs and dipped out some of the meaty liquid of the stew, which she fed to Perry. It was a slow, tiring process, which required most of her strength to support him as he sipped the soup. It sapped Perry's strength, as well, for after a few minutes he closed his eyes and slipped back into sleep.

However, he woke up less than an hour later with a trifle more color in his pale cheeks and a clearer look to his eyes. This time she managed to prop him up on pillows into a half-reclining position, and it was easier then to spoon the fortifying broth down him.

"No," he said, when she moved to help him lie back down when he had finished. "Let me stay up a bit. I fancy a little time spent awake."

"Good." Nicola stepped back, pleased. "As long as you don't exert yourself."

"I don't think I could if I wanted to," he retorted. "I feel weak as a kitten."

"You will get your strength back before long. Don't fret about it. Resting is the best way to let your body heal itself."

"I would say that your work had something to do with it. Jack told me you pulled out the ball."

Nicola made a face. "So I did, and no doubt I made a terrible mess of it. I apologize for causing you pain."

"I scarcely remember it. One of the benefits, I presume, of lying at death's door."

"I suppose you could call it that." Nicola smiled. "Well, since you are awake and feeling so well, I shall take the opportunity to change your bandage." She went over to the small bedside table and began gathering her supplies.

"Tell me what happened," Perry said. "With you and Jack, I mean. He told me only that you had seen his face. He's depressingly closemouthed."

Nicola had to smile. "Don't you know that it's not polite to pry?"

"So my mother tried to tell me. Fortunately, I have managed to ignore most of her precepts. One so rarely finds out anything if one doesn't pry."

"There is little to find out in this case. Jack removed his mask, and I saw who he was. I realized that he had let me believe for ten years that he was dead, when all that time he was alive. He also told me that he thought I was a liar, as well as shallow, traitorous, devious and generally wicked."

"I see."

"I doubt that," Nicola replied briskly, laying the bandaging and salves on the bed beside him. "You know only what Jack has told you, and since he knows nothing of the reality of it, you cannot, either."

"Indeed." Perry cast a somewhat wary eye upon the materials, but said only, "It had always seemed to me that he had a fairly good grasp of what happened."

"No doubt he did—of what happened to *him*. He sent me a note via his grandmother and the farmer's child. And Richard, I am sure, showed up and told him those things about me and turned him over to a press gang. Richard is capable of almost anything. However, Jack knows nothing of what I did or thought or knew—because he saw fit to believe the words of a man who tried to kill him, who had him kidnapped."

She was untying Perry's bandage as she spoke, her fingers moving ever more quickly and forcefully as her words grew in anger, until Perry let out a grunt of pain. Nicola glanced down, instantly contrite. "Oh, I am sorry. I did not mean to hurt you. I should not have been talking about Jack. It only makes me angry."

She sighed as she removed the pad and bent over to inspect the wound closely before she reapplied her ointments and placed a new pad over it. "Still red, but no pus. I think you are healing nicely, Mr.—"

"Just call me Perry. I have become unused to more polite forms of address. So you are saying that the things this Richard told Jack were not true? You did not turn the letter over to him and—"

"Of course not. I never received any letter. If I had, I certainly would not have given it to Richard. I hated the man! I thought he had killed Gil—Jack." She retied the bandage and set the salve back on the table.

Perry frowned. "But Jack did not believe him without reason. His grandmother had taken the letter to you. He knew you had it, and then Richard had it. It was not unreasonable to—"

"Unreasonable? No. Jack was quite reasonable. Anyone who did not love and trust me might have thought the same. Anyone who did love me—indeed, anyone who really knew me—would have known that it was impossible. So you see—I have found out that a great deal of what I have based my life on was false. I thought Gil dead, but he was alive. I thought that he had loved me as much as I loved him, that at least, if I was to be alone all my life, I would have had a great and rare love. But I did not. I gave my heart to a man who did not love or trust me. I have held in my heart for ten years a memory of a love that didn't really exist." Tears sparkled in her eyes.

"No!" Perry said anxiously, reaching toward her. "Do not believe that. Jack loved you. He loved you more than life itself. I know it. I heard how he talked of you. He was devastated."

Nicola took the man's hand and patted it. "Shh. Please, don't get in a taking. It is not good for you. Let us not talk of this any longer. You need to rest."

"Devil take it, but I'm weak!" Perry admitted, falling back against his pillow. His face was paler, and sweat dotted his forehead.

"Yes. It was only two days ago that I took the ball out of your shoulder. So, please, stay calm. Don't think about Jack or what happened. Just go back to sleep."

He sighed and closed his eyes. "All right. For now. But later…"

"Yes, later." Nicola watched as his breathing grew shallower and he slipped back into sleep.

She sincerely hoped that she would not be here too much later. What she would have liked to do was ride straight back to Tidings right now and hide in the comfort of her bed. She did not want to have to see Jack, and she dreaded having to talk to him. However, she knew that she could not leave just yet. Not only did she have a patient to tend to—who, although obviously improving, was not entirely out of danger yet—but she also had to wait for Jack's men to return with Nurse.

Fetching Nurse had, after all, been her excuse to both

Deborah and her aunt for leaving their houses. She could not return without her—or, at least, without her refusal. Jack had sent a man with her note to Nurse the night she had taken the ball from Perry's chest. It would not take a man riding on horseback longer than a day to get to Larchmont, but escorting Nurse back would be another matter. Not only would she travel more slowly, but it would doubtless take her some time to get her affairs in order and to pack, provided, of course, that she decided to come. Nicola could not imagine her arriving before tomorrow evening at the earliest, which meant that Nicola would have to endure at least another day of being in this house with Jack. All she could hope was that he would try to avoid her as hard as she planned to avoid him.

Those hopes were dashed later that night, when the door opened and Jack came into the room. Nicola's eyes went to him immediately, and she felt again the shock of seeing the man she had thought long dead. Her heart bounded, and she knew a quick rush of pleasure at the sight of his face. Following on its heels, of course, came the hurt and anger, the sense of vague humiliation at having been duped. She turned away, looking at Perry's face.

Jack stood just inside the door for a moment. "I came to relieve you. I will look after Perry for a while. You go and get some rest."

"I'm fine."

"So am I." Jack came over to the bed and stood across from her. Nicola avoided his eyes, assiduously studying her hands, linked in her lap.

"I slept while you were watching Perry, and now it is your turn."

"There is no need for you to watch him."

"There is no need for you to exhaust yourself, either.

What good would you be to him then?" Jack pointed out reasonably.

"You are right, of course. I shall go lie down." Nicola stood up, and her eyes slid involuntarily to Jack. He was watching her, and she wondered what he was thinking. *Had her words swayed him at all? Or did he still believe her capable of such treachery?* Nicola reminded herself that it really did not matter; what was important was that he had not trusted her to begin with.

She started toward the door. He said her name and started after her, reaching out his hand to take hold of her wrist. Nicola stopped, acutely aware of his nearness. She could not look at him. Memories of their kisses, ten years ago and just the other day, crowded her mind, and it was humiliating to her that she should feel such a jangling rush of emotions for him when he felt so little for her.

"I want to talk to you," he said in a low voice, his breath brushing her hair.

Nicola shivered. "I—I see no reason to. It is clear what you think of me. What else is there to say?"

She managed to make herself look up into his face. He was only inches from her. His eyes were the same: bright and dark and alive with wit. *How could she not have recognized them?* She knew with a horrible certainty that if he kissed her, her knees would buckle.

"We cannot escape what is between us that easily," he replied.

"There is nothing between us but pain. And I have no need to feel any more of that. I would like to leave here as soon as possible."

Nicola moved around him and walked out the door. She hoped he would never know how much it had cost her to do so.

CHAPTER TWELVE

JACK WATCHED NICOLA WALK AWAY, something hard and heavy forming in the area of his chest. He had been in a turmoil all day. He kept seeing Nicola's face when he took off his mask, the utter and complete shock that had pervaded her features. He had known she would be startled, but he had not expected her to faint. Then there had been the flash of joy when she opened her eyes and saw him. He remembered the way she had cried out his name and thrown her arms around him, kissing him ecstatically. He thought of the things she had said, the questions she had asked, her initial cry that he was alive. *How could any of that have been feigned?*

But if she was not pretending her reaction, that meant that everything he had believed for the past ten years had been wrong. And that was equally impossible. Jack thought about the night when Richard and his men burst into the farmer's house and dragged him out of bed. He had been asleep, content despite his bruises from being dragged along the stony River Lyd, because he knew that soon Nicola would come to him and they would leave for a new life together.

Then Richard had stormed in, and all his rosy dreams had come crashing down. Richard had looked at him, his face stamped with contempt. "What? Surprised to see me?

Who were you expecting? Miss Falcourt, perhaps?" His laugh was scornful. "Did you really think that she would marry you, you worm? It's all very well to dally with a peasant, but marriage? I can see her now, living in a hovel, a babe on one hip and another in her belly, sweating over a mess of gruel. You are a fool."

"What are you doing here?" Jack had gasped out, dazed and struggling to sit up from where they had thrown him on the ground. "How did you know—"

"Trifle slow, aren't you? Good gad, what did Nicola see in you? How do you *think* I knew? Nicola told me. She showed me your pathetic little letter, driveling on about marrying and going to live in blissful poverty. Thank God she has more sense than you. She knows that she will marry a peer, an equal. It is the life she knows, the life she expects to lead. She would never throw herself away on the likes of you. Of course, when she read your letter, she could see that getting rid of you would be a problem, so she came to me, asking me to send you away. Which is precisely what I intend to do, as I plan to be the peer she marries."

Jack remembered the slashing pain that had pierced him at the Earl's words, worse than any physical pain that Richard's men had inflicted on him as they tied him and gagged him and tossed him callously in the back of a wagon. At first he had struggled against the truth, refusing to acknowledge that Nicola could have betrayed him. But on the long ride to the port of Plymouth, he had had nothing to do except think about it, and he had realized that Exmoor's words must be true. *How else had Exmoor gotten hold of the letter?* He trusted his grandmother implicitly, and she had said that she would take his note to Nicola. She would never have taken it to the Earl. It had to be Nicola who had given it to Exmoor. Denial had gradually settled into despair.

Despair had turned into anger and hatred for both Exmoor and Nicola. He had survived the ordeal of his enforced service in the British navy by focusing on his determination to somehow make the two of them pay. Even after all the years since he had escaped the cruelty of the naval ship, his hatred had burned fiercely. Becoming a success in the New World had not been enough to satisfy him. He had burned with a desire to inflict actual damage on Exmoor, and so he had returned with Perry and his men to hurt Richard in one of the few ways he could be hurt, by taking his money. His intent with Nicola had been less clear. He had known only that he had to see her again to prove to himself how dead his feelings for her were, how glad he was that she had not agreed to marry him.

He had been sure he would find her married to some bloated lord, years older than herself and thoroughly obnoxious. Her looks would have faded after ten years and several children. She would be shallow and boring, having turned into a copy of her mother from years of living that way of life. He had not been prepared to find her still beautiful, a little less vibrant, perhaps, with a touch of sadness in her wide gray eyes, but achingly lovely, and neither married nor a typical noblewoman. He had not expected a huge fist of longing to slam into his gut when he first saw her, nor had he thought that images of her would haunt him, both waking and sleeping, distracting him from his purpose.

He had been unprepared for the jealousy that seared him when he thought she was married to Exmoor, as well as the intense relief that had flooded him when he found out that it was her sister, not she, who was Lady Exmoor. He had been even less ready to deal with the fact that, from the moment he saw her, all he wanted to do was kiss her and caress her, a desire that owed little to revenge and much to simple need. Even worse, he was reluctantly finding that he liked her, just as he had when he first met her. He enjoyed talking to her; he admired the things she did. And now this...

Burning with desire for her and irritated by his own attraction to a woman he was supposed to hate, it had snapped the last bit of his self-control when he heard her use *himself* as an excuse for not giving in to passion. She had dared to claim that she was still faithful to her first love, spinning a touching story that he had died—with no mention of the fact that, if so, it had been because she helped send him to his doom. Anger had surged up in him, and he had ripped off his mask. *Let her see that the man she held comfortably dead was anything but that.*

It was not the way he had planned to reveal his identity, if he ever did. But it certainly had had an effect on Nicola. The only problem was that the effect was not satisfactory. There had been no guilt, no shame, not even an admittance that she had been caught in the middle of a lie. Instead, Nicola had turned it all around on him, leaving him feeling empty and confused and somehow in the wrong.

She could not be telling the truth. It must have happened the way he had always thought it did. And yet... He could not get out of his mind the look in her eyes when she saw him.

NICOLA HAD TROUBLE SLEEPING. After two hours, she sighed and got out of bed and dressed again. She would go and sit outside for a while, she thought. No doubt part of her restlessness was due to the fact that she had been cooped up inside this house for so long. There would be enough moonlight that she would be able to see. Wrapping her cloak around her, not bothering to pin her hair up, she moved quietly down the stairs and out the back door.

The night was quiet and chilly, the woods wrapped in dark silence. She could hear the distant hooting of an owl. Silvery moonlight filtered down through the canopy of the trees. Not far from the back door was the stump of a tree long ago cut down, and after standing for a moment, she walked over to it and sat down.

There was the scrape of a boot heel behind her, and she jumped up, whirling around, her heart pounding. Jack stood a few feet away from her, his hands in his pockets. The moonlight touched his face, lighting the planes and casting his eyes into shadow. He looked so much the same, yet so different. Nicola wanted to look at that face for hours, to reach out and touch it. She wanted to smooth her thumbs along the sharp lines of his cheekbones, to trace his brows, his lips. She curled her hands into fists, keeping them resolutely by her sides.

"Sorry," he said quietly. "I didn't mean to startle you."

"What are you doing here?"

"I saw you from Perry's window. It's a little late to be out, don't you think?"

Nicola shrugged. "I couldn't sleep. What's the matter? Did you think I was trying to escape?"

"No. I—" He stopped. "I don't know what I thought. I thought—that I would join you."

"I can't imagine why," Nicola retorted tartly. "Feeling as you do about me."

"You must have noticed that I—" He glanced away. "I seem to have trouble staying away from you."

"I have noticed that you have a perverse desire to

torment me," Nicola snapped back. "Is that why you returned to Dartmoor? To punish me, as well as Richard?"

"I wanted to punish Richard. I am afraid I never had a very clear idea what I wanted to do with you." He grimaced. "I expressed that badly. I think we both know what I want to do with you. I should have said, I had no plan for revenge."

"Why not?" Nicola asked, looking him squarely in the eye. "You think that I turned you over to a man who hated you, who had tried to kill you once already. I would have said that that would make me worse than Exmoor. After all, he at least was straightforward in his intentions. I, on the other hand, was a deceiver. A liar. A coward. Why stop at the Earl? Why not wreak havoc on my life, as well?"

"I thought about it, believe me," he shot back, his eyes glittering. "I played out many scenes in my head that had you down on your knees, begging for my forgiveness. However, most of them involved things I would not do in real life. Too, most of them involved breaking your heart, and I did not think you had one to break."

Fury and hurt welled up in Nicola, and her eyes blazed. "Indeed, I would have said you were right, for when I thought you were dead, my heart died, too. Or, at least, I thought it had until this morning, when you broke it all over again. Congratulations. Even if you did not intend revenge on me, I think you have accomplished it."

She whirled and started for the house, but his hand lashed out and grabbed her wrist, pulling her back around to face him.

"Do you honestly expect me to believe that?" he asked, an odd note in his voice. "That you loved me all this time? That you didn't—"

"I don't expect you to believe anything except whatever

you wish to. That is what you have done for the past ten years. And, frankly, I don't really care whether you believe me. I know now the quality and extent of your love, how easily it is severed and how weak it is under duress." Tears hovered at the edge of her voice as she spat out her words to him, and she was all but quivering under the force of her emotions. "You are not *worthy* of my love! You are not capable of giving or receiving it."

"Not capable!" His dark eyes flamed, and he jerked her roughly to him. "I'll show you how capable I am."

His mouth came down on hers, and his arms went around her like steel bands. She could feel heat flare up suddenly in his body, and her own flesh flamed in response. His kiss was familiar and exciting, at once the old Gil and the new Jack, the haunting sweet kiss of the boy she had loved and the harsh, searing one of this stranger who wished to punish and defeat her. She wanted him. She wanted to kiss him back and wrap her arms around his neck, give herself up to the treacherous power of her desire.

But something in her, some strength or pride or will, would not let her do so. She would not be the weak vessel he obviously thought she was, ready to melt with desire for him no matter how he had hurt her or how little he loved her. She was not the kind of woman he believed her to be, the sort who would betray the man she loved, then fall back into his arms like some trollop.

Nicola pulled back, and when his arms stayed tightly around her, not letting her go, she stomped sharply with the heel of her shoe on his instep. Breath hissed out of him as he jerked back, his arms falling away from her.

"Bloody hell, woman! What are you trying to do?"

"I am trying to get away from you!" Nicola responded.

"Did you really think that you could treat me as you have treated me, say the things to me that you have said, and I would just swoon in your arms? Well, I won't! I am not here for you. I am here because your friend Perry needed help. I will take care of him, and then I will leave. I won't betray you and your men to Exmoor—and if you think that I couldn't find my way back to this cottage, then you are a far stupider man now than Gil ever was—any more than I would have betrayed you to him ten years ago. But what I will *not* do is dally with you. Don't try to kiss me. Don't try to touch me again. Or I swear that you and all yours here will find yourselves subject to a sudden and violent illness. Do I make myself clear?"

She did not wait for his response, just turned on her heel and marched back into the house.

JACK WATCHED HER GO, SLIGHTLY STUNNED. He sat down heavily on the stump where Nicola had been seated and put his elbows on his knees, resting his head on his hands. He sat that way for a long time, then finally rose and made his way back into the house and up the stairs to Perry's bedroom.

As he walked across the dimly lit room, he could see that his friend's eyes were open and his color better. Perry had already awakened once while Jack was sitting with him and had managed to drink more liquid from the stew and even swallow a few bits of meat.

"You look better," Jack said as he plopped down in the chair beside Perry's bed.

"You don't," Perry replied bluntly.

Jack groaned and shook his head. "Oh, Perry…what if I have made a mistake? What if I was wrong about her all those years ago?"

Perry did not need to ask about whom he spoke. He

looked at his friend sympathetically. "I think you may have been, my friend."

Jack shot him a black look. "You are so kind."

"Merely truthful. Obviously you are thinking the same thing yourself."

"I was right," Jack insisted. "I had to be. It is only—I don't know—her face when she saw me. She couldn't have been prepared for it, and I don't see how she could have put on an act, not so quickly. But there was no dread in her face, no fear, as I would expect if someone that I had done that to had reappeared years later. She looked stunned and then…"

He closed his eyes, thinking of the way Nicola's soft gray eyes had shone when she cried "You're alive!"

"She seemed…happy," he continued in a low voice. "And now she is so indignant, so furious…."

"I did not see her face or hear her indignation," Perry said, "but, frankly, I have noticed little about the lady that seems treacherous. First, it is clear that she is not close to Exmoor. Everyone says that this is the first time since her sister's marriage to the man that she has come to stay at their house. The gossip—and I hear this on the best authority, namely Lydia Hinton at the inn—is that she detests her brother-in-law and objected strenuously to her sister's marrying him. It doesn't seem likely that she would confide in a man she despises, much less ask him to do a favor, does it?"

Jack's only answer was a shrug.

"Secondly," Perry went on, ticking the points off on his fingers, "she has given no indication of being the sort of person who would betray anyone, much less the man she loved. After all, the villagers have nothing but the best things to say about her. It is my understanding that she has bound up poachers' wounds with nary a word to Exmoor or even to Lord Buckminster, her own cousin. Thirdly, she came here to save my life—even returned all on her own and without a word to Exmoor. It would have been quite easy to have notified him and let him have someone follow the two of you right back to this house."

"I was careful. I kept a lookout."

"Yes, and you didn't see anyone, did you? Because he sent no one. Because she did not tell him. Instead, she apparently made up a tissue of lies to both her sister and her aunt and put herself to a great deal of trouble just to return to make sure I pulled through. That is hardly the action of an informer."

"It was an entirely different situation ten years ago. She was much younger."

"And her personality was so different? Back then she was selfish and cold? Someone who lied and betrayed those who loved her? Yet now, ten years later, she has become someone warm and compassionate, a woman who devotes her time and money to helping the unfortunates of London? Who tries to save others with her skills in herbs and who does not even give an adequate description of a man who robbed her so that he can be found? Really, Jack, I don't think it will wash. It was easy to believe what you said before I met the woman. I have known many a lady with a heart of stone, capable of the greatest treachery. But now that I have met her…"

"You have based all this on knowing her for two days?" Jack asked with sarcasm. "Most of which time you've been unconscious."

"It does not take a long time if one is looking with unprejudiced eyes," his friend pointed out.

"You think I don't know what a good and kind woman she can be?" Jack asked, goaded. "You think I don't know what she does for others, how she helps the lowliest people who have no claim on her? Dammit, man, why do you think I love her? *Loved* her. She has plenty of fine ideals, and she even acts on them. She was well able to dally with a stable lad. It was when it came to marrying one that she balked. That is what sent her running to Exmoor."

Perry took a last sip of stew and waved it away. He leaned back on his pillows, regarding his friend, and after a moment said, "I imagine that it would have been enough just to tell you no. A woman who looks like Nicola Falcourt has had ample experience with turning down marriage proposals, even at seventeen. Why not write back a letter telling you that she had changed her mind? Or just not show up where you asked her to meet you? Why send Exmoor to do you in? I mean, really…one day she was kissing you, the next she was sending you to be imprisoned in the bowels of a ship?"

"She may not have known what Exmoor would do," Jack admitted. "She may have intended only that he warn me away, but Exmoor seized the opportunity to do more."

"She didn't know? When he had just thrown you over a waterfall?" Perry retorted sarcastically.

"Her reputation was at stake. She was afraid that I would make a scene, that everyone would know about her relationship with me. It would have ruined her chances at a good marriage."

"Yet she never married, even though she was so careful not to ruin her chances. And she was so concerned about her reputation that she came here alone to an outlaw's lair to live for several days."

"Dammit! Whose side are you on?"

"Yours," Perry replied simply. "If you are so sure that you were right, why are you having doubts now? I like the girl, and I don't want to see you throw everything away because you refuse to admit that you were wrong."

"That is not why I—" Jack stopped, shaking his head. "Don't you think I *want* to agree with you? That I wouldn't give anything to say 'Oh, yes, there must have been some kind of mistake'? Perhaps that is why I saw honesty in her eyes when she told me she thought I was dead—just because I want to believe that I was wrong. She is a woman who could make any man doubt reason." He set his jaw. "But I am not a fool. I refuse to deceive myself. I will not let myself fall under her spell again—as you so obviously have—only to find my heart trampled beneath her feet another time. I went through that pain once, and there is no way I will again."

"Then is it that you are afraid?" Perry let out a chuckle at the fire that flamed in his friend's dark eyes at his remark. "No. Don't take my head off. Remember, I am a poor, defenseless, bedridden—"

Jack snorted. "You are never defenseless, with the way your jaw flaps. And, yes, I am afraid. You would be, too, if it had been your heart that was torn out."

"Perhaps I would. Unfortunately—or perhaps it is fortunately—I have never sunk so deep in love." Perry sighed. "But, you know, if you were wrong about her ten years ago, then it isn't a risk."

"How could I have been?" Jack asked, a note of despair in his voice. "My grandmother wrote me back and said that she would deliver the letter to Nicola."

"But you don't know that she actually gave it to her."

Jack fixed him with a cold gaze. "Are you saying that my grandmother lied about it?"

"Of course not. Don't be a fool. But you don't know what happened after she sent you that letter. You never heard from her again. You were seized and taken to the ship. What if something prevented her from delivering the note to Miss Falcourt? What if Nicola is right, and it was somehow intercepted by Exmoor?"

"How?"

"I don't know!" Perry exclaimed in exasperation. "You are the stubbornest man alive. The only person who knows the truth is Exmoor, and somehow I doubt that you are going to get him to tell you. Maybe you will never know for sure. But sometimes you simply have to go on faith."

"If that were true—if she did not get the letter…" Jack swung around and walked away, stopping at the window to stare out broodingly. "Then I was an utter fool and threw away ten years of my life."

"It will be better to know that than to continue to be one and throw away the rest of your life."

"She would never forgive me," Jack said quietly. "How could she?"

"You won't know unless you ask her."

Jack shot his friend a dark look. "You don't understand. She hates me now. She threatened to poison me tonight if I touched her again."

Perry let out a bark of laughter. "I knew I liked that girl. At last, a woman you cannot charm."

"I wouldn't laugh so heartily if I were you," Jack told him sourly. "She threatened to poison you, too."

NICOLA REMAINED AT THE BANDITS' hideaway for another two days. As her patient improved, caring for him settled into the usual, rather boring routine of sitting beside his bed, coaxing him to eat and drink periodically, and giving him a few doses of medicine. She had gone through such periods many times at bedsides, of course, but always before she had had something to occupy the empty time while the patient slept. But now she had no book or needlework or even a pad to sketch on while Perry dozed, and when she was relieved by one of Jack's men or the girl Diane, she had nothing to do in her room, either. She took a few brisk walks around the outside of the small house, but as the days were rather chilly and misty, there was little enjoyment in that.

Jack did not intrude on her, either when she was sitting with Perry or any other time. She was, she told herself, grateful for that, of course, but that, too, made the days more boring. She realized after a time that Jack was going so far as to have one of the others come in to take over in the sickroom from her, after which he would quickly relieve them, thereby avoiding running into Nicola. For some reason, the fact that he did so irritated her, even though she knew it was easier if she did not have to see him or speak to him. He was, she thought to herself, taking the cowardly way out.

In the way of all patients, Perry grew more restless and fretful as his condition improved. By the third day he felt too good to sleep three-fourths of the time as he had before, but he did not feel up to doing much more than sitting up in bed and feeding himself. His wound was healing nicely, but he complained that it itched. He grew tired of every position in which he could lie or sit, yet whenever he changed position, it made his shoulder hurt. He could not concentrate well enough to play a game of cards with Nicola, and there were no books for her to read to him.

Finally, in an effort to distract him, Nicola asked him about his life.

"Dead boring," he told her. "Wastrel son of a good

family, that sort of thing. I am sure you've heard a dozen tales like it."

"But few of them wound up being highwaymen," Nicola pointed out mildly.

Perry chuckled. "Blame that on bad companions. My father always told me they would lead to my downfall."

"You have been friends with Jack for a long time, I take it."

He cast her a considering look. "Yes. For years. We were impressed at the same time. Fortunately, for some reason he decided to help me, or I am sure that I would have been dead within months of being thrown on board. Gentlemen's sons do not do well as swabbies, I'm afraid."

He paused, then added, "We escaped together and have worked alongside each other ever since. He has yet to lead me astray."

"I fear he has this time," Nicola said quietly. "The Earl hates him—and he doesn't even know who he really is. I fear if he found out, he would be even more determined to destroy Jack."

"No doubt. Will you tell him?"

"I?" Nicola glanced at him in amazement. "Of course not. But someone is bound to see him without his mask sometime and recognize him. Many of the villagers would recognize him. They are quite curious about his identity, too. And Richard has been offering bribes for information about him. Eventually he will find him, and—" She stopped, shrugging her shoulders.

"And would you care if he were captured? Hanged?"

A shudder ran through Nicola at the thought. "Of course I would. I would hate to see any man hanged. And I know Jack. I—I once loved him. No matter how I feel about him now, I would not want him to die."

"How do you feel about him now?"

"You are certainly full of curiosity today."

"I am always full of curiosity. Well? How do you feel?"

"I don't know," Nicola admitted in a low voice. "It has been so long, and I—I am angry at what he did, how he left me, how he assumed I had betrayed him. Anyway, it scarcely matters how I feel about him. He feels nothing for me except contempt and anger."

"I doubt that that is true."

Nicola made no reply, simply looked at her hands, clasped together in her lap.

"You know, men can be utter fools at times," Perry said.

Nicola smiled and glanced up at him. "True enough. What brought you to that insight?"

"Sad experience, in general. But what I am talking about now is Jack. Sometimes, when you want something tremendously, when it is terribly important, that is the thing you mishandle the most. You are so anxious about it that you do exactly the wrong thing, bring about the thing that you feared."

"You are saying that is what he did in this instance? That Gil, I mean Jack, loved me so much, he decided I had betrayed him?"

"I am saying that love can cloud one's thinking. Make you believe things that perhaps you would not logically. Let us say that you feel unworthy of a certain woman— beneath her in station, for instance. You worry about losing her, about her seeing how little you deserve her, how foolish it is of her to love you. And when you find out that that very thing has happened, it doesn't surprise you. You don't question it. It is what you have feared all along. So even though you hate her for it, even though it breaks your heart, you believe it. You accept it. The fact that you have learned it from an untrustworthy person doesn't make you doubt the information. You are filled with too much pain for that. All you can see is that what you feared would happen has indeed happened."

Nicola made a face. "Jack? Uncertain? Feeling unworthy of me? Really, Perry… You would do better to find someone who did not know him to try that one on. He is one of the most confident men I have ever met. He knew I loved him. We were mad for each other. It would have taken a fool to have mistaken it."

"No matter how cocksure a twenty-year-old boy may act, I can assure you that deep down he is uncertain about a great many things, at least where women are concerned. I am sure he knew that you loved him, or at least were infatuated with him. But you were a member of the upper class. You belonged to a different world than he did. Lords' daughters do not marry stable boys. Believe me, he had had it drilled into him all his life that he belonged to an inferior class, one that would never mingle with ours. We aren't talking about a schoolmaster's son, someone genteel but not of the nobility. We are discussing someone raised in the servant class, someone, moreover, whose mother and grandmother had ceaselessly warned him to stay away from nobles—a not unreasonable notion when one is talking about someone like the Earl of Exmoor. How could he expect you to marry him? He knew that to even ask it of you was wrong and selfish, for he could never hope to provide you with the kind of life that you were used to living. No one, even your most indulgent kin, would have approved of the match. You know that—why else were the two of you sneaking around, meeting secretly?"

Nicola frowned, looking troubled. "I know that

everyone else would have disapproved. But he knew I didn't care for that! I had told him time and again. We had made plans for the future."

"Yes, he hoped. He daydreamed. He wanted to believe, and so he did. But, deep down, he knew how much of a risk it was, how little likelihood there was of your actually marrying him. It couldn't have surprised him that you had reconsidered your rash promise."

Nicola looked at him thoughtfully. "Perhaps you are right. I suppose he could not have known for sure until I actually married him. But couldn't he have trusted me a little? Given me the benefit of the doubt? Why did he immediately assume that I was wicked? How could he have known me and thought that I would do that to him? Even if I had changed my mind about marrying him, even if I had somehow lost my love for him—in the space of twenty-four hours!—how could he believe that I would give him up to Richard? How could he think that I would have wanted him thrown into such a hellhole? I would have had to be a monster! He believed me to be deceitful...sadistic...faithless...." Tears welled in her eyes. "How could he believe that of me? He could not have loved me and thought so little of me."

"Jealousy and anger can make a fool of any man," Perry replied. "I cannot answer for why he did what he did then. I only know that from the day I met him, you are what he has talked about."

"Yes, because he blames me for what happened to him!"

"Perhaps so. But I have seen him talk about the time before that happened. I have seen the way his face looked when he spoke of you. I would stake my life on his having loved you greatly."

Nicola blinked away the tears that suddenly sprang into her eyes. "It doesn't matter now, anyway," she told him huskily. "Whatever love he felt—or I felt, for that matter—is long dead now. All that is left are the bitter feelings."

Perry snorted. "If you believe that, then *you* are as big a fool as he."

Nicola cocked her eyebrow at him. "Have you had this sort of conversation with him?"

"Something like it," Perry admitted.

Nicola looked at him quizzically. "Have you appointed yourself the Cupid of this little group?"

He grinned. "Someone had to. It is obvious that if I left it to the two of you, this dismal mess would just continue."

Nicola sighed. "I don't think there is much that even Cupid can do now."

"Why not?"

"Too much has happened. Too much blame and anger and dislike. I—what do we have left after all these years?"

"Love?" he suggested quietly. "It is something very precious. I have never known it, not the kind you had. You loved him for ten years even though you thought him dead. Do you really think it could then just disappear?"

Nicola shrugged and turned away. "I don't know what I think anymore."

"You'll figure it out," Perry told her and smiled. "I have faith in you."

NICOLA COULD NOT KEEP THE OUTLAW'S words out of her mind the rest of the day. *Was he right? Had Jack's actions sprung from his love for her rather than from the lack of it?* She knew that anger and recriminations were common enough responses when one was hurt. She had only to think about her own reactions the day before when Jack had revealed who he was and what he had done. Her first instinct had been to flare up into rage and to accuse him of not really loving her. She realized with a little bit of a shock that she had immediately assumed that he had only pretended his love, that he had acted deceptively, just as Jack had assumed that she had deceived him.

On the other hand, Nicola knew that it was quite possible that she was merely deceiving herself. She *wanted* to believe that Jack had really loved her. She did not want to face the fact that she had spent the last ten years of her life pining for a man who had known her so little, loved her so little, that he would believe anything about her, even the words of his worst enemy.

That way was folly, she told herself. It was pointless to find excuses for him. It was madness to let herself believe that this man had loved her deeply…might still love her, beneath all the hurt and anger. That love was gone, could not be brought back any more than the past ten years could be given back to her. It was better just to let it go. Jack was obviously avoiding her. When she went back to Tidings, she would probably never see him again. That would be best for everyone concerned. And someday, *someday,* her heart would stop hurting.

CHAPTER THIRTEEN

SHORTLY BEFORE NOON THE NEXT DAY, as Nicola sat chatting with Perry, the door opened and Jack stepped in. Nicola glanced up, her heart beginning to beat harder, as it always did when he appeared. She supposed if she was around him long enough she would grow accustomed to seeing Gil suddenly standing in front of her, older and even more handsome, but she certainly did not intend to spend enough time with Jack for that to happen.

"Jack!" Perry said with delight. "Come join us. We were just discussing the time you and I spent in Boston."

"It was cold, damp and stuffy," Jack said shortly. He looked at Nicola. "One of my men just came in. Your nurse has arrived."

"She is here?" Nicola asked, surprised.

"No. I will take you to her. Perry is well enough now and…" His voice trailed off, and he glanced away.

"Yes. It is time that I went home. It probably already seems suspicious to Richard that I have been away this long." Nicola tried to ignore the cold lump that was forming in the pit of her stomach. "I, uh, I'll just go pack my things."

It did not take long to pack; she had brought little besides her medicines. She left behind packets of meadowsweet and feverfew in case Perry's fever returned, and a small jar of marigold cream, as well as a little woundwort to aid in the healing of his wound. Afterward, she changed the bandage one last time.

"Make sure that you change this frequently," she told Perry. "Don't let anyone else do it but Jack—or you when you are feeling better. And make sure that your hands are freshly washed. I have explained that to Jack, too. That wound must be kept clean."

"I understand." Perry smiled at her. "I wish you were not leaving. Your company is much more enjoyable than these fellows'."

"Well, perhaps we will meet again sometime—in better circumstances."

"You mean when I can come up to your front door to call?" he asked, his pale blue eyes dancing.

"Exactly." She turned to leave, then swiveled back. "Remember what I told you about Richard and how determined he is to get all of you. Please talk to Jack. He would rather die than listen to me, but he will pay attention to you. I don't want anything to happen to you." She managed a crooked smile. "I would hate to see all my hard work go to waste."

"I will try," Perry agreed, his voice serious for once. "Believe me, I have little desire to dangle at the end of a rope."

"Good. Take care of yourself." She had grown rather fond of this man in the days she had been tending to him. Now she bent down and kissed his cheek lightly. "Goodbye."

She left the room and hurried down the stairs. Jack was waiting outside with the horses. He held out his cupped hands to toss her up into the saddle. Nicola raised one brow.

"No blindfold?"

"It is beginning to seem a bit absurd," Jack said. "I am not fool enough to think that you could not lead Exmoor to the general area. And I doubt that you would sacrifice Perry's life after all you did to save him, however you might feel about me."

"That is true," Nicola responded coolly. It was not exactly an admission of trust, but it was better than having him wrap that scarf around her eyes again. She put her foot in his cupped hands and swung up onto her horse.

Jack mounted, and they started off.

Through the woods, they rode single file, with Jack leading the way. There was little opportunity for speech, which was just as well, for Nicola was not feeling in the least talkative. The cold lump in her stomach was growing with each passing moment. It was a lovely ride, and at another time she would probably have enjoyed the woodland beauty of brooks and glades and towering trees, but today she barely saw it.

They emerged from the woods on the north side, instead of where they had entered the other day, and Nicola wondered exactly where they were going. Obviously he was not headed straight back to Buckminster Hall. They followed a narrow rocky stream through pasture and trees, finally emerging close to one of the stone hills that dotted the region. There, at the bottom of the tor, nestled among trees and almost hidden from view, lay a quaint cottage.

Nicola pulled up short, her heart suddenly swollen with emotion. "Granny Rose's!"

"Yes. It seemed a safe enough place. No one ever goes there. It is quite deserted. Your nurse is waiting for you inside. I shall leave you here."

"Oh." Nicola turned to look at him. The realization that she might never see him again burned in her chest. If Perry could persuade him to stop this dangerous, foolish game he played, they might leave here soon…and she would never even know that he was gone. "Well…thank you—for fetching Nurse, I mean. Remember to change Perry's bandage."

"I will."

"All right. I, uh…"

"It is I who should thank you," he said stiffly, turning his gaze away from her. "You did me a great service—and at risk to yourself. I am fully aware of how much you did. Perry would not have made it without you. He is lucky to have met you."

And what about you? Nicola wanted to cry. *What are you feeling? Are you glad you saw me again?* But she said nothing, realizing that such questions were foolish. She merely nodded and turned away, digging her heels in so that her horse started forward.

"Nicola!"

She twisted in her saddle, looking back at him. But he only shook his head. "Nothing. I am sorry. Goodbye."

"Goodbye." Her throat would barely open enough to get the word out. Nicola turned back and rode toward the cottage.

Jack remained where he was, watching Nicola's figure grow smaller and smaller as she approached the cottage. He watched as she reached the cottage and dismounted. She tied her horse outside and walked into his grandmother's house, something he had watched her do time and time again. His throat felt raw; his eyes burned. He wondered if he was a wise man or a fool. He turned and rode away.

NICOLA BLINKED THE TEARS OUT OF her eyes as she rode toward Granny Rose's cottage. She refused to look back and see Jack riding away. She also refused to acknowledge the fact that it felt as if her heart was being torn out of her body. The love between them was over. This momentary pain was nothing but a twinge, a reminder of what it had been like ten years earlier when she had lost him. *That* had been the true end of their love.

She saw as she drew nearer that Granny Rose's cottage had become almost totally overgrown. Ivy climbed the white stone walls and reached the thatched roof, just as it always had, but now it splayed across the shuttered windows, as well, almost burying the tiny place. In front of the house, Granny's flowers had gone to seed, spreading in no order and in most places choked out by weeds. The side garden looked to be in little better shape, the neat rows of carefully cultivated herbs lost among weeds and twining rosebushes and the stalks of flowers. Since it was winter, the flowers and shrubs were bare, which made the cottage look even more desolate.

She would come clean the place up, Nicola thought. It hurt her to see it in such disrepair. Granny Rose had loved her little house, speaking with pride of how it had passed down through generation after generation of herbally wise women. The herb garden, she had assured Nicola, grew from former ones planted as far back as the days of King Henry VIII and perhaps even further. Granny would be horrified to see it looking so, and Nicola felt a trifle guilty that she had never even thought to see to Granny's beloved cottage. She had lived in London the last two years of Granny's life, after Gil left, not returning to Dartmoor except briefly for her sister's wedding. The first time she had visited her cousin and aunt after Granny's death, she had ridden over to the cottage, but it had sent such pain stabbing through her that she had not come back since. But now she thought that she had been selfish and unthinking.

Contemplating the task that lay before her, she dismounted and tied her horse to the low fence, then pushed open the gate. She picked her way through the dead vegetation. The narrow path between hollyhocks that had once led to the door was no longer even discernible.

Before she reached the front door, however, it opened, and a short, plump, beaming woman bustled out of it, spreading out her arms to embrace Nicola.

"Nicky! My child! Oh, I am so happy to see you!" Nurse enfolded her in a hug, smelling, as Nicola remembered fondly, of lavender. She held Nicole away from her, looking her over. "As beautiful as ever, I see. I was so delighted when that man brought me your note."

Nicola smiled at the other woman. There were more wrinkles in her face, and gray had spread like wings along her temples, but otherwise she looked much the same as when Nicola had last seen her.

"Of course I came immediately," Nurse continued. "As if I could have denied my baby when she was in trouble. Poor little lass." She heaved a sigh. "So sad. To have lost all her babies." She shook her head. "Ah, well, mayhap I can help her this time."

Nurse's mount, a placid old mare, was tethered in the small yard behind the house, chewing on the plentiful overgrowth. Nurse's bag and bandbox were tied on behind the saddle, and she was eager to go, despite the fact that she assured Nicola it had been a long and tiresome ride from her house.

"You would have thought both those men were mute, the amount they talked," she said as Nicola led her horse to a rock so Nurse could scramble onto it.

Nicola smiled, thinking that she was sure Jack's men had heard more words spilling from her old caretaker's mouth than they had probably heard in the past month. She led her own horse over to the rock and mounted, and they started for Buckminster Hall. Nurse continued to talk, describing her life, her own snug cottage, the odd way Nicola's men had left her here at this desolate house, all scattered with questions about Nicola and Deborah.

At the Hall, Nicola's aunt was pleased to see them and typically unquestioning about the details of their journey. "Exmoor was here yesterday," she told them, looking irritated. "Stayed so long I didn't get in my morning ride. Devilish nuisance."

"What did you say about me?"

"Told him you'd gone down the village. Should have said something else. That's why he stayed so long. Said he'd just wait for you. I said you were probably dosing people and would be quite a while, but still he stayed, talking. Beautiful sunny day, too." She shook her head in regret.

"I'm sorry."

Lady Buckminster shrugged. "Ah, well, can't be helped. It's awkward, though, talking to Exmoor. I never liked the man, but now, given how the Countess feels about him…" The Dowager Countess of Exmoor, who despised Richard, was one of Lady Buckminster's friends, and now that her son Bucky was marrying the Countess's granddaughter, Penelope, they would also be family. "'Course, with my niece married to the man, can hardly snub him, either. Social niceties can be the very devil to work out."

"It is a problem," Nicola agreed, smiling. "I had best get back to Tidings as soon as possible, then, to allay his suspicions. Thank you, Aunt Adelaide." She gave her aunt an impulsive buss on the cheek. "You have been a lifesaver."

Her aunt gave her a warm hug. "Come back and

actually stay next time. You know, Bucky wrote me saying that he's coming soon."

"Really?"

"Yes. Apparently Penelope and her family will be at the Dower House before long, and then Bucky's coming a few days after. 'Course, the wedding's only a few weeks away now." She sighed, looking pained. "I shall have to talk to Ursula and the Countess about wedding things."

"Don't worry. I am sure that Penelope and the Countess will take care of everything."

"I hope so," Lady Buckminster replied candidly. "Never much liked talking about flowers and dresses and such." She brightened. "Did I tell you I'm thinking about giving Penelope a phaeton and team as a wedding present? Found a nice pair of bays."

Nicola grinned. "I am sure she will love it."

She took her leave of her aunt, and she and Nurse rode on to Tidings. Nurse was obviously weary of being in the saddle, for she was no rider, but she was too eager to see Deborah to complain. Though she had taken care of both girls from the time they were small and loved them both, it was Deborah who was her special favorite. Nicola had always been one who disliked supervision, wanting to explore, to ride, to be on her own, whereas Deborah was far more docile, even clinging, and Nurse had remained as Deborah's maid even after she had reached the age where she no longer required a nurse or even a governess. Indeed, when Deborah had gotten married, it had been the first time that she had ever lived without her nurse.

This fact, apparently, was a sore spot for Nurse, who, among a dozen other topics, explained to Nicola how much she had always disliked the Earl of Exmoor.

"It weren't my Debbie that didn't want me to go with

her," she said with some heat. "The Earl insisted. She told me so herself, almost in tears, she was, but she said he wanted to give her some fancy ladies' maid, and she was that excited that he wanted to do it for her." Nurse grimaced. "More like he just didn't want me there. I never liked the man, and I told her she shouldn't marry him. Ah, well. No doubt she's found that out." She turned to Nicola. "Is she happy? Does she love him still?"

"I don't know," Nicola answered honestly. "I have wondered the same myself. I think she may still love him. She doesn't talk about it. But I would not say she is happy. I think her marriage has…not been what she hoped it would be."

Nurse nodded sagely. "Well, mayhap a babe will make her life happier."

"I hope so. I only hope she is able to carry this one to full term."

"Aye. Well, I'll do everything I can to make sure she does." Nurse set her pudgy jaw determinedly.

DEBORAH WAS AS HAPPY TO SEE her old nurse as the woman was to see her. She came out of the drawing room and hurried down the hall toward the older woman, her arms outstretched, tears of joy streaming down her cheeks. "Nicola, you brought her! I knew you would!"

Nurse enfolded Deborah in her warm, motherly embrace. Richard followed his wife into the hall at a slower pace, watching his wife's reunion with her nurse.

"Touching…" he murmured, and turned his gaze to Nicola. "How fortunate that you were at Buckminster Hall when the nurse arrived."

"Yes, wasn't it?" Nicola replied blandly. "She arrived this morning."

"I hope you were able to help Lady Buckminster with the wedding. She seemed a little…shall we say, ignorant?…of exactly what you were doing."

Nicola forced a laugh. "Yes. Aunt Adelaide cares little for such things. That is why she needed my help. I think we made a start on it, and, now, with Bucky and Penelope and the others coming soon, she will be able to turn all the preparations over to them."

"Of course." His tone indicated a certain doubt, but Nicola ignored it. Richard had obviously grown somewhat suspicious about Nicola's visit to her aunt, but she was sure that he knew nothing about what she had actually been doing. The odds were that he would assume it had something to do with Nurse's arrival, and as long as she said nothing, all his speculation would be useless.

So she merely smiled at him and went to join Deborah and Nurse.

IT WAS WONDERFUL TO SEE HER sister happy and content. Their former nurse was quick to soothe Deborah's fears and worries, for she spoke with authority on all subjects regarding pregnancy and infants. Under her care, even Deborah's morning sickness seemed to subside. She took over most of the food preparation for Deborah's morning and noontime meals, unerringly choosing things that did not aggravate her nausea and coaxing her into eating them. She was also able to pull Deborah out of her gloom, encouraging and helping her to sew and knit for the coming baby's layette, talking about the wonderful antics of children she had known, and generally increasing Deborah's optimism.

Nicola quickly found that their ongoing discussions of babies left her a trifle bored, and though she helped them sew, her stitching skills were not of a quality to do the fine work, leaving her with the duller work of seams and hems. Deborah had shifted her dependence from Nicola to her nurse, freeing Nicola from constant attendance on her, but she had little else to do to occupy her time.

She cast about for something and hit upon the idea of sprucing up Granny Rose's cottage. It had saddened her to see it in its current condition, and it was the sort of active task she enjoyed.

So a few mornings after she brought Nurse to Tidings, she had her horse saddled, tucked her work gloves and a few gardening tools in a bag, and set out for Granny Rose's cottage.

Nicola was prepared this time for the overgrown state of the cottage, but it still made her sad. She wondered if Jack had come by to look at his grandmother's house and how he had felt when he saw it. Nicola wondered if Granny Rose had ever received any more communications from him before she died or if she had died, wondering what had happened to him. It made her feel even sadder to think of that.

She tethered her horse in front of the cottage and exchanged her fine leather riding gloves for coarser cloth ones. Then she set to work on the garden. Taking out her small pruning shears, she began on the shrubs, but she quickly found that she needed something larger. She searched in back of the cottage and found a small shed that contained larger tools. Taking out a larger set of shears, she began to clip away the vines that grew over the windows. It was more physical labor than she was used to, but today Nicola welcomed the work. It took her mind off her obsessive thoughts, and that was surely an advantage, for sitting at Tidings the last few days, she had thought of little except Jack Moore.

Once she had cleared the windows of vines and opened the shutters so that light could enter the house, she went inside to investigate. Granny Rose's furniture stood exactly where she remembered it, giving an eerie impression that the old woman had just stepped out and might be back at any minute. She was pleased to find that it was not as dusty as she had expected, but there was still plenty of work to be done to make it clean. She hauled the rugs outside and hung them over low branches of trees, then applied the rug beater she had found inside. Puffs of dust billowed out, and she kept swinging until the rugs were clean. By the time she finished, her arms ached. But she went on to dust the furniture and sweep and mop the floor.

She had brought a basket of food with her, knowing that it would be a long hard day, so she ate a cold luncheon in the middle of the day and even had a cup of tea and biscuits at teatime. After she ate, she returned to work, and by dark the house was mostly clean inside and she was bone weary. Though she had done her fair share of manual labor at her charitable houses, she was not used to doing quite this much of it at one time. Still, it felt good to work and to have a clean house to show for it.

She returned eagerly to the cottage the next day and picked up where she had left off. She located the cabinet filled with the beakers, vials and jars that Granny had used in her remedy-making, and she took them out and washed them. It pleased her to return Granny's little work area to the state she remembered it. She decided to celebrate with a rest and cup of tea. She had just set the kettle on to boil and put tea leaves in Granny's plain teapot when there were noises outside. At first she thought it was simply her horse moving about restlessly and whinnying, but then she realized that if her horse was that agitated, there must be something wrong.

Nicola went to the window and looked out. Jack was dismounting from his horse and leading it around the side of the house toward the back. Her stomach constricted, and she felt suddenly hot, then cold. One hand flew to her hair, tied up in an old kerchief while she cleaned, and she realized in horror how she must look—dressed in old clothes, her hair a mess. She whirled and ran for Granny's bedroom, whipping off the kerchief and apron as she went. She straightened her hair as best she could and rubbed a smudge of dirt from her cheek.

"Nicola?" Jack's voice came from the front door.

Nicola's heart jumped into her throat, and she went to the door of the bedroom. Jack stood across the main room of the tiny house, just inside the door. Nicola thought suddenly of the times she had seen him this way when they had met here ten years ago under Granny's less-than-approving eye.

"Hello." Her voice came out much softer and more fluttery than she would have liked.

"What are you doing?" he asked.

Nicola raised an eyebrow. His abrupt question and flat tone had chased away the breathless feeling inside her. "I might ask you the same thing."

"It is my grandmother's house," he pointed out.

"And it was my friend's," Nicola responded. "When I saw it the other day, I knew that I could not leave it in this condition. Granny Rose would have hated it, especially the garden going to seed."

"This isn't the garden."

Nicola grimaced. "Are you afraid I'm stealing Granny's old pots and pans? I started work in here. Why does it matter?"

"I don't know," he responded honestly. "I—it just surprised me to see your horse tethered outside."

In fact, it had made him think of the times when they had met at his grandmother's when they were young and in love. He remembered how his heart would rise when he came around the curve in the road and saw Nicola's bay mare tied in front of the house. For a moment he had felt back in that time and place, his pulse jumping with anticipation, his lips widening involuntarily into a grin. It had been decidedly irritating.

Jack closed the door and advanced into the room. "Have you thought that perhaps I liked the cottage being so inconspicuous?"

"Leave the ivy, then. You don't have to have weeds as tall as I am in your yard. Especially the herb garden. It is disgraceful. Granny Rose had the finest herb garden in all Dartmoor."

He shrugged, but Nicola could see a vaguely guilty look steal into his eyes.

"What does it matter if the garden is cleared?" Nicola pressed her argument. "It isn't as if you were living here. No one is going to search for you at Granny Rose's cottage, and even if they did, you wouldn't be here. Where's the harm in making it look nice?"

"There is none, I suppose. Maybe I have been suspicious for too many years." He glanced around at the room in which they stood. "It looks much nicer. What did you do?"

"Just cleaned it—beat the rugs, mopped the floors, things like that."

His brows rose. "You?"

"Yes, me." Nicola put her hands on her hips pugnaciously. "Why shouldn't it be me? I am quite capable of cleaning a house."

"I wouldn't have thought you had ever even swept a floor."

"Well, it isn't how I normally spend my time, but I have cleaned a few houses. The places I bought for my women were not exactly sparkling."

"I would have thought you hired people to do that."

"In general, I find the money is better spent on other things, such as food and clothing. We try to do as much of the work as possible. Once we have a house set up, the women who live there keep it clean."

He looked at her for a long moment. Just as he started to speak, the kettle began to whistle sharply, startling them both. Nicola jumped, then laughed.

"I was about to have a cup of tea. Would you like some?"

Jack hesitated, then smiled. "All right."

He followed her into the kitchen, leaning against the door frame and watching as she poured water over the tea and left it to steep, then bustled about, getting out cups and spoons and taking a tiny bag of sugar from her basket. Jack leaned over and looked into the basket and grinned.

"I must say, you come well-prepared."

"I intended to spend the day."

"Did you bring enough for two?" he asked.

Nicola looked at him, feeling suddenly as if her lungs had stopped working. "Probably. Why?"

"I thought I might stay and help you. Out in the yard, I mean. I would think much of the work is too heavy for you."

A smile curved Nicola's mouth and warmed her gray eyes. She felt so suddenly, eagerly happy that her knees turned shaky. She strove to keep her voice light. "Why, thank you. I think I could manage to find enough food to make it worth your while."

He returned her smile, and for a moment Nicola

thought that he was going to say something else, but then he pressed his lips together and turned away. "Uh, are there tools still around?"

"Yes. Everything seems to be pretty much as she left it. I guess there were no heirs other than you, and no one knew what to do with it."

"There are few people who would want to live here," he explained. "People always came to Granny, but they feared her, too. They thought she came from a long line of witches. That was one reason why she enjoyed your visits. You were the only one who wanted to learn, who viewed her as a…a sort of doctor, I suppose, instead of someone who made magical potions."

"I never knew that." She looked at him. "Do people view me that way?"

"Not that I know of. I listened when people spoke of you, but I tried not to ask questions. I thought they might find that strange."

"Oh. I see."

"Not the best policy. It resulted in some misinformation." At Nicola's questioning look, he added, "At first I thought you were Lady Exmoor."

"Oh." She looked away, uncomfortable now, with the estrangement between them suddenly intruding on what had been a pleasant, even friendly time.

"I have been thinking the last few days…" he began, looking down at his hands as though they had suddenly become fascinating. "What if I have been wrong about other things? What if I was too—too hasty in my judgment?"

"And have you decided anything?" Nicola asked, her breath uneven.

"No," he replied honestly, and this time he lifted his

head and looked her in the eyes. "I don't know what to think. I look at you, I think of you, and all I can see is how beautiful you are, how good you are, how kind and hard-working and generous…and I think, I was a fool! I was the one who wasn't true. I doubted our love. And you."

He clenched his jaw and pushed himself away from the door frame, walking away from her. "But then I think that it is now that I am being a fool, that I am believing what I *want* to believe, not the evidence. That if I let myself trust you, I shall fall into that pit all over again."

"That is how you think of our love? As a pit?"

"No. The pit was the pain afterward, the bone-aching loss, the realization that I wished my life was over because I felt as if everything in me had already died." His voice was harsh, his eyes blazing. "That is the pit I lived in for years, when the only thing that kept me alive was hating you and Exmoor." He slammed his fist into the wall. "Bloody hell!"

"If that is what kept you alive, then I am glad you hated me," Nicola said.

He glanced at her, surprised. "I thought you despised me now, thought me a coward and a fool."

"No, I thought you were a man who never loved me as I loved him."

"I loved you more than anything in the world!" he shot back.

"Then why did you not believe in me? Why do you even yet not trust me? Do you think that I have never married because no man of my class wanted me?"

"Of course not."

"Then why? Why would I never have fallen in love, or, if I am the venal, wicked person you think me, why would I not have snared some wealthy lord for his money and his position? I had the opportunity."

"I am sure you did." Jack felt as if a huge fist was clutching his chest, squeezing his lungs until he could not breathe.

"Then why?" Nicola demanded tartly. She reached out and prodded his chest when he did not answer. "Why did I find no other man? Why did I remain a spinster? A virgin! Why, Jack?" She poked him again, her voice rising. "Why? What other possible reason could there have been except that I loved you too much ever to love anyone else! I had had the greatest love I could have known. I could not settle for less. Can you understand that? How can you think that I would have betrayed you? I have been faithful to you for ten years, even though I thought you dead!"

Her voice broke on a sob, and she whirled around to run away, but Jack's hand lashed out and gripped her arm, holding her back.

"No! You cannot just say something like that and run away!" he told her gruffly. "Look at me. *Look at me!*"

Nicola whipped around, holding her head high, her chin up and her huge eyes defiant.

Jack let out an incoherent noise and jerked her to him, his mouth coming down to cover hers.

CHAPTER FOURTEEN

NICOLA CLUNG TO JACK, LOST IN A burst of sensations and emotions. The love she had felt for Gil swept over her, mingling with the desire that her mature self had known with Jack. She wanted, she hungered, she melted with love. His hands dug into her back, pressing her closer and closer against him, so that his body was imprinted on hers, melded so intensely that his heat became hers, her scent his. They held on, lost in memories and passion, their yearning swift and thundering, pounding through their veins.

Thought and hesitation vanished, swept away in a torrent of elemental hunger. They kissed over and over again, relearning the pleasures of each other's mouths. They touched and explored, their hands roaming where they would, remembering and discovering, trembling under the force of their desire.

His lips were soft, his teeth sharp, his mouth hot and wet, and Nicola felt newly alive wherever he kissed her. Slowly his mouth moved from hers, trailing languid, velvety kisses across her cheek until he reached the lobe of her ear. He took it between his teeth, worrying it gently, laving and nipping and arousing her until Nicola moaned from the pleasure of it.

She caressed his body, bolder than she had ever been

as a girl, her hand slipping beneath his shirt and exploring the hard plane of his chest, the softer flatness of his stomach. With her every touch, she could feel the excitement ratcheting up a notch in him. His breath caught and shuddered out when her eager fingers found the flat bud of his nipple. Teasingly, she played with it, reveling in the sounds she pulled from him.

He said her name as he unfastened the buttons of her dress, breathed it like a prayer as he pushed back the open bodice, shoving it off her shoulders and down her arms. He stopped, his eyes going to the ring that hung on a long chain, usually hidden by her clothes. Slowly he reached out to touch it.

"My ring? You have my ring?"

Nicola nodded, watching him. Emotions flitted across his face too swiftly for her to be sure what they were. "Yes. I went back later—just to sit there. And I saw it glint. It had landed on a ledge below the edge of the Falls."

"You kept it all this time…." His voice hoarsened as he said the words, and his eyes went from the ring back up to her face. A flame burned fiercely in his dark eyes. Not taking his gaze from hers, he placed his hands flat on her chest, sliding them down under her chemise and onto the soft white orbs of her breasts, and all the while he watched the pleasure that took her at his caresses. He moved over and under her breasts, pushing the chemise down out of the way. Her breasts were creamy white against his hard, tanned hands, startling and arousing in the contrast. He caressed her pink-brown nipples with his thumbs, watching them harden and elongate, eager for his touch. Nicola gasped when he touched her there, a shock running down through her from her nipples to explode in her abdomen, turning her insides molten. The desire that she had felt for him in the past was as nothing compared to the tidal wave of passion that ran through her now.

She knew that she loved him. What he had done or what he believed about her could not change how she felt, even as the intervening years could not alter it. She loved him; she would always love him. He was part of her and had been from the moment she met him. No matter what happened, he always would be. Beyond that knowledge, there was no thought—no question of right or wrong, of smart or foolish. What was happening between them was all emotion and sensation, and it had been inevitable from the moment he had stopped her carriage.

With a wordless noise, he swept her up in his arms and carried her into the bedroom. There he laid her down gently on the bed and knelt beside it. He began to kiss her, working his way down her throat to her chest and onto the lush mounds of her breasts. He explored her breasts with his tongue and lips, teasing her nipples as his fingers had done. Nicola moved restlessly, digging her fingers into his arms and shoulders, sliding her hands up and into his hair, clenching her fingers when a sizzle of pleasure even more intense than the others struck her. But he did not even feel the slight nip of pain when she tugged at his hair, so lost was he in pure sensation.

With a noise of frustration, he pulled back long enough to unbutton his shirt and pull it off. Nicola watched him, her breath catching in her throat at the sight of his tanned chest, lightly covered with dark curling hair. As he moved back to her, she stretched out her arms eagerly to meet him, and when her fingers touched his flesh, he let out a shuddering groan and buried his face in her breasts.

They loved each other with hands and mouths, heedless of time or place. Neither thought of the unlocked door or

of the tasks that waited outside. The only things that
mattered at this moment were their hunger and the slow,
sweet lovemaking that would satisfy it.

His mouth fastened upon her nipple while his fingers
sought out the dark heat between her legs. He slid over the
slick, tender flesh, arousing them both. Nicola's breath
rasped in her throat. His heat surrounded her, and she felt
lost in an endless, swirling haze of pleasure. With every
breath she took, every beat of her heart, her pleasure grew,
equaled each time by another leap in the intensity of her
hunger. She felt his response, the same wild, furious heat
that bloomed within her. It was as if their hearts beat in
time, their blood coursed between their veins, their flesh
melted into each other's. They were consumed and fed by
the same yearning.

Hastily they stripped away the remnants of their
clothing, and he moved over her. She opened her legs,
taking him inside her, and the flash of pain hardly registered against the urgent, intense pleasure of being joined
with him. They moved together in an ancient, timeless
rhythm, seeking what they had missed years ago. Tears
formed in Nicola's eyes and rolled silently down her
cheeks. She didn't know why she cried, only that what she
was experiencing was so beautiful and pleasurable it
bordered on pain. She wrapped her arms tightly around
him, her hands digging into his back, and buried her face
in his shoulder.

Jack let out a hoarse cry, shuddering to his fulfillment,
and Nicola clung to him, stunned by the wave of pleasure
rushing through her. She loved him with all her heart and
soul, and in that moment she did not know whether she
was fortunate, foolish, or doomed to a life of despair.

He collapsed against her, his chest heaving, his skin

damp with sweat. He let out a faint laugh and rolled over onto his back, wrapping his arms around Nicola and pulling her with him so that she lay on top of him.

"Sweet Jesus, I had not expected that," he said. His hand stroked down her hair, which had come tumbling down somewhere along the way. It was like golden silk beneath his hands, and he closed his eyes at the pure sensory pleasure of touching it. He felt alive to every sensation— the feel of Nicola's skin against his, the sound of her breathing, the taste of her on his lips, the wetness of her cheeks…. "Here…what's this?"

He reached up and stroked his thumb across her cheek. "Are you crying? Did I hurt you?"

"No." Nicola shook her head. She wanted to add "not yet," but she did not. She had known the likelihood of getting hurt when she lay down with him; she would not blame anyone but herself for whatever happened.

"Why are you crying? Are you sad?"

"Maybe a little. For the past ten years. But it's more from joy, I think."

"Good. I…don't want to hurt you."

Nicola raised her head and looked down into his face. He looked more like the boy she had known—his face relaxed and alight with happiness, the crooked smile she had loved so much spreading across his face, his dark eyes bright and mischievous. She smiled and laid her head back down on his chest, letting out a sigh. This moment, right now, was enough. She pressed her lips against his bare chest, then snuggled into him. Soon she heard the steady rhythm of his breathing and knew that he had fallen asleep. She smiled again as she, too, drifted into slumber.

When she awoke, he was gone. She sat bolt upright, a little panicked, and her dress, which he had laid over her for warmth, slid down. She scrambled into her clothes and grabbed all the hairpins she could find, pinning up her tresses as best she could. She hurried through the house to the front door. As soon as she opened it, she saw Jack near the gate, wielding a hoe against some stubborn weeds. She relaxed with a sigh, telling herself that she was being foolish. *Did she think he had just vanished?*

Jack looked up and saw her, then smiled and gave her a wave of the hand. Nicola smiled back in what she hoped was a nonchalant manner and went out to join him.

For the rest of the day they worked together in the yard in cheerful amity, digging weeds and cutting back shrubs and flowers, joking and talking. It was as if the last ten years had fallen away. They did not speak of love or the Earl of Exmoor or the past, by unspoken consent steering clear of anything that could cause unpleasantness.

The tea was long since ruined, but they ate Nicola's lunch together, and later that afternoon, she brewed another pot of tea and they sipped it in tired silence, sitting on the front stoop of the cottage and looking out at what they had accomplished.

When Nicola rose to take the cups back inside, Jack reached up and curled his hand around her wrist. "Will you be coming back tomorrow, then?"

Even his voice sounded more like his old self, with the faintest touch of an accent.

"Yes." Nicola avoided looking at him, afraid of his answer. "And you?"

"Aye, I will be here." He stood up. "If you are."

Nicola looked up at him. He was gazing at her, his face solemn now. He reached up a hand and cupped her cheek. "If you're wanting answers, I don't know what to say."

"I don't need answers," Nicola replied promptly. "I don't even want to ask questions right now."

"Nor I." His grin was quick and warm. He took the cups from her hands and set them down on the stoop, then pulled her into his embrace.

Being in his arms was wonderful, Nicola thought. Before long, she might want more, but right now this was enough. This was all she wanted.

He laid his cheek against her hair as he hugged her tightly to him. "You are the most beautiful woman I have ever known." He kissed her on the mouth, a hard, quick kiss. "I'll see you tomorrow."

And he was gone as suddenly as he had arrived, striding around back to get his horse. She heard the jingle of the bridle, but she did not see him leave. Nicola sat down on the stoop again, feeling bereft. She wrapped her arms around her knees and pulled them up close to her body, resting her chin on her knees.

Her life had changed irrevocably today, she realized, and she was not even sure how she felt about it. She loved a man whom she was not sure loved her back—or trusted her. A man who could be gone in a day or a week and she would never know what happened to him. He was danger-ous and daring, and most people, she supposed, would consider him a scoundrel.

But he was the only man she had ever loved, and she had realized something today: she would not, ever again, let her chance to love him slip away unheeded. She would seize the moment as it came along, and if and when it was over, she would at least have memories. She would at least know that for a while she had truly lived. She would not live with regret for the rest of her life.

THE FOLLOWING WEEK WAS THE HAPPIEST of her life. She rode to Granny Rose's cottage every day—except for one afternoon when it rained too hard to make any excuse for riding out feasible—and she took with her a basket of food. Sometimes Jack was there when she arrived, his horse tethered in back of the house where it could not be seen, and sometimes she got there first and was already working when he came up noiselessly behind her and wrapped his arms around her, nuzzling her neck.

They worked in the yard the first few days, weeding, pruning, planting. She laid out the herb garden as she remembered it. Some of the plants were still there, grown wild, like the apple-smelling German chamomile, and she was able to trim them, restoring them to their neat mounds and rows. She cultivated the ground, thinking that in another two months she would be able to plant the rest of the plants—the marigolds and comfrey, the onion, garlic and rosemary, the delicate white-flowered yarrow. Nicola liked to think of how the garden would look this summer, and then she would catch herself and remind herself how pointless it was to make plans.

There was no future here, no past. There was only the present and the little magical, secluded world of Granny Rose's cottage. That was all she needed. She asked no questions and gave no explanations. She did not try to argue away Jack's suspicions; she simply ignored them, and so did he. Nor did she try to determine the extent and intent of his feelings for her. For the moment it was enough to work alongside Jack, to talk and laugh and be with him. To sit at the table with him and eat, to pour his tea, to look into his face and see the light in his dark eyes as he looked back at her. To slip off to the bedroom and make love with him, sometimes in a rush of heat, other times slowly and gently, driving each other mad with long, lazy kisses and caresses. She loved him; that was the only knowledge that she needed. None of the rest of it mattered now.

When the garden and yard were finished, they still came to the cottage, meeting and going for a ride, or simply spending the afternoon together before a fire.

One afternoon, when Jack walked in, he was wearing his mask. Nicola's eyes went to it, and an odd thrill ran through her.

"Oh. Sorry." Jack reached up and untied the mask, stuffing it into the pocket of his coat. "I went into the village today. It's better if they aren't able to recognize me. I forgot I had it on."

"No. Don't take it off." Nicola started toward him, her gray eyes warm with sensuality. She stopped before him, looking up at him in an unmistakable invitation, and reached her hand into his pocket, pulling out the black satin mask. "You know, when you took me in front of you on the horse that night…when you kissed me, I could feel your mask against my skin, soft and cool, and it was… exciting."

His dark eyes flared with light. "Was it?" he asked huskily.

Nicola nodded, one corner of her mouth lifting in an alluring way. "It's a little dangerous, your identity hidden like that."

"Mmm…I see. And here I always thought you were such a proper girl." Jack smiled with pure sexual anticipation. Taking the mask from Nicola's hand, he put it on again, tying it in the back, transforming himself once more into the highwayman.

Nicola could not deny the shiver of delight that ran through her. There was something primitively stirring about seeing him this way—himself and yet a stranger, a dangerous stranger, who took what he wanted, wild and free—until her touch tamed him. She did not move, merely smiled at him, her face beckoning, challenging.

He wrapped one hand around her wrist and pulled her to him until she was flush against his body. He took her other arm in his hand and pulled both her arms behind her, holding her without pain, but helpless and vulnerable to him. He gazed down into her face, his eyes blazing through the holes in the mask.

"You are mine." His voice was low, darkly vibrant. "Now and always."

"I am no man's," she challenged.

"Indeed?" He smiled, amused, and his mouth came down to claim her.

His kiss was deep and voracious, as though he could summon up her very soul through it. Nicola was limp, breathless, shaking with the force of her desire. She moaned, struggling to free her hands so that she could touch him. But he would not let her go. Instead, he put both her wrists into one of his large hands, holding her securely, and brought the other up to travel over her body. His hand roamed over her freely, caressing her through her dress, cupping her breasts and teasing the nipples to aching hardness. His lips explored the tender flesh of her throat, arousing her with frustrating slowness, teasing and stoking her passion, until she writhed against him, moaning.

"Please…" she panted. "Let me touch you. Let me…"

A long shudder of desire ran through him at her words, and his skin flamed hot against her even through their clothes. He released her hands, his arms going around her and lifting her up into him, grinding her pelvis into his. Nicola gasped with pleasure, her hands going to his shoulders. She caressed his chest and back and shoulders, sliding up his neck and tangling in his hair. Her fingers found the slick, cool cloth of his mask, and the touch stirred her sensually. Heat bloomed deep inside her, pooling like liquid fire between her legs. She kissed him, wrapping her legs around him and pressing the aching seat of her desire against him. Her fingers dug into the cloth of the mask and pulled it from him, tossing it aside.

He walked with her to the bed and laid her down upon it. Roughly, his fingers clumsy with hunger, he stripped her undergarments from her and unbuttoned his trousers. With a primal groan of satisfaction, he sank deep inside her. Nicola cried out and jerked, pleasure rippling through her already. He waited, teeth clenched, until the waves of her passion died away.

"Oh, no, my sweet, that's not nearly enough." He began to stroke within her, slowly, steadily building the hunger inside her again. His hands caressed the smooth bare skin of her buttocks beneath her skirts, lifting and guiding her, holding her to the same steady pace until she was groaning and clawing at his arms, aching for the surcease only he could give her. Twice he brought her to the edge, then retreated and began again.

Nicola moaned his name, clamping herself tightly around him, and he could hold back no longer. With a cry, he plunged deeply, his seed spilling into her in a supreme rush of pleasure. Nicola gasped as she hurtled into her own maelstrom of passion, clinging to him.

Jack shuddered and collapsed against her. They lay there on the bed, damp and depleted, recovering from the violent release of their desire.

"We're still dressed," Nicola murmured with a chuckle, amazed at the storm that had swept through them.

"Mmm hmm." Jack propped himself up on his elbow

and looked down at her, his face replete with satisfaction. "Next time, we shall play out *my* fantasy."

Nicola grinned. "And that would be?"

"It would definitely involve a blindfold."

IT WAS SOMETIME LATER WHEN NICOLA'S horse, tethered in front, whinnied. Nicola scarcely noticed the noise, but Jack's arm beneath her head tensed at the sound. He pulled it away and rose, striding across the room to peer out the window. Nicola sat up.

"What's the matter? What is it?"

"Probably nothing. Just wondered why your mare—" He stiffened. "There's a rider, coming this way."

"What?" Nicola hurried over to join him. "Oh, my God!" Jack turned to her. "Who is it?"

"It's Stone—the Bow Street Runner that Exmoor hired. He must have followed me." She paled, her stomach constricting with fear. "Oh, no... Deborah was teasing me at the dinner table the other night about being gone so much. I didn't think anything about it, but it must have made Richard suspicious. Stupid, stupid! I didn't even think to look to see if anyone was following me!"

"It doesn't matter." Jack was already crossing the room, grabbing his jacket as he strode past the sofa. He sat and pulled on his boots. "He won't find me."

He stood and cast a long look around the room for any sign of his occupancy, then turned to Nicola. "Can you handle him on your own?"

"Of course. I don't like the man, but I don't think he would dare offer me any harm. I *am* his employer's sister-in-law, however little I like Exmoor. But what about you? How are you going to get away? There isn't a back door."

A smile lifted the corners of his mouth, and his eyes

sparkled with mischief. It occurred to Nicola with a flash of irritation that he was actually enjoying this. "Ah, but Granny Rose's house has a secret." He went to the side of the fireplace and bent down, sliding one of the hearth-stones out. Then he reached into the space where the rock had been and twisted a lever. There was a loud click, and Jack reached up and tugged on the rock beside the fire-place. A narrow section of it slid open, revealing a tiny room the size of a narrow cupboard. Jack shoved the rock back into place, concealing the lever.

"I told you that people always thought her ancestors were witches. They knew they might need protection."

There was a jingle and scrape outside. "Hurry!" Nicola looked out the window. "Hurry! He's getting off his horse!" She ran to the door and shoved home the lock. What fools they had been to leave it unlocked!

Jack gave her a salute, stepped into the space beside the fireplace, grabbed a handle on the other side of the secret door, and pulled it too. There was nothing, not even a crack to show where the door had been. Nicola went through the room, glancing about to make sure that there was nothing that looked as if two people had been in the house.

The handle turned on the front door, and Stone shoved against the wood. It rattled but did not move. Nicola went into the kitchen and looked around, quickly putting one teacup and plate back into the cupboard.

There was a knock at the door. She started toward it, calling, "Who is it?"

"It's Stone, Miss Falcourt."

"Mr. Stone?" Nicola unlocked the door and opened it, putting a puzzled expression on her face. "What are you doing here? Has something happened to Deborah?"

"No, miss." He took off his hat. "I, uh, came to see if you were all right."

"All right? Whatever do you mean? Of course I am all right." She stepped back, allowing him to enter. The sooner he saw that Jack was not here, the sooner he would leave. She didn't want Jack to have to spend any longer time in the boxlike room than was necessary. "Why wouldn't I be all right?"

"There is a highwayman roaming the area, miss," Stone reminded her as he walked past her into the room. His eyes darted around the room as he walked to the kitchen.

Nicola followed him. "Yes, I know. That is why I locked the door. I am quite careful, you see. How did you know where I was?"

He glanced at her, his face impassive. "His lordship told me to follow you, make sure you were all right."

Nicola doubted that those had been exactly his instructions, but she pretended to believe him. "Richard worries too much about me. As you can see, I am perfectly fine. I do not think the highwayman would stop me again. It is obvious when I am riding horseback that I have no jewels or valuables with me."

"There are other things a man might want," he reminded her darkly, striding back through the parlor to the small bedroom. He went to the wardrobe and opened it, peering in.

Nicola saw with horror that Jack's mask lay upon the floor. Quickly she kicked it under the bed.

"You think he's hiding in the wardrobe?" Nicola asked, putting a tinge of sarcasm in her voice. "Really, Mr. Stone…"

He lifted his head. "What was that?"

"What?"

"I heard a horse." He turned toward the blank back wall.

Nicola's nerves began to jangle. *Jack's horse!* He always tethered his horse in back, with the innate caution of those who live outside the law. Thank God there was no window in the back, so Stone could not see the horse, but all he had to do was walk around the house. Once he saw it, he would know that someone else was here, and he might search more thoroughly. *Would Granny's hideaway stand up to a careful search?* She had never noticed it, but then, she had never really looked.

"A horse? Oh, that must be mine."

"Yours is in front."

"Well, sometimes I don't tie it well enough, and it roams around. Fortunately, it is a very docile animal and never wanders far."

Stone ignored her words and strode quickly through the house and out the front door. Nicola hurried after him, trying desperately to think of some excuse for Jack's horse being there. *Could she say a friend from the village had come here to visit her? But then where would she be?*

Stone glanced over at her horse, which was standing placidly, tail swishing, outside the low fence, where it had been all along. He cast a glance back at her.

Nicola tried to smile. "Ah, there she is. Then you couldn't have heard her behind the house. It must have been a trick of sound."

"It was a horse." Stone started through the garden and around the side of the house. Nicola went after him.

She could admit to secretly meeting a lover here. Perhaps the scandal of the story would distract Stone enough.... No, no one would be fool enough not to question where the man was.

In front of her, Stone came to a halt. "Damn!"

Nicola looked at the small area in front of them, behind the house and the hill. There was no horse. Nicola struggled to keep her face blank. *Where had the animal gone?*

"You see? There was no horse. It was a trick of sound. That often happens where there are hills, I've noticed. You probably heard my horse—or yours—out front, and it sounded as if it were coming from the back." She realized as she talked that the hidden cupboard must have had a back way out. Jack had meant to leave the house, and she had assumed he was going to hide in the secret room. She had to bite her lip to keep from grinning.

Stone walked forward a few more feet and squatted down. "There are hoofprints here. There was a horse."

"Sometimes I tether my horse back here, and, as I told you, she has gotten loose once or twice and wandered around."

Stone paid no attention to her, walking around until he found a set of tracks leading off. Nicola went with him, making sure to scuff through the horse tracks as she walked. The hoofprints led to a patch of ground a few feet away and disappeared.

"Damn!"

"Really, Mr. Stone!" Nicola exclaimed, putting on a shocked look. "Your language!"

"Sorry, miss." His stormy face looked anything but sorry. He turned, his eyes drilling into her. "Who was here? I know there was someone here. Are you helping to conceal that highwayman? It is a crime, you know, and—"

"Oh, please, Mr. Stone." Nicola infused her voice with amused contempt, doing her best to sound like Lady Morrow, a vain, cold Society beauty. "You are becoming infected with Richard's delusions. He assumes that I am having affairs with every man I meet. I fear he still has not gotten over the fact that I rejected him years ago." She shrugged elaborately. "However, I can assure you that I would scarcely be dallying with a highwayman. When I take a lover, I stay in my own class."

"Yes, miss."

'Now, I would appreciate it if you would leave. I am afraid that I come here every afternoon for the much more mundane purpose of drying herbs and making infusions and such, and I have work to do. Goodbye."

She strode back into the cottage, then watched from the window while Stone mounted his horse and rode off. Nicola presumed he would try to find the tracks where they came out on the other side of the rock, but she was confident that Jack would be far away and would have covered his tracks well enough that Stone would have no success.

Her first thought was to go home and give Richard a piece of her mind for having her followed. She was furious—primarily at herself for not having thought about the fact that Richard would wonder about her frequent absences from Tidings—and it would be a great relief to take that anger out on someone she despised as much as Richard.

However, she soon rejected that notion. In her anger, she just might let something slip that would let Richard know that the highwayman was really Gil. That would only make matters much worse. If he had looked for Jack with intensity before, it would be nothing compared to how he would search for him now. To find out that the highwayman who had made a fool of him and stolen his money was the very same man who had, to his way of thinking, stolen Nicola from him would be the ultimate insult. Nicola had no illusions that Richard had ever really loved her; she did not believe the man was capable of actual love. But he had desired her and had wanted to make her his wife, and she knew that it must have eaten at him all this time that she had preferred a common stable boy to him. Why else would he have gone to such lengths to get rid of Gil?

Besides, it would probably only confirm his suspicions about her and the highwayman if she reacted with such emotion. It would be better, she reasoned, if she reacted mildly, perhaps even treating it as a joke. Richard hated to be laughed at, and if he thought that she was amused by his actions, he might just stop them. At the least, it ought to give him pause and make him wonder if his suspicions were correct.

So she packed her things without haste and rode back to Tidings. There, she bathed and changed and avoided Richard until dinner.

Then, when the three of them were seated, their soup in front of them, she said lightly, "Really, Richard, don't you think it was a bit...shall we say, deéclassé to have your man follow me this afternoon?"

"Follow you?" Deborah looked at her. "What are you talking about?"

"Mr. Stone—you know, that Bow Street Runner— followed me on my afternoon ride."

"But why—is that true?" Deborah turned toward her husband, a puzzled expression on her face.

"Not exactly as Nicola put it," Richard replied easily. "I have been a trifle concerned about your sister's safety, since she insists on riding out every afternoon without a groom when there are bandits lurking about. So I did ask Stone to keep an eye on her, make sure no harm came to her."

"No doubt that is why he was looking in cupboards and behind doors."

"In cupboards?" Deborah repeated. "In cupboards where? What are you talking about?"

"At Granny Rose's cottage," Nicola explained, watching Richard for any sign of reaction at the mention of Gil's grandmother.

There was a moment of silence. Richard's expression did not change, though Nicola thought she saw something flicker in his eyes.

"Granny Rose!" Deborah exclaimed. "But—but she's dead, isn't she? Has been for years."

"Yes, she is. Her cottage stands vacant. It was in terrible shape. One day when I was out riding I went there, and when I saw how overgrown it was, I could not bear for it to look like that, so I went back and worked in the yard. That is where I have been the past few days, restoring her herb garden. She has a wonderful little space inside for working with remedies, too, and I have been using that. Making salves, drying herbs, things like that." She sighed. "I suppose that is ruined now. I shall always be looking over my shoulder, expecting one of Richard's men to pop in on me."

"They won't harm you. I only want to make sure you're safe."

"Mmm." Nicola put just a tinge of disbelief in her tone. She turned toward her sister. "I think the truth is, Deborah, that Richard believes I am clandestinely meeting the highwayman. Mr. Stone was terribly disappointed not to find him, I'm afraid."

Deborah looked at her blankly. "Why would you be meeting the highwayman?"

"I am sure I don't know," Nicola replied. "I believe it is Richard who thinks that."

"I don't think that," Richard said, watching her intently. "It is you who brought up the subject."

"I don't understand," Deborah put in plaintively. "We seem to be talking in circles."

"Yes. Rather tiring, isn't it?" Nicola said carelessly. "Why don't we speak of something else? How is that lovely blanket you're knitting coming along?"

Deborah's face brightened at the mention of her latest project with Nurse, and she began to chatter animatedly. Nicola responded enough to keep the conversation going and wondered if she had made any headway in deflecting Richard's suspicions.

NICOLA KNEW SHE COULD NOT SEE Jack again for a while, not with Stone following her wherever she went. It was, she realized the next morning, a depressing prospect.

She spent the next day with Deborah and Nurse, working on baby clothes. As she worked and listened to them talk, she remembered exactly why it was that she had decided not to help them but to go clean up Granny's cottage instead.

The next afternoon she went back to Granny's cottage. She knew that Stone would follow her, and she wanted him to see her spend her afternoon working at the cottage alone. If she stayed away from the cottage now, it would rouse Richard's suspicions even more. She was certain that Jack would not be there. He was far too smart to return after yesterday.

Somehow, working at the cottage by herself was even worse than staying at Tidings. Here she missed Jack all the time, and everything she saw or did reminded her of him. Pulling up stray weeds that were defiantly poking through the soil again, she remembered him working there, cutting and pulling and chopping the weeds with a hoe. When she brewed tea in the kitchen, she pictured him sitting at the kitchen table, talking and smiling. If she sat on the sofa she thought of them sitting there or lying in front of it, warming themselves by the fire. When she left the cottage a few hours later, shutting the door behind her, she decided that she would not come back for a few days.

She spent the next morning idling about the house, sitting with Nurse and Deborah for a while, then looking through the library for something to read. Finally she took three books back to her room and settled down. But she found it difficult to concentrate. She kept thinking about Jack and wondering how and when she was going to be able to see him again.

The knock on the door startled her from a daydream about Jack, and she jumped, the book sliding from her lap onto the floor. A parlormaid entered with a note on a silver tray, and Nicola took it eagerly. *Perhaps her aunt needed her for some reason.*

With even greater delight, she recognized the handwriting as that of her friend Penelope. Eagerly, she tore open the note and began to read.

Dearest Nicola,
After a long and somewhat harrowing journey, Cousin Marianne, Grandmama, Mama and I have arrived safely at the Dower House.

Nicola smiled, knowing exactly how harrowing it would have been to have been stuck in a carriage for two days with Penelope's mother, the vocal, opinionated and domineering Lady Ursula.

Since Mama insisted on bringing along her lapdog, Fifi, who, you may recall, is rendered nauseous by carriage travel, there were moments when I was not sure that we would make it. When Fifi drooled all over Grandmama's slippers, she threatened to send Fifi back to London with one of the servants, which put Mama into such a pet that she did not speak to any of us for the next hour. Fortunately, Marianne persuaded Mama that Fifi would be much less sick riding in the open air, so we were able to put her in a basket on top of the coach and let the footman tend to her.

Now we are safely ensconced at the Dower House. Cousin Alexandra and her husband, as well as Lord Lambeth, delayed their trip a few days—I cannot imagine *why,* since they could have ridden in caravan with us—and should be arriving with Bucky at Buckminster Hall soon.

Please come to see us at your first opportunity, as we are all eager to see you.

Love, Penelope

It came as no surprise to Nicola that her friends had sent a note rather than coming to call on her and her sister. The Countess had not stepped foot in Tidings since the day she had moved out more than twenty-two years ago, unable to bear seeing it in the hands of Richard instead of her dead son. Now that they had found out the details of Richard's treachery all those years ago, the Countess and her family despised him. None of them would think of coming to call on anyone at his house.

Eagerly Nicola bounced to her feet and hurried to the wardrobe to pull out her riding habit. It seemed like ages since she had seen her friends, and she was bursting with news to tell them. It took her only a few minutes to dress and tell her sister about the Countess's arrival. Then she flew down the stairs and out to the stables, and soon was on her way to the Dower House to see her friends.

CHAPTER FIFTEEN

THE DOWER HOUSE LAY AT SOME DISTANCE from Tidings, on a separate piece of property from the rest of the Exmoor estate, north of the village and rather closer to both it and Buckminster Hall than to Tidings.

However, Nicola did not mind the long ride. She was eager to see her friends again. She had not realized until she received Penelope's note how much she wanted to talk to someone about Jack. She could not say anything to her sister about it. After all, Deborah was married to the Earl, and she could not risk her repeating something to Richard. But Penelope and Marianne were people to whom Nicola felt she could say almost anything.

She arrived a trifle flushed from the ride, her hair somewhat disarrayed, but she knew that Penelope and Marianne would not mind. Lady Ursula, of course, was another matter, but Nicola had learned long ago to put that overbearing woman's remarks out of her mind as soon as she heard them.

She handed over the reins of her horse to one of the grooms and started toward the front door. As she rounded the corner of the garden, a small redheaded form burst out of the bushes, shouting, "Boo!"

Nicola gasped, her hand going to her heart, then smiled as the young girl before her burst into a fit of giggles.

"Did I scare you?" Rosalind asked, her dark blue eyes gleaming. Rosalind was Marianne's nine-year-old daughter, and she had her mother's coloring and tall, graceful body. Nicola had no doubt that one day Rosalind would be one of the great beauties of the Ton. Right now, however, she was an engaging hoyden.

"Rather," Nicola said emphatically, knowing that Rosalind would be delighted to hear it. "Didn't you know that you are supposed to treat us older people with respect?"

Rosalind giggled again. "You aren't old. Grandmama is old. But she is very beautiful, don't you think?"

Nicola nodded. Rosalind's grandmother, the Countess of Exmoor, was in her seventies, and her tall frame was becoming a trifle bent with age, but there was no mistaking the beauty in her face. "Yes, I do. Is your mother at home?"

"Yes. They sent me outside with my governess."

"Your governess?" Nicola made a great show of looking about and seeing no one. "Where is this personage? Is she invisible? What a remarkable woman!"

"No. She's down at the other end of the garden."

"Looking for you?" Nicola tried to look severe, but it was spoiled by a smile.

Rosalind nodded. "Mama says I should be kinder to Miss Northcutt. I try, I really do, but she is such a gabster! And she never talks about anything interesting. Just boring old kings and things. Did you know that she said the mark of a great lady is the way she sits! Do you think that's true?"

"Not really," Nicola admitted. "I would think it is her character."

"*I* thought it was a silly thing to say, myself.

Although—" Rosalind considered the matter "—Grandmama does sit awfully straight."

Nicola smiled. "That is true. But I think there are probably a good number of other women who sit equally straight but haven't half the Countess's character. You really like your new grandmother, don't you?"

"Oh, yes. She's ever so interesting. She lets me look through her jewels sometimes, and she tells me stories about them, how they came into the family and everything. Of course, she's not like Gran," Rosalind said, referring to the eldest woman of Marianne's former and quite unusual "family." "Grandmama doesn't know how to mark an ace, and I can beat her at whist lots and lots of the time. Still, I have fun with her."

"It's nice that your grandmothers are different," Nicola replied, seeing the child's vague expression of guilt. "It wouldn't be much fun if they were just alike. You and Gran can do some things together, and you and your Grandmama can do others."

"That's true." Rosalind skipped ahead of her and darted up the front steps to grab the door knocker and send it crashing into the door three times in quick succession. She grinned at Nicola. "I always go in the kitchen door, but you must come in the front because you are company. I'm glad. I haven't been able to use that knocker since I got here."

A footman opened the door to them almost immediately. "Miss Falcourt. Miss Rosalind." He delighted the child by bowing to her as gravely as he did to Nicola. "If you will sit down, I will tell Miss Castlereigh that you are here."

He ushered them into a pleasant drawing room, decorated in dark mahogany furniture and accented with blue in the drapes and chair cushions. Rosalind, plopping down on one of the brocade-cushioned chairs, offered to stay to keep Nicola company.

"That is very kind of you."

Rosalind nodded, bouncing on the cushion. "Mama will make me leave," she said without rancor. "She says I am unkind to poor Miss Northcutt. But don't you think Miss Northcutt could make a bit of push to be more fun?"

"Mmm. Perhaps. But you must remember that sometimes people are nervous when they first know one. She may be afraid that you and your mother will be disappointed in her. Maybe she wants to make sure you realize that she knows a lot of things."

"Afraid?"

"Why, yes. If she lost this job, it would probably be very difficult for her."

Rosalind considered this. "Oh." After a moment, she slid off the chair. "Perhaps I had better go down to the end of the garden and find Miss Northcutt. I truly didn't mean to worry her."

"Of course not. That would be nice of you."

Rosalind flounced out of the room, intent on her new good deed.

Almost immediately afterward, Rosalind's mother swept into the room, followed by her cousin Penelope, both of them beaming and reaching out to Nicola. The contrast between the two women was striking. Marianne was tall and voluptuous, with flaming red hair and dark, midnight-blue eyes. She was, Nicola thought, the most beautiful woman she had ever met—except for her sister Alexandra, whose vibrant dark looks were equally arresting. Penelope, on the other hand, was small, slender and pale, the sort of woman who generally receded into the background wherever she was. Penelope had, however, blossomed the past few months. There was now a glow to her cheeks and a gleam in her eyes, brought about largely, Nicola knew, by her newfound love.

Even though Nicola had known Marianne for only a few months, in some ways she felt closer to her than to any of the aristocrats with whom Nicola had lived for years. Because Marianne had spent her youth in an orphanage and had even gone into service when she left that institution, completely unaware of her noble family, she did not have the snobbery and class consciousness of many of Nicola's peers. She found Nicola's work among the poor women of London admirable, without expressing even a tinge of distaste. She had entered into Nicola's endeavors, donating some of her newfound wealth and, perhaps more important, several days of her time to assisting at Nicola's charitable house.

Marianne had a ready, warm sense of humor and was fiercely loyal to those whom she loved. She enjoyed a good shopping spree with Nicola, but she was equally happy discussing books with Penelope. There were times when Nicola felt as if she had known her for years instead of only a few months, and she was one of the few people on whom Nicola felt she could rely.

"Nicola!" both women cried joyfully, and Nicola stepped forward to hug each of them.

"It seems as if it's been months, not weeks, since you left London," Penelope told her. "We persuaded Grandmama to come down here early." Lowering her voice, she added, "Mama, too."

Nicola could not imagine Penelope's mother letting even the smallest of wedding details go on without her. She suspected from the rather harried look in Penelope's eyes that Ursula was causing a good bit of disruption.

"Disagreements over wedding plans?" she asked lightly.

Marianne rolled her eyes expressively. "There have been moments when I thought that Grandmama and Aunt Ursula might come to fisticuffs."

Penelope giggled. "Grandmama did start banging her cane on the floor one day. I don't think I have ever seen her do that before."

Nicola felt sure that if anyone could drive the dignified Countess into slamming her cane, it would be her opinionated daughter.

"It is fortunate that it is a double wedding, actually," Marianne said. "When Aunt Ursula is causing too much of a disruption in the plans, Lambeth will turn very future duke-ish and say that that is the way it is done in his family." Even as she arranged her face in a turned-up, snobbish pose, there was a light that warmed her eyes at the thought of her fiancé.

"That's true," Penelope agreed. "Mama has always been a trifle in awe of Lambeth."

The three of them sat down in a cozy cluster on a small sofa and a matching chair at right angles to it and proceeded to catch up on the most recent gossip. After a few snippets of what new lover Lady Armbruster had taken and what lord's son had fallen in with cardsharps and who had lost a fortune at White's on a bet over a race between bugs, Marianne paused, looking at Nicola thoughtfully.

"I don't think you are terribly interested in this, are you?" she asked, her eyes narrowing.

"No, of course I am," Nicola protested without much conviction.

Penelope laughed at her tone. "Marianne's right. I am surprised I didn't see it." She leaned forward, looking into her old friend's eyes. "There's something going on with you. What is it?"

Nicola smiled. "Well…yes, there is. I—I don't know where to begin."

"You are in love!" Marianne exclaimed.

"No! Nicola, is that true?"

"How did you know?" Nicola asked, startled.

"Then it *is* true!" Penelope cried in delight. "Marianne, you're so clever. How did you guess?"

The lovely redhead shrugged. "Just something about her face." She turned to Nicola. "You are always beautiful, but I don't recall ever seeing such a glow on your face." She paused, smiling, then added, "It is the way I feel inside."

Nicola chuckled. "You are right. I am in love. But I don't know whether he loves me, and it—oh, it's all such a tangled mess. I don't know what to do."

"That sounds like love," Marianne said wryly. "Tell us all about it." The two women edged closer to her.

"I shall try. Do you remember when I told you that Richard had killed the man I loved years ago?"

"Yes, of course," Marianne replied. "You said you thought it was an accident at the time, but you were no longer so sure."

Nicola nodded. "I have found out since that it definitely was not an accident."

"That man is wicked!" Penelope cried out, clenching her small fists. "If only there were some way to expose him! What did he do?"

Nicola told them about her love for the Tidings stable boy and how Richard had found out and struggled with him atop Lady Falls, finally sending Gil over the edge. Penelope, who had heard most of the story over the years, nodded, while Marianne listened in rapt silence.

"Then, about two weeks ago, I found out that he didn't murder him. Gil didn't die. He came back."

Both her friends listened, slack-jawed, as she told them what Gil had revealed to her about Richard and how he had had Gil impressed into the navy.

"But that is almost as good as a death sentence!" Marianne exclaimed.

"It's typical of Richard," Penelope added bitterly. "Look at what he did to you. He doesn't usually have the courage to kill, but he ruins people's lives without compunction. He has no heart."

"I think you're right," Nicola agreed. "I despise him. I wish to God my sister were not married to him! But what about Gil? How could he have loved me and still believe what Richard said about me?"

Penelope frowned. "I don't know. How did he explain it?"

"I don't know that he did, really. I don't think even yet that he is sure I didn't turn him over to Richard. We don't know how Richard got hold of his letter to me. Gil's grandmother would not have given it to him, but I never received it."

"I imagine he is afraid to believe you," Penelope said shrewdly. "If he admits that you did not get the letter, he has to face the fact that he threw away the last ten years for both of you because his faith in you wasn't strong enough."

"I don't know that it was his faith in Nicola," Marianne put in. "No matter how much he loved you, he knew that there was this practically unbridgeable gap between the two of you. You probably don't understand that part of how he felt, but I do. I grew up a servant, you know, and the ruling class was so far away from us. It was absurd to think that one of them might love you, marry you. The nobility may use us—may, on occasion, even love us—but they don't *marry* us. It was your background, your status, that he distrusted, not you."

"Maybe so, but how can we go on if he cannot trust me, even yet? Will he always be questioning me, distrusting me? Will every little mistake I make be seen as some betrayal of him?" Nicola sighed. "Yet when I am with him…we are so happy. We don't talk about any of that, and everything is…blissful."

Marianne smiled. "That is what I see in your face."

"But you have not heard the worst of it," Nicola continued.

"There's more?" Marianne asked, startled. "There's worse?"

Nicola nodded. "He didn't just come back here to live. He—he is a highwayman. He has been stealing from Richard for months."

There was a long silence as the other two women stared at her.

"You see?" Nicola said unhappily. "I told you it was a terrible tangle. As if it weren't enough that I am in love with a man whom I'm not sure loves me, he is also a criminal and likely to be seized and hanged at any moment. I have to sneak around to see him so that Richard and his man Stone won't find out. I am a fool, aren't I?"

"But a very intriguing one," Penelope teased. "I think your story tops even Alexandra's or Marianne's."

"But this highwayman…" Marianne said. "Is he our highwayman? The one who saved Justin and me—you remember, when Fuquay made the mine cave in on us, a mysterious man dressed all in black dug us out. And Lambeth felt sure he was the highwayman everyone had been talking about, that he probably had some of his goods stored in the mine entrance."

"That's right!" Penelope exclaimed. "I remember. Don't you, Nicola?"

"I'm not sure I ever knew who it was that saved you. So much happened right after that, with the other attacks on your life and then finding out who you really were. Did he tell you his name? He calls himself Jack Moore now."

"Yes! Jack! That's it," Marianne said, nodding. "Well, he isn't your typical highwayman, I can tell you that. Justin and I owe him our lives."

"I know. He is a good man, really. It is only that he despises Richard—it is almost always things related to Richard that Jack seizes. But they will hang him for it, anyway, if he is caught."

"Won't he stop?" Penelope asked. "I mean, now that you and he are—"

"I don't know what we are. And I'm not sure whether he will stop, either. Getting revenge on Richard seems to have driven him for the past ten years. I don't know that he can give it up now."

"If he loves you, he will," Marianne said quietly. "You cannot hope for a life together as long as he continues to be a highwayman."

"I know." Sudden tears sparkled in Nicola's eyes. "I suppose that that is the only way that I can learn if he still loves me. If he gives up his attacks on Richard so that we can be together." She looked from one woman to the other. "A pretty clear-cut test, isn't it? What does he want more— me or revenge?"

THE NEXT MORNING, NICOLA WAS in her sister's sitting room describing Penelope's and Marianne's wedding plans to Deborah and Nurse—though not as all-consuming a topic as babies, weddings were always of major interest—when they were interrupted by the quiet entrance of one of the footmen.

"There is a…person, my lady, at the kitchen door asking to speak to Miss Falcourt."

"Me?" Nicola looked up. "Who is it?"

"A lad from the village, I believe." The footman's tone clearly expressed his low opinion of sorts such as village boys turning up asking to talk to one of the ladies of the house.

"Oh. Someone must be sick."

"Yes, miss. I believe that is what the boy said."

"I'll see him in the kitchen." Nicola excused herself to Deborah and hurried through the hallway after the footman into the vast kitchen of Tidings.

A boy of about ten whom she had seen before but could not place was seated on the hearth beside the great kitchen fire, looking with awe all around him. At Nicola's approach, he jumped up, twisting his cap in his hand.

"Miss? Maggie Falkner sent me. Her babe is sick, and she's fair discombobbled about it. She says you'd know what to do. Will you come, then?" He finished his little speech and visibly relaxed his shoulders.

"Yes, of course I shall come. I just have to gather my remedies. Do you know what ails the child?"

"Me mam says 'tis only colic and Maggie's too green to know, but Maggie, she's worried somethin' sick about it."

"Well, we'll see. Run back and tell her I am coming."

The child left, visibly relieved to escape the grandeur of the great house, and Nicola went upstairs to change into her riding habit and get her bag. No matter what the boy's mother said, Nicola could not imagine Maggie Falkner, a steady-headed young woman if ever there was one, would be calling for her help for nothing more than colic. She felt sure it was imperative to get there as soon as she could.

She hurried down to the stables, where they saddled the horse she had been riding since she came to Tidings, and soon she was on her way. She did not glance back to see if Stone was following her. She assumed he was, and, indeed, she rather hoped so. *Let him spend an afternoon standing out in the cold watching the Falkners' house.*

She made good time to the village. She imagined that she had beaten the neighbor boy back, in fact, even though the way by foot was shorter than taking the road, as she had. She dismounted, and Maggie's husband hurried out to take her horse and tie it for her.

"How is the baby?"

Falkner nodded his head. "We'll all be fine, miss, now that ye are here."

Nicola went into the house, calling out softly as she stepped inside, "Maggie?"

The young mother came bustling toward her. "Upstairs, miss." She motioned for Nicola to go before her up the narrow, twisting little stairs that led to two small rooms. Nicola went lightly up the stairs, wondering at Maggie's attitude. She looked far less worried than Nicola would have imagined.

"What is wrong with the baby?" she asked, twisting back to look at Maggie. "What is she doing?"

"Ye'll see, miss. I can't explain it that well." She pointed to the door in front of them. "Go on in."

Nicola turned the knob and walked into the room. In the instant that her mind registered that there were only a bed and a chest in the room, with no cradle or baby in sight, the door slammed shut behind her. Nicola jumped, letting out a squeak of surprise, and an arm wrapped around her waist and a hand came up to cover her mouth.

"Don't go yelling now, or you'll give the game away,"

a low, masculine voice murmured in her ear before the hand over her mouth fell away.

"Jack!" Nicola whirled around, delight bubbling up in her. "Oh, Jack!" She threw her arms around his neck and went up on tiptoe to kiss him.

After a long, satisfying moment, his arms loosened around her, and she slid back down and looked up at him, her eyes shining. "What are you doing here?"

"I had to see you. Hal Falkner's one of the village men who rides with me. So I asked a favor of him and his wife. The babe's not sick, just asleep in the room next door."

Nicola's eyes widened. "Oh, Jack…" She reached up a hand and smoothed it down his cheek. "I'm glad you did. I have been racking my brain trying to think of a way to see you. But I couldn't even get word to you if I had thought of a way. That Stone fellow trails me everywhere I go." She drew a sharp breath. "Oh, my God! He's probably outside right now, watching the house!"

She started toward the window, frowning, but Jack caught her wrist and pulled her back with a smile. "Don't worry about him now. He'll see nothing, standing out there watching this house. I have been here since before first light, and my horse is nowhere around. No one knows I am here except Hal and Maggie, and they certainly won't be telling him. He won't come to the door, and even if he did, they won't let him in."

Nicola let him pull her back into his arms. "All right. If you're sure…"

"I am."

She leaned against his chest, luxuriating in the warmth of his arms and the steady beat of his heart beneath her ear. "I missed you."

"I missed you, too. God!" He squeezed her tightly

against him. "It seems like weeks since I've been with you. I kept thinking about you, wondering what you were doing, wishing you were with me." He kissed the top of her head.

Nicola smiled. "Me too."

"I don't like being cut off from you. Not even being able to write you a note…"

"I know."

"Mmm, you smell good." He breathed in her perfume, nuzzling her hair.

Nicola let out a sigh of pure pleasure as his lips moved down to her ear and trailed slowly over her cheek, velvety and hot. "Jack…"

"How did I live without you all those years?" he murmured. "Oh, Nicola…"

His mouth found hers, and they kissed lingeringly, re-discovering each other as if it had been weeks instead of days since they last kissed. Nicola's hands slid up Jack's chest and around his back, caressing the smooth curve of his muscles through his shirt. She thought about slipping her fingers beneath his shirt and touching his skin, and the idea made her shiver with desire. As though he knew her thoughts, Jack's body surged with heat, and he wrapped his arms around her tightly, lifting her up off her feet. He began to walk toward the bed.

Nicola tore her mouth away, whispering, "Jack! No. What about Maggie and Hal?"

"They won't be coming in here. And they wouldn't let anyone else, either."

"Yes, but they'll know…."

"Know what?" He kissed his way down her neck.

"That we—that—" She let out a sigh as his lips touched the soft upper curve of her breast.

"Mmm?" He set her down on her feet beside the bed, and his hands slid up her body to cup her breasts. He looked down into her eyes, his thumbs circling her nipples, bringing them to life. He bent to kiss her lips while his fingers caressed her breasts. "That we what?"

"I forget…." Nicola tugged his shirt from his trousers, slipping her hands up underneath the material. His flesh, smooth over rock-hard muscles, seared her fingers. She could think of nothing right now but him—his scent, his touch, the incredible sensuality of his mouth on hers.

They tumbled onto the bed, lost in a haze of passion, the rest of the world receding. Limbs twined together. Hands and lips explored, aroused, soothed. Had an army burst in at that moment, they might not have noticed, so wrapped up in their passion were they.

They made slow, sweet love, kissing, murmuring, taking their time to bring out each ounce of pleasure. Nicola, shuddering under Jack's skillful touch, wondered if anyone had ever felt the stunning sensations that ran through her now. And when at last their blissful torment had built to its highest peak, release burst through them like a tidal wave, joining them in a dark, mindless pleasure.

Jack lay back on the bed, his heart pounding, sweat drying on his skin, and he pulled her close to him. "I don't want to let you go," he whispered.

Tears sprang into Nicola's eyes, and she snuggled even closer to him, as though she could somehow crawl right through his skin and become part of him. "I don't want to go."

"The last few days, all I could think about was you. I didn't want to. I tried not to. But nothing worked." He paused, then continued, "What if…what if there were no Jack Moore, gentleman highwayman?"

Nicola's heart stuttered. "What do you mean?"

"I mean, what if he disappeared? And then what if one day—not long from now—Gil Martin returned. Older, wiser, back from America. A man with a past and a future, a man no one was hunting."

Nicola sat up, turning to look down into his face. "Jack, are you serious?"

He nodded. "I don't want to live like this, hiding, meeting you in secret. I want...I want to call on you. To go riding with you in broad daylight." He reached up and took a strand of her hair in his hand, twining it around his fingers. "I want to squire you to the opera. Or a play. And I don't think that The Gentleman can do that."

"You're right." Nicola took his other hand, linking her fingers through his.

"You know, I have been a highwayman only the past few months. Before that Perry and I owned a business in Maryland. I am really a rather dull fellow."

"What about Richard?"

He grimaced. "I will never beggar him. All I can be is a thorn in his side. It has been amusing, but that hardly seems like enough for a life." Jack looked at her. "I hated him the most for taking you away from me. Now that I have you again..."

Nicola leaned forward and kissed him. After a few moments, she said, "What are you going to do? Is 'The Gentleman' just going to disappear?"

"We are going to carry out one last raid. Day after tomorrow, early in the morning, Exmoor has a wagon leaving the mine. It is going to be carrying a lot of money, more than we've ever gotten off him before. He has been storing it in a safe there, afraid to send it for two months because of the damage we've done him. He thinks to escape detection by sending it early in the morning and with no guard, disguising it as a common ore wagon. But we have informers inside the mine. So we will be waiting for it."

Nicola sat up, uneasiness stirring in her. "Are you sure? Must you make a last theft?"

"I could leave it. I told you, I had a business. We sold it, and I have the money. I could set up something here or back in the States. But I want to give the men one last big payoff. It will keep them going for a while. I hate to leave them at the mercy of Exmoor's jobs again."

"I see." It still made her uneasy. But Nicola understood his desire to make sure that his men were taken care of. It was one of the things she admired about him.

"Then The Gentleman will disappear," Jack said lightly. "After that, I believe that Gil will appear—in London, perhaps? It might be better to have some time between the two events here."

Nicola nodded. "I am usually in London, anyway. But Deborah wanted me to stay with her through the birth of her child. And I have to stay here for a wedding next month."

"I don't think I want to be in London without you that long," Jack mused. "Perhaps Gil will have to return to his home after all." He grinned. "At least you've fixed up my inheritance for me."

Nicola rolled her eyes. Then she leaned against him, curling her arm around his waist. "Promise me that you will be careful."

"I will." He kissed the top of her head.

"I must leave soon," she said with a sigh. "Stone will get suspicious if I stay in the Falkners' house much longer."

"I know." He slid his hand down her hair, then touched his lips softly to hers. "I will see you soon."

"When? How?"

"I'm not sure." He grinned. "Perhaps I shall simply show up at your front door."

Nicola left soon after that, blushing a little as she passed through the main room of the house, where Maggie sat, holding her baby and rocking. But Maggie only smiled at her and stood up to walk her to the door.

Nicola turned at the door. "If that man Stone should come here asking about my visit—"

"That one!" Maggie made a disgusted face. "He'll not learn anything here."

"Don't hold back so much that it seems suspicious. You can say that the wee one had an earache, but that I soothed it with drops and now she is all right."

"He won't be surprised at our not talking. No one in the village will talk to him. Thinks he can buy us. Get us to betray our own for money!"

"Thank you." Nicola smiled at the woman and opened the door. "Take care."

"Yes'm, you too."

Nicola did not see Stone, but she had little doubt he was there. Hal came up to untie her horse and help Nicola into the saddle, nodding to her and smiling. Nicola thanked him also, then turned her horse and headed into town. She had no desire to see anyone. She only wanted to hug her happy knowledge to herself, to ride home and think about Jack and their future. However, she knew that at any other time, if she had ridden into town on an errand of mercy like this, she would probably also have taken the opportunity to drop by and visit some people—the vicar's wife, for instance. Besides, it was difficult to resist the impish urge to make Mr. Stone spend even more of his day uselessly.

However, today she did not think she could bear the vicar's wife, who was sweet but rather dull. She was much too excited for that. So she rode over to the inn for a bit of refreshment and a little chat with Lydia, the innkeeper's lady. After that, she allowed herself to turn homeward.

The most difficult thing, she found, was damping down her excitement in front of her sister and Richard that evening. She could scarcely go around grinning at nothing without arousing their curiosity, and she had no explanation for her sudden happiness. So she strove all evening to appear calm and unexcited, succeeding above her expectations, apparently, for Deborah worriedly asked her if she was feeling well.

Nicola seized the opportunity to admit that she had a headache and say that she thought she would retire early and put lavender water on her temples. Then she fled upstairs and closed herself in her room, lying down on her bed and at last allowing herself to contemplate the rosiness of her future.

Jack had as good as said that he loved her, hadn't he? He was, after all, giving up his revenge on Richard in order to be with her. She smiled dreamily, remembering his words about missing her and wanting to be with her. *Perhaps he had not mentioned marriage or love, but he was committing himself to her. Surely he must have realized that he had been wrong about her betraying him.*

She lay looking up at the tester over her head, imagining introducing Jack to Marianne and Penelope, to all her friends. She chuckled as she pictured Richard's reaction when he saw him. He would be angry—and perhaps just a tad frightened that Jack might reveal the perfidious thing he had done to him ten years ago. She stopped for a moment, worried that Richard might try to kill Jack to keep him from talking, as he had obviously done with Mr. Fuquay a few months ago. But, she reassured herself, Fuquay would have been able to implicate him in more serious crimes, crimes committed against members of Society—things that would have gotten him ostracized from his own class at the very least. A former stable boy's assertion that Exmoor had had him pressed into the navy would hardly cause even a ripple among the Ton. And even Richard was bound to have gotten over his jealousy in the past ten years.

A more realistic concern was whether he might connect Jack's sudden reappearance with the disappearance of The Gentleman. But she did not see how he could be certain of it. Only Perry and the men Jack had brought with him knew that he was one and the same person. The local men—except, now, for Hal Falkner—had never seen him without a mask, according to the town's gossip. So even if someone could be persuaded to talk, they would not know that Jack was the highwayman. Richard would not have any proof. And suspicions would not be enough to get Jack arrested.

So she settled back into a rosy contemplation of the future.

She remained in her happy state throughout the next day—until late in the evening, when her sister came into her room to say good-night. Deborah looked a little troubled, but shrugged it off when Nicola asked her what was the matter.

But after a few moments of small talk, she said, "Nicola...do you think there are men from the village among the highwaymen?"

Nicola, who had been only half paying attention to her, turned to her sharply at that statement. "What? Why are you asking?"

"Because I heard Richard talking to that fellow Stone."

"And?"

"Well, I guess it's not really—I mean, he needs to protect his property and all, but this seems so cold-blooded!" Deborah raised troubled eyes to her sister.

"What seems cold-blooded?" Nicola asked, her nerves tightening in her stomach. "What did he say?"

"They were talking about their plans. It has gotten out, apparently, that Richard is shipping a large amount of money tomorrow morning. But it's only a ruse. The wagon isn't full of money. It will be full of men—with guns." Deborah bit her lip and looked at her sister. "He has put out lies about the wagon carrying a lot of money, and when the highwaymen open the back of the wagon, the men will open fire. They're planning to kill the highwayman and all his men!"

CHAPTER SIXTEEN

NICOLA FELT AS IF SHE COULD NO LONGER breathe. "They—what? They are going to simply shoot them all down?"

"As many as they can, I suppose," Deborah answered. "I know that they are criminals, and they have been stealing from us. And if they get caught, most likely they will hang. But at least they will have had a trial first. This…" She shivered. "I don't know, it seems more like murder."

"It *is* murder," Nicola retorted grimly. "I can't believe that anyone, even Richard— What am I talking about? Of course Richard would. His money is more important to him than other men's lives." Nicola began to pace. "Deborah, we cannot let this happen."

"How can we stop it?" Deborah asked. "I came to tell you because it bothered me. I mean, what if they kill some of the men from the village? But I don't know how I could stop it. Richard would not listen to me—nor, I think, would he care for your opinion. Sometimes he seems to unaccountably dislike you."

"No doubt he does. However, I don't really need to persuade Richard not to have the men shot," Nicola pointed out. "He cannot shoot them if they are not there. If they know it is a ruse and do not fall for his bait…"

"You are going to tell them?" Deborah asked, wide-eyed. "But how?"

"I can find them," Nicola said grimly, starting toward her wardrobe.

"You know who they are?" Deborah asked. "Where they live? How? Richard said that you were thick as thieves with them, but I didn't believe him." Deborah frowned, troubled. "They are criminals, Nicky. I know that you are very fond of—of some odd sorts of people, but…I mean, highwaymen! They have been taking money from us for months now."

"And Richard has been taking money from everyone for years and years!" Nicola snapped back, whipping her nightgown off over her head and pulling on the skirt of her riding habit. "Honestly, Deborah—do you have no idea what your husband is like? Or how people feel about him?"

"What are you talking about?" Deborah asked, paling.

"I am talking about the fact that Richard is a wicked man! No, I cannot condone their taking money from him or anyone else. But much of the money they have taken goes to people in the village, people Richard has wronged! He squeezes money from his tenants. He is universally disliked. He pays the men who risk their lives down in the mines a mere pittance. He lays them off if they are ill. Have you any idea what it is like to have no food? To watch your children starve? Of course they despise him. Of course they are happy to take his money. They feel as if they are getting some of their own back. Why do you think the villagers protect these men? Hide their identity? They would not do the same if it were Bucky's money they were taking."

"No…" Deborah said weakly, staring at her sister.

"I haven't the time to talk about this now," Nicola said, finishing up her buttons. "I have to get to them tonight. But promise me one thing, Deborah." She went to her sister and took her by the arm, staring earnestly into her eyes. "Do not go to your husband about this. Don't tell Richard that I have gone to warn them. You know that it is wrong of him to kill them in cold blood like that. If he should try to come after me, to stop me—" Her gray eyes blazed.

"I will not tell him," Deborah promised. "But you will take care...please."

"I will be as safe as I can." Nicola turned away to sit down and pull on her stockings and boots. "But I have to slip out of the house unnoticed. I cannot let Stone follow me. Does he watch my movements this late at night? Do you know?"

"I don't know. Richard said only that he worried about you, that he wanted someone competent to watch over you. You *are* his responsibility, you know, because you are under his roof. And you are my sister."

Nicola started to dispute Richard's motives, but she stopped. There was no point in trying to make her sister see the truth about Richard now, and there was no time for it, either. "I cannot afford to have him follow me tonight. I must make sure he does not."

"How?"

"I'm not sure." Nicola glanced around. "Do you have something heavy in your room? A paperweight?"

Deborah nodded. "Yes, I have a paperweight."

"Good, let me have it. I may need to have a weapon. More and more I think Alexandra is right. I should carry a gun."

"A gun!" Deborah stared. "You're joking."

"No. Alexandra carried one in her reticule when she was in danger in London. She told me that I should, too, when I venture into the seedier parts of London. I see her point now."

Deborah blinked. "I must say, Nicola, the Countess's new granddaughter sounds a trifle odd."

"She grew up in America," Nicola explained.

"Oh." Deborah seemed to take that as explanation enough.

She went with Nicola to her room and handed her a small, heavy lead crystal paperweight, which Nicola tucked into her pocket. Then they slipped down the stairs, unlocked the side door, and Nicola went out into the dark garden.

She heard her sister close the door after her. She hoped that Deborah would have nerve and family loyalty enough to not go to her husband with the news that Nicola was betraying his plan to the highwaymen. Hopefully, even if Deborah told Richard, she would wait long enough that he would not be able to catch up with her.

Nicola walked quickly through the dark garden, sticking close to the side of the house, where, wrapped in her dark cloak, with the hood pulled far forward to hide her face, she was little more than another shadow among the shadows. When she reached the corner of the house closest to the stables, she stopped and looked across the yard toward the stables. The yard looked immensely long. With not even a tree or bush between the stables and the house, she would be exposed to any watching eye. She could only hope that neither Stone nor Richard would be up, watching. She started to step out of the covering trees, and it was then that she saw the dot of red light flare and die about twenty feet away from her.

She froze. It came again, and she realized what it was. Someone was smoking a cigar, standing beneath one of the oak trees. The red flare came every time he inhaled. Nicola edged closer, making her way to another tree and peering

out from behind it. She was close enough now that she
could make out his features, and she was almost certain
that the man was Stone. He stood leaning against the tree
trunk, where he could see the kitchen entrance to the
house, as well as the stables and the yard in between the
two. *Did he do this every night on the chance that she
might sneak out of the house and ride to meet Jack? Or
perhaps he was simply enjoying an evening smoke before
turning in for the night.* Whatever the reason he was here,
she could not risk him seeing her and following her.

Nicola reached beneath her cloak and put her hand in
her pocket. Her hand closed around the oblong glass paperweight. Pulling it from her pocket, she crept noiselessly through the dark. She hated the thought of attacking
a man who was not expecting it, but desperation drove her.
When she was directly behind him, she raised her hand and
brought it down full force upon his head. Stone made an
odd noise and crumpled to the ground.

Nicola stepped around him and ran toward the stables.
They were dark. She felt sure that the grooms had all gone
to bed; they had to rise early in the morning. She could
sneak in and get her horse, she thought. She knew that she
could saddle and bridle it; she had done so before. The
only problem would be making little enough noise that she
did not wake one of the grooms and bring him down to investigate. She also had to move quickly. There was no
telling how long Stone would be knocked out. She wished
fleetingly that she had had something to tie him up with.

Softly she tiptoed down the center corridor to her
horse's stall. Grabbing a bridle, she slipped inside the stall
and put it on, then led the animal out. As silently as she
could, she put a saddle on the mare, her nerves jangling
the whole time, expecting at any moment for a groom to

come down the stairs. No one did, however, and she led the horse out the door and through the yard. Across the way, she could see a dark shape on the ground beneath an oak. Stone was still unconscious.

She continued leading the horse until they were some distance from the stable. She climbed up onto a low stone wall to mount, and then, with a last glance back to make sure no one had seen her, she kicked the mare in the ribs and started off.

Nicola rode swiftly along the path and through the meadow, knowing that it would be slow-going once she got to the woods. She prayed that she really could remember the way to the hideout. She had paid attention that once because she had felt challenged to remember it, but the next two times, when Jack had been with her, she had not paid full attention. Also, those times she had been going from the hideaway to Granny Rose's cottage, not the Exmoor home.

The moon was up, and she made good time, though she dared not give her horse its head. Once she reached the woods, she perforce had to slow down. She wound her way through the trees, crossing the brook. Once she took a wrong turn, and for a few minutes she was afraid that she was lost, but then she recognized a fallen tree ahead. She was simply on the wrong side of it, so she was able to cross it and get back on her course.

She could hear the rustle of night animals and sometimes the crack of twigs. Once an owl hooted not ten feet from her and made her jump. She kept on, ignoring the night sounds, and finally, up ahead of her, she saw the small house. She let out a little cry of relief and pushed her horse toward the dark cottage. When she reached it, she slid off, tying her horse to the railing, and ran up onto the stoop, crying out Jack's name. She pounded on the door, calling him.

A moment later there was the thunder of feet on the stairs inside and the sound of a bolt being shot back. Jack opened the door. He wore trousers and had hastily donned a shirt, for it hung unopened. His hair was rumpled, his eyes sleepy.

"Nicola!" He pulled her inside and closed the door. "What is it? What's the matter? What are you doing here?"

Behind him, Perry and two other men came down the stairs, rubbing their faces and staring at her.

"You cannot go tomorrow morning!" Nicola cried. "It's a trap."

"A trap! What do you—the load of money?" Jack asked.

"Yes! Deborah overheard Richard and Stone talking. There is no money. The wagon is going to be full of men, and they will shoot you or seize you. You can guess which is more likely."

He let out a curse and ran his hand back through his hair. Nicola reached out and laid her hand on his arm.

"You can't go."

"I understand. It's just—I am still trying to take it in." Suddenly, behind them, the door was flung wide open and several men rushed in. Nicola whirled and saw the men running at them, guns in their hands, and she let out a shriek. A shot rang out, the ball smacking into the wall above the stairs, stopping everyone where they stood.

Richard strode into the room, saying, "Well, well, Nicola, good work. You led us right to them." He looked past her toward the stairs. "Now, who have we—"

He came to such an abrupt stop that the small man following him bumped into his back. The blood drained from his face. In any other situation, his expression would have been comical. "Holy Christ! You!"

"My sentiments exactly," Jack replied crisply.

"I never thought I would see the day," Richard said, almost musingly. Then he snapped out an order to his men. "Tie them up. We're taking them back to gaol." He cast a glance at the small man who had followed him in. "Well, Constable, I hope you are pleased with what we've netted here."

"How could you do this?" Nicola started toward Richard, fists clenched. "How could you do this? You used me!"

When the men rushed in, she had realized, with a sickening feeling in her stomach, how Richard had manipulated her. It was the *story* of the trap that had really been the trap. Richard had cleverly induced her to run to Jack, thus revealing his location to Richard's men, who had obviously followed her. *Had even Stone's watching for her been part of the ruse?* Once she had disabled him, she had not even thought to watch for anyone else following her.

"You are despicable! How can you call yourself a human being?" Nicola said furiously while Richard watched her, a faint smile on his face. "You made me think that he was in danger so that you—I could kill you with my bare hands."

"Well, Nicola." Jack's voice cut through her words, low but deadly, and Nicola swung around, stung by the tone of contempt with which he spoke her name. When she saw the sneer on his mouth, her heart went cold inside her.

"You have managed to do it again," Jack continued, looking at her as he would at a snake. "I never thought you could, but somehow you did. You made me believe you, even after what you had done to me. And you betrayed me again."

"No!" Nicola's word came out a whisper. She felt as if he had punched her in the stomach. *Jack thought she had led the men to him on purpose!* "I didn't!"

"I'm not that big a fool," Jack said bitterly.

"It's not true," Nicola protested, tears welling in her eyes. "Please, Jack, don't look at me like that. I did not betray you!"

"Really, Nicola," Richard said smoothly. "Why bother to lie to him now? It's obvious that you gave him to me, just as you did ten years ago." He glanced at Jack, saying, "Talented, isn't she? I am sure any number of men have fallen under her spell."

"Stop it! How dare you say that I helped you?" Nicola cried out. "I would as soon help a snake!" She whipped back around, saying, "Jack, please…"

"Take me out of here, Constable," Jack said, looking away from her. "I cannot stand the stench of treachery in this room."

Nicola felt as if her heart had died within her. Jack did not believe her. Once again he was lost to her, hated her. Even worse, she *had* betrayed him to his enemies, however unknowingly. He had every right to hate her. She had been foolish and impulsive, so driven by her fear for him that she had not stopped to think. She had been an easy pawn for Exmoor to use. And now…now Jack would die because of her mistake.

She watched in horror as the constable and the hired men led Jack and the others out the door. More men were coming toward them from the small building in back, and another man walked with them, hands tied. Nicola walked to the doorway and stood, watching numbly, as another man led out several horses. Jack and his men were mounted, hands tied behind their backs. Richard strode past her and got on his horse. The procession started out, with Richard and the constable in front. Only Nicola remained behind, standing on the front stoop, watching Jack disappear from her life again, hating her.

The tears began to flow in earnest, and she could not stop them. She sank down onto the stoop, sobbing.

AFTER HER BOUT OF TEARS, Nicola went inside the small house and wandered upstairs. She went into Jack's room and sat down on his bed, closing her eyes. She could sense him all around her. There was the faint scent of him on his pillow, a shirt that he had worn thrown across a chair, the rumpled, turned-back bed that he had hastily left.

Nicola swallowed hard and squeezed her eyes shut. She had indulged her tears, and she refused to do so again. She had to do something. She thought for some time and finally rose with renewed purpose. She was not going to let Jack rot in gaol, much less hang. Whatever it took, she would get him out.

She rode to Buckminster Hall. Penelope had said that Bucky and the others were planning to arrive the evening before. She hoped that they had. When she arrived at Buckminster Hall, it was the middle of the night, and it took a long, steady pounding of the door knocker to finally bring a sleepy-eyed footman to the door. His powdered footman's wig was clapped crookedly on his head, and he had misbuttoned his livery jacket. He stared at her for a long moment.

"Miss Falcourt?" he asked finally.

"Yes. I have come to see my cousin. Is he here?"

"Lord Buckminster? Why, yes, miss, he rode in last night, him and Lord Lambeth. Lord and Lady Thorpe came, too, in a carriage."

"I have to talk to Lord Buckminster."

"Now, miss?"

"Yes, of course now." Nicola gave him a level, commanding look. "Are you going to keep me on the step or let me in?"

"Oh, miss, I'm that sorry." He stepped back, looking alarmed and contrite. "I'm not thinking well. Please come in. But, miss, did you know it was three o'clock in the morning? His lordship's been in bed these two hours."

"I wouldn't have thought him that easily accustomed to country hours. I am sorry, but you will have to wake him up. I must speak to him. It is urgent. Or, if you like, I will wake him myself. I know where his room is."

"Miss!" The bewigged young man looked shocked. "That would never do. I will tell him you are here."

She cooled her heels in the entryway for a good fifteen minutes before Bucky appeared, dressing gown thrown over a nightshirt and billowing out behind him as he walked. He was frowning anxiously.

"Nicola! What is it? What's the matter?"

"Everything." Nicola rose to meet him. "I must talk to you. I did a terrible thing tonight, and I sincerely hope that you can make it right. I need for you to go to the magistrate and see him about a prisoner."

"Prisoner!" He looked dumbfounded. "Whatever are you talking about?"

"It's the highwayman. The constable arrested him and his men tonight, and it was all my fault. Richard tricked me into it, and I was too stupid to see that it was a trick."

"I am afraid you have lost me. What does Richard have to do with all this? Now that I think of it, what do you?"

"I told you, it was my fault that he was arrested." Quickly she explained how Richard had tricked her, getting her to lead his men to the outlaw's hideout.

"But who is this chap? Why do you know him?" Bucky asked.

Nicola hesitated. No matter how kind and good her cousin was, Bucky was still an aristocrat and a male relative, and she did not think that he would be overjoyed to hear that she was in love with a highwayman. Finally she said, "He is Granny Rose's grandson. Do you remember her?"

"The old woman who cured people? By Jove, yes, sent my valet to her for one of my colds once, and she fixed me right up. Weren't you forever going over to her house?"

"Yes. I was very fond of her, and she of me. She taught me so many things, and—and I cannot let her only grandchild be hanged. Please, Bucky, I beg of you. Use your influence. The magistrate is good friends with your mother, and I know he would do you a favor."

"I suppose he would."

"Jack will leave here and never return. I am sure he will promise that. He would even agree to leave the country if necessary. He has lived in the United States the last few years."

"Then what the devil is he doing here, being a highwayman?" Bucky asked reasonably.

"It is much too complicated to explain. But, believe me, he does not deserve to hang. He doesn't even deserve to be in gaol. I swear to you that he has harmed no one—well, except Richard, and that was only financial. Richard, of course, talks as if he is the most dangerous highwayman since Dick Turpin, but he is a good man. Really."

"I shall talk to the Squire." Bucky referred to Squire Halsey, the local magistrate. "Tomorrow morning," he added hastily. "Wouldn't do to wake him up, you know."

"Yes, you're right." Nicola had to admit the logic of that, even though she wished that he would get dressed and ride to the magistrate's house right now and haul him out of bed.

"Best if you stayed here and went to bed, too, you know," Bucky pointed out. "Not the thing to be tearing about in the middle of the night."

Nicola knew that he was right. She did not feel in the least sleepy, but she knew that there was nothing that she could accomplish in the middle of the night. Nor could she return to Tidings right now. She wanted to see Richard, but no doubt he had gone to bed, and no amount of bullying would get him awakened as it had her cousin. She refused to sleep another night under his roof. So, finally, she agreed to stay in her old room at Buckminster Hall.

She slept little, however, too troubled and unhappy to give way to sleep. Early the next morning, she dressed in the same habit she had worn the night before and started back to Tidings.

Although it was early, Richard and Deborah were up. Nicola could hear the sound of their raised voices coming from the dining room, and she turned in that direction. She paused in the doorway. Exmoor and her sister were standing, quarreling, their food ignored on the grand table beside them.

"But you cannot leave her alone there!" Deborah was saying with some heat, her cheeks flushed with anger.

"She's lucky I didn't have her arrested, too, for aiding and abetting a criminal!"

"She has a kind heart."

"She has a meddlesome nature and an unnatural proclivity for the lowest sorts of people."

Nicola stepped into the room, saying, "She is right here."

Richard and Deborah swung around to face her.

"Nicola!" Deborah cried, starting toward her, arms outstretched. "I was so worried about you!"

"Did you know his plan?" Nicola asked coldly, stopping her sister with a look. "Did you tell me that about the trap because he told you to?"

Deborah looked hurt, and her hand came up to her chest. "No! Nicola, how could you think that I would send you into danger like that? I had no idea. I overheard them talking, so I went to you."

"I am sorry." Nicola went to her sister, opening her arms, too. It occurred to her that now she understood some of what Jack had felt ten years earlier when Richard had said Nicola had betrayed him. She had been doubting her sister from the moment the real trap was sprung. All night, beneath her distress, was the disturbing fear that Deborah had helped Richard to trick her.

Thankfully, she drew her into a hug now. "I know you would not hurt me," she whispered to her sister. "I just— I scarcely know what to think right now."

"I know. You must be exhausted. Where have you been?"

Nicola shook her head. "It's not important."

"You should go to bed. Come, I'll go up with you."

"No. I came to talk to Richard." Nicola straightened, releasing her sister and turning grimly toward Exmoor. "I have come to beg you to let him go."

"Let him go?" Richard gaped at her. "You must be joking."

"I have never been more serious. You do not need to do this. He was about to leave the area, anyway." Nicola moved closer to him.

"Of course he was." Richard sneered and turned away.

"Haven't you done enough to him?" Nicola cried, tears springing to her eyes. "I know you recognized him. You know what you did to him ten years ago. You ruined his life. Is it any wonder that he hated you? That he wanted some vengeance on you?"

"What are you talking about?" Deborah asked. "I don't understand. Richard *knows* this man?"

"Yes, he knows him. 'The Gentleman' is Gil Martin."

"Gil Martin?" Deborah repeated blankly.

"Yes. Granny Rose's grandson."

Deborah drew in her breath sharply. "No! Gil? The boy that Mother—"

She stopped abruptly. Nicola turned to her, curiosity aroused. "That Mother what? What did Mother ever have to do with Gil?"

Deborah looked uncomfortable, and she glanced toward her husband. He simply folded his arms and gazed back at her sardonically.

"Yes, Deborah, why don't you tell your sister about what your mother had to do with Gil? What you had to do with it."

"You?" Nicola took a step toward Deborah, her hand going to her sister's arm. "You had something to do with Gil? And Mother? Tell me, Deborah."

Deborah looked away. "I...you were locked in your room, and one of the maids, Mary Broughton—you know, the girl you usually used as your personal maid—brought a letter to me. She said you wouldn't answer her, and Granny Rose had given her this letter for you. Granny Rose had come to Buckminster Hall to see you—with this letter."

"What—what did you do with it?"

"I didn't know what to do with it, so finally I—I read it." She blushed and looked at Nicola a little defiantly. "I'm sorry. I didn't know what was in it, and I thought I would see if it was something important, something you would want to be disturbed for, or just some little something Granny Rose wanted of you. Then I—I saw that the letter was really from Granny's grandson and—and it scared me. I didn't know what to do. I was afraid that you would run away and marry a stable boy! It would have been a terrible scandal and I would never have seen you again. I knew Mother would go into a horrid decline. The family would have been disgraced." She looked away and added softly, "I knew that no one would ever want to marry me, with a scandal attached to our name."

"No one? You mean Richard."

Deborah nodded, looking wretched. "I am sorry, Nicola. I was young and—and I had no idea. You had never spoken of him."

"Of course not. I knew how you and Mother would have reacted."

"But I didn't know how much you loved him. I thought it was just calf love. Shallow and quickly gone. I didn't know that you would never marry. That you would be so unhappy and go off to London to live. And then...when I saw how you felt, I was afraid to tell you."

"So you gave the letter to Mother?"

"Yes. She sent a note to Richard, and he came around. They talked. I didn't hear what was said. But Richard left, and we never heard from Gil Martin again."

"No. You wouldn't have. Richard gave him to a press gang, and they threw him into the hold of a naval ship."

Deborah's eyes widened. "No! Oh, Nicola..."

"Yes. A rather severe punishment, don't you think, for loving someone above his station. But, then, that wasn't the reason, was it, Richard?" Nicola swung back to him, her face hard and her eyes fiery. "You put him into servitude in the navy because he had taken the woman you wanted for yourself. Isn't that right? He had thwarted you. So you punished him—and punished him further by telling him that *I* was the one who had turned him over to you. You weren't content with sending him into hell. You had to break his heart, as well."

"Did you honestly think I would let him have you?" Richard thundered. "That I would let that—that scum touch you? Possess you? You were mine!"

"I was *never* yours!" Nicola shot back. "You would have known that if you hadn't been so arrogant. I never gave you the least encouragement. I let you know in a hundred different ways that I did not want you, but you would never acknowledge them."

"I knew you would have—if only he hadn't been in the way. It was all because of him. You were the only woman for me, the only woman I have ever loved! And that black-guard stole you from me!"

Deborah drew in her breath in a sharp hiss at his words. Nicola swung around. Deborah was pale, devastated by her husband's harsh words.

"Richard?" she asked tremulously, like a lost child. Her eyes filled with tears, threatening to spill over. "What do you mean? Did you never love me?"

"Oh, Christ!" Richard exclaimed in disgust, swinging out his hand and sending a vase toppling off a table. "Must you forever be mewling and whining? Of course I did not love you! Only a fool like you would have thought so! And *I* was a fool for having thought that you could replace her. Because you were her sister, I thought you must be like her, that you would have her wit and grace and spirit. I looked past all the insipid girlish airs and the foolish co-quettry. When you were married to me, when you were older, I thought you would be like her. But you were not. You couldn't even bear me an heir! You were useless! It didn't even make her jealous."

Tears streamed from Deborah's eyes, and she brought her hands up to hide her face as, sobbing, she sank into a chair.

He turned to Nicola, saying bitterly, "Why didn't you see what you had missed? I was sure you would regret your decision, would burn at seeing your sister have all the things that you could have had—money, Tidings, power!"

"I didn't want those things. All I wanted was the man I loved," Nicola replied fiercely. "You were a fool. You still are. Your wife is the only woman who loves you. Don't you know that? Look at how you treat her!"

Richard glanced at Deborah's huddled, weeping form and waved her away. "Do you think I care for that? She is a weak, sodden, missish girl. What do I care if she loves me? She isn't you! It was always you—you who plagued my dreams, who drove me wild. You were the woman I loved. She was nothing but a bad substitute."

"Love? You didn't love me! You wouldn't have the least idea how to love anyone. Your pride was wounded, perhaps. You were obsessed with the one thing you could not get by fair means or foul. That is the only reason why you wanted me. You didn't love me. The only person you love is yourself!"

"I should have turned you over to the constable, too! I wish to God I had."

"You would never do that. Then you wouldn't have been able to hurt Jack again. You had to trick him into thinking that I had betrayed him, make him hate me again. You would never have passed up that opportunity just for the sake of putting me in gaol. You are evil, Richard. I know you, and you are black to the core."

"Then leave!" he shouted. "Get out of my house. Go live with your beloved aunt—or maybe the Dowager Countess! You're thick as thieves with her now, aren't you?"

"Don't worry. I *am* leaving. I could not stay in the same house with you. You taint everything." She turned toward her sister. "I am sorry, Deborah. I know I promised you I would stay with you. But I cannot. I cannot live under the same roof with this monster."

She turned and started toward the door. Her sister's voice stopped her.

"No, wait!" Nicola turned back. Deborah looked at Nicola pleadingly, holding out her hand. "Wait," she said again. "I am leaving with you."

CHAPTER SEVENTEEN

IF NICOLA'S COUSIN AND AUNT, OR ANY OF their assorted guests, found anything peculiar about Nicola, her sister and their former nurse arriving with a few bags of their clothes piled on top of the carriage just as the Buckminsters and their company were sitting down to breakfast, they were all far too polite to say so. Aunt Adelaide was in the midst of describing in great detail the matching pair that she was purchasing for her future daughter-in-law when the butler ushered in her two nieces, his perfectly even voice indicating none of the surprise he had felt when he saw Miss Falcourt and Lady Exmoor, both looking a trifle bedraggled, standing on the doorstep of Buckminster Hall.

Aunt Adelaide, her mind still on the horses, smiled with real pleasure and said, "Nicola! Deborah! Come in. Sit down. How wonderful to see you. Would you like breakfast? Huggins, lay another two places."

"Thank you, Aunt, but no, please, if Deborah and I could just go to our rooms—that is—" Nicola broke off, glancing at the three guests awkwardly.

The two men, Lord Thorpe and Lord Lambeth, regarded them with British aplomb, not even raising an eyebrow at their sudden intrusion. The third person, Lady Thorpe, had been raised an American and was a great deal more forthright than the others. She stood up quickly, going over to the women.

"Nicola. Are you all right? What's happened?" Alexandra was a tall woman, with a statuesque figure, a cloud of dark curling hair and one of the most beautiful faces in the country. She could present an imposing figure, especially given her often blunt speech and unreserved American ways. However, she also had a kind heart and a ready warmth, and now she curved her arm around Nicola's shoulders, saying sympathetically, "You look all done in. I am sure you must need to rest."

"Yes, of course," Aunt Adelaide agreed. "You do look tired. No one's in your old rooms. Huggins, take them up."

"Thank you. I am sorry. I *would* like to rest, and Deborah is exhausted." Deborah, who had gotten little sleep the night before, having spent it pacing and worrying about her sister, and who had cried all the way over to Buckminster Hall in the carriage, was slumped against Nicola.

"Of course. Here, I'll help you," Alexandra said. With her usual efficiency, she took over, hustling the other women upstairs and putting them to bed, introducing herself to Deborah as she did so and carefully avoiding any prying questions about their disheveled appearance.

Once Alexandra had Deborah settled in her old room, with Nurse to care for her, she took Nicola to her room and helped her out of her dress and into bed, sending the maid for a pitcher of water and a glass, as well as a bite of breakfast. Then she sat down on the bed beside Nicola and looked her in the eye.

"What happened? It's Exmoor, isn't it? What has he done this time?"

Alexandra was not as close a friend to Nicola as

Penelope or Marianne. Although she was Marianne's sister
and the Countess's granddaughter, she had arrived in
England only a few months ago. During the time that Nicola
had met Marianne, Alexandra had been on her honeymoon
in Europe with Sebastian. However, she had a friendly,
frank way that put Nicola at ease, and Nicola suspected that
if she spent any time around her, she would grow to like her
as much as she liked Marianne. She was also not one to
mince words about a topic, a quality that Nicola admired.
Alexandra went straight to the heart of a matter.

Nicola found herself pouring out the entire story of
what had happened, starting with her love for the stable
boy and Richard's wicked interference. When she reached
the part about the highwayman, Alexandra exclaimed,
"The highwayman? *Our* highwayman?"

Nicola stared. "That is what Marianne said. How is he
your highwayman?"

"He helped Thorpe and me. Remember that balloon
ride we got trapped on? He was the one who gave us
shelter that night." She grinned impishly. "Of course, he
managed to take Thorpe's wallet, too, which I don't think
he has yet forgiven. We had to ride the mail coach all the
way back to London."

Nicola smiled, tears suddenly springing to her eyes.
"That sounds like Jack. Oh, Alexandra, what am I to do?
I love him! And he's in gaol—and he despises me,
anyway!"

"Well, tell me the rest of the story. How did he wind up
in gaol? I warrant that was Richard's doing."

"Of course. He hates him." Nicola explained how
Richard had tricked her into betraying Jack's location and
Jack's assumption that she had meant to do it.

"What a coil," Alexandra said, when Nicola had finally

wound down. "Well, I will make sure that Bucky goes over to this magistrate today and pleads your highwayman's case. I'll send Lambeth and Thorpe, as well, for they both owe him for what he has done for them. Three lords ought to intimidate a squire, don't you think?"

Nicola smiled. "I am sure they will."

Alexandra smiled back and gave her a reassuring hug. "Don't worry. I will get right on it. You just get some sleep. You'll see. It will all look better when you have had some rest."

NICOLA DID FEEL BETTER WHEN SHE awoke that afternoon. She was at least rested. However, the sleep had done nothing for her anxiety over Jack, and she dressed quickly, sweeping her hair up into a simple bun, and went downstairs to see what Bucky had been able to accomplish.

She found him down in the formal drawing room, along with all the others. Marianne and Penelope had come over, having learned that Bucky's group had arrived. Marianne was happily ensconced next to her fiancé, her blue eyes glowing and her hand tucked into his. Lambeth, a handsome man with blond hair and cool gray eyes, was obviously entranced by her. Penelope, shyer and more reserved, contented herself with looking at Bucky lovingly.

Alexandra, sitting beside her dark, sardonic Thorpe, was obviously teasing the lovebirds with all the worldliness of a woman married three months. When she saw Nicola in the doorway she smiled, saying, "Come in, Nicola, and save us from all this prenuptial bliss."

"As if you didn't still turn all gooey and glowing whenever Sebastian comes into the room," her sister Marianne retorted good-naturedly. "Hello, Nicola. It's good to see you again."

There were all the greetings to get through, but Nicola was interested in only one thing, and when at last she had said hello to everyone in the room, she turned to Bucky, her eyes intent on his face. "Well? Did you talk to the magistrate? What did he say?"

Bucky looked uncomfortable. "Frankly…it wasn't good. I pressed him, Nicola. So did Justin and Sebastian. Thing is, Exmoor's out for the man's blood. He is adamant about keeping him in gaol and charging him. Poor Halsey's too scared of Exmoor to thwart him. Well, Richard is the wealthiest and most powerful landowner hereabouts. I am only a baron, not an earl, you know, and our lands are not as extensive. And Justin and Sebastian aren't local, so even though Justin's a marquess and all, his pleas don't weigh as much with the local magistrate. I am sorry, Nicky. Normally I think Halsey would let him out despite his crimes if Mother and I asked him to, but with Exmoor watching him like a hawk, he doesn't dare."

"I hate that man!" Nicola exclaimed with venom. "Richard doesn't even deserve to live. It is shameful that he can have so much control over other people's lives!" She whirled and began to pace the room.

Marianne and Alexandra glanced at each other and Penelope worriedly. All of them hated to see their friend so forlorn, and it seemed especially awful in the face of their own great happiness. Penelope rose and went to her friend.

"Nicola…"

Nicola turned. "No, I'm all right. You cannot do anything for me. I am not in despair. I know what I have to do." Her face was set and grim, her gray eyes blazing with determination.

"Nicky?" The look on her face unnerved Penelope. "What do you mean? What do you have to do?"

"Set him free," Nicola replied evenly. "If influence won't do it, then I have to use a more direct route."

"Nicola! You're going to get him out of gaol? But how? That's illegal!"

"As if I care for that. I'm not sure how, just yet. I have to think about it."

"Nicola!" Penelope looked toward the others for help. "Marianne, tell her."

"Well," Marianne said reasonably, "I can't see what else she can do, really."

"Marianne!" The redhead shrugged. "I'm sorry. But it's the truth. If Justin were in gaol, that is what I would do."

Alexandra nodded. "Me too."

"Alexandra!"

"Wouldn't you? If Bucky were facing certain hanging?" Penelope looked at her for a moment. "Well…yes. But it's so dangerous."

"Quite right," Lambeth spoke up. "We can't have Nicola dashing about breaking into gaol."

Penelope turned toward him gratefully. "There. You see?"

"So I shall do it," Lambeth continued calmly.

"What?" Nicola turned to him. "But you—why?"

"The man saved Marianne's life. Mine, too. I promised him then that if I could ever do him a good turn, I would. I certainly can't turn my back on him, and I hardly think talking to a magistrate discharges me from my obligation to him."

Marianne looked at him, a worried frown on her face, and Nicola thought that Marianne would exclaim that he could not do it. Instead, she said, "But it is dangerous. You should not do it alone. I will go with you."

"You?" Lambeth's brows drew together thunderously.

"Absolutely not. You are staying right here. I shall need an alibi, and you can provide it."

"But you cannot go alone—" Nicola began.

"He won't be alone," Lord Thorpe put in. "I shall go with him. I owe the man, too. It will be much better with two of us."

"Three," Alexandra corrected him calmly. "I dare swear I am as good a shot as either of you, and I certainly am not letting you go without me."

"Nor I," Marianne agreed. "We shall all four go."

Sebastian and Justin immediately burst into protests, and Bucky and Penelope chimed in, unwilling to let their friends go without them. The next thirty minutes were spent in fruitless argument over who should and should not go, until finally Thorpe let out a roar that silenced everyone.

"All right," he said, when everyone fell silent and turned toward him. "Now. Lambeth, I have learned through bitter experience that there is no stopping Alexandra once she has made up her mind. I dare swear her sister is the same way."

Lambeth scowled. "Yes. She definitely is."

"I might as well tell you that I am, as well," Nicola spoke up. "Jack is the man I love, and I am the one who is responsible for his getting caught. There is no way on earth that I am going to let you go rescue him without me."

"Oh, the devil take it!" Bucky exclaimed. "We shall all go. We'll be a bloody gang."

It took some talking after that, but finally it was agreed upon and a plan worked out. Marianne and Alexandra would provide the distraction for the gaoler. Lambeth and Thorpe would do the actual entering of the gaol and releasing of the prisoners. Nicola, much to her dismay, had to be content with riding with the men and·standing watch, holding their horses. They would be masked, but her form was unmistakably feminine, and her presence at the gaol would be a dead giveaway if anyone saw them. Penelope and Bucky, in the meantime, would provide the alibi for the entire group. They would make sure that the Countess and Lady Ursula, Penelope's mother, went to dinner with Lady Buckminster, getting them out of the Dower House. Then Penelope and Bucky would have a dinner at the Dower House, with the collusion of one or two trusted servants, which they would pretend was attended by all of them.

Nicola wanted to do it that evening. She could not get Jack out of gaol fast enough. However, they all agreed that it would have to wait until the following night. It would take a while to arrange for the Countess and Lady Ursula to be out of the house, and that was an essential part of the plan. So, finally, Nicola agreed to wait.

She managed to get through the rest of the day. She and the other women persuaded Aunt Adelaide to invite the Countess and her daughter Ursula for a dinner and card party the next evening, which was not a difficult task. To further move things along, Nicola offered to pen the invitation for her aunt, one of the many social obligations her aunt disliked. After that, there was little she could do. It would be up to Penelope and Marianne, who were staying at the Dower House, to get things set up with the servants there. And Thorpe, whose servants were intensely loyal— and handier in a fight than run-of-the-mill servants— would have his coachman arrange for the extra horses for the escapees.

The only thing left that Nicola could do was to visit Jack in gaol. They agreed that it would be helpful if Jack and his men knew that rescue was on the way, so that they would be ready to run. Nicola was the only person among the group who was known to be acquainted with the highwayman. It would be better if there was no hint that either Lambeth or Thorpe knew him.

So early the next morning Nicola set out for the village gaol. She was greeted with astonishment by the constable, who was sitting with the gaoler in the large front room.

"Miss Falcourt! What are you doing here? This isn't a fit place for a lady."

"I have come to see the prisoner. Jack Moore."

"But, miss, ladies don't come here."

"I do."

"But, miss…it just ain't proper, like."

"Why don't you let me worry about the proprieties, Constable?" Nicola said with a cool smile. "Just take me to the prisoner."

The constable glanced around the room as if seeking help, then sighed and said, "Yes, miss."

Picking up the large key ring that sat on the gaoler's desk, he led her to the back of the gaol, where a barred door separated the cells from the front part of the building. One large key on the ring opened the door, and the constable passed through it. Nicola followed on his heels. He turned, startled, then sighed again and walked the rest of the way to Jack's cell.

There were four barred cells in the small gaol, and all of them were occupied by Jack and his men. Jack's men stood up as they walked by. Nicola glanced at Perry, and he winked, which raised her spirits a trifle. They stopped in front of the last cell. Jack was seated on the narrow bed, his back against the stone wall, legs stretched out in front of him. He sprang to his feet when he saw the constable, with Nicola at his shoulder.

"What the devil are you doing here?" he burst out. "Bloody hell! What did you let her in for?" He strode to the barred door to confront the constable, who stepped back a foot even though bars separated them.

"Uh, the lady is here to see you."

"I don't want to see her," Jack retorted, not looking at Nicola. "Take her away."

"Jack, please…just listen to me…."

"I am through listening to you!" He turned to her, his eyes blazing. "I refuse to listen any longer. Go away. I don't want to see you."

Pain slashed through Nicola's chest like a knife. "No. I didn't mean to harm you. You must believe me."

"I don't know what game you are playing," Jack said coldly. "If you are trying to get more information from me for your brother-in-law or what. But I have been tricked enough by you and your kind. I know how you and the Earl colluded to capture me. I'm not a fool. Even that day at Granny Rose's cottage, you had set me up for Stone to catch. You just hadn't counted on my knowing an escape route."

"No!" Nicola cried, aghast.

"Shut up!" Jack roared, overriding her words. "Get her out of here. I won't speak to her. I won't see her. Even a prisoner has some rights, doesn't he? I don't have to be plagued by her."

"Jack…" Nicola whispered. Her insides were as cold as ice; she wasn't sure if she could move or even if her lungs would continue to work. Clearly Jack hated her. There was no way she could convince him that she had not betrayed him to Richard. "I'm sorry." Tears welled up in her eyes and spilled over, coursing down her cheeks.

"Save your tears for someone who is more naive," Jack told her bitingly, and turned away, walking back to his cot.

Nicola whirled and ran back down the hall.

THE TWO WOMEN SHIFTED IN THE seat of the gig. It was late that afternoon, and it was growing dark. It was almost time for their charade to begin. Marianne lifted the opened pocket watch from her lap and looked at it again.

"That is the fifth time in the last two minutes that you have looked at that thing," Alexandra remarked, a faint smile curving her mobile mouth. She arched an eyebrow at her sister. "It's hard to imagine you being a thief, given your nerves."

"I'll match my courage against yours any day," Marianne shot back, but her smile took any sting from the words. "Just because I like to do everything right doesn't mean—"

"I know," Alexandra replied, regarding her sister with affection. "I didn't mean that. I meant that you must have suffered more than you enjoyed it."

"You're right about that," Marianne agreed. "Frankly, I am just as glad to leave a life of crime behind me," she said, referring to the years she had spent living with a family of thieves. She reached over to squeeze Alexandra's hand, "I'm also very glad to have found a sister."

"I am, too." Alexandra grasped her hand tightly.

They were silent for a moment. Marianne steadfastly did not look at her watch. It was Alexandra who broke first, saying, "All right. I give in. Is it time yet?"

With some relief, Marianne picked up the watch and looked at it. "One minute. Justin, Sebastian and Nicola should be leaving now."

They thought of the men they loved and the woman

who was their friend, riding toward the edge of town to wait in darkness for Alexandra and Marianne to do their job. Alexandra shivered, and Marianne thought she saw her lips move in a silent prayer.

"They will be all right," she said with more assurance than she felt.

"As long as we do our part well," Alexandra agreed, her jaw setting. It would, Marianne thought, take more than one poor gaoler to stop Alexandra when Sebastian's life was at stake.

"We will." Marianne straightened, the dancing nerves in her stomach giving way to the familiar excitement as the moment of action drew near. It had always been this way: she would be sick with nerves beforehand, but when the game began, she would be filled with confidence, excited but focused coolly on her objective. "Let's go."

Alexandra picked up the reins, which had been lying loosely in her lap, and slapped them over the horse's back. The animal stepped out smartly, opening up into a trot, then a run, at Alexandra's urging. They flew down the road at a smart pace. Marianne gripped the rail at the side of her seat and held on tightly as they whipped around a curve in the road. Alexandra had driven her own vehicle for years, she said, and her husband had been instructing her in the finer points of handling a team. Marianne felt sure she was an excellent driver. However, she was not so accustomed as her sister to this rapid form of conveyance and, frankly, her heart felt as if it were in her throat.

As if sensing Marianne's thought, Alexandra turned to her and grinned, her eyes sparkling with excitement. The wind caught her bonnet as she turned back and tore it from her head, sending it skittering down the road behind them. Alexandra laughed, unconcerned, as her hair began to tumble down. They were, after all, supposed to look as if they had been terrified by thieves. However, she pulled back on the reins, slowing the horse. It was dusk and growing increasingly dark, and she would not risk injuring her horse for the sake of an exhilarating ride.

She pulled him to a stop at the edge of town, and the two women got out of the carriage. The village, as she had expected, was quiet, with no one on the streets. It was dark, and all good citizens would be home enjoying their suppers. That was why they had planned it this way.

Alexandra's cheeks glowed pink from the ride and excitement, and her thick, curling black hair tumbled around her shoulders. She looked beautiful and faintly exotic as she grinned at her sister and unbuttoned the top two buttons of her dress, exposing an impressive cleavage.

"Are you ready?" Marianne cast an expressive eye at Alexandra's décolletage. "Did you stuff your chemise?"

"Nicola said we must distract them," Alexandra pointed out, her grin widened. "But I didn't stuff. Penelope, of all people, showed me a way to wrap a binding down and around and tie it, and *voilà!*"

"*Voilà* indeed," Marianne commented dryly.

"It isn't exactly as if you are unendowed," Alexandra pointed out as Marianne pushed the sides of her cloak back, exposing a low-cut evening dress over which the tops of her soft white breasts spilled.

"I know." Marianne glanced down and had to giggle. "I pinned my dress in the back so it was too tight. It has been bloody difficult to breathe, I'll tell you."

"But well worth it," Alexandra said. "Here, take that off. We want him to see all that glorious fiery hair, after all." She reached over and pushed Marianne's hat back, so that it fell off and hung dangling behind her by its ribbons. "There. I think we look perfect. Ready?"

Marianne nodded, and the sisters climbed out of the gig. Going to the horse's head, Alexandra backed him up, talking soothingly to him, until the left wheel of the little conveyance was hanging perilously in open air over the ditch. Another few steps and the vehicle would probably tumble over. Marianne ran to stick a rock under the other wheel to lock it so that that very thing would not happen. They needed a disabled vehicle, but also one that they could leave in quickly. Alexandra tied the reins around the nearby railing of a fence to keep the horse on a short lead.

Having secured things as best they could, Marianne and Alexandra looked at each other, lifted their skirts and started running down the street. They ran to the gaol, not a long distance, but carefully out of sight of the gig. They threw open the door to the gaol and staggered dramatically into the room, shrieking.

The gaoler, a middle-aged man of bovine appearance, sat at a desk across the room, in the midst of eating a cold supper. He looked up at the sudden entrance of the two women, and his jaw dropped. He stared dumbly, adding to his resemblance to a cow.

Alexandra, who had kept her skirts clutched up to expose the lower part of her legs, dropped them and lurched forward, her hand going to her breast like an amateur thespian in the throes of great emotion.

"Oh, sir!" she cried, her husky voice reverberating through the room. "You must help us! We have been attacked!"

"Attacked!" She would not have thought it possible, but the man's eyes grew even larger and rounder.

"Yes!" Marianne added her voice to the scene, and she

and Alexandra rushed toward the gaoler, their hands extended. "By highwaymen. It was awful! Awful!"

"Highwaymen! But there ain't any highwaymen now," the gaoler protested, looking confused. "They're all locked up."

"I tell you they attacked us!" Alexandra cried, reaching out and seizing the man's hand. She took a step closer to him, her bosom heaving. The gaoler's eyes went immediately down to her breasts and fastened there.

"Uh…mmm…that is…"

"You must help us," Marianne said, stepped up beside him and laying her hand entreatingly on his arm. "Lambeth will be furious when he hears about this."

"Lambeth?" The name caught his attention. The gaoler turned to look at her.

"Yes. The Marquess of Lambeth, my fiancé."

"The Duke of Storbridge's son," Alexandra added for emphasis.

"Sweet Lord," the beleaguered man breathed. "Then you—you're the one staying with the Countess? Her granddaughter, they say?"

"Yes. And I am her other granddaughter, Lady Thorpe," Alexandra supplied.

The gaoler looked thoroughly stunned now, reeling from the double blows of their titles and their amply exposed bosoms.

"You must help us," Alexandra repeated, impatience beginning to creep into her voice.

"Yes, you must!" Marianne hooked her hand beneath the gaoler's arm and started propelling him toward the door. "You must come with us."

"Where?"

"The scene of the crime, of course," Alexandra explained, linking her arm through the gaoler's other arm.

"Oh, of course. But best I fetch the constable," he said, stopping, his brow furrowing in thought. "And the magistrate."

"What good can the magistrate do?" Alexandra exclaimed. "We need help now! And we need someone young and strong."

"Yes, we must hurry," Marianne urged, pulling him forward. "We might still be able to catch them."

"What?" The gaoler came to a dead stop again, his face paling. "Catch them!"

"Don't be silly, Marianne," Alexandra said quickly, seeing the man's expression. "The thieves won't have hung around for us to bring help. They are long gone, I am sure. But we must get the gig out of the ditch."

The gaoler looked relieved. "Oh, aye. Wait—I nearly forgot. The keys." He turned back to the desk, on which lay a large ring of keys.

Alexandra let out a gusty sigh, rolled her eyes and flopped over against his chest.

"Oh, no, she fainted!" Marianne cried. "Oh, dear! What shall we do? Lord Thorpe will be furious with me. It was all my idea to take a turn in the gig this afternoon, you see, but then we waited too long, and dusk came, and…"

Marianne continued to chatter while the gaoler looked around, obviously at a loss as to what to do with a member of the nobility fainting in his arms. Finally he lowered Alexandra to the floor and looked up at Marianne for guidance.

"Get some water," she suggested, and the man took off at a shambling run. Marianne dropped to her knees beside Alexandra, and Alexandra opened one eye.

"Is he gone?" she hissed, and Marianne nodded. "We cannot let him take those keys with him!"

"I know. If he does get them, just faint again, and I'll sneak them off his belt. Da taught me a few tricks."

She pulled a vial out of her reticule as she spoke, and Alexandra eyed it suspiciously. "What's that? Not smelling salts!"

Marianne grimaced. "No. I've never fainted in my life. It's a little bottle of perfume, but I'm going to pretend it's smelling salts. Else we'll have that man tossing a glass of water in your face."

"Oh, Lord!" Alexandra grabbed the vial from her and held it to her nose, letting out a loud moan. "Oh, my! What happened?" she asked, sitting up, just as the gaoler came pelting back, carrying a cup from which water sloshed with every step he took.

"You fainted, my lady!" the gaoler exclaimed. "Mayhap you'd better sit down here, and I'll send someone to fetch his lordship."

"Lord Thorpe!" Alexandra exclaimed, looking as if the man had suggested sending for the Devil himself. "No, you mustn't." She rose agilely to her feet and grabbed the man's wrist, sending the last remaining bit of water to the floor. "He will be furious if he finds out what we have done. He said I must not take the gig. We must get home! We are expected at a dinner party, and we're late."

"Yes!" Marianne agreed emphatically, sticking her vial of "smelling salts" back into her reticule and seizing the gaoler's other arm. "We must go. Hurry! Lord Thorpe has a terrible temper," she added, casually maligning Alexandra's husband.

The gaoler looked a trifle apprehensive at the idea of a bad-tempered lord coming storming into his domain, and he turned at their urging and hustled out the door, leaving the keys still lying on his desk.

"HAVE THEY LEFT? WHAT'S GOING ON?" Justin, Lord Lambeth hissed. He was standing behind Lord Thorpe, who was positioned at the corner of the gaol.

"No, they're still inside," Sebastian reported. "What's taking them so long? It was a mistake to let them help us."

Sebastian let out a soft snort, having all the experience of a husband of almost three months. "I would like to have seen you stop them. Once Alexandra gets the bit between her teeth, I haven't a prayer."

Lambeth, who had had a few encounters of his own with his fiancé's feisty nature, knew that Sebastian's words applied to Marianne almost as much as to Thorpe's head-strong American wife.

"Wait!" Sebastian said softly, straightening a little. "The door is opening. Yes, it is they." He watched his wife emerge, glancing around her, and he smiled to himself. Even in the dim light cast by the lantern the gaoler carried, he could see the excitement in her face. *She was utterly beautiful, and she was having a grand time.* He wondered if she had the least notion what fear felt like. He had never seen it in her. And he was certain that there was no man as lucky as he.

"They are walking away," he continued in a whisper. "They're going around the corner." He waited, his muscles tensing, giving them an extra allowance of time, just in case the gaoler took it into his head to come back for some reason. Mentally he counted to ten. He could sense Lambeth's rising tension behind him. "All right. Let's go."

The two men eased around the corner, using no light, their eyes well accustomed to the darkness. They moved lightly and quickly, concealed by their dark clothes and masks. They reached the door to the gaol and went inside. A lamp still burned in the lobby of the gaol, and by its light they could see the gaoler's desk, on which lay the great ring of keys.

"Good girls." Justin's lips curved up in a smile as he crossed the room and grabbed the ring. Sebastian took the lamp to light their way.

With Sebastian close behind him, Justin unlocked the door in the opposite wall and stepped into the corridor beyond. It was a narrow corridor, not very long, and it was lined on either side with cells, each of them with a barred door, locked securely. They went to the first door and looked in. Two men lay on narrow cots in the small, primitive cell. Justin felt a sympathetic shudder run through him at the thought of being shut up in this little room.

He took the key ring and tried first one key in the door, then another, until he found one that fit. By the time the lock turned and he swung the door open, the men were standing looking at them. "Who are you?" one of the occupants asked in tones as cultured as Justin's own voice. "What are you doing?"

"Letting you out. If I were you, I wouldn't ask questions."

"Indeed not," the other man agreed, seeing the sense of this suggestion. He came out into the corridor, followed by his companion. Justin opened the next door with the same key. Two men emerged from it, rubbing their faces sleepily and looking dumbfounded.

"Wot's goin' on, Per?" one asked, turning toward the occupants of the first cell.

"It appears we are being released," Perry replied, still watching Justin and Lambeth as they moved down the row.

The third door opened to reveal the first face that looked familiar to Justin and Sebastian: the tall, dark-haired highwayman who had helped each of them at different times.

"Who the devil are you?" he asked suspiciously.

"Looking a gift horse in the mouth, are we?" Justin retorted lightly. "I think it is best if we do not bandy names about. Suffice it to say that I am someone whom you once helped out of a rather sticky situation in a mine." He nodded toward Sebastian, who smiled and tipped his hat. "And he has reason to wish you well, too. You gave him and his lady shelter one night."

Jack's eyebrows rose. "The devil you say." He looked at Sebastian and grinned. "The balloonists? Well, I guess that good deeds really do come back to one."

"They might have come back sooner if you had not lightened my pocket before you left," Sebastian reminded him grimly.

Jack laughed. "Aye, so I did. Sorry, sir. Sometimes I have a little difficulty controlling my impulses."

As Justin opened the last two cell doors, Jack strode to the end of the corridor and peered out into the empty lobby. "Took care of the gaoler as well, did you?"

"For the moment," Sebastian replied. "But we need to make haste before he returns."

"We shall. Come on, men."

Jack started across the room, but Sebastian called out. "Wait." He hurried to catch up with him. "We have something more of a plan than just releasing you into the night. There are horses waiting. Follow us."

Jack looked at him for a moment, then glanced toward Lambeth. He shrugged. "Lead on. I suppose we have little choice except to trust you."

"Quite right." Sebastian threw open the door and gave a quick look outside, then stepped out into the street, motioning to the others.

They ran down the street toward the alley. Sebastian rounded the corner followed by Jack's men, with Jack and

Lord Lambeth in the rear. Just as the last of them were almost to the corner of the building, there was a loud cry from behind them. Justin muttered a curse and grabbed Jack's arm just as a pistol shot rang out.

CHAPTER EIGHTEEN

AS THEY LEFT THE GAOL, ALEXANDRA COULD not resist a quick look around, but she saw no sign of her husband or Justin. Marianne, more accustomed to carrying out a charade, did not even glance about, merely tucked her arm more tightly into the gaoler's and strode along briskly, chattering all the while like a vacant-headed, frightened female. They whisked the gaoler around the corner of the building and down the street to the edge of town, where their horse and gig stood waiting.

"You see?" Alexandra cried as they approached the vehicle. "We are in the ditch! We were almost killed!"

She dragged the man around to the ditch side of the gig to point out their wheel resting on nothing but air, while Marianne slipped over to the other side and unobtrusively kicked away the rock that they had placed under the wheel to stabilize it. The gaoler examined the gig, distracted by the increasingly hysterical Alexandra. It would have been an easy problem to fix, requiring only that one of them lead the horse away from the ditch; at worst, the gaoler might have had to add his shoulder to pushing the gig forward until the wheel found purchase. However, the two women managed, with their constant chatter and cries and occasional bouts of tears, to make the procedure take twice as long as it should have.

When at last the gaoler got the gig several feet away from the ditch, Alexandra collapsed into grateful tears, seizing the gaoler's rough hand and declaring over and over that he had saved her life. She found, a little to her surprise, that the tears came quite easily, for worry and fear for Sebastian gnawed at her beneath her flamboyant performance. *Had they gotten into the gaol without incident? Had they had enough time to release the prisoners? What if they had been delayed, and when the gaoler went back to his post, he walked right in on the escape attempt?*

The gaoler started back to the gaol, and the two women went along, doing their best to delay him. They were not sure how long it had taken the men to enter the gaol after they left or how much time they needed to unlock and empty the cells. It would be disastrous if they let the gaoler return to the place too soon. As it was, just as the three of them rounded the corner of the gaol, they saw the last of the prisoners emerge from the front door and dash down the street.

The gaoler gaped at the sight for a moment before he realized what was going on. Then he let out a roar, pulled a pistol from his waistband, raised and fired. One of the men staggered, but kept on running, rounding the corner of the building and disappearing down the alleyway. The gaoler started to go after the men. Marianne and Alexandra shrieked and threw themselves against him, holding fast to his arms.

"The prisoners escaped!" he said excitedly. "I got to catch 'em!" He paused and looked down the dark alleyway, then added uncertainly, "Yeah, I'd better go after them."

"No! You might get injured!" Alexandra cried. "They could wait lurking at the end of the alleyway and attack you, several against one, and you have already shot your pistol."

"That is right," Marianne added. "I know that the danger to yourself would not stop you, but think about us. You mustn't leave us alone. What if they came back to get us? What if there are more of them inside the gaol, waiting to murder us?"

The gaoler looked at the two women, then down the long, dark alley. "It would be wrong to leave you two ladies unprotected…." he agreed thoughtfully.

Marianne suppressed a grin. "That's right. And Lord Lambeth will be ever so grateful to you for staying with us instead of chasing after those criminals, as I am sure you would like to do. It takes a man of true courage to remain at his post and do his duty when all his instinct urges him to follow those dangerous men—no doubt armed to the teeth—through the dark night. To catch them and fight them, risking life and limb—I understand that that is what you long to do."

The gaoler swallowed, mumbling, "Er…yes, I guess I do."

"But to stay here with us instead!" Alexandra exclaimed. "That is the action of a truly courageous and honorable man."

The gaoler raised his head, sticking his jaw out manfully. "You're right, my lady. I cannot follow me heart. I must stay here and protect you."

Looking noble, he turned and strode back down the street to the gaol. The door stood open, and they walked cautiously inside, looking around. The front room looked just as it had when they left it, except that an empty space occupied the portion of the desk where the large ring of keys had lain earlier. The gaoler walked through the room and into the corridor beyond, where the row of cells lay, with

Marianne and Alexandra right on his heels. They relaxed with sighs of relief when a glance down the short corridor revealed only empty cells, the barred doors hanging open. The ring of keys still hung in the last of the cells.

The gaoler looked at the key ring with a thunderstruck expression. "My keys!" His hand went instinctively to his belt, but the keys that usually hung there were gone. "They opened them with my keys! But how—"

"You mean you left your keys here?" Marianne exclaimed, turning to him with a haughty expression worthy of a future duchess. "Sitting out there where anyone could get them? How could you be so careless?"

"But I—you—" the man sputtered, looking from one woman to the other, trying to recall exactly how it had happened that he had left his keys behind.

"That's all right," Alexandra reassured him. "We shall tell the magistrate what a splendid job you did. After all, you kept us safe, despite all these lurking highwaymen. Lord Thorpe, I know, will be very grateful to you."

"You know," Marianne added confidentially, coming down from her lady-of-the-manor pose, "I think this was all a plot."

"A plot?" the gaoler repeated stupidly.

"Exactly. Those highwaymen stopped us not to rob us but to get us to do precisely what we did—come running to you! Where else would we have gone for aid? Of course we came here, and when you so bravely went to help us, they were no doubt lurking about outside and sneaked in to free their compatriots. There must be many more of them than anyone realized."

The gaoler looked much struck by this thought. "You're right…there must be. Why, it'd take several men to risk breaking into the gaol."

"Especially given the fact that you are guarding it," Alexandra put in admiringly. "After all, they could not count on our distracting you. Why, we might not have even come here at all! Then they would have had to face you. I imagine there must have been—oh, four or five of them, at least."

"At least," Marianne agreed. "Maybe even more." The gaoler nodded. "You're right. It must have been a great gang of men. There's no telling how many of those scoundrels are still around here."

"Six or seven," Alexandra added.

"I suppose I should go after them…." the gaoler said, somewhat less than enthusiastically.

"By yourself?" Marianne looked shocked. "You are a brave man, indeed, but I really do not think you should. Why, think how many of them there are—the ones who rescued them, the ones who were here in jail—why you yourself said it must be a large gang. And they are bound to have guns, too."

"Yes, if they came to get their friends out of gaol. Certainly they are armed…to the teeth. Perhaps you should go to the constable."

"Oh, aye!" The gaoler's face cleared. "The constable must be told first. And the magistrate. Lord Exmoor…" His face took on a troubled expression at that thought.

"The magistrate will go to tell Exmoor, I am sure, considering what an important man Lord Exmoor is," Alexandra reassured him.

"You're right. It will be up to Squire Halsey." That thought seemed to afford him some relief. "Well, I had best be going out to the Squire's house to tell him now."

"Absolutely. And we must go home," Marianne said. "Lord Lambeth and Lord Thorpe will be worried about us. We are already dreadfully late for our dinner party."

They slipped away before the gaoler could recover his wits enough to recall that they should wait and lodge a complaint with the magistrate about the supposed attack on them this evening. They hurried back to the gig, Alexandra rebuttoning the top buttons of her dress and twisting her hair back into some semblance of a knot as they strode along. Marianne, too, reached back beneath her cloak to unpin her bodice, drawing a huge breath of relief as the dress loosened about her chest.

"Do you think they're all right?" she asked Alexandra as they climbed into the gig. "Did the gaoler hit anyone when he fired?"

"It looked to me as though he did. One man jerked and hesitated, I thought, but I could not tell who it was. They were too far away, and they were all dressed alike. Dark hats, masks…"

"I know." Marianne looked over at her anxiously. "It could have been Justin or Sebastian who was hit."

"Don't think that way. Anyway, whoever it was, it can't have been too bad a wound. He continued to run."

"Still, let's get home as fast as we can. I want to see Justin."

Alexandra nodded; she, too, felt the cold grip of fear in her stomach. She slapped the reins sharply, and the horse started off.

JUSTIN JERKED AS THE BALL FROM THE pistol seared across his upper arm. He staggered briefly, but recovered and continued to run. The men raced down the narrow alleyway, Sebastian in the lead, until they emerged on another quiet street. They ran down the street, making as little noise as they could, and turned into a narrow lane. Sebastian slowed to a walk now, and the others followed suit. Jack glanced over his shoulder, wondering why the gaoler was so slow in pursuing them.

"Don't worry about the gaoler," Justin said in a low voice. "The girls will take care of him."

"The girls?" Jack cast him a curious look.

"Yes. You met one of them with me not too many weeks ago."

"The redheaded beauty?" Jack asked in amazement.

"The same. She is soon to be my wife." He fixed the highwayman with a hard look.

Jack chuckled. "Ah, I see. So I am not to notice her beauty anymore?"

Justin smiled. "I imagine that would be too much to ask. Anyway, she has a sister who is almost as lovely as she, and the two of them, um, shall we say—distracted the good gaoler."

Jack's brows rose. "But—isn't that rather dangerous?"

Justin's smile broadened. "I am afraid it would have been even more dangerous for me had I refused to let her play a part. I am afraid that you will find out that there are certain women who won't be dictated to."

Jack grimaced. "I have already discovered that, thank you."

Justin chuckled. "I dare swear you have."

"Were you hit? I heard a pistol."

At these words, Sebastian turned and looked at them. "Lambeth? You were hit?"

"Just a scratch," Justin assured them. "It didn't go into my arm. Stings like the devil, but I'll be all right."

They were approaching a large, spreading oak tree, and now they could make out a dark clump of shapes beneath it, which resolved as they drew closer into several horses. Jack realized with some astonishment that they were waiting for him and his men. At second glance he saw that they were his own horses, "liberated" earlier that evening from the village stables. He looked at the masked man beside him, scarcely able to believe that this nobleman, who was virtually a stranger to him, would do so much to ensure his freedom.

Sebastian turned toward the others and said, "We are going to divide up. It will make you harder to find. Jack, you come with us." He turned to Perry. "You take the others and ride as hard and as fast as you can for Exeter. I have sent instructions to someone I know there to help you into hiding. He'll do a good job. Just go to the Blue Boar Tavern and ask for Murdock. You should have a good hours' head start, at least. And unless I miss my guess, the authorities will not be chasing you. They will be after him." He nodded toward Jack.

"Wait…" Jack began, annoyed at this assumption of command over his own men.

"What? Do you want to go with them? It will ensure that they will be pursued. You know as well as I that Exmoor wants only you. The rest he really doesn't care about."

Jack hesitated. He could see the sense in what the man said, and he certainly was not going to endanger his men just because he did not like having his authority usurped. Still… "But how will they know that I am not with them?"

"Oh, I think they will know exactly where to look to find you," Justin drawled. "I doubt Richard will even bother with tracking us."

"Come on, man," Sebastian said. "We are wasting time. Which is it to be?"

"Perry, do as he said," Jack replied. He had some doubts about this whole bizarre rescue, but he knew that the most important thing was that Perry and the others not suffer for his decision to seek revenge against the Earl of Exmoor.

AS THEY REACHED THE HORSES, JACK saw that there was a lad, clad in a dark jacket and with a dark cap pulled low on his face, who stood with the horses, holding their reins. Quickly the lad began handing the reins to Perry and the others. After a quick consultation with Sebastian, Perry and the other men mounted and took off. Justin took the reins of the three remaining horses from the stable lad and handed one set to Jack.

"I know you are full of questions," he said. "We shall answer them all later, but for now, I think it is imperative that we get away."

Jack nodded, taking the reins and turning toward his horse. Sebastian went to the lad, saying, "Justin was hit."

"What?" the lad exclaimed in a cultured, feminine voice, and strode over to Justin to inspect his arm.

"It's nothing," Justin insisted. "The ball merely grazed me. I'm fine. We need to go."

Jack stood staring at the woman, dressed like a lad, speechless. He had recognized the voice immediately. It was Nicola.

"You!" Jack exclaimed in astonishment, striding forward to face her. "Good God! What are you doing here?"

"Hello, Jack," Nicola answered calmly.

"How could you have let her come?" Jack snapped, fixing Justin with a furious glare. Calmly Justin took off his mask and gazed back at him.

"I would be interested in hearing how you think we could have stopped her."

"But it's too dangerous! She could have been hurt! Killed! My God, man!"

"It's not a question of their *letting* me come," Nicola pointed out. "I was planning to break you out of gaol. They insisted on coming along."

Jack stared at her. "You planned to break me out of gaol by yourself? My God, have you run mad?"

"Please!" Justin hissed. "If we continue standing here arguing, we shall all be in gaol in another moment. My arm will last until the Dower House. You can fuss over me there, Nicola. And the two of you can continue to argue there, as well. But I, for one, do not intend to stay here and get caught."

With those words, Justin swung up onto his horse, and the others, seeing the force of his argument, followed suit. They rode in silence, skirting the village and striking out across the fields. They could not ride at a fast pace for fear of injuring their mounts in the darkness, and it seemed to take a maddening amount of time.

But at last a large house loomed up before them. They rode up to the stables, which lay between them and the house, and dismounted. Immediately a man stepped out of the shadows and came toward them.

Sebastian turned toward the man and handed him his reins. "Ah, Harris, good man. Is my wife home?"

"My lord." The man sketched a slight bow to him. "Aye, her ladyship's here, and in fine form, too, if I may say so."

"I am sure I could not stop you from doing so."

The large man ignored his employer's dry quip, going on to say, "I let one of the lads here put away the horse and gig, seein' as how it wouldn't matter. What with everybody knowin' about her adventure. But I'll do these myself, real quiet, like."

"Good. If any of the other lads question you—"

The heavyset man smiled faintly. "Lord love you, them

lads won't go askin' *me* questions. And if I tells one of 'em to keep his trap shut, he won't be openin' it. You can be sure of that."

"I am, Harris."

The man gave a quick nod and began gathering the reins of the others' horses. While he walked silently back into the stables, leading the horses, the three men and Nicola hurried across the yard to the kitchen door. Jack looked up at the side of the house as they approached it, a strange sensation moving through him. The tan stone house seemed somehow welcoming—no, more than that, almost familiar.

"Whose house is this?" he whispered.

"The Countess of Exmoor's."

"Your sister?" He turned toward Nicola, puzzled.

"No. The Dowager Countess."

"Exmoor's mother?"

"Oh, no!" Sebastian inserted. "Don't say anything like that to the Countess. She despises the man. He is a distant cousin, inherited Tidings when her husband and son died.

"Did you not ever see her when you lived here? She used to live in Tidings long ago, when we were children, I suppose, but after her husband died, she moved here, to the Dower House." Nicola paused. "Although I guess she was not here much. She stayed primarily in London after…the tragedy. That is where I got to know her."

They reached the kitchen door and slipped inside. The large kitchen was deserted except for a lone man at the table, who jumped to his feet when he saw them, relief spreading over his face. "Lord Thorpe! Lord Lambeth! Miss Falcourt. I cannot tell you what a relief it is to see you."

"Thank you, Mulford. I understand the ladies are here."

"Indeed, sir. As well as everyone else."

"What?" Lambeth took a step toward the man. "What do you mean?"

"Never mind that now," Nicola said. "We need to get Lambeth's arm cleaned and bandaged. Mulford, get me a clean rag, a bandage and a small bowl of water.

"Yes, miss." The butler turned and hurried off to do as she bid.

"I'm just going to clean it with water now, Justin. We haven't time for anything else. Later I'll put something on it. But right now we have to hide Jack and get into our evening clothes. I suspect it will not be long before Richard and his men are here."

The butler returned with the supplies, and Nicola ripped off Justin's torn sleeve and began to clean the arm. At that moment, the door to the kitchen opened, and Bucky stuck his head in, looking anxious. When he saw the group in the kitchen, his expression changed to one of almost comical relief.

"Lambeth! Thorpe! Thank God." He opened the door wider to admit his large frame. "We are in the suds now. Oh, I say, Lambeth, what happened to you?"

"Hallo, Bucky." Justin greeted him with little concern. He was aware, as were Nicola and Sebastian, that their friend was somewhat apt to be thrown for a loss by the slightest change in plans. "I'm fine. Don't worry about it. What happened here to get you in a twit?"

"Lady Ursula is here," Bucky said, turning paler at just the thought.

"Good gad!" Justin exclaimed, stiffening.

"Hold still!" Nicola admonished him.

"What the devil is she doing here?" Sebastian asked. "She was supposed to be safely away with the Countess and Lady Buckminster."

"I know!" Bucky looked aggrieved. "That is what I told them. And Lady Ursula asked if I didn't want them here. Well, I mean, what could I say? Truth was, I wished them at the devil, but I could hardly say that, could I?"

"Them?" Sebastian asked, looking more alarmed. "Do you mean the Countess is here, too?"

"All of them!" Bucky exclaimed. "The Countess. My mother. Lady Exmoor."

"Deborah!" Nicola stopped her dressing of Justin's arm and turned to stare at him. "But how—why—"

"They took it into their heads to join us. Decided it would be more fun, the whole group of us together. I ask you—how could it be more fun to have Lady Ursula here?"

"Quite true."

"Who is Lady Ursula?" Jack asked.

"Penelope's mother," Nicola explained.

"My future mother-in-law," Bucky added sadly. He looked at Jack more closely. "I say, are you the highwayman, then?" He extended his hand in his usual friendly manner. "Pleased to meet you. Or, well, I suppose, not meet you, exactly. You stopped my carriage a few weeks ago, but, well, we were not really introduced."

"True." Jack suppressed a grin and shook the other man's hand. "Pleased to make your acquaintance."

"So what did you tell them?" Sebastian asked. "About our not being here?"

"Oh! Well, I was at a dead loss, I'll tell you. But Penelope made up a pack of lies." He grinned in admiration. "I always knew she was a downy one, but I never realized just how clever she was. She said you had all gone to look for Alexandra and Marianne because they were late. And then she acted worried. She carried it off,

but I could see she felt bad… you know, for worrying the
Countess."

"I am sure so," Nicola said feelingly. "Blast it! I did not
want to drag the Countess into this."

Sebastian grunted. "And God knows what any of them
will say if Exmoor shows up, looking for the escaped
prisoner."

"The Countess won't say anything that she thinks
would help Richard," Nicola said.

"True. But Lady Ursula is always a wild card. And none
of them will know how much their words could endanger
us."

"Well, there's nothing for it now," Justin pointed out.
"We're done here. Nicola, you had better get our friend
upstairs. Thorpe and I will change and join the others."

Nicola nodded and turned to Jack. "We are going to
stow you away up in the attic."

"Perhaps I had best show you, miss," the butler began,
but Jack had already turned and was headed toward the
servants' staircase.

"We'll find it," Nicola told him. "And I am sure that you
will be needed in the drawing room." The butler, like Sebastian's coachman, was an old family employee and would
have done anything for the Countess and her granddaughters, so he had been taken into their confidence. He was the
only servant waiting on Penelope and the others tonight.

"Yes, miss."

Nicola followed Jack, with Sebastian and Justin on her
heels. Bucky, with a martyred sigh, returned to face Lady
Ursula. Jack led the way up to the second floor, where the
stairs ended. They emerged onto the main hallway, and
Jack, without hesitation, went down the corridor a few
steps and turned right at a small hallway that branched off

the main one. Sebastian and Justin parted from them there, going down to Marianne's room, where their evening clothes lay waiting for them. Nicola, however, went with Jack. She was a little surprised to find a narrow staircase at the end of the short hallway. Jack started up it confidently, and she followed.

The third floor hallway was darker and narrower, with more doors opening off it. It was, as in most houses, where the servants resided, and consequently it was plainer, with much smaller rooms. Once again Jack strode confidently down the hallway.

"Wait," Nicola said. "We need to find the attic stairs."

"Past the nursery," Jack said, pointing ahead of him.

"What?" Nicola stared at him. "How did you know that?"

"Why, you can see them," he said as they reached the farther end of the hallway, where, indeed, a very narrow, very steep set of stairs led up to a small door.

"You must have better eyes than I," Nicola said. She had been unable to distinguish the steps at this end of the dark hallway. "But how did you know that was the nursery back there?"

Jack, who had gone up the stairs, paused at the door, frowning. "I don't know. It's odd. I just—somehow knew where to go, where the rooms were."

He turned the doorknob and went into the attic, with Nicola on his heels. The candle he carried made a small pool of light in the vast darkness of the attic. He held it up and peered around as far as he could. "It looks like it would be hard to find someone in here."

"That's what Penelope said. She said it always scared her to come up here, it was so big and full of trunks and old furniture and all sorts of things."

"Oh, no, it's a grand place to hide." A peculiar look crossed his face.

"What is it? What's the matter?" Nicola asked.

"I don't know. Nothing. It's just…I feel so strange. As if I'd been here before. As if…I suddenly saw a place in my mind—a little area behind a great big trunk, and there's an old rocking horse there, most of the paint peeled off him, and…"

He started walking through the attic, winding his way around sofas and chairs and trunks of clothes, the detritus of centuries of family. The light of his candle fell eerily on the nearest objects, leaving the back of the huge room in gloom. Jack circled around some boxes, then stopped, looking confused. He turned and shoved aside a hatbox and peered over the chest on which it had lain. There stood a large, humpbacked trunk and, next to it, an old red rocking horse, one runner broken, the paint worn thin and peeling. Nicola stared at it, an icy feeling in the pit of her stomach.

"Jack…how did you—"

"I don't know." He turned and looked at her. "I don't know how, but I seem to know this place. Perhaps—perhaps my mother used to work here when I was young. Before we moved, before I was ill. I don't remember anything before that illness—it's as if the fever burned away all my memory. But I was at Granny Rose's when I was sick—I remember that. So perhaps we lived with her till then. My mother could have worked for the Countess, I suppose. Maybe I came with her sometimes. Maybe we even lived up here in the servants' quarters."

"That would be odd," Nicola said. "I mean, to have a maid with a child living with her. But the Countess isn't like other women. She is a compassionate woman. Perhaps she let your mother keep you here with her. That must be it."

Jack nodded, looking thoughtful, and they turned and made their way back to the attic door. They stopped at the door, and Nicola turned to Jack.

She hesitated, then said, "I want you to know that I did not mean to lead Richard to you. I swear to you. Richard tricked me. He made me think that you were in danger, and I panicked and ran to warn you. It never occurred to me that it was a trick, and I didn't think to look for anyone following me. I was stupid, but I swear to you, I meant you no harm."

To her surprise, Jack smiled. "I know." He reached out and put his hands on her arms. "I never thought you had betrayed me."

"What?" Nicola gaped at him. "But you said—you wouldn't even see me at the gaol!"

"I was trying to protect you. You, of course, stubbornly refused protection, but—"

"You were trying to protect me?"

"Yes. I couldn't let them arrest you, too, and you were without question aiding and abetting a criminal. I thought if I pretended that you had done it to betray me, the constable would think you were not one of us. I figured if I acted wounded and betrayed, Richard would so delight in it that he would back me up and pretend that you had indeed been in on the plan, just to make me suffer. That's why I said the things I did. I hated the hurt on your face, but I couldn't let you go to gaol. Nor could I let you ruin it all by coming to the gaol to visit me."

Nicola stared at him for a long moment, tears welling in her eyes. "Then you believe me? You know?"

He nodded. "I finally got smart. I started listening with

my heart, not my head, and I knew that I loved you. All I wanted was you, and if I hadn't been so damned self-pitying, I could have cleared it all up years ago. It was I who kept us apart the last eight years, not Exmoor. Revenge didn't matter, Exmoor didn't matter, nothing mattered but you."

"You love me?" Nicola repeated, a radiant smile breaking across her face.

"I love you."

"Oh, Jack!" Nicola threw her arms around him. "I love you, too!"

He wrapped his arms around her, squeezing her tightly to him. "Nicola, tell me you forgive me."

"Of course I do. I love you."

He bent, and their lips met in a long, sweet kiss. Nicola trembled in his arms, knowing that at last she was home with her love.

Finally he raised his head, giving her a brief kiss on the forehead, and relaxed his arms. He sighed. "You had best get back to the others."

"Yes." Nicola nodded, wiping away her tears. It was difficult to keep the wide smile from her face. "There will be ample time for this later. I expect Richard to come after me first. So I had better be ready for him."

"I hate hiding and letting you face him!" Jack said explosively. "Maybe I—"

"Don't be foolish," Nicola told him, putting her hands on his arms and looking up earnestly into his eyes. "You cannot face him yourself. You will only prove that we helped you escape if you do that. The best thing you can do for any of us is to stay up here and not let them find you."

He sighed, the muscles in his taut arms relaxing. "I know. I just feel so useless, sitting up here."

"I will come back up as soon as I can," she promised. "But now I have to hurry."

"I know."

She went on tiptoe to brush her lips against his. But his arms went around her tightly, pulling her to him for a long, deep kiss. "I love you," he said huskily when at last he pulled back. "Oh, God, I was a fool for so long."

"It doesn't matter now." Nicola wrapped her arms around him and squeezed him tightly. "All I care about is that you're free. And I love you."

Then, with a last brief kiss, she tore herself away from him and hurried out the door.

CHAPTER NINETEEN

NICOLA RACED DOWN TO PENELOPE'S room. She had ridden over to the Dower House this evening in a carriage with Lambeth, Bucky and Lord Thorpe. They had all been wearing formal evening attire, as befitted their supposed dinner party. Once they got to the Dower House, they had all changed into their "working clothes," and Nicola had left her elegant gown in Penelope's room. The dress was still spread out on the bed where she had left it, along with a heap of petticoats. Swiftly she peeled off the boots and boy's clothing she had worn for disguise.

The door opened, and she whirled around with a gasp. She went limp when she saw that it was only Marianne who had slipped inside the door. "Sorry to frighten you," Marianne said. "I thought you could use some help dressing."

"I could," Nicola said with heartfelt relief. Buttoning the tiny row of buttons up the back of her gown was difficult to do by herself under any circumstances; with the pressure of time, it would have been nearly impossible.

With Marianne's help she slipped into her petticoats and tied them, and Marianne lowered the green silk dress over her head. Quickly Marianne began to fasten the long row of pearl buttons.

"How is everything downstairs?"

"Confused," Marianne replied succinctly. "But still polite. I can see that Aunt Ursula is going to begin hammering us with questions at any moment. The only thing that has saved us so far, I think, is the fact that she already thinks Bucky is such a fool that she isn't surprised when what he says makes little sense. Then Alexandra and I bombarded her with our story, which rather distracted her. But when I left, I could see her frowning, and I think she is going over all the holes in our stories. As long as Penelope and Bucky don't cave in, though, we can bluff our way through. Even *she* is reluctant to interrogate a future duke, and I rather think Thorpe scares her a little."

"I didn't think anyone scared her," Nicola said as she smoothed her hair back into place, repinning the strands that had come loose beneath her hat.

"There. All done." Marianne stood back and inspected Nicola.

"Do I look all right?"

"Lovely, as always. No one would guess that you hadn't spent the evening in your parlor."

"How is Lambeth?"

A shadow crossed Marianne's face. "He looks perfectly all right, quite elegant and cool. But I think his arm hurts him. He favors it a bit—I've noticed that he keeps it resting on the chair arm. But at least the bandage was not bulky. It doesn't show."

"It was only a graze," Nicola reassured her. "I am sure he will be fine, and I will put something on it after this is all over."

Marianne nodded. "Yes, just so long as Richard doesn't notice that he is weak in his arm."

"We'll just have to keep him distracted from it." Nicola said firmly. "Well, shall we go down and face the dragon?"

"Aunt Ursula?"

"Who else?"

They linked arms and went downstairs, where they found the rest of the group in the formal drawing room. Sebastian stood next to the chair on which Alexandra sat, one elbow casually propped up on the mantel, and at the other end of the mantel, like a bookend, stood Lord Buckminster, gazing at his future mother-in-law with a hunted expression. That good woman, a middle-aged family tyrant dressed all in blue, with a bosom like the prow of a ship, was sitting several feet away, frowning at her daughter, who was on the other side of an elderly, regal-looking woman. The aged woman was the Countess of Exmoor, Lady Ursula's mother and the grandmother of Marianne, Alexandra and Penelope. The Dowager Countess, who had obviously been quite a beauty in her day, was tall and slender and sat ramrod straight in her chair. There was the faintest line of worry etched into her forehead. Penelope sat with her hands clenching her fan, obviously waiting in dread. Slightly behind the others were Nicola's sister, Deborah, and their aunt, Lady Buckminster, who looked faintly puzzled, which greatly increased her resemblance to her son. Beside them was an empty chair, and next to it, Lord Lambeth lounged, looking as if he hadn't a care in the world.

He sprang up when Marianne and Nicola entered, saying, "My dear. And Nicola. The wait was well worth it. You look lovely." He swept them a bow.

"Always a handy one with a compliment, Justin," Nicola retorted, smiling.

"There you are, Nicola," Lady Ursula said. "You know, I cannot fathom why you went with Lambeth and Thorpe to look for the girls."

"You know me, Lady Ursula," Nicola said easily. "I

never was one to sit at home and wait. How are you this evening? You are looking quite well."

"Just what I was telling her," Lambeth said easily. "If you get any younger-looking, Lady Castlereigh, you shall have people asking if Penelope is your sister, not your daughter."

Lady Ursula could not help but smile at his remark, though she remarked with as much sternness as she could muster, "You *are* a flatterer, Lambeth. I shouldn't wonder if you lead my niece quite a dance."

"I am afraid it is the other way around, my lady."

Nicola crossed the room to where her sister sat and bent down to kiss her on the cheek. "I am glad you came, Deborah. I did not expect to see you."

"I was a trifle surprised myself," Deborah admitted, smiling a little wanly. "But when the Countess and Aunt Adelaide suggested it, I thought, well, why not? A game of cards or some conversation would be nice."

Nicola smiled and made a pleasant reply, her mind elsewhere. Should they tell the Countess and the others everything, she wondered, and hope that family loyalty would keep them silent when Richard came to question them, as she was sure he and his Bow Street Runner would? The Countess, she knew, would never do or say anything that would aid Richard, and her family loyalty was well-known. And if she remained in ignorance of the night's events, there was always the possibility of her saying something wrong inadvertently, especially because she did not know what was at stake. If it were only the Countess involved, Nicola thought that she would have told her everything without a second thought.

But Lady Ursula was another matter. One never knew what she might do or say. Anyone who badgered as sweet a person as her daughter Penelope had to be perverse, and everyone knew how much she had fought against believing that Alexandra was her long-dead brother's child. On the other hand, she had no liking for Richard, either, and she had grudgingly admitted at last that Alexandra and, later, Marianne were her true nieces. Surely family loyalty and the fear of scandal should ensure that she not reveal that her nieces' husband and fiancé; had been involved in a gaol break, but Nicola was a little afraid to rely on that.

Worst of all, she knew that she did not trust her own sister not to reveal their secret if she told her. Even though Deborah had left Richard's house in bitter tears, vowing never to see him again, she was, after all, his wife. She had loved him and, for all Nicola knew, still loved him despite her pain and anger. He was also the father of her unborn child, a fact that weighed heavily with a woman. Nicola was not sure what Deborah would say if Richard wheedled her with sweet words to tell him what Nicola had done.

Nicola looked at Marianne. She wished she could talk to her and the others privately.

"It seems odd to me—" Lady Ursula began.

Alexandra cut into her words as if she had not heard her. "A game of cards does sound nice, Deborah," she said, retrieving the thread of conversation Deborah had started. "Why don't we repair to the card room? Sebastian? Marianne?"

"Yes, why don't we?" Nicola agreed, thinking that perhaps they could snatch a bit of conversation together as they changed rooms. She stood up.

At that moment, the sound of loud voices came from the hallway beyond. Nicola tensed, and Lambeth rose to his feet, turning toward the door and starting forward, as did Sebastian, then Bucky.

The doors to the hallway were flung open, and the Earl

of Exmoor barged in, followed by his Runner, Stone, then by the constable and the magistrate, Squire Halsey, wringing his hands and protesting in a useless way. After them came the butler, saying, "My lord! You cannot—"

"Don't tell me what I cannot do," Exmoor snarled at the man. He turned to face the occupants of the room. Behind them, Nicola could now see several other men, all carrying muskets. She recognized none of their faces, and she supposed that they must be the men Richard had hired to help him capture Jack.

"What the devil do you think you're doing?" Sebastian snapped as he, Lambeth and Buckminster moved to stand between Richard and the women in the room.

"Oh!" Squire Halsey groaned. "Lord Thorpe. Buckminster. Lord Lambeth…so sorry to intrude. Really, Exmoor, we cannot just accost innocent people."

"Especially not when they will be dukes one day?" Richard asked bitingly. "Buck up, man, grow a spine. You have a legal right to be here."

"I dispute that, Exmoor," Lambeth said coldly. "I know of no right that you or the Squire has to burst into the Countess's home and frighten her guests. I would suggest that you leave at once."

"We want only to talk to her." Richard turned, fixing his gaze on Nicola. "The rest of you I have no quarrel with."

"Oh, but I am afraid you do," Thorpe said in a silky tone. "If you think that I am going to allow you to drag a lady from this house and browbeat her, then you are more of a fool than I took you for."

"Richard." The Countess's voice cut across the room, as icy as a winter's day. All eyes turned toward her. She had stood up, a tall, regal figure, her elegant white hair crowning her head, and she looked at Richard with a cool imperiousness that was guaranteed to make any man feel like an errant schoolboy. "You dare to come into my home with armed men?"

Even Richard had the grace to flush at her words. "It is nothing to do with you, my lady. We seek—"

"Nothing to do with me?" The Countess's eyes flashed blue fire. "You come in here, dragging the Squire along with you, bringing your company of men to invade my home, and you say it has nothing to do with me?" She turned her gaze to the magistrate, who gulped audibly and took a step backward. "Why are you here, Squire? Have you come to arrest me? Or are you content, as Richard said, with merely harassing those under my protection?"

"Countess…my lady…"

"Yes?"

"We mean no disrespect to you, my lady," the Squire said feebly, mopping his forehead with his handkerchief.

"Perhaps you do not mean any," the Countess allowed graciously. "But that is what you have demonstrated, nevertheless. Did you think you could troop in here and treat my guests and me as if we were common criminals and not give offense? Send your men out, and perhaps we can discuss this matter like civilized people. Otherwise, I am afraid that you will hear nothing from anyone in this house. Even if you drag us out and haul us down to gaol."

"My lady!" The Squire looked striken. "Oh, no, goodness gracious. This is awful. Awful." He turned toward Richard. "Lord Exmoor, send your men out. You have no authority here. This is trespass, and I told you that it was not proper—"

"Stop blubbering, Halsey," Richard said with contempt. "I will send my men outside. They can stop anyone leaving well enough from there. But I am not leaving here until I get some answers."

He turned and barked an order at Stone, who turned and left the room, gesturing to the men in the hall to follow him. The Countess looked at Richard with contempt.

"You shame the name of Exmoor," she said bluntly, and for the first time emotion tinged her elegant voice with a tremor.

"Oh, Grandmama…" Penelope cried out in sympathy, rushing to her side and taking her arm.

"Have you not harmed her enough already?" Alexandra asked, her lip curling. "Must you come in here and—"

"No, no!" the Squire said, wringing his hands in distress. "We mean no harm to the Countess. Not at all. It's the escaped prisoner we are chasing. That is all we want."

"And precisely why would you come to the Countess's house looking for a *prisoner?*" Lady Ursula asked bitingly. "Eh? Speak up, man, and tell me that."

"It is Nicola," Richard said once again, looking at Nicola.

"Nicola Falcourt?" Lady Ursula repeated in tones of amazement. "The girl has always been a trifle odd, I will admit, but I can assure you that she is *not* a prisoner. Do you have bats in the belfry, man? Halsey, how can you be such a fool as to listen to this?"

"No, no, Miss Falcourt is not a prisoner, my lady," the Squire hastened to assure her.

"At least not yet," Richard said.

"Then what in heaven's name are you talking about?" Lady Buckminster asked, speaking up for the first time. "You do realize, Squire, that you are talking about my niece?"

"That's right," Bucky agreed, adding, "I would watch my step if I were you, sir, before I went slandering my cousin."

"Oh, no. My lord—my lady—I would never—I did not mean—"

"Do shut up, Halsey," Richard interposed. "They are trying to distract you. Everyone knows that Nicola was not a prisoner. It is the highwayman we are after."

"The highwayman?" Penelope asked, looking puzzled and supremely innocent.

"The one who accosted Lady Thorpe and Miss Montford this evening?" Sebastian asked. "Frightened them half to death. I say, Squire Halsey, crime seems to run rampant here. I meant to come see you tomorrow about it."

"Not the one who 'accosted' the ladies," Richard said, with a thin smile that made clear his disbelief. "'The Gentleman,' he is called, and he was in gaol, but his accomplices let him out tonight while the gaoler was distracted... coincidentally...by Lady Thorpe and Miss Montford."

"Exactly what are you trying to say, Exmoor?" Sebastian asked in a voice as hard as glass. "I warn you, you are treading on thin ice."

"It seems an odd time for two young ladies to be out driving alone."

"My wife is quite competent with the reins," Sebastian said, "and when they left, it was still afternoon. Obviously they did not plan to stay out so late. In any case, what my wife does is my business, not yours."

The two men glared at each other, the tension in the air rising palpably.

"Gentlemen, please," the Countess interrupted crisply. "Could we return to the matter at hand? My granddaughters told us about the incident. It sounded quite harrowing, but I scarcely see how any of it has anything to do with this house. I am sure you can wait to question the young ladies until tomorrow, can you not, Squire? Surely they can tell you little to help you track down this escapee."

"Perhaps not," Richard replied, casting a long glance at Marianne and Alexandra, who gazed back at him blandly. "But I feel sure that Miss Falcourt can help us."

"I fail to see how I can help you," Nicola replied calmly. "I was not even with Marianne and Alexandra."

"I am sure not. More likely you were at the gaol itself."

"Are you saying that the escape of the prisoners was effected by a young gentlewoman?" Lord Lambeth asked, amusement tinging his elegant drawl. "Really, Exmoor... don't you think that is a little far-fetched?"

"Not if you know Nicola."

"Ah, but I do. I have known her for years," Lambeth replied. "And I think I can say without doubt that Miss Falcourt was not in that gaol tonight."

"Of course not," Penelope spoke up. "She was here, with us, all evening. We were having a dinner party."

Nicola waited, her entire body stretched with tension. What if Lady Ursula spoke up and pointed out that Nicola had not been here most of the time she had been in the house? Or even her own sister? Nicola wanted desperately to turn and look at Deborah, to send her a pleading, warning glance, but she dared not. Richard would see the look and know where to attack.

"I think we can all attest to that," the Countess put in. "We had a small gathering of family and friends. Unfortunately, two of my granddaughters were delayed, but they did arrive, safe and unharmed, thank heavens. Is that what you wanted? A statement of our whereabouts this evening?"

She turned an acid look upon the hapless Squire Halsey. "Perhaps you think that *I* was at the gaol this evening, unlocking prisoners, instead of here in my own home."

Nicola relaxed. She did not think Lady Ursula or the others would say anything contrary to whatever the Countess said.

The Squire's face reddened, and he looked as if he wished the earth would open up and swallow him. "My lady, please, no, you must not think that. I—I have only the deepest regard for you. And your family," he added, glancing apologetically at Lady Ursula and the Countess's granddaughters.

"Do you?" the Countess asked quizzically. "If that is true, why are you invading my home and asking my family and guests questions about an escape from gaol that we obviously had nothing to do with?"

"Quite right, Mama." Lady Ursula said, rising from her seat and walking forward to face the Squire and the Earl. Tall, like everyone in the Montford family, and large, with that jutting bosom, Ursula was an imposing figure, and when she strode through a room, people tended to step back, especially when, as now, she was fairly quivering with indignation. "It's damned impudence, I say, Squire Halsey, and I wonder that you have the nerve to come in here and insult my mother like that."

"Insult!" The Squire looked as if he might faint right there. "No, no, my lady, I meant no insult."

"It is bad enough," Ursula continued, building up a fine head of steam, "that she should have to bear the insults of certain family members—" She shot a look at the Earl of Exmoor that would have felled many men. "But to have you add your presence to this—this inquisition—well, that's the outside of enough. Do you think this highwayman is here with us? Perhaps you would like to search the house—paw through all our possessions. Or perhaps you intend to search us all, right here, just in case we have the fellow hidden about our persons."

"My lady, please," Halsey groaned. "No, of course not. We have no intention of searching the house."

"That's good, since you have no right to—and since you would have to go through us in order to do so." Sebastian turned toward Exmoor. "If your purpose in coming here was to alarm and upset the ladies, then you have done an admirable job," he said, ignoring the obvious fact that most of the women in the room, other than Deborah, looked more ready to engage in battle than give way to feminine hysterics. "What the devil do you have to do with any of this, anyway? I would think it is a job for the constable or the magistrate."

"It is my goods upon which the thief has primarily preyed," Richard snapped back. "So I hired a Runner to track him down."

"The same one you hired to follow my fiancé a few months ago?" Lambeth asked with deceptive mildness.

"I don't know what the devil you're talking about."

"I think we both know that you do. You know, I believe that I would very much look forward to talking to this Runner in person."

"No doubt you will get your chance."

"I think it is time for you to go, Exmoor," Sebastian said, laying a restraining hand on Lambeth's arm. "And take your mercenaries with you."

Richard turned toward Nicola. "Congratulations, Nicola, you have managed to involve a great many illustrious names in your sordid scandal." He looked at the Countess. "Given your dislike of me, my lady, I am sure that you were quite eager to help her play out this charade. However, I wonder how you will feel when you and our family name are dragged through the courts because you chose to join in Miss Falcourt's scheme to save her highwayman lover."

There were several audible indrawn breaths at his statement, and a small smile played over Richard's lips.

"Ah," he said. "I see that she failed to tell you that fact. Or you, Buckminster, when she persuaded you and the others to pressure the magistrate for his release. No doubt she told you only what a villain I was and how I had entrapped this poor man. But not a word of how he has been preying on commerce and travelers for the past few months. Not a word of how he and she have—"

"I say!" the usually easygoing Lord Buckminster barked, taking a step toward the man. "You better be prepared to meet me at dawn tomorrow if you missay my cousin."

"Thank you, Bucky," Nicola said with a smile.

"I am sure that Lord Exmoor is well aware of the consequences of saying anything slanderous," Sebastian added warningly.

"It is no slander. Everyone knows that she ran to warn him. That is how we were able to capture the scoundrel. And obviously she knew where his hideout lay—and how else would she know it except if she met him there?"

"That is enough, Richard," the Countess interrupted. "No more threats and posturings. Miss Falcourt has told me nothing," she added truthfully. "I will not allow you to stand here in my own house and accuse me of lying. It is time for you to go. Past time. Squire Halsey." She turned an icy stare on that poor man. "Take your friend and go. I suggest that you not return unless you are invited."

This subtly veiled threat did not go unnoticed by the Squire, whose overbearing and socially ambitious wife would make his life a living hell if she were snubbed by the Countess during the upcoming wedding festivities. The man paled and beat a hasty retreat, hooking his arm through Richard's and pulling him out the door with him.

The group they left behind stood in silence until at last they heard the front door close. They turned almost as one to face the Countess. Her piercing, regal gaze swept over her assembled family and came to rest on Nicola.

"All right, child. I suggest that you tell us exactly what is going on. And none of this twaddle that the lot of you have been talking so far. I want to know the truth."

"Absolutely right, Mama," Lady Ursula agreed, nodding her massive head. "A more silly story I never heard—out riding in the gig at dusk! Accosted by highwaymen!"

"Let them tell it, Ursula," the Countess said calmly.

"Oh, my lady, I am so sorry!" Nicola cried, hurrying toward the Countess. "I should not have involved any of you. I should have done it myself. The last thing I wanted was to bring any harm to you."

"I would like to see you try to have done it without us," Penelope said stoutly.

"That's right," Alexandra agreed. "We all owed the highwayman a great deal. There was no chance that we were not going to return the favors that he has done us."

"Who is this highwayman? What do you mean, you all owe him?" Ursula asked.

The Countess sighed. "I can see that this is going to take a long time in the telling. I believe I will sit down." She did so, raising an aristocratic finger to point at Alexandra. "First you. How do you owe a highwayman anything?"

"He was the man who helped Sebastian and me when we were lost in that balloon," Alexandra explained. "You remember us telling you about him."

"Yes, of course."

"He found us and gave us shelter and food, then took us to the village to catch the coach the next day."

"Hardly sounds like a highwayman," the Countess murmured.

"I know. He speaks and acts just like a gentleman. That is why they call him The Gentleman."

"He did even more for Justin and me," Marianne added. "If it had not been for him, we would probably have died in that mine. It was Jack who dug us out. So you can see that when we heard that he was in gaol, we could hardly stand by and let the man hang, even if he is a highwayman. When Nicola came to us—well, really, to Bucky—for help, we all insisted on helping her."

"I see. It did not occur to you to help in the form of a good barrister?" the Countess asked. "Or in applying the pressure of several prominent families to obtain his release? You had to break into the gaol and haul him out?"

"We did try our influence first," Sebastian protested, looking a trifle sheepish, but Lambeth only grinned and replied, "It did seem rather more fun."

"Influence wasn't enough," Nicola assured her. "Bucky, Justin and Sebastian tried to help him because I asked them to, but neither the constable nor the magistrate dared go against Richard. He was adamant about seeing Jack go to trial—he has a personal vendetta against him."

"Mmm. It sounds as if this 'Gentleman' had something of a vendetta against Richard," the Countess pointed out.

"It's true. He did," Nicola admitted. "But he is not a bad man. I swear to you. Richard wronged him many years ago. Wronged him terribly. Richard almost killed him, and when he found out that he had not succeeded, he sent his men to kidnap Jack and give him to a press gang."

"Good Lord!" Lady Buckminster exclaimed.

"That sounds vicious enough for Richard," the Countess said. "What did he have against the man?"

"He wasn't even a man then. He was a boy. Only a few years older than I. And the reason Richard hated him…" She cast a hesitant glance over at her sister.

"Go on," Deborah said with a sigh. "I am well aware of how Richard felt about you."

"Richard wanted me. He had offered for me. Then he found out that I was in love with Jack—he was known as Gil then, and…and he was a stable boy at Tidings." She raised her chin defiantly. "I know you will think ill of me, my lady, for loving beneath my station. But I do not care for that! Jack was—is—the only man I have ever loved. He is a wonderful, good man—funny, handsome, brave, compassionate. I know that if you knew him, you would like him."

"I think I would like to meet this young man," the Countess responded. Nicola smiled, and the Countess continued, "But tell me what happened between him and Richard."

"Exmoor found us one day where we would meet, up at the head of Lady Falls. He and Jack struggled. It was horrible, bloody, and I could not get them to stop, and finally Jack slid backward over the Falls. Richard said it was an accident, but Jack says it was not. He pushed him."

"I do not doubt that."

"We could not find him at the bottom of the Falls. I heard nothing from him for years. I thought he was dead. But he didn't die. He was swept downstream and managed to crawl out. A farmer helped him. Jack—Jack sent me a letter, but I did not receive it. My mother got it and gave it to Richard instead. So Richard had him taken from the farmer's house, and he told Jack that it was I who had betrayed him. All these years, Jack thought I was treacherous. I believed he was dead. I had nothing of him but the ring he had given me."

"An engagement ring?"

"No. It is a man's ring. Quite ordinary-looking, really, but it meant a great deal to Jack. You see, it was all he had of his father." Nicola went up to her, pulling the chain out from beneath her dress and slipping it off over her head. She held it out to the Countess, saying, "I have kept it with me all these years. It—what's the matter? My lady?"

The Countess had taken the ring in her hand, then had gone dead still, her face draining of color. She stared at the ring, not speaking.

"Mama?" Lady Ursula crowded in beside her anxiously. She looked down at the ring, then exclaimed, "Good God!"

"What? What is it?" Nicola looked from one to the other.

"What did you say Jack said about this ring?" the Countess asked her, her eyes bright, two red spots of color suddenly bursting on the paleness of her face.

"Why, only that he knew little about it. His mother told him that it was his father's, a keepsake. He never knew his father, so it was precious to him."

"Where is this man?" the Countess asked. "This highwayman. I want to see him."

"Right now?" Nicola asked.

"Yes, of course."

"Grandmama, what is wrong?" Alexandra asked as she and Marianne joined the little knot.

"Nothing." The Countess stood, holding up a hand as if to deflect all conversation. She turned to Nicola. "Where is he?"

"Here. I—I can fetch him if you wish."

"I do wish it. I must talk to him."

CHAPTER TWENTY

JACK WAS NOT IN THE ATTIC. EVEN WHEN she called his
name, he did not answer. Panic rose in Nicola's throat, and
she turned and hurried back down the stairs to the hall
below. She started down the hall, and as she did, she
noticed that one of the doors stood open. She went to the
doorway and looked inside. It was obviously the nursery,
long unused, with toys and books put neatly away into
cabinets. Jack sat at the child-size table, and even as
worried as she was, Nicola had to laugh at the absurdity
of his long legs doubled up as he sat in the little chair. He
turned, startled, and gave her a sheepish grin.

"Whatever are you doing in here? You scared me."

"Sorry. I'm not sure exactly what I'm doing," he
replied, frowning. "I feel…unsettled. I wanted to look at
things." He shook his head and smiled. "I'm being stupid.
What I should be doing is riding away. I can't stay here
and endanger these people. It was risky enough for them
to get me out of gaol. To stay here and continue to put them
in danger would be the work of a scoundrel."

"They want to help you. You once saved their lives, and
they feel that they are returning the favor. Besides, there
is not a person in this house with any fondness for Exmoor.
You cannot leave yet. Exmoor was just here. He and his
men are out searching everywhere. Give it a day or two,

and when the hunt has died down, you can go—and I will go with you."

He turned to her, and there was a look in his eyes of such love and longing that it made Nicola's heart twist in her chest. "No. I cannot ask that of you. It is too dangerous."

"Do you not want me with you? When you said tonight that you loved me, did you not mean it?"

"Of course I meant it," Jack retorted roughly. "I love you. I have loved you for ten years. Even when I hated you, I loved you. But you cannot marry a highwayman."

"Do you intend to continue this vocation?"

"Of course I'm not going to continue. I shall go home— well, back to America."

"I will go with you."

"Nicola—think. I am not poor, but I have nothing like the sort of wealth that you are accustomed to."

"*Still* you think that matters to me? Have you learned nothing? I love you, and I want to be with you, and that is all I care about!"

Jack reached out and grabbed her arms, pulling her to him fiercely. "My beautiful, wonderful girl," he murmured in a low voice. "How could I ever have doubted you? I was such a fool." He bent and took her lips in a long, searing kiss.

When at last he raised his head, his voice was a trifle unsteady. "If that is truly what you want, we will marry and go back to the United States. But I will send for you when I am safely away. Or we can meet in London. You can go home, and I will come to you. But I refuse to allow you to ride out with me. What if we did not make it? What if they captured you? I could not let you be caught aiding and abetting a thief. Or worse—you could be shot."

"None of that will happen, because we will wait here until the hue and cry dies down. Then we will go, and no one will stop us. I will not let you go again, Jack, not even for a few days. I have seen what fate can deal out. I lost you once, and I will not risk losing you again."

"You will never lose me," he promised, and wrapped his arms around her again, pressing her to his chest. "Not even if you try."

"Then you agree that I will come with you when you leave?"

"I agree that we will talk about it further," Jack replied in an amused voice. Reluctantly, he released her and stepped back. "Now, tell me about Exmoor. What happened?"

Nicola quickly related the events of Exmoor's visit, concluding with the Countess's sending him on his way. "You should have seen her, Jack. She was magnificent. Not a single intimation that she knew we were all lying through our teeth. Didn't turn a hair at all of Richard's accusations. Just looked like a queen and dismissed him and the Squire. Poor Squire Halsey looked as if he wished he were anywhere but here."

"She sounds like quite a lady."

"She is. And she wants to meet you."

"Me?"

"Yes. After Richard left, of course she wanted to know what was going on, and we explained about you, and she said that she wanted to meet you. That is why I came up here, to take you down to see her."

Jack looked uneasy. "I don't know. I have never met a countess before."

"Don't be absurd. You've met higher than that. Lambeth is a marquess. He will be a duke and Marianne a duchess one day.

"That was different."

"Come on." Nicola took his hand and pulled him toward the door. "I have never seen you back down before anyone yet. She is a woman. I am sure that you will charm her silly."

WHEN THEY WALKED INTO THE DRAWING room, the tension in the air was palpable. Jack came to a halt, and Nicola glanced up at him. He wore an odd expression as he looked around the room. His gaze finally settled on the Countess, and Nicola felt his arm go rigid beneath her hand.

The Countess rose, her eyes fixed on Jack. "Come here."

Jack hesitated, then started toward her, Nicola by his side. Nicola glanced around at her friends, but their faces, all turned toward Jack, gave nothing away. They reached the Countess, and Jack swept her an elegant bow.

"Jack Moore, my lady, at your service."

"Mr. Moore." The older woman's voice was tight, almost breathless. "I hope you will not think me rude, but I need to ask you a few questions."

"Of course, my lady. I shall do my best to answer them."

The Countess opened her hand to reveal Jack's ring, lying on her palm. "This ring—where did you get it?"

Jack looked surprised; this was obviously not the sort of question he had been expecting. "Why, from my mother, my lady. It belonged to my father, she said, and I was to keep it forever."

"So this was nothing that you found, say? I promise you, I do not care if you took it or found it. I just need to know."

Jack frowned. "No, I did not find it—or steal it, if that is what you are saying. I will swear an oath, if you like. My mother gave it to me, and those were her words. I cannot swear to you that what she said was the truth. I think she often tried to…I don't know, make me feel better."

"Better? What do you mean?"

"I was very sick when I was a child."

Lady Ursula drew a sharp breath, and Jack glanced at her. He stared at her for a moment, his forehead creasing. But the Countess drew his attention sharply back to her.

"You were sick? How old were you?"

"I—I'm not sure. Eight or nine, I guess. I don't remember much from it, but those are the earliest memories I have, of being very sick, and of Mother and Granny Rose taking care of me. I was weak for a long time afterward, and I was…unhappy much of the time. I guess it was because I couldn't go out and play for so long. I'm not really sure. I just remember being sad. I hated being confined to the bed, but I was too weak to do much of anything. So Mother would tell me stories, and once she gave me this ring and told me that it was my father's and that I must keep it."

"Did she…tell you anything about your father?"

Jack shifted his feet, looking embarrassed. "Only silly stories, nothing real."

Everyone, absorbed in what Jack was saying, was looking at him and the Countess. No one even heard the faint sounds in the outer hall, but then the door crashed open, and everyone jumped, whirling around to face the door. In the doorway stood the Earl of Exmoor, the magistrate on one side of him and the Bow Street Runner, Stone on the other. Exmoor held a pistol in his hand, and Stone, a musket. Behind them stood the other men, looking uncomfortable.

"There you are, Halsey!" Exmoor said, his voice rich

with satisfaction. "I told you he was here. I knew they were hiding him."

The Squire wrung his hands, glancing guiltily toward the Countess. "Still, sir, we have no right to be here...."

"The devil take it!" Richard said impatiently, starting forward, shoving the pistol into his waistband and stretching out a hand to seize Jack.

The Countess rose, her blue eyes blazing, and swept in front of Jack. "You will not touch him!" she commanded, looking for all the world like an avenging angel. "If you lay a hand on this man or harm him in any way, I promise you that I will not rest until you are utterly destroyed."

Everyone in the room stopped, staring at the Countess, taken aback by the vision of fury. Then Alexandra's crisp cool voice rang out, "I have him, Grandmama."

She stood there in her elegant gown, a small pistol aimed directly at Richard's heart.

"No, Mr. Stone," Lord Thorpe said. "Raise that musket and you're a dead man."

Stone, who held a musket loosely in his hand, glanced at Lord Thorpe. Thorpe, too, held a very serviceable dueling pistol, aimed directly at Stone. Stone's eyes moved a fraction and he saw that Lord Lambeth, too, held a gun leveled at Richard.

"You will die first, Exmoor," Lambeth said casually. "You know that I am a crack shot, and I have it on the best of authority that Lord Thorpe is no slouch with a pistol, either. Or Lady Thorpe, for that matter. American, you know."

"Don't be a fool. You wouldn't shoot me. You would hang."

"I expect that I would receive a medal, rather," Lambeth replied. "At any rate, you would not be around to see it. You would have a ball in the head and another in the heart."

"Put down your gun, Exmoor," Lord Thorpe commanded, and Richard, with a blazing glance of hatred toward him, dropped the pistol to the floor.

"You, too, Stone."

With an oath, the Bow Street Runner set down his musket on the table. The Squire let out a little moan and plopped into a chair, mopping his brow.

"Oh, dear," he murmured. "Oh, dear."

"Do stop dithering, Henry," Lady Ursula said impatiently to the Squire. "And try to act like a representative of the Crown. You are the legal representative here, and I think you had better listen."

The Squire, like most people, straightened at Lady Ursula's tone of command. "Yes, of course, Lady Castlereigh. It is just—what am I listening to?"

"You will see." The lady turned her gimlet eye toward the roughly dressed men standing uncertainly in the doorway, their weapons dangling at their sides. "Well, what are you lot standing about for? Get out of this house this instant."

Thorpe, a smile playing at his lips, said, "She's right. I suggest that you throw down your arms and leave."

The men glanced uncertainly toward Stone, then the Earl, obviously at a loss. Lambeth cocked his pistol, saying, "Richard...you know I am an impatient man."

"Yes, all right!" Exmoor snapped. "Do as they say. Stone, take the men and leave."

Shrugging, the men dropped their weapons and trooped out, Stone shepherding them. Bucky walked to the door, closed it and turned the lock. "There! Now perhaps we can have a little privacy."

"Go on, my lady," Thorpe told the Countess. "You were asking Jack a few pertinent questions."

"Yes." The Countess moved back to her seat. "Now, Jack, you were saying that your mother told you stories about your childhood. What sort of stories?"

Jack shifted uncomfortably, glancing toward Richard. "Why, fairy-tale sort of things, about how my father was a rich, powerful man, much admired. Sometimes he was a king or a prince, other times he was a warrior. They were fanciful stories."

"Did she say how he died?"

"There were many different ways. Sometimes he died in battle, sometimes she said that treachery brought him down." A wry smile touched his lips. "But, whatever it was, he always died bravely."

"Think carefully, now. She never said a name or gave a hint as to who he was?"

Jack looked at the Countess, puzzled. "My lady, I don't understand. Why are you so interested in this ring? Or in my mother's stories?"

"Please, indulge me. This is exceedingly important to me."

Nicola looked at the Countess, whose eyes were bright, her whole body tense, then over at Lady Ursula and on to Alexandra, whose attention was riveted on Jack. Suddenly she understood what was going on. She pressed her lips together to hold back a gasp, and she turned to look wonderingly at Jack. *Was it possible?* Suddenly things began to fall into place.

"All right," Jack said, and it seemed as if he braced himself. "Frankly, my lady, I do not think that my mother knew who my father was. After I was grown, some of the whispers I heard—well, I believe that she was not as virtuous as she should have been."

Exmoor let out a derisive snort.

"I think she wove those stories because she wanted to believe that my father was a great man, not just someone in a tavern to whom she had given her favors," Jack continued, his cheeks blazing red. "There is even some possibility that it is worse."

"Worse? How?"

"When she lay dying, she told me that I should seek my fortune, that I had a 'heritage.' She was delirious much of the time. She kept crying and saying she had wronged me, assuring me that she loved me. I tried to calm her down, telling her that she had been a good mother, but she only said that she thought she was keeping me safe, but perhaps it was that she wanted what she could not have. It was...rather unintelligible much of the time, but finally she said that I was the earl's son. I—when I came to live with my grandmother after Mother's death, I asked her what she had meant, and Gran told me not to talk about it. She said it was better if I let it drop. I think—" he glanced again toward Richard, then away, finishing in a rush "—well, it is possible that I am Exmoor's by-blow." His mouth twisted grimly. "It is not a heritage I desire to have."

"Ha!" Richard's voice cracked out contemptuously. "As if I would have touched that doxy!"

Jack started toward the other man, his eyes blazing, but Nicola caught his arm and held on. "Jack! No. Forget him. You need to finish this. It's...very important."

"She—she said you were the earl's son?" The Countess looked suddenly much older and frailer.

"I think so. Or perhaps it was the earl's heir. I don't remember exactly."

"Oh, Grandmama!" Alexandra cried, her face lighting up, and she hurried over to where they stood. "It is he! It must be!"

Jack looked at Alexandra as if seeing her for the first time, and the blood drained from his face.

"What is it?" the Countess asked, her eyes on Jack like a hawk. "You looked—"

"I—I am sorry. It—for a moment I felt quite queasy. Forgive me, my lady, perhaps I am coming down ill. I have felt very strange the last few hours."

"Strange in what way?"

Jack frowned, searching for words to describe the peculiar thoughts and emotions that had been impinging on him ever since he came into the house. "I'm not sure. Almost...sick. Yet happy and excited, in a way. And sad, too, all at the same time."

"And what did you feel when you looked at Alexandra just now?" the Countess pressed.

"I'm not sure. Startled...and shaken. I have met the lady before, but suddenly, seeing her in this room—it was as if something flashed through my head, but I could not catch it."

"And what did you feel when you looked at Ursula?" the Countess asked, motioning toward her daughter. "I saw your face when you looked at her earlier. A very odd expression appeared on your countenance."

Jack looked hounded and embarrassed. "It was absurd."

"Please tell me." The old woman looked at him entreatingly.

"A thought popped into my mind. 'I didn't break it.'"

"What?"

Jack shrugged. "That's what I thought. 'I didn't break it.'"

"Break what?"

"A little glass horse." If possible, Jack looked even more uncomfortable than before. "I am sorry—" he began, but Lady Ursula stood up, her sharp voice cutting him off.

"My God!"

Everyone turned to look at Ursula, who was staring wildly at Jack. "The unicorn. It was a unicorn. A crystal unicorn. I brought it for the baby. I showed it to Simone, then we went upstairs and left it sitting on the table here. In this room. And later I found it broken. I was—I was certain John was playing with it and dropped it. But he kept protesting that he did not do it. And Chilton—" She stopped, tears pooling in her eyes. "Chilton said that if his son said he did not break it, he didn't break it."

The room was filled with stunned silence. The Countess looked as if she might faint, and suddenly her shoulders shook and tears began to run down her face. "It is you. Johnny. You're alive."

Suddenly the room was filled with excited voices. Much to Jack's astonishment, Alexandra threw her arms around him, followed a moment later by Marianne, both of them crying.

"What nonsense!" Richard exclaimed, his voice cutting across the babble.

"Wait. Stop! Just a moment. Delightful as it is to have two beautiful women hugging me, I am afraid I haven't a clue what's going on."

"You are my brother!" Alexandra exclaimed. "Our brother. Marianne's and mine. We thought you were dead, but…"

Jack gaped at her as if she had lost her mind. "I beg your pardon." He turned toward the Countess and saw in the quiet, tear-streaked happiness on her face confirmation of Alexandra's words. "My lady…no. It isn't possible. This is absurd!"

"For once he has spoken the truth," Richard said sarcastically. "This man could not possibly be John Montford, returned from the dead. He is merely a local boy, raised by a witch and a tavern wench. No doubt he heard the local stories about Chilton and his children, and he came up with this intriguing story to get your sympathy and support, my lady."

"You have no voice in this matter," the Countess told him coldly. "Anyway, Jack is not the one telling the story," she pointed out. "I think it is quite clear that he knows nothing about what we are saying."

"But, Countess…" Squire Halsey spoke up for the first time, his interest overriding his earlier discomfort. "I'm not sure I understand what's going on. Are you saying you think 'The Gentleman' is your grandson—the one that was killed by the Mob in Paris twenty-some-odd years ago?"

"He wasn't killed. None of the children were. Don't you remember how two months ago we discovered that Marianne was my granddaughter? It was after that party at Lord Buckminster's."

"I remember the turnup at the ball," Halsey allowed. "And all the to-do afterward. But I thought everybody said that the boy had died."

"That is what we thought. But I think now that they were wrong. We were all wrong. I don't know if you remember, but my son, Chilton, lived in this house from the time that John was about two. John lived here for five years. It was his home. As you heard my daughter recount, there was a contretemps right in this room over whether he had broken a crystal unicorn. It turned out later that a careless maid had knocked it over." Her mouth quivered, but she pressed on. "And this man remembered that incident. He just told us about it."

"No doubt one of the others fed him the information," Richard sneered. "This proves nothing except that he is a good actor."

"This proves something!" the Countess exclaimed, holding up the ring Nicola had handed her. "You recognize it, don't you, Richard? The ancestral ring of the Montfords?" She turned to Jack, saying, "This ring was my son's. It has been in the Montford family for generations. It is by tradition worn by the heir to the title—in this case, my son. It would have been *his* son's when Chilton died. And you have the ring."

Jack looked stunned. "But—but it's impossible. How could I be your grandson? My mother was a tavern wench."

"I'm sorry," Alexandra said. "I know we aren't explaining this well." She launched into the story of the Countess's family, how they had been caught in the French revolution and how all of them had been believed killed, and how only recently it had come to light that the children had escaped the riots and been carried safely back to London, by their mother's friend, Rhea Ward, only to be whisked away and kept secret from their grandmother, the Countess of Exmoor.

"It fits, don't you see?" Marianne added excitedly. "The man who took me to the orphanage was not essentially a bad man. It was just that Richard forced him to get rid of the children."

"That is not true!" Richard shouted, starting forward, but Sebastian waved his gun at him as a reminder, and he stopped. "You are making slanderous statements, and I warn you—"

"It isn't slander if it's true," Lambeth pointed out.

"You have absolutely no proof of any of the things you're saying."

"Mrs. Ward told me that she gave Marianne and John to my companion, Willa," the countess said. "And Willa told us that she gave the two children to you."

"The word of a lunatic and that of a dead woman. That is certainly impressive."

"Rhea Ward was not mad!" Alexandra exclaimed, her dark eyes flashing.

"Isn't it convenient how everyone who could testify against you dies?" Lambeth added. "The way Mr. Fuquay died—at your hand. Before he could tell us anything." There was a soft gasp from the direction of Deborah, but no one paid any attention, including her husband. He merely rolled his eyes and said, "This is nonsense. There is no proof whatsoever."

"What about the jewelry?" Penelope asked, surprising everyone.

"What?" Marianne asked.

"The jewelry that your mother gave to Alexandra's mother when she gave her the children. You remember, Mrs. Ward said that Lady Chilton gave her several of the Montford family jewels, as well as some of the jewelry Lord Chilton had bought for her."

"That's right," Alexandra agreed, her eyes lighting up. "Mama said that she gave the jewelry to Willa. I suspect Willa turned the jewelry over to Richard, too."

"If that jewelry is in Richard's possession, that would go to show that he took the children, as well," Sebastian agreed. "What were the jewels, Alex?"

"A sapphire pendant," the Countess answered for her. "I remember when Chilton gave it to Simone. A diamond choker. A string of large, lustrous pearls that had been in the family since the fourth earl. An emerald brooch…jet earrings."

"A topaz ring," Deborah said suddenly, standing up, and everyone in the room turned to look at her. "A parure of rubies? An enameled bracelet of blue and gold?"

"Yes!" Lady Ursula exclaimed, astonished. "All those things were Simone's. How did you know?"

"Because I saw them," Deborah said. She looked straight at her husband, speaking to him rather than the others. "I saw you take them out and look at them one night. You thought I was upstairs asleep, but I wasn't. I saw you pore over them, then hide them back away in your safe. I was curious, so I went back one time when you were gone to London and I took them out."

"Shut up, Deborah!" Richard exclaimed. "Don't be a fool."

"I am not a fool, though you have always thought me one. No doubt you thought I was so stupid that I didn't know where you hid the key to your safe or even where the safe was. But I knew. I saw many more things than you ever realized. I took out the box, and I went through it. It was full of jewels, beautiful jewels. I was devastated because you had never given them to me, never allowed me to wear them. I had no idea that it was because—"

All the color drained from Richard's face as she spoke. "That proves nothing," he protested feebly.

"It proves that what my mother said was true," Alexandra said in a hard voice. "That what Willa said was true. She gave you the children and the jewels."

"You told Mr. Fuquay to kill me, didn't you?" Marianne said to Richard. "But he didn't have the heart. Perhaps he was supposed to kill John, too, but instead he decided to give John to someone. The boy was very sick. Fuquay could have thought that he would ease out of the responsibility for his death—leave it to fate, so to speak. What if he gave him to Jack's mother? I mean, the woman who reared Jack."

"But…" Jack raked his hands back through his hair, looking shaken.

"Don't you see? It makes sense," Nicola said, putting her hand on Jack's arm. "You were ill, just like the Countess's grandson. The fever and illness no doubt burned away your memory. Or perhaps it was all too horrible to remember. All your memories come from after that time. Yet you knew this house when you came here tonight. Remember how you knew the way to the attic and where the nursery was? It is no wonder—it was once your home. And your mother—Helen, I mean—when Fuquay gave you to her, she took you home to her mother, knowing that if anyone could heal a child so ill, it would be Granny Rose. And she did heal you."

"But surely this man would have come back. Or Exmoor. They would have found out I was still alive," Jack protested.

"Not if she told them that you were dead," Alexandra supplied. "She must have suspected that Fuquay was up to something havey-cavey. Why would a single gentleman be foisting a desperately ill child onto someone? Perhaps she even figured out who you were. I mean, they—we— lived close by. She could have seen you before, known who you were. She would have known, too, what sort of man Richard is. Perhaps Fuquay even told her that Richard wanted you dead. So if she wanted to keep you safe, what better way than to tell them that you were dead?"

"No doubt that is why she moved away," Nicola added. "To make sure that Richard never saw you, because he might suspect the truth. So when you were well, she took you and left Granny Rose's. It always seemed an odd thing for her to have done, but now it makes sense."

"But why didn't she take me to the Countess and tell her who I was? The Countess would have recognized me."

"She was poor and ignorant," Marianne pointed out. "She would not have had the money to travel to London, and how could she have gotten in to see the Countess? No doubt she was scared of Exmoor and his power, afraid that he would find out who you were and harm you. The easiest thing would have been to hide you from him."

"And perhaps she did not want to give you up," Nicola added gently. "You remember how you said she talked about having done wrong by you? And do you remember how Exmoor acted when he found you and me together?" Nicola turned to Richard. "I assumed you were jealous. Maybe you were. But you became truly enraged only when you saw Jack's ring hanging from the chain around my neck. You grabbed it and jerked it from my neck and threw it away. You realized then who he was, didn't you? That is the real reason you tried to kill Jack. When that didn't work, you had him impressed into the navy, which, if it did not kill him, would certainly have ensured that he would never return to Dartmoor. And now…" She paused, a smug smile tugging at her lips. "Now you must be absolutely frantic, knowing that Jack is alive and free. No wonder you were so eager to have him thrown in gaol and hanged."

"You think I am scared of a stable lad? Or of that ring? It proves nothing."

"No? Then why did you break into my room to search for it?"

"What? I don't know what you're talking about."

"I think you do. Remember when someone mysteriously broke into my room one night? It was so odd—the intruder was searching through my vanity. But now it makes sense. It was you, looking for my ring. I always suspected you—I knew it wasn't Jack, as you said, and the man was your height and build. You had easy access to any room in the house. But I couldn't understand why you would have done that. Now it's clear. You must have seen the ring around my neck at some point, and you were trying to steal it. But you could not find it because I wear it around my neck. Always."

"The ring means nothing," Richard snapped. "Anyone could have found it anywhere. Even if it is the precious Montford family ring, it scarcely proves that the person holding it is Chilton's son. You haven't said anything that would stand up in a court of law."

"No?" The Countess stood up, a smile of triumph on her lips. "I think this will, though. John Montford had a birthmark. It is noted in the family records. It was brown and shaped something like a crescent moon. It is located on his back, on the right shoulder blade. I have seen it. I can identify it." She started toward Jack, saying, "I am afraid you will have to take off your shirt. I'm sorry."

Jack stared at her with a stunned expression on his face. He turned and unbuttoned his shirt as she bade him to, exposing his broad back. There on his right shoulder blade was a small, crescent-shaped birthmark.

"By Jove!" Squire Halsey exclaimed.

"John!" the Countess said, her eyes swimming with tears. "Oh, Johnny, you've come home." She reached up a trembling hand to cup his cheek.

Everyone's eyes were on the Countess and Jack, even Lambeth's and Thorpe's. Richard whirled and ran for the door, knocking the Squire out of his way. Lambeth whipped around and raised his pistol, but Jack was already across the room, a feral, wordless cry erupting from his lips. He threw himself the last few feet and crashed into Richard, knocking him down.

The two men rolled across the floor, punching and grappling, crashing into tables and chairs and sending knick-knacks flying. Richard managed to struggle to his feet, and he landed a kick in Jack's side, but Jack lashed out with his hand, grabbing the other man's ankle and sending him crashing to the ground. Jack crawled across the floor after him and finished him off with a right upper cut to Richard's jaw. Richard went limp.

Jack staggered to his feet, breathing heavily, and Nicola ran to his side. "Are you all right?"

"I'm fine."

But Nicola was not satisfied, alternating between examining each cut and red mark and hugging and kissing him. They turned and began to walk back toward the Countess.

Everyone was babbling excitedly as they watched Jack and Nicola cross the room toward the Countess, so no one noticed when Richard twitched, then moved on the floor. He raised his head and glanced around. His eyes fastened on Jack, whose back was to him, his hand linked with Nicola's. Richard's eyes narrowed, and he made a noise low in his throat. Stealthily he stood up, lunged toward the pistol that Alexandra had abandoned earlier on one of the tables, and grabbed it.

Penelope saw him move and let out a shriek. Everyone turned, including Jack and Nicola. No one was close enough to reach Richard in time to take the gun away, though Sebastian and Justin both ran toward him. Richard and Jack simply stared into each other's eyes, the moment frozen in time. Then Richard raised his hand and aimed.

A shot rang out, and Richard jerked backward, a look of astonishment on his features as a red stain blossomed across the front of his white shirt. He crumpled to the ground, dead. Everyone whirled around. The Countess stood there, slim and elegant, holding Sebastian's pistol in her hand.

"May you rot in hell," she said quietly, and dropped the pistol to the floor.

EPILOGUE

NICOLA FLUFFED OUT PENELOPE'S VEIL AND stepped back to admire her handiwork. "You look absolutely beautiful."

Penelope smiled. "Thank you."

They turned to Marianne, who was equally radiant in her wedding gown. Her sister, Alexandra, was adjusting her veil, tears in her eyes. Alexandra smiled at Nicola.

"In two months we shall be doing this for you," Alexandra said. "Won't that be grand? We shall all be sisters."

"You know, a few months ago," Marianne mused, "I had no family at all. Now I have a grandmother, a brother, sister, cousins, aunts—and soon a sister-in-law." She reached out and took both Nicola's hands in hers. "I am so happy."

"I am, too."

It had been a month since Richard died, and much had changed since then. All charges had been dropped against Jack. The man who had pressed charges was dead, and, moreover, no one found it reasonable to charge a man with stealing property that turned out to be, by rights, his own.

Jack was now living at Tidings, along with the Countess and Ursula, who expected to remain until his wedding to Nicola in two months. He had been spending the last month correcting the abuses against the Exmoor tenants and workers that Richard had perpetrated. It would take some time before he would have everything the way it should be, but he was enjoying the work, and the people of the area loved him. He had brought Perry and his other men back to Tidings, where they now worked for him in more legitimate endeavors. Perry was now managing the mine for Jack.

"It's like going from hell to heaven," Maidie Thompson had told Nicola the last time she had been in the village, bringing old Mr. Holliwell tea for his rheumatism.

Nicola smiled to herself. The past month had been like going from hell to heaven for her, too. The love that had been snatched from her ten years earlier had been restored, and she was blissfully happy. Soon she would marry Jack and become part of a warm family whom she loved. Life could not, she thought, be more perfect.

"Well," said the Countess from where she sat, surveying the process of dressing the brides, "you are both lovely. I think that my life is complete. To watch two of my grand-daughters marry today. To have you back with me after all these years..." Her eyes filled with tears.

Nicola reflected that the aristocratic old woman had never uttered one word of regret for shooting Richard, at least not in Nicola's hearing. She suspected she never would.

In truth, there were few people who mourned Richard's passing. Only Deborah had loved him, but even her sadness had eased over the past month, and she had, out from under his dominance, begun to blossom and glow in a way she never had before. Some of that glow, Nicola thought privately, was due to the fact that Jack's friend Perry had returned to the area after Richard's death and had begun to visit the mother-to-be with some frequency. She was also further along now in her pregnancy, and she was increasingly hopeful that this baby, at last, would be brought to full term. It certainly would, Nicola knew, if Nurse had anything to do with it.

"Time to go." Aunt Ursula bustled in. "The carriages are waiting, and I'm sure the church is full by now."

The women had dressed at Tidings, and now carriages would take them to the church in the village. They left the bedroom where they had changed and swept down the staircase to the grand entryway below.

Jack stood waiting for them at the bottom of the staircase, and he swept them an elegant bow. "I definitely have the most beautiful family in the world," he said with a grin. "You, Grandmama, are the loveliest of them all."

"Dear boy." The Countess pinched his cheek lightly and smiled. "I always knew you would turn out to be a charmer."

She moved past him toward the door, her daughter and granddaughters walking with her. Jack turned to Nicola. He smiled, his eyes caressing her face. He reached out and took her hand and brought it tenderly to his lips.

"I'm not sure I can wait two months," he said, turning her hand over to kiss her palm. "I never get to see you enough." He leaned close to her, murmuring, "I want to go to sleep with you at night and wake up beside you in the morning."

"I want that, too," Nicola confessed, a little catch in her voice. "But we will have that for the rest of our lives."

"I am counting on it," Jack replied, and bent to kiss her.

Nicola leaned into him, losing herself, as she always did, in the pleasure of his mouth. Finally he raised his head, looking down into her starry eyes.

"It's been grand, suddenly being an earl, having a family, all that," he said quietly, his eyes serious for once.

"But the best thing that has happened to me since I came here is finding your love again."

"Time to go!" Aunt Ursula trumpeted from the front door.

Jack and Nicola grinned at each other. She slipped her hand in his, and together they started forward.

REQUEST YOUR
FREE BOOKS!

2 FREE NOVELS
FROM THE ROMANCE/SUSPENSE
COLLECTION PLUS 2 FREE GIFTS!

YES! Please send me 2 FREE novels from the Romance/Suspense Collection and my 2 FREE gifts. After receiving them, if I don't wish to receive any more books, I can return the shipping statement marked "cancel." If I don't cancel, I will receive 4 brand-new novels every month and be billed just $5.49 per book in the U.S., or $5.99 per book in Canada, plus 25¢ shipping and handling per book plus applicable taxes, if any*. That's a savings of at least 20% off the cover price! I understand that accepting the 2 free books and gifts places me under no obligation to buy anything. I can always return a shipment and cancel at any time. Even if I never buy another book from the Reader Service, the two free books and gifts are mine to keep forever.

185 MDN EF5Y   385 MDN EF6C

Name _____ (PLEASE PRINT) _____

Address _____ Apt. # _____

City _____ State/Prov. _____ Zip/Postal Code _____

Signature (if under 18, a parent or guardian must sign)

Mail to **The Reader Service:**
IN U.S.A.: P.O. Box 1867, Buffalo, NY 14240-1867
IN CANADA: P.O. Box 609, Fort Erie, Ontario L2A 5X3

Not valid to current subscribers to the Romance Collection,
the Suspense Collection or the Romance/Suspense Collection.

Want to try two free books from another line?
Call 1-800-873-8635 or visit www.morefreebooks.com.

* Terms and prices subject to change without notice. NY residents add applicable sales tax. Canadian residents will be charged applicable provincial taxes and GST. This offer is limited to one order per household. All orders subject to approval. Credit or debit balances in a customer's account(s) may be offset by any other outstanding balance owed by or to the customer. Please allow 4 to 6 weeks for delivery.

Your Privacy: Harlequin is committed to protecting your privacy. Our Privacy Policy is available online at www.eHarlequin.com or upon request from the Reader Service. From time to time we make our lists of customers available to reputable firms who may have a product or service of interest to you. If you would prefer we not share your name and address, please check here. ☐

BOB07